Debī Chaudhurāṇī,

or

The Wife Who Came Home

Debī Chaudhurāṇī,
or
The Wife Who Came Home

BANKIMCHANDRA CHATTERJI

Translated with an Introduction

and Critical Apparatus by

Julius J. Lipner

OXFORD
UNIVERSITY PRESS
2009

OXFORD
UNIVERSITY PRESS

Oxford University Press, Inc., publishes works that further
Oxford University's objective of excellence
in research, scholarship, and education.

Oxford New York
Auckland Cape Town Dar es Salaam Hong Kong Karachi
Kuala Lumpur Madrid Melbourne Mexico City Nairobi
New Delhi Shanghai Taipei Toronto

With offices in
Argentina Austria Brazil Chile Czech Republic France Greece
Guatemala Hungary Italy Japan Poland Portugal Singapore
South Korea Switzerland Thailand Turkey Ukraine Vietnam

Published by Oxford University Press, Inc.
198 Madison Avenue, New York, New York 10016

www.oup.com

Oxford is a registered trademark of Oxford University Press

Library of Congress Cataloging-in-Publication Data

Chatterji, Bankimchandra, 1838–1894.
[Debi Chaudhurani. English]
Debi Chaudhurani, or, the wife who came home /
Bankimchandra Chatterji ; translated with an introduction
and critical apparatus by Julius J. Lipner.
p. cm.
Includes bibliographical references and indexes.
ISBN: 978-0-19-538836-7
1. Chatterji, Bankimchandra, 1838–1894. Debi Chaudhurani.
2. Brahman women—India—Fiction. 3. Married women— India—Fiction.
4. Brigands and robbers—India—Fiction. 5. India—Social conditions—18th century—Fiction.
I. Lipner, Julius. II. Title. III. Title: Debi Chaudhurani. IV. Title: Wife who came home.
PK1718.C43D39 2009
891.4'434—dc22 2008055911

1 3 5 7 9 8 6 4 2

Printed in the United States of America
on acid-free paper

For my grandchildren (to date): Amalia Lakshmi, Luke Xavier,
Christian Paul, and Maximilian Julius.
śiśavo jagan modena pūrayanti
("Children fill the world with gladness")

Preface and Acknowledgments

Debī Chaudhurāṇī is the second of the famous nineteenth-century Bengali novelist, Bankim Chatterji's, last three novels—the so-called *trayī* or triad purportedly illustrating in narrative form the ideology Bankim developed in later life to undergird the polity of an India emerging into modernity. As I have indicated in the Introduction to this translation, there is truth to the view that these three novels are meant to be of a piece ideologically. In 2005, my treatment of the first of the trilogy, *Ānandamaṭh*, was published. It had a lengthy Introduction, full English translation, and an extensive Critical Apparatus. I have followed this pattern in my treatment of *Debī Chaudhurāṇī*. Since many preliminary matters concerning Bankim and his times, not to mention my philosophy of translation, were discussed in the Introduction to *Ānandamaṭh*, I have not repeated them here; it might be helpful, therefore, to dip into the previous discussion to supplement what is said in the present one. In essence, however, both books are meant to be read as self-contained works, and I have made no assumptions about any previous knowledge that the reader is expected to bring to the reading of this one.

Once again, it is a duty and a pleasure to acknowledge help received toward the completion of this book. It is impossible to mention all concerned, but my thanks again in particular to the Ramakrishna Mission Institute of Culture at Golpark in Kolkata for hospitality and assistance, especially to Gopa Basu Mallick, Library Assistant, who delved successfully into the archives when hope was fading, to the Librarian, Swami Gitatmananda, for issuing enabling permissions, and to Swami Prabhananda, the then General Secretary, for presiding over it all. Many thanks to Kumud Ranjan Biswas, retired Indian Administrative Officer, for information on the history of land tenure in Bengal; to Richard Widdess, Professor of Musicology at the School of Oriental and African Studies, University of London, for sharing his expertise; to the two readers of the manuscript appointed by the Press for their helpful feedback; to the Managers of the University of Cambridge's Foreign Travel Fund and to the Managers of the funds of the Divinity Faculty for financial support; and to my good friend Pradip Bhattacharya of the Indian Civil Service for ferreting out the seemingly unferretable. A special word of thanks to David "DB" Goode, Computer Officer of the Divinity Faculty at Cambridge, not only for ready and cheerful assistance in the ordinary things, but also for unassuming and crucial computer wizardry when it came to the extraordinary matter of converting (ancient) files into modern ones (diacritics and all). A computer dinosaur like me can only stand back and wonder gratefully. Special thanks too to the Press' Commissioning Editor, Cynthia Read, who came to the rescue at a critical time, and to the rest of her team for their courtesy and efficiency.

Very many thanks to Rachel McDermott, friend and distinguished scholar of Bengali culture in her own right. She read the whole manuscript of this work prior to publication and made many helpful suggestions and comments, which I was glad to follow up. She also very kindly sent me a photocopy of Subodhcandra Mitra's English translation of *Debī Chaudhurāṇī,* which I was unable to procure myself. I refer to this act of particular kindness again in the Introduction.

But most especially, I would like to thank my chief confabulator in this project, Sajal Bandyopadhyay, who gave so generously of his time, goodwill, and knowledge. The mistakes that remain are attributable to me alone. The dedication speaks for itself: a grandfather's lot is truly a happy one.

Procedural Note

As in the case of its predecessor, *Ānandamaṭh*, or *The Sacred Brotherhood*, this work is in several parts: there is a substantial Introduction, placing the novel in context and discussing its content; this is followed by an English translation of the sixth book-edition of the novel (the "standard edition"), which is followed in turn by the Critical Apparatus, two Appendices, and further material. In the translation of the novel, I have kept footnotes to a minimum; such footnotes as do exist have, I believe, a clarificatory function, enabling the reader to follow the narrative through some of its more obscure, time- or culture-bound references. Since there have been no less than seven editions of the story—if one includes the (partial) serial version—a number of significant variants of sections of the narrative exist. Some of these variants are of negligible import for the development of the story (e.g., changes of spelling and verbal forms); but others are more significant. In the Critical Apparatus, under the heading "Variants" for a particular chapter, I have noted the changes I believe to be of significance. Variants are signaled by an asterisk in the body of the translation; on encountering an *, the reader may turn to the "Variants" section of the corresponding chapter in the Critical Apparatus and consult how the text differed in a previous (indicated) edition. In this way, changes to the development of the narrative may be traced. The "Variants" section of a chapter in the Critical Apparatus is followed by that of the "Notes," in which certain words, ideas, or themes of the story are explained. The two Appendices contain more extensive variants found in the (incomplete) serial version of the novel. As in the case of *Ānandamaṭh*, Bengali terms have generally been given what I call "phonetic" diacriticals, viz. marks that will guide those familiar with Sanskrit or Bengali to a recognition of the original words.

This work may be approached in one of two ways: either (1) the reader may read the story first, aided by the Critical Apparatus and Appendices, and then go on to peruse the Introduction in an effort to place the narrative in context, or (2) he or she may begin with the Introduction and then proceed to the story, guided in the process by reference to the Critical Apparatus and Appendices. Notice that in both cases I have included the Introduction as a necessary part of the process. I recommend the second approach: Can one enjoy the main course on offer without first whetting the appetite by recourse to an appropriate starter?

Contents

Abbreviations

(See the Select Bibliography for further details.)

AM(L):	J. Lipner's *Ānandamaṭh*, or *The Sacred Brotherhood*
BcJ:	Amitrasūdan Bhaṭṭācārja's *Baṅkimcandrajībanī*
ChUp:	The *Chāndogya Upaniṣad*
DCB:	Debprasād Bhaṭṭācārya's *Debī Caudhurāṇī* with Notes
DCM:	Subodh Chunder Mitter's translation of *Debī Chaudhurāṇī*
DCsv:	*Debī Caudhurāṇī*, serial version
DT:	Bankim's *Dharmatattva*
KaUp:	*Kaṭha Upaniṣad*
SBA:	*Saral Bāṅgālā Abhidhān* edited by Subalcandra Mitra
skr.:	Sanskrit

Introduction

Bankim Chatterji (1838–94) began *Debī Chaudhurāṇī* as a serial in the December 1882 issue (Bengali Era (B.E.): Pauṣ 1289) of the monthly journal, *Baṅgadarśan,* which he had created ten years earlier.[1] Ostensibly, it is a tale set in the last quarter of the eighteenth century in the district of Rangpur situated in the northern sector of the greater Bengal of the day. A young, beautiful Brahmin woman—all of Bankim's leading young women are beautiful—Prafulla by name, has been married off to the son of a rich landlord. The latter has refused to take her in as the result of a misunderstanding that is not her fault. He is a bigoted man who accuses his daughter-in-law of having lost caste. Consequently, she has no recourse but to live with her widowed mother in dire poverty. Before long, news reaches her in-laws that she has died. Prafulla, however, is very much alive: she had been abducted, but has escaped.

After an adventure or two in a dense forest in the course of which she finds a hoard of buried treasure, Prafulla meets a learned bandit-chief (also a Brahmin), Bhabani Pathak, who in the manner of Robin Hood robs from the rich and corrupt to give to the poor. Bhabani Pathak persuades Prafulla to dedicate her life and her treasure to helping the needy. Over ten years the chaste Bhabani trains Prafulla to become a hardy member of his gang. Prafulla, now known as Debi Chaudhurani, becomes notorious in the region as the Queen of Bhabani's followers. She lives with her female attendants in a lavishly decorated barge which roams the numerous watercourses of the region. However, her opulence and queenly image are only a front. Her training under Bhabani has made her as selfless and dedicated to his cause as he. Still, Debi, who has preserved her integrity as a faithful (though cast-off) wife under Bhabani's protection, hankers for a life of domesticity with her rather feckless husband, Brajesvar, who is devoted to his father, the landlord Haraballabh (the villain of the piece). Neither Brajesvar nor Haraballabh (who had turned Prafulla out of the house a decade earlier) knows that Debi is really Prafulla. Haraballabh hatches a plot to capture Debi, pocket a reward and ingratiate himself with the English rulers of the region. Needless to say, Debi evades capture. All sorts of wonderful complications arise which result in Debi, Bhabani, Brajesvar, Haraballabh, and Brenan, the English officer in charge of the force sent to apprehend Debi (not to mention a few others), finding themselves thrown together on Debi's escaping barge. Though by now Debi is known to her husband, she succeeds in concealing her identity from her father-in-law. From here the story moves rapidly to its denouement. The English lieutenant is sent packing, Debi's followers are soon disbanded, Bhabani Pathak departs a sadder and wiser man, and Prafulla is accepted back in her in-laws' house at the instigation of her doting husband. The errant wife has finally come home.

[1] Strictly speaking, the Bengali transliteration of the novel's title should omit the "h" after the "C," viz. *Debī Caudhurāṇī.* But since the Bengali consonant *c* is pronounced as in the English "Ch," I shall write *Chaudhurāṇī* for phonetic convenience.

The novel was not completed as a serial. It ceased to appear in this form at the end of Part II in January 1884 (the B.E. Māgh 1290 issue of the journal). It was then revised, completed, and published as a book for the first time in May 1884, with subsequent minor revision up to and inclusive of the sixth book-edition in 1891. In due course we shall take note of the significance of these changes or variants.[2] Here I wish to point out that there are undercurrents to the overall story that at times rise openly to the surface, thus giving the lie to the "ostensibly" with which I began its description. *Debī Chaudhurāṇī* is really a thinly disguised tale of *dharma,* in the sense of the new social order that its by now famous author envisaged for the Bengal and India that were coming to terms with modernity under British rule.

In fact as a literary exercise, the novel is a mixed bag. Some critics do not like it at all. "*Debi Chaudhurani* is the weakest of all that Bankim wrote," opines Sisir Kumar Das. "Its story is sketchy and unrealistic, its characters controlled by Bankim's religious ideas and not by the natural laws of fiction. . . . The artist Bankim surrenders completely to a weak propagandist" (S. K. Das 1984:174, 177). But, notwithstanding one's puzzlement as to what "the natural laws of fiction" might be, this judgment is unduly harsh in my opinion, and fails to take account of the context of the times. No doubt the novel has a blatant didactic ring to it, but it also has a number of redeeming literary features. The plot itself involves river-bandits and forests, buried treasure, mistaken identity, and rescue, not to mention a battle or two. A gamut of experiences, raw and more nuanced, is described: grief, desolation, self-sacrifice, devotion, fidelity, treachery, bigotry, simmering passion, love, to name but some. There is also, as one would expect from Bankim, a fair amount of humor: the descriptions of the decline of the staff (*lāṭhi*) as a weapon and instrument of authority in Bengal, of the excitement created in the village when Brajesvar (pronounced "Brajeshor" in Bengali) visits his father-in-law's house, of the breathless curiosity among the villagers to see the "new bride" when Prafulla finally returns, are classic vignettes of Bengali literature, besides providing insightful glimpses into the culture of the times. While there is perhaps a depiction or two in more ponderous traditional mode, for example, that of the Teesta river in flood as a reflection of Debi's voluptuous

[2]I have given the variant readings worth noting from the serial and other versions in the two Appendices and Critical Apparatus at the end, to enable the reader to trace the development of the novel as a literary creation. As stated, the serial version was begun in *Baṅgadarśan* in December 1882, when Bankim was no longer the journal's editor. His older brother, Sanjibcandra, now acted in this role. When the novel was discontinued in its serial form (January 1884), the journal was being edited by a Candranath Basu in a way that greatly disappointed Bankim so that he no longer wished it to continue. This resulted in the closure of the journal and the suspension of the novel (*Baṅgadarśan* was revived in April 1901 under the editorship of Rabindranath Tagore). The translation in this book follows the sixth book-edition after the text edited by Brajendranath Bandyopadhyay and Sajanikanta Das, and published by the Baṅgīya Sāhitya Pariṣat (the Literary Society of Bengal). The variant readings of the serial version, abbv.*DCsv* in this book, which are substantial on occasion, are surprisingly omitted under the variant readings given in the Baṅgīya Sāhitya Pariṣat edition.

beauty and unrequited passion, Bankim also writes with a light, idiomatic touch, a pioneering feature of his art as a novelist. And then there are those passages that draw the reader in, provoking a response for the first time perhaps of psychological recognition, an immersive exploration of emotion that the reader had not perceived so clearly before. This is how Bankim describes Brajesvar's feelings when, some time after he had spent a night with Prafulla, Brajesvar thinks that he has lost her forever:

> Not much more was said that day. Even Grandaunt Brahma didn't understand fully, for it wasn't that simple. Prafulla was incomparably beautiful, and while it was true that it was by her beauty that she had captivated Brajesvar's heart, he also realized that day he'd met her that she was more beautiful and sweet within than outside. If Prafulla had, as his wife, lived with him in her own right... then this intoxicating infatuation would have turned into the tenderest love. Infatuation for her beauty would have given way to infatuation for her virtues. But that didn't happen. The lightning that was Prafulla flashed but once, and then dissolved forever into the darkness, so that that intoxication multiplied a thousandfold. So much for the simplicity of the matter.
>
> As to its complexity—there was an intense compassion to preside over it all! After that golden icon had been deprived of its rightful claim, and been insulted and falsely given a bad name, it had been cast out forever. And it was now desperate for food. Perhaps it would die of starvation! Add to that deep attachment this profound compassion, and the measure was full. Brajesvar's heart was overwhelmed by Prafulla—there was room for nothing else. The old lady didn't understand as much. (Part 1, ch.14)

No other Bengali novelist had written like this: confronting the reader, penetrating analytically the complexity of emotion in its cultural specificity. This is why, after its serial beginning, the novel became popular and was published no less than six times in book-form during Bankim's lifetime. Sisir Kumar Das, in the quotation given earlier, speaks of Bankim's intention in this novel as "propagandist." There is no doubt, as has been stated earlier, that by writing this novel Bankim wished to convey a message. Deciphering what this might be will be our chief task in this Introduction.

Debī Chaudhurāṇī is reckoned as Bankim's thirteenth novel. It was preceded by *Ānandamaṭh*, a story of a band of forest-dwelling warrior-monks who fight to rid Bengal of foreign rule (both Muslim and British),[3] and succeeded

[3]The serial version began in *Baṅgadarśan* in March 1881; the novel was first published as a book in 1882. I have given an extensive Introduction to the novel, with a full English translation and Critical Apparatus, in *Ānandamaṭh* or *The Sacred Brotherhood*, Oxford University Press, New York, 2005 (abbv.: *AM*(L)).

by *Sītārām,* whose eponymous antihero seeks to establish a kingdom in which Hindus and Muslims can live in harmony, only to see it destroyed by his obsessive lust for his wife Sri, who has turned into an ascetic immune to his blandishments.[4] All three novels are set more or less in the same period, about a hundred years before the last decade of Bankim's life; all three become vehicles for expressing, through their events and characters, the neo-conservative vision of *dharma* (the right religious, social, and political order that must imbue the new India) that Bankim shaped toward the end of his life. This was a *dharma* supposedly rooted in Hindu tradition but modified and updated (in this sense it was a new form of the Eternal Law or *sanātana dharma*) to meet the requirements of modernity as moderated by current Western ideas and mediated by British rule. It was a *dharma* under the sovereignty of a theistic Absolute (*īśvar*), with the figure of a reconstructed Krishna regarded as historical and shorn of its supernatural accretions acting as moral exemplar, in a context in which both men and women equally were to seek happiness in this life by striving to cultivate as fully as possible their physical, mental, and aesthetic capabilities. With special relevance to our analysis of *Debī Chaudhurāṇī,* this last requirement did not entail resorting to a kind of reductive gender-equality where women should attempt to be "as good as men" in all aspects of life, but rather cultivating in a disciplined way the full range of powers which they shared as human on the one hand, and which were specific to their sex on the other. We shall return to this point later. Here we note that no room seems to have been made in this scheme for a partnering role in creating the new India for other long-standing dwellers in the land, such as Muslims and Christians, and this strikes me as a fateful flaw of the project. But we cannot dwell on this here.[5]

In teasing out this idea of *dharma* for a specifically Hindu polity, Bankim was particularly influenced on the Hindu side by the *Bhagavad Gītā,* a religious Sanskrit text famous in Hindu tradition from about the beginning of the Common Era and which Bankim describes in the novel as the "best of all works" (*sarbbagranthaśreṣṭha,* Pt.I, ch.15), and on the Western side, by the humanistic thought of A. Comte, Herbert Spencer, and J.R. Seeley among others.

The interpretative tradition of Bankim's works has grouped these three novels into a loose triad (or *trayī*) expressing in concrete form—through the events and characterization of narrative discourse—the *dharmic* ideology of the later Bankim. As indicative of this trend, already in July 1884 in his Bengali fortnightly, the *Samālocak*, Thakurdas Mukhopadhyay could write in an early review as follows (since *Sītārām* had only just begun its serial existence, it could not be included):

---

[4]*Sītārām* was begun as a serial in the first issue of the monthly journal, *Pracār*, in July 1884. It was first published as a book in 1887.

[5]For fuller consideration on this matter with reference to Bankim's work, see *AM*(L), Introduction (esp. Parts III and IV), and my essay, "'Icon and Mother': an inquiry into India's national song," *Journal of Hindu Studies*, 1:26–48, 2008.

> What the sage [Bankim] has shown through...the narrative of *Debī Chaudhurāṇī,* we see nowhere else...Selfless action (*niṣkām karma*)—the great driving force of Aryan life, the refreshing fruit—overflowing with the nectar of immortality—of the best of all works, the holy *Bhagavad Gītā*...is the basis of the book, *Debī Chaudhurāṇī.* And it is to explain the *dharma* of selfless action which benefits everyone, to create a sense of integration with the world, that Bengal's...chief author is now occupied. The first fruit of his endeavour was *Ānandamaṭh,* and the second is *Debī Chaudhurāṇī.* In other words, *Debī Chaudhurāṇī* provides a conclusion for *Ānandamaṭh*. The sage ended *Ānandamaṭh* with the words: "The flame that Satyananda had lit before departing did not die out easily. If I get the chance, I'll tell you about that some other time."[6] He has told it in *Debī Chaudhurāṇī. Ānandamaṭh* and *Debī Chaudhurāṇī* are trees from the same seed, depictions from the same mould....The events of both works took place at about the same time...[and] in the locations of both, the country lacks proper rule and the people are oppressed....In the first work, knowledge (*jñān*) lies at its action's root as its secondary objective, while devotion to one's country as the motherland is the first. Both these things occur at the root of the action of the second work....Debi [demonstrates] action imbued with knowledge (*jñānātmak karma*); in *Ānandamaṭh* we find but a trace of the knowledge on which this action is based. Since Debi Chaudhurani follows only the course of action [in her life]...we could say that the knowledge [of *Ānandamaṭh*] and the recourse to action [of *Debī Chaudhurāṇī*] reflect each other....In *Debī Chaudhurāṇī* a most beautiful, vivid portrait of the action-part [of the equation] has been painted.[7]

So here we have a critic who rather likes *Debī Chaudhurāṇī,* and who sees it as completing to some extent the thinking considered to underlie *Ānandamaṭh* (recall that *Sītārām* was in its first stages at the time). But other commentators, after *Sītārām*'s completion, went on to integrate, more or less closely, the ideology of Bankim's last novel with that of the preceding two (see, e.g., S.K. Das [1984:ch.12]).[8] This ideology receives conceptual development largely in two theoretical projects Bankim was occupied with at this time: (a) the articulation of his new idea of *dharma* (published as a book entitled *Dharmatattva*—"The Essentials of *Dharma*"—in 1888, but already begun in essay-form in 1884), and (b) a lengthy disquisition on the nature of Krishna Vasudeva, here denuded

[6]This was how the novel ended in the first edition. In addition to a line or two of the conclusion of that edition, it was omitted from the ending of the fifth and standard edition; see *AM*(L):279–80.

[7]Quoted from A. Bhattacarja, 1991:639–40 (abbv.:*BcJ*).

[8]Indeed, the action of *Sītārām* also falls into the time frame of the other two novels.

of the divine attributes ascribed to him by tradition and depicted instead as a historical figure fit to act as the most superior moral ideal for humankind (this work was published under the title of *Kṛṣṇacaritra*—"The Nature of Krishna"—in 1886). In other words, one could say that the trilogy of novels is the narratival counterpart of the late theoretical writings.[9] It would be a useful exercise to attempt conceptually to interlink in detail these two projects, the narratival and the theoretical, but that is not our task in this Introduction.[10] So, after having provided the larger context for *Debī Chaudhurāṇī*, let us proceed to more particular considerations for our understanding of the novel.

The action in *Debī Chaudhurāṇī* spans a period of over ten years, that is, from about 1775 to 1785.[11] The location, as noted earlier, is the jungles and waterways of the Rangpur region in the north of the greater Bengal of the day. As the text avers, neither Muslim nor British rule held sway at the time. The point is that, politically, this is contested territory: there is no local or national power that effectively rules the land. I have pointed out in my earlier work that the same applied narratively for *Ānandamaṭh*,[12] and just as this uncertainty creates space in *Ānandamaṭh* for Bankim, writing with hindsight about a hundred years later, to justify the intervening period of history under British rule *politically* in his own terms, and to suggest a political future for the motherland that subtly alters the trajectory of history, so in *Debī Chaudhurāṇī* this hiatus creates space to justify and endorse a kind of *socio-religious* reform in Hindu society to meet the demands of modernity. But this is not the deracinating reform associated with the Western-orientated Brahmo Samaj or Young Bengal who were

[9]From the point of view of Bankim's Bengali writings, one could add here Bankim's incomplete commentary on the *Bhagavad Gītā* (for a treatment of which, see Harder [2001]). But this was very incomplete, Bankim's commentary reaching only the fourth chapter (out of eighteen) of the *Gītā;* some of the commentary was published serially in *Pracār* in 1886–8.

[10]Indeed, in *Dharmatattva* Bankim makes explicit reference to *Debī Chaudhurāṇī* as illustrating a point or two. Thus in ch.8 of *Dharmatattva*, Bankim is recommending the disciplined cultivation (which he calls *anuśīlan*) of one's physical powers (*bṛtti*). In the course of his discourse with his Teacher (*Guru*), the disciple says: "So for the person who cultivates his or her physical powers, it is not enough to be only healthy and strong; he or she must be skilled in physical exercise…" The Guru answers: "Make sure you add wrestling to this exercise, for this is particularly strengthening. It helps particularly to protect both oneself and the other." Here there is a footnote in the original which says: "In the book *Debī Chaudhurāṇī* written by the author, the young woman Prafulla has been portrayed as an example of this disciplined cultivation (*anuśīlan*). So even though she's a woman she's been made to learn how to wrestle."

[11]In Part I, ch.8 of the novel, the author writes: "The region had no proper ruler at that time: Muslim rule had passed, while British rule had not been properly established. Besides, a few years earlier the famine of '76 had devastated the land…." The "famine of '76" denotes (in the reckoning of the B.E. of the text) the great Bengal famine of 1770–1. If that had passed "a few years earlier" (*bachar kata haila*), the action now is in, say, 1775. Prafulla undergoes specific training under Bhabani Pathak for ten years after this, and the story continues again; so that would give a time span from about 1775 to 1785 for the story to unfold.

[12]See *AM*(L):59–60.

perceived generally to ride roughshod over the continuities of Bengali Hindu tradition, rather it is a more sober transformation, sensitive to ancestral norms and effected through a considered dialogue with Western ideas.[13]

This is why Bankim is keen to assert that the novel, though not lacking completely in historical basis, is not meant to be a historical novel. In a Notice at the beginning of *Debī Chaudhurāṇī*, he writes:

> Only a portion of *Debī Chaudhurāṇī* was published in *Baṅgadarśan*. The whole book is published here.
>
> After *Ānandamaṭh* was published many wanted to know if there was any historical basis to that work. The *sannyāsī*-revolt was historical no doubt, but there was no special need to make that known to the reader, and it was with this in mind that I said nothing about it. Since it was not my intention to write a historical novel, I made no pretence about historicity. . . . Similarly, there's a slight historical basis to *Debī Chaudhurāṇī*. Whoever wishes to be apprised of the facts can do so if they read the historical evidence pertaining to Rangpur District in the "Statistical Account" of Bengal collated by Mr. Hunter and promulgated by the Government. There's not much in this respect, and there's very little connection between the historical Debi Chaudhurani and the book. The names Debi Chaudhurani, Bhabani Pathak, Mr. Goodlad, and Lieutenant Brenan are historical, as indeed are the few facts that Debi lived in a boat, and that she had "fighters" and armies etc. But that is all. If the reader would be so kind as not to consider *Ānandamaṭh* or *Debī Chaudhurāṇī* a "historical novel" (*aitihāsik upanyās*), I'd be most obliged.

[13]The Brahmo Samaj, founded in the first quarter of the nineteenth century in Calcutta and eventually developing into a fragmented movement seeking change in Bengali society by responding to Western, British-mediated influences (see Kopf [1979]), could generate the following perception (as quoted in Jones [1976:42–3] from the *Arya Magazine*, May 1882): "Some [Brahmos] took unhesitatingly to coats, hats, and pants without any censure from their co-labourers. Thus indirectly encouraged they went further, and began to indulge freely in the habit of resorting to hotels and eating with forks and knives on tables. In a word they commenced to imitate the customs and manners of Europeans. . . . [They] began to exchange presents in Christmas, to which they saw no objection. They thus saw all evil in everything national, and all good in everything European." As for Young Bengal, that body of rebellious youth in the first half of the nineteenth century, their reputation for flouting ancestral ways was even more radical. As one newspaper report put it, they showed their contempt for traditional Hinduism by "cutting their way through ham and beef and wading to liberalism through tumblers of beer." Perhaps the passage quoted above from the *Arya Magazine* criticizing the Brahmo movement is somewhat tendentious since its founding source, the Arya Samaj, was a rival reform movement. No doubt too some Brahmo leaders (e.g., Debendranath Tagore and even the founder of the Samaj, RamMohan Roy) wished to be seen as reforming Hinduism from within. The point is, however, that in theory at least Brahmos sat lightly to those forms of *dharma* that upheld caste-distinctions, and they inveighed against such traditional practices as image-worship and other forms of religious ritual; here they rejected both form and content. As we shall see, in these respects Bankim, who was not a Brahmo, generally sought to retain form but transform content.

It will help to glance here at the "slight historical basis" (*ekṭu aitihāsik mūl*) of the novel, the better to try and understand what Bankim set out ideologically to accomplish. As Bankim indicates, this basis can be gleaned from the important statistical account of Bengal produced by W.W. Hunter (1840–1900), the well-known civil servant who labored for many years in the area. In Vol.VII, which deals with the Districts of Maldah, Rangpur, and Dinajpur, Hunter quotes from a Report produced by a Collector he refers to as a Mr. Glazier. This Report, we are told, pertains to "the close of the last [viz. 18th] century" (p.158). So the period of the Report coincides with that of the novel.

> Rangpur, writes Glazier, as a frontier District bordering on Nepal, Bhutan, Kuch Behar, and Assam, was peculiarly liable to be infested by banditti, who ravaged the country in armed bands numbering several hundreds.... The tract of country lying south of the stations [viz. administrative centres] of Dinajpur and Rangpur, and west of the present District of Bogra, towards the Ganges, was a favourite haunt of these banditti, being far removed from any central authority. In 1787, Lieutenant Brenan was employed in this quarter against a notorious leader of *dakaits* (gang robbers), named Bhawani Pathak. He despatched a native officer, with twenty-four sepoys [Indian troops under European command and training], in search of the robbers, who surprised Pathak, with sixty of his followers, in their boats. A fight took place, in which Pathak himself and three of his lieutenants were killed, and eight wounded, besides forty-two taken prisoners. Pathak was a native of Bajpur, and was in league with another noted *dakait*, named Majnu Shah, who made yearly raids from the southern side of the Ganges. We catch a glimpse from the Lieutenant's report of a female *dakait*, by name Debi Chaudhurani, also in league with Pathak. She lived in boats, had a large force of *barkandazs* [armed fighters, bodyguards] in her pay, and committed *dakaitis* on her own account, besides receiving a share of the booty obtained by Pathak. Her title of Chaudhurani would imply that she was a *zamindar* [landlord], probably a petty one, else she need not have lived in boats for fear of capture (Hunter 1876, Vol.VII:158–9).

That is more or less it. Further detailed information about the *dramatis personae* is scarce, and this gives Bankim the freedom to build characters and weave a plot unencumbered by historical verisimilitude, in the service of the message he sought to convey. Indeed, Bankim's own creation goes against even the little information we glean from Glazier's Report. Bankim makes no mention of Majnu Shah (unless he has been transformed into Rangaraj, Bhabani's chief lieutenant, in the novel), nor apparently is Bhabani Pathak a non-Bengali (he is described in very Bengali terms in the story, and is a bandit with a social conscience), and he does not die in the novel in the way the statistical account records;[14] further, I doubt very much whether the Debi of history was the chaste wife of Bankim's story! Be that as it may, the glimpsed romance of Glazier's account becomes fertile ground for development in a number of interesting ways at Bankim's hands.

In short, Debi exemplifies through the machinations of event and plot, Bankim's ideal of the *dharmic* person as spelt out in the treatise, *Dharmatattva* (*DT*). As such, she is the counterpart (being female), as well as the reduced image with her human frailties, of the perfect, rounded individual, Krishna Vasudeva, the *dharmic* ideal of *DT*, and the subject in his own right—as a historical personage provisionally denuded of his traditional divine attributes—of Bankim's text, the *Kṛṣṇacaritra*. This is not fanciful thinking. Bankim seems to have made this identification in as many words in the last chapter of the novel. Here Debi's (or the transformed Prafulla's) practice of the path of selfless action (*niṣkām karma*)—for Bankim the central teaching of the *Bhagavad Gītā*, "the Song of the Lord (Krishna himself)"—comes to full fruition.

Bankim first assures us that she has succeeded in her practice.

> "It was after [Prafulla] came into the family that she became a true renouncer (*sannyāsinī*)," he writes authorially. "She had no selfish desires; all she sought was to engage in work. The goal of selfish desire is to seek one's own happiness, while work's goal is to seek the happiness of others. Prafulla was selfless, that is, intent on work, so she was a true renouncer. This is why whatever Prafulla touched would turn to gold."

As the novel relates, of Prafulla's golden touch there can be no doubt. After she has cheerfully given up the command of armies in order to instruct her maidservants about their household chores and relinquished the queenly wealth of previous years to wash dishes and sweep the floors, she is able to reconcile all family differences, previous rivalries, and the competing demands of her wifely duties. Her unassuming learning and shrewdness of intellect enable her to give advice on the management of her father-in-law's estates so that "the family's wealth and prosperity grew with each passing day." She establishes a hostel called *Debinibas*, "Debi's Home," till finally, "surrounded by her children and grandchildren, Prafulla died, and the people of the region felt that they had lost a mother." Can one end one's days more perfectly than this? But this is not intended to be realistic; it is a translation from the mortal state to the immortal, a passage from raw humanity to the perfection of wisdom and action. Prafulla has realized the *Gītā*'s teaching of selfless service, and in this sense she is a Krishna reborn. As if to accentuate this, Bankim ends the novel with these words:

> So come now, Prafulla! Return to our world once more and let us behold you. Why don't you confront this society of ours and say: "I am

[14]"The real Bhabani Pathak was a Bihari Brahmin, a Bhojpuri [Glazier's 'Bajpur'] from the Ara district": Jadunath Sarkar in the "Historical Introduction" to B. Bandyopadhyay and S. Das' centenary edition of the novel, p.1.

> not something new; I go back in time. For I am that very same Voice of the past. How often have I come to you, and you have forgotten me, and so I have come again! *To protect the good, to destroy the wicked, and to establish right order (dharma), I take birth in every age.*"

The words in Italics are the words of Krishna himself uttered in the fourth chapter of the *Gītā* (vr.8). Prafulla's transformed life memorializes the Krishna of the *Gītā* and his teaching; Bankim calls each of us to follow her example to the best of our ability, so that we too can become, in our individual circumstances, an embodiment, as he saw it, of Hinduism's *dharmic* ideal.

But how does this transformation take place? As mentioned earlier, and as explained in the *Dharmatattva*, it is achieved by the disciplined cultivation (*anuśīlan*) of our physical, mental, and aesthetic capabilities (*bṛttis*) in a spirit of proper love (*prīti, bhakti*)—in ascending order of priority—for ourselves, our families, the society, and birthland in which we live, and the whole world of inorganic and organic being, all encompassed in and orientated to the love of God (*īśvar*). This is what the *Gītā* teaches. But there must be a balance, a harmonization (*sāmañjasya*) of these loves; one cannot be emphasized at the expense of another. Western patriotism has done just this, viz. seeking the aggrandizement of one's own country at the expense of other peoples (hence colonialism); Hindus have gone the other way: loving all creation at the expense of a proper patriotism and self-love (hence meekly accepting foreign rule). The *locus classicus* for the development of this integrated love, its theater for a proper maturity, is not the life of the wandering renouncer or ascetic (*sannyāsī*), but society. For it is amid the relationships of society that self-love and other love, love for one's country and love for the world as encompassed in love for God, can be properly articulated and perfected.[15]

A concrete exemplification of this discipline—albeit narratively—is Prafulla/Debi/Prafulla, or rather, the raw Prafulla, disciplined into Debi, and finally transformed into the mature, re-domesticated Prafulla. Bankim spends two chapters of the novel illustrating how this disciplined cultivation or *anuśīlan* of the faculties might take place. After Prafulla, barely out of her teens, has escaped from her abductors and found the hoard of treasure in a derelict mansion in a forest, she meets Bhabani Pathak and agrees to throw in her lot with him and use her wealth as he thinks fit (she seems to have little alternative). But for this she needs to be instructed by him. The initial instruction takes place over five years (described in Part I, chs.15 and 16).

The focus in these chapters is on Prafulla's physical, mental, and spiritual training. Thus, her thirst for knowledge is fed by acquiring basic skills of reading, writing, and mathematics, which culminate in the mastering of Sanskrit grammar and literature, not to mention studying "a little Samkhya philosophy,

[15] See *DT*, especially chs.20–5.

Vedanta, and traditional logic—but only a little. After introducing Prafulla to these philosophical systems, [Bhabani] occupied her in the detailed study of the Yoga texts. Finally, he made her study the *Srimad Bhagavad Gita*, the best of all works" (I.15). All this in five years—wonderful! One continually hopes for students as responsive as this (no doubt, though, artistic license had a part to play in reducing the time required for Prafulla's academic achievements).

But note the Sanskritic nature of this instruction. Prafulla seems not to have spent any time familiarizing herself with masterpieces of Muslim thought in, say, Urdu or Persian (after all, a culturally sophisticated Muslim presence in these languages had been developing in India with its outreach in Bengal for long centuries by the time the novel's action takes place), or even with the well-known Bengali versions of the great epics, the *Mahābhārata* and the *Rāmāyaṇa,* attributed to the savants Kāśīrām (17th century) and Kṛttibās (*c.*15th century) respectively. Where higher learning was concerned, she appears to have been instructed exclusively in the Sanskritic tradition. This is a reflection, of course, of Bankim's own contemporary evaluation of the traditional sources of knowledge requisite for a dialogue with the West to prepare for the India of the future. But why the Sanskritic tradition? As I have written elsewhere: "In the eyes of the-then Bengali intelligentsia, Sanskrit afforded a link of continuity, culturally and religiously, with the ancestral tradition of the majority. As such, the judicious application of Sanskrit was a psychological marker of cultural ballast, of legitimizing authority…and of a sense of Hindu national identity."[16] Another marker of Bankim's exclusively "neo-conservative" Hindu project.

But while Bhabani Pathak was educating Prafulla's mental faculties (*mānasik bṛttis*, to use *DT* terminology), he was also seeing to the development of her physical powers (*śārīrik bṛttis*). The regime he imposed required unquestioning obedience; it was calculated not only to harden Prafulla physically but also to encourage her to choose a life of strict discipline as her preferred course of action. Here are some examples:

> "With regard to dress, for the first year she was allowed four items of clothing; for the second year, just two. During summer in the third year she had to wear a thick, coarse cloth; it was to be washed and dried while she was still wearing it. During winter she had to do the same with a thin piece of Dhaka cotton. For the fourth year, she had to wear a cloth of Dhaka silk.…For the fifth year, she could wear whatever she wished: Prafulla continued with the thick, coarse cloth. From time to time she'd wash it in alkaline water.

[16]In my essay, "'Icon and Mother': an inquiry into India's national song" (see note 5). See also Victor van Bijlert, "Sanskrit and Hindu national identity in nineteenth century Bengal," and Corstiaan van der Burg, "The place of Sanskrit in neo-Hindu ideologies: from religious reform to national awakening," in Jan E.M. Houben (1996).

> The same applied with regard to doing her hair. For the first year, she was not allowed to use oil: she had to tie her hair unoiled. During the second year, she was not allowed even to tie her hair; day and night her dry tresses would hang disheveled. During the third year, in accordance with Bhabani Thakur's instructions, Prafulla shaved her head.[17] In the fourth year, her hair grew again, and Bhabani Thakur ordered her to rub her hair with perfumed oil and keep it dressed continually. For the fifth year she was told to do as she pleased. That year, Prafulla never even touched her hair," and so on (see Part I, ch.15).[18]

After this training, Bhabani discourses with Prafulla on the teaching of the *Gītā* (Part I, ch.16), driving home philosophically and morally the need for a life of selfless action. It was only in this way that she could live with her public image as a prominent member of his band and dispose of her immense wealth for the benefit of the poor. The wealth in reality, taught Bhabani, belonged to Sri Krishna, the Lord of heaven and earth, the possessor of everything, the fitting recipient of the fruit of all her actions. Since the Lord pervaded and indwelt all being and had a special predilection for the needy, by distributing her wealth to the needy, she was in fact returning to Krishna what was really his. Bhabani explained in graphic detail the abuses the poor had endured from the rapine and greed of the local landlords and their minions.

> Prafulla's heart had melted when she heard this harrowing tale of the people. She thanked Bhabani Thakur a thousand times and said, "Yes, I'll go with you. If I'm entitled to spend this wealth, then I'll take some of it with me, and give it to those who suffer."
>
> Bhabani said, "I've said we'll need to dissemble to do this work. If you come with me, you'll have to dress up a bit. This job can't be done in the clothes of a renouncer."

> "I have offered my actions to Sri Krishna," replied Prafulla. "So the actions are His, not mine, and the pleasure and pain that arise from getting the job done are His alone, not mine. I'll do whatever is necessary to get His work done." Bhabani Thakur was well-satisfied. (Part I, ch.16).

This complements Bankim's main thesis in the *DT* like a glove. At the end of the chapter, Prafulla is given a further five years to learn how to implement this teaching through a life of action as Debi Chaudhurani. So, using the Sanskritic tradition especially in the form of the *Gītā*'s teaching as a prime spiritual

[17] "Thakur" here is used as a term of respect for Bhabani.

[18] It is also clear that Bhabani did not neglect Debi's "aesthetic" capabilities (in *DT* terminology, her *cittarañjinī* powers; see ch.5) which are in full evidence during her playing of the *vīṇā* in Part II, ch.3 of the novel.

resource, valorizing a life of selfless action on the grounds of returning to God (in the person of Krishna), who indwells all, what is really God's, that is, being *in* the world but not *of* the world, and affirming withal, as the text relates, her continuing state as a chaste, married woman, may all be regarded as Prafulla's (in fact, Bankim's) acknowledgment of the norms of a reconstructed Hindu tradition (there were others, as we shall see). These pointers reflect Bankim in "conservative" mode, as an affirmer of tradition. But there were also differences in the reconstructed Hinduism he shaped that may justify our description of him as a "neo" conservative. This came about as a result of his dialogue with ideas emerging from the West. Let us inquire briefly into this.

The "dialogue" of which we speak took place on several fronts. Consider first the role of caste in *Debī Chaudhurāṇī.* Bankim did not repudiate caste out of hand; granted that caste existed, he repudiated as something sacrosanct the preservation of caste-privilege arising from birth. Himself a Brahmin, in his satirical writings especially, as is well known, he derided mercilessly the image of the ignorant, arrogant, greedy, indolent (one could go on!) Brahmin male who invoked his status as a Brahmin by birth to justify the arrogation of privilege. In "Hindu Dharma," the first part of a lengthy tract entitled, "The nature of deity and Hindu dharma" (*Debtattva o Hindudharma*), published in the first issue of his monthly journal *Pracār,* he writes:

> First one must ask, what is Hindu religion (*hindudharma*)? We observe many types of Hindu orthodoxy (*hinduyānī*). There's the Hindu who doesn't step out if he sneezes, who answers "True! True!" to the clicking call of a gecko, who snaps his fingers if he yawns. Is all this Hindu religion (*hindudharma*)? One musn't sleep facing this way, or eat sitting like that, or start a journey if one sees an empty jar.... Is all this Hindu religion?
>
> We knew a landlord, a Brahmin by birth and very Hindu in his observance of rules. Every day he would rise at dawn—whether in winter or the rainy season—take an early-morning ritual bath and immediately sit down, mind totally focused, to his ritual worship till quite late in the morning. If there was the slightest obstacle to this worship he'd think he'd been struck by lightning. Then at midday he'd eat a vegetarian meal and remain without food for the rest of the day. When he'd finish eating he would sit down to his work as a landlord. Then, which of his tenants he would destroy, the possessions of which defenceless widow he would seize, which debt incurred by him he would evade, which innocent person he must fraudulently send to jail, which lawsuit to prepare under false pretences—these were the things he'd concentrate on and be occupied with. We know that this individual was completely devoted to his worship and his rituals, to his gods and the Brahmins—there was nothing phoney about this. Even when forging something he'd intone Hari's name. He thought that if

> he remembered Hari at this time the forgery would certainly be successful. Now is this individual a Hindu?
>
> Let me tell you about another Hindu. There's virtually nothing he doesn't eat. He eats everything except what's bad for health, and though a Brahmin he even drinks liquor (though not much). He'll accept food from a person of any caste (*jāti*). He doesn't object to eating with Muslims (*jaban*) and Christians (*mleccha*). He practises no daily rituals of worship etc. Nor does he ever tell an untruth, and if he does then . . . it's an untruth that is in effect true in so far as it is intended to act for the common good. He gives to others and seeks their welfare without ulterior motive (*niṣkām*). He controls his senses as best he can and worships God (*īśvar*) in his heart. He deceives no one and never covets what belongs to others. Considering the sky etc. and Indra and the other deities as images of God and expressions of power and beauty, he pays mental homage (*mānasik upāsanā*) to them all, and ascertaining in the revered Krishna spoken of in the *Purāṇa*s the expression of the God (*īśvar*) who possesses all good qualities, he reckons himself a Vaishnava. In accordance with Hindu *dharma* he respects his elders, looks after his wife and children lovingly, and is kind to animals. . . . Is this individual a Hindu? Who among these two persons is a Hindu? Or is neither a Hindu? . . . One individual has fallen from *dharma,* the other has lapsed from its practices. Are the practices *dharma* or is an upright life *dharma* (*ācār dharma, nā dharmai dharma*)? And if the practices are not *dharma* and an upright life is, then one will have to call the upright person who has lapsed from the practices a Hindu. How can one object to this?

This was published in 1884 at about the time of *Debī Chaudhurāṇī.* What Bankim has done here, through the person in the second description, is to speak implicitly in favor of universalizing Hindu *dharma* as a creed that is not totally a function of caste and ritual; further, in effect, Bankim is saying that this is what it means to be truly a Brahmin. It is still a description of a *Hindu* way of life, of Hindu *dharma,* in so far as Hindu images and symbols play their part in portraying and granting access to the Almighty, but it is not Hindu in any obvious sense of the term. (In fact, it is also—and one has but to study what Bankim wrote and professed, to appreciate this—a covert description of the kind of Hindu Bankim perceived himself or wished to be.[19])

So for Bankim the Brahmin was required to discharge responsibilities, not to enjoy entrenched privileges. The Brahmin found himself, on the cusp of a new era, socially and ritually privileged *by the weight of tradition.* This was not his personal

[19]On a theological basis. There is enough evidence to show that on a personal level Bankim was quite happy to attend rituals in the presence of a religious image in the family residence at Kāṭalpāḍā when he visited or stayed. How he interpreted these rituals from a theological point of view is another matter.

achievement for which he could claim credit. He was to use this privileged position, therefore, to discharge the responsibilities of leadership in society for the good of all. He was to do this in a spirit of selfless service (*niṣkām karma*). Without abandoning the cultural genius of his own Hindu tradition, he was to educate himself in the philosophical wisdom and scientific knowledge of the West, now accessible under the influence of British rule, so that his compatriots could share in the fruits of this knowledge and come to terms with the demands of modernity. Nothing stood still—not even the hoary and trusted norms of ancestral Hinduism.

Bankim's trilogy of final novels endorses Brahmin leadership under this rubric. Much is made in *Debī Chaudhurāṇī* of Brahminness: we are left in no doubt that Bhabani Pathak is a Brahmin, that his chief lieutenant, Rangaraj, is a Brahmin, that Debi comes from Brahmin stock as do her in-laws. Her father-in-law is reviled for his sense of Brahmin self-preservation and his bigotry; he is not the sort of Brahmin Bankim favors. Debi, however, is a "self-made" Brahmin in the mode Bankim endorses. At the beginning of the novel she loses caste in her father-in-law's eyes, but without due cause. She is rejected as an outcaste and lives in a forest. As I have noted in my Introduction to *AM*(L), "Just as the forest is able to change form itself, so it is the locus of changing identities in others (43).... In Hindu tradition... the forest is a classic arena of liminality and transition (55, see further)." It is in the forest that Prafulla meets her instructor, Bhabani Pathak, and it is there that she begins her transformation from being a raw, uneducated young woman with potential, to becoming the erudite, resourceful Debi Chaudhurani. Further, it is through her activities as Debi in the forest and its waterways (it is in a clearing in the forest that she holds court and distributes her wealth to the needy) that she meets her long-lost husband and is re-instated as a fitting Brahmin wife for him.

Prafulla's Brahminness, through the resources tradition has made available to it at Bhabani's hands—and not by the privilege of birth (for these were denied to Prafulla)—comes to fruition in a domestic context. From being a nothing—outcasted, cast-off, and so "unmade" as a Brahmin—she has realized her full potential but contingently, that is, by chance circumstance (which any other upper-caste Hindu might have accomplished), and she is able to implement this transformation by devoted service in circumstances suitable for her as a woman. It is this fulfilled potential that brings true happiness to herself and to others. This rite of passage is available to each properly primed Hindu, regardless of birth, in his or her own right, even perhaps to those of the lower castes, since the relevant source-text, the *Gītā,* being part of general tradition (*smṛti*) rather than of the canonical scriptures or Veda (*śruti*), was open to all for perusal and imitation. In this sense everyone can emulate the "self-made" Brahmin and be of service to community and country. "Everyone," that is, within reason, in accordance with the constraints of the context of the times.

Bankim could hardly have made Prafulla an outcaste or untouchable by birth if she was to develop as she did; that would have been utterly unrealistic to his readers. But he came close by the literary device of outcasting and then re-instating her, notwithstanding the ritually transgressive experiences she underwent. But this was radical thinking enough for the time, and it helped lay the foundation for even greater socio-religious advances effected by subsequent reformers such as Vivekananda (1863–1902), who was emboldened to speak quite openly and with approval of living in "the age of the Shudra," a coded phrase for all, regardless of caste.[20]

The strong Comtean influence in this humanistic rewriting of Hindu *dharma* is not hard to find: insisting that one's conception of *dharma* must develop into a more universal, altruistic mode to meet the needs of the times (cf. the final section of the long extract quoted above), endorsing Brahmin leadership under a rubric not of birth but of responsibility, and affirming that society was the prime locus of social and moral transformation, were all emphases, illustrated in the novel, that Bankim derived from his reading and adaptation of Comte. From Herbert Spencer came the endorsement of continuous "progress" in the advancement of human knowledge; as for J.R. Seeley, one cannot but recognize his influence in Bankim's stress on the human attributes of Krishna, the more easily to instal Krishna as a moral ideal (so different from the heavily theologized, docetic deity of other forms of Vaishnavism current in Bengal). Hence the references to works by Seeley and Comte in the fronting quotations of the novel.[21]

But the reconstituted Brahmin of the story was a woman! Another innovation of Bankim's "neo-conservative ideology," and, no doubt, one of the most salient features of the novel. Comte's view on women was an important facet of his thought in nineteenth-century eyes. In the essay on Comte in the 1910–11 edition of the *Encyclopaedia Britannica* (Vol.VI:821b–822a), the author writes:

> From earliest manhood Comte had been powerfully impressed by the necessity of elevating the condition of women... and in the reconstructed society women are to play a highly important part. They are to be carefully excluded from public action, but they are to do many more important things than things political. To fit them for their functions, they are to be raised above material cares, and they are to be thoroughly educated. The family, which is so important an element of the Comtist scheme of things, exists to carry the influence of woman over man to the highest point of cultivation. Through affection she purifies the activity of man.

This essay was written close to the time and context of Bankim's own reading of the French philosopher. There is no doubt that this interpretation had an important influence on the creation of Debi. But the reader must not think that Bankim's

[20]Vivekananda, whose thought had immense influence far beyond his native Bengal, was himself a non-Brahmin. He came from a respected caste in Bengal, that of the Kayastha, whose ritual status was nevertheless reckoned by some authorities to be Shudra or not "twice-born," unlike the Brahmin, Kshatriya, and Vaishya strata of the caste hierarchy.

[21]More detailed remarks on Bankim's knowledge of Seeley and Comte are made in the appropriate place in the Critical Apparatus.

preoccupation with the role of women in Hindu society was not prefigured in the concerns of the Bengali intelligentsia earlier in the nineteenth century. This was already a chief concern in the thought of Rammohun Roy (1772?–1833), who had begun the process of modernizing Hindu belief and practice, if we can put it thus, in the early part of the century. Rammohun sought to topple the wandering, socially detached ascetic or renouncer (*sannyāsī*) from his perch as the undisputed ideal of Hindu wisdom and practice in the Sanskritic tradition, and bring the male householder (*gṛhastha*) together with woman as his partner to the fore in this respect. Dermot Killingley, a leading authority on Rammohun, writes:

> While Śaṅkara [a seminal 8th-century theologian of the Sanskritic tradition] considers that only the saṃnyāsin is capable of true knowledge of Brahman [the Supreme Reality], Rammohun says that this knowledge is possible for the householder.... Rammohun's ideal person was not the saṃnyāsin but the "godly householder" (brahma-niṣṭha-gṛhastha); in 1826 he published a tract defending this ideal, using arguments and quotations from Manu [an ancient but still influential law code at the time] which he had already used in previous tracts.[22]

By this time Rammohun had tapped into and prioritized, in terms of his Indian context, a wider global discourse about domesticity and women, of which Comtean ideas became an influential part. Rammohun gave the emancipation of women from their lowly status in Hindu society, subject as they were to the travails of poor education, child-marriage, widowhood, suttee, etc., a high priority in his thought and activities (see Crawford 1987:especially pp.101–15, 222–30). Subsequent Bengali thinkers, Hindu and Christian, followed suit by highlighting these themes in their work.[23] In general, as the nineteenth century progressed, they were party to an intellectual shift, in western-educated circles of Indian thought, from what has been called "old patriarchy" to the "new."

> "Where an older Hindu patriarchal tradition had demanded that women remain illiterate and uneducated, confined to the inner recesses of the home...," writes Judith Walsh, "colonially modern Indian men imagined a new order....To this end, proto-nationalist reformers of the period [viz. the last four decades or so of the nineteenth century] offered women participation in a 'new patriarchy' [here Walsh acknowledges the work of Partha Chatterjee]; 'new' because it challenged indigenous patriarchal traditions by allowing women's literacy and education, and by encouraging them to travel outside the home; but 'patriarchy' because it maintained women in

[22]See Killingley's doctoral thesis, *Rammohun Roy's Interpretation of the Vedānta*, University of London, 1977, pp.233–4. The tract was written in Bengali and entitled "Brahmaniṣṭha Gṛhasther Lakṣaṇ" ("The defining traits of a householder devoted to Brahman").

[23]Such thinkers included the Christians Krishna Mohan Banerjea (1813–85) and Lal Behari Day (1824–84), and otherwise ideologically opposed Hindus such as Radhakanta Deb (1784–1867) and Keshabchandra Sen (1838–84). For an analysis of the status of women in Bengal, see Borthwick (1984).

> a dependent and subordinate status within Indian society (3–4)....Central to new patriarchy was the idea that the husband's authority over his wife should be supreme. The husband, not the family elders, must be the wife's guide on all matters of conduct and behaviour (64)." (Walsh 2004)

In his writings, Bankim too was party to this shift; later we shall inquire into what role *Debī Chaudhuraṇī* may have played in this context. My point here is that Bankim's reappraisal of the role of women and of society in his vision of a reformulated *dharma* for the future was not original. What was original, at least in *Debī Chaudhuraṇī*, as we shall see, was the way he blended old ideas and new in a dynamic that seems quite distinctive.

An eminent Bengali woman Professor once remarked to me, with a tone of disappointment in her voice, that the returning Prafulla was re-instated into domesticity, thereby assuming once more a role that was traditional for women. "What was the point of it all?" she asked. The answer is that for Bankim, Debi, or rather the regenerate Prafulla, returns as the new woman. From a position of utter dependency on the goodwill and charity of others (thus reflecting the abject status of women in some perceptions of traditional Hinduism), she has developed progressively into an autonomous agent, disbursing her wealth as she thinks fit (cf. Part II, ch.11), standing up to Bhabani Pathak and his lieutenants when the need arises, and hatching ingenious schemes to rescue her hapless husband and cowardly father-in-law from their troubles; *she* has chosen to give up this form of autonomy and return to her husband's home in the role of compliant wife. But the compliant wife here is a radically altered woman, her compliance self-initiated, and a source of strength and wisdom. She has returned newly disciplined and energized to undertake her domestic role, and the result is that the transformed woman successfully transforms the lives of all she encounters. In serving she really rules—effectively and for the benefit of all. One may still disapprove of the domestic context as this new woman's preferred element in Bankim's eyes, but Bankim was writing in the late nineteenth century about a context—marriage and the Bengali household—that was a necessary component of societal life.

Here we may mention that Prafulla was not the only current wife of her husband, Brajesvar. It was the practice of the times, especially for Brahmin males of the highest ritual status, known as *kulin*s, to take many wives. Such marriages conferred on the prospective wives and their children a highly desirable caste status, as well as relieved the brides' parents of a pressing obligation to marry their daughters off to their best advantage. Needless to say, as has been amply recorded, this practice could be, and often was, subject to abuse of different kinds, since there was no set limit to the number of marriages a *kulin* could enter into.[24]

[24]See K.M. Banerjea's, "The kulin brahmins of Bengal," 1844, for a poignant description, when the practice was still current, of some of these abuses. Also see the relevant endnote under ch.8 of Part III in the Critical Apparatus.

Brajesvar, however, had only three wives, Prafulla being the most senior. The relationships between Prafulla and her co-wives, Nayantara and Sagar, comprise an important dimension of the story. After tentative, and in Nayantara's case, conflictual interaction earlier on, Prafulla returns home as a model of amity and guidance for her co-wives, who live with her in the same household. The point is that the transformed Prafulla is now empowered to negotiate the potential minefield of co-wifely interaction without problems. This becomes a kind of marker of the success of her perfected *anuśīlan* or disciplined cultivation of human faculties:

> When Prafulla did have disagreements it was with Brajesvar. Prafulla would tell him, "I am not your only wife. Just as you belong to me, you belong to Sagar and to Nayan[tara] also. I shan't see to your needs by myself...." But Brajesvar wouldn't listen. Brajesvar's heart was filled with Prafulla alone. She would say, "If you don't love them as you love me, your love for me will remain incomplete. For they are one with me." But Brajesvar couldn't understand that. (Part III, ch.14)

Not only has the new wife overcome the internecine and hierarchical rivalries so often associated with women family-members in the old and new patriarchies, but she also eschews an exclusive love with her (uncomprehending) husband which is hers for the asking, and which was perceived in the period in which Bankim was writing as disruptive of the values of the traditional extended family. In short, for Bankim, the appropriate context of *dharma* for the reconstituted woman, however educated and disciplined she might be, is an *inclusive* domesticity. This is inclusive in two senses: (a) it includes an equitable, balanced relationship between husband and wife (rather than one of simplistic equality), and (b) it does not shut out other members, especially female members, of the extended family. Let us inquire briefly into each.

(a) In her own right, the new wife is a partner to her husband, which means that she does not need to vie with him in every respect. The ideal is that she must continue to act as wife and mother, but as a helpmate in a partnership, "carry[ing] her influence over man to the highest point of cultivation," as the article on Comte quoted earlier affirms, and "through affection purify[ing] the activity of man." The *DT* (ch.23) clarifies Bankim's view on this. In a conversation between the Guru and his disciple, the Guru says:

> Society (*samāj*) is necessary for upright living and right order (*dharma*), and a pre-requisite for the formation of society is the custom of marriage. The essence of the marriage-custom is this, that husband and wife, becoming one, apportion and carry out domestic matters. Each should undertake what is appropriate to them. The man's share is to provide for and protect....The wife is not capable of providing for and protecting her husband, but she is capable of serving him and making him happy. That is her *dharma*. Other *dharma*s are incomplete; Hindu

> *dharma* is the best of all and complete. In Hindu *dharma* the wife is called the [husband's] partner in *dharma* (*sahadharmiṇī*).[25]

"Then the equality (*sāmya*) between husband and wife that the Westerners seek to establish," asks the disciple, "is that just social pretence?"

"Is equality possible?" counters the teacher. "Can men give birth or suckle infants? And for their part, can women engage in battle in command of troops?"

"So the cultivation (*anuśīlan*) of the physical powers that you spoke of earlier doesn't apply to women, is that it?" persists the disciple.

"Why not?" replies the Guru somewhat sarcastically. "Let everyone cultivate the powers they have. If a woman has the capacity to fight let her cultivate that, and if a man has the capacity to suckle let him cultivate that...." An uncontoured "equality" or sameness may not be desirable, whereas the balanced equity of a partnership is.

(b) The re-domesticated Prafulla endorses the principle of "each to his/her own" between husband and wife wholeheartedly, but in a way that encompasses other members of the household. "It's not the *dharma* of women to rule," she tells Sagar, her co-wife. "It's the family life you've described that's a hard duty (*kaṭhin dharma*); there's no yoga harder than that. Just think how many illiterate, self-seeking, ignorant people we've constantly got to deal with. And our task is to see to it that none of them are put out, that each one is happy. Is there any form of renunciation (*sannyās*) more difficult than this? Any virtue (*puṇya*) greater than this? This is the kind of renunciation I want to embrace" (Part III, ch.13). And this kind of renunciation derives from a discipline that is based—putatively—on the teaching of the *Gītā* about the oneness of all being and the selfless action that perceives and effects this oneness in the Godhead, Krishna. I say "putatively," because while it is true that such principles of thought and action could be located, without too much difficulty, in a re-interpretation of a Hinduism of the ancient past, it was also true that it was catalyzed by, and incorporated, modern western influences, as we have seen. In the novel Bankim may have been writing ostensibly about a bygone age, but in the process he was writing very much in the context of, and for, an audience of his time.

So Prafulla had become the "*karma-yogī*," the doer of unitive selfless action, *par excellence*. This was not a political involvement—encouragement to a form of which was the underlying aim of *Ānandamaṭh*, Bankim's preceding novel. It was, rather, endorsement of a kind of social activism for the welfare of the (extended) family and society, and by this means of the country, soundly constituted as it must be by right social order. *Debī Chaudhurāṇī* is a patriotic novel only by implication, cohering with *Ānandamaṭh* on the basis of a synoptic vision.

[25] I have changed the order of some sentences to make the point more clearly.

This implicit larger patriotic goal is hinted at in a number of ways in the depiction of Debi's character. She affirms her wifely status, even in the face of opposition, throughout the novel, thus attesting to an irrevocable plank of the traditional social order that constitutes the well-being of the country. While undergoing Bhabani Pathak's strict regime of training in the forest, she obeys his injunctions concerning food and drink to the letter but insists on one exception: the observance of *Ekadashi,* that is, the eating of fish on the eleventh day (*ekādāśī*) of the lunar fortnight which Bengali women whose husbands were alive practiced in order to demonstrate their current wifely status. This observance in the novel acts as a link between the early Prafulla, Debi the bandit-queen, and the transformed wife who finally came home. It signifies Bankim's respect for the ethical basis of traditional customs that were likely, in his opinion, to build up and maintain society.

But this wife, who cared not only for her husband but also for her co-wives and extended family, was also a mother, not only to the bandit gang who were instructed by Bhabani Pathak to call her "mother,"[26] but also to the wider community of the needy who benefited from her largesse. This is why, in singing her virtues at the end, Bankim can write in the final chapter that when Prafulla died, "the people of the region felt that they had lost a mother." She was the nurturing mother, and in this role she performed the function of the Goddess of Plenty, Annapūrṇā, whose image was installed—not by accident, one would think, from the literary point of view—in the guesthouse called *Debinibas* ("Debi's Home"), that Prafulla (or Debi) established after she was re-instated in her father-in-law's residence. In fact, "*debī*" means "Goddess," and Bankim is not above weaving the semantics of this historical fact into the weft and warp of his story. In this sense Debi, virtuous mother and wife, represents the emergent motherland, lauded so famously in *Ānandamaṭh*. In order to develop this point somewhat, we now need to summon her husband, poor put-upon Brajesvar, to take part in our discussion.

In the Śākta or Goddess strand of traditional Hinduism, the woman is identified as a symbol and representative of the Goddess as Power or *śakti*. Understood thus, the Goddess is the empowering mode of her male consort, who is represented as inert and passive. Theologically there is but one Supreme Being, no doubt, but artistically and mythologically the one Deity is portrayed in the two interlinked modes of male and female. The male represents the continuing presence or stasis of the Deity, while the female is its active power and outreach. In this sense the female functions as vigilant consort and nurturing mother of creation. Perhaps this is why Debi, who on several occasions in the story is likened to a real Goddess, is associated with the waterways of Rangpur. As I have pointed out in the Critical Apparatus to ch.3, Part II:

---

[26]See Part I, ch.11 toward the end, and also under the Critical Apparatus for this chapter for the significance of this appellation.

> Debi Chaudhurani is intimately associated with the river: she lives on the river and is at home on it. In a way, she is the Goddess of the river...and a representative of Bengal. As such, her actions of "banditry" are legitimated, as she is engaged, in the dire circumstances of the time, in liberating Bengal from the oppressions of poverty, the rigidities of custom (a Comtean idea), and misrule. She will help bring the new Bengal, and by extension a new India, into being.

In the novel, Debi, in her roles as bandit-queen and re-instated wife, functions as the active counterpart of the rather passive, feckless Brajesvar. This role appears somewhat at odds with Bankim's protestations in the *DT* that women, even after they have developed their capabilities by *anuśīlan*, should not try to compete with men in the performance of "manly" activities such as fighting on the battlefield and so on. But there Bankim is speaking in generalities, while here in the novel he has a point to make. After all, Debi is using her developed capabilities to "serve and make her husband happy," as the *DT* requires. This objective overrides what are only counsels of prudence to the contrary in the *DT*. Further, as I have noted earlier, Debi enacts the role not only of the nurturing, but also of the avenging mother, seeking justice on behalf of and distributing wealth to her "children"; with these powers, she is also the protective Goddess-consort of her feckless husband. This added, culure-specific dimension of Debi/the regenerate Prafulla, in the role of Goddess as protective mother, takes Bankim's ideal of the new woman beyond that of Comte, for whom, in terms of the quotation given earlier, woman only "purifies the activity of man... through affection." The new Prafulla has surpassed that. But the new Prafulla has also surpassed the ideal of the Indian woman commonly constructed in the new patriarchy. "New patriarchy imagined the husband's role and authority as total; it defined older women as irrelevant and younger women as completely subservient to their husbands" (Walsh 2004:111). But the Prafulla who has returned to domesticity, disciplined by her decade-long training, embraces and harmonizes the regulating agents of both patriarchies—the women elders of the family as well as the husband—in a triumphant synthesis that one might perhaps call a "new matriarchy!"

But why does Brajesvar play this generally passive role in the story? Bankim's literary device is what can only be called Brajesvar's inordinate devotion to his father, Haraballabh. Haraballabh, as we saw earlier, is an avaricious, unscrupulous, cowardly landlord, who as head of the family is given unquestioned authority in his household. Brajesvar is in awe of his father, but he is also devoted to him. As such, he is unable to stand up to him. When Haraballabh banishes Prafulla from his household without due cause, Brajesvar is deeply unhappy but does not object openly; when Haraballabh is on the point of ruin because of his profligacy, Brajesvar strains every nerve to save him; when Haraballabh seeks to betray Debi to the English authorities, Brajesvar insists that Debi save both herself *and* his father, notwithstanding the latter's perfidy. These incidents occur progressively as the story unfolds, and the reader burns with indignation at the way Brajesvar seems to take his father's repeated acts of unfeeling arrogance lying down. The story justifies Brajesvar's stance by seeming to hold him up as an example of traditional filial devotion.

After Haraballabh has banished the destitute Prafulla, we are informed that:

> One day, the annual rites to commemorate the death of Haraballabh's father came round. While Haraballabh was performing the rite, Brajesvar happened to be there for some task or other when he heard the priest make Haraballabh recite at the end: *A father is heaven, a father is duty, a father indeed is one's highest concern. All the gods are pleased when a father is satisfied.*
>
> Brajesvar learned these words by heart, and whenever he felt like weeping for Prafulla, he'd console himself by saying: *A father is heaven, a father is duty, a father indeed is one's highest concern. All the gods are pleased when a father is satisfied* (Part I, ch.14).

The serial version of this chapter ends ruefully as follows:

> Aryan devotion to one's father (*ārya pitṛbhakti*) no longer exists in the land of Bengal. Through the deadly poison (*halāhale*) of English education, Bengal's ancient code of practice (*prācīn dharma*) has been shattered. One's most revered, worshipful father, whose lotus feet one lacked the courage to touch in the past, has now become "My dear father"! He is no longer the object of devotion (*bhakti*), only of reproach (*anujog*). And the Bengali who doesn't refer to him as "the old man" is now reckoned a virtuous son. Perhaps this society is making progress and not going to ruin, now that the Bengali has learnt to give speeches! Instead of our traditional code of practice (*dharma*), we've now got lectures—what great gains we've made! [27]

When Brajesvar returns with the money, acquired, to say the least, in unorthodox fashion, to redeem Haraballabh's pressing debt, the serial edition of the novel (Part II, ch.12 of that version) develops the situation as follows:

> Now if Brajesvar had replied, "I didn't get the money," then this would clearly be a lie. If he were a child of today with an English education, I cannot say what he would have decided here about the "Lie direct"; but since he was a child of that time, he had no particular objection

[27]In the serial version of the novel, this was the conclusion of ch.15 in Part I. It is a good illustration of the way variants, in this case material omitted in later versions of the text, can help reveal new facets of the author's original intentions.

> to a situation involving a "Lie direct." Nevertheless, wherever else he might be able to utter a falsehood—not in his father's presence! He had never done so in the past. Brajesvar was unable to say that he hadn't got the money, so he remained silent.
>
> When he saw that his son gave no reply, Haraballabh despaired and sat with his head in his hands. Brajesvar realized that even his silence was equivalent to uttering a lie, for he *had* brought the money, but since he gave no answer his father thought that he had not. The foolish Brajesvar believed he was deceiving his father! But the subtle intellect of our smart, refined, elegantly shod English-educated student of today would have thought instead: "I've told no lie! Whatever little I've said is nothing but the truth! I'm not *obliged* to say anything about Debi Chaudhurani's money since there was no question of bringing that money in the first place, and there's been no mention of it. Besides, that money comes from banditry so if he accepts it the pater will be sunk in the mire of sin. So it's incumbent on a pure soul like me to say nothing about it. The main thing is I've not told an untruth. What can I do if father goes to jail!"
>
> But Brajesvar wasn't such a pure soul, and he didn't think this way. His heart began to break at the sight of his father sitting there silently with his head in his hands.

No doubt Bankim is taking a swipe here at the deracinating influence of the English education of the times, and no doubt he also wishes to affirm an important element of traditional Hindu practice: filial devotion. But this devotion is also a narratival device to render the submissive Brajesvar effectively helpless so that his wife, Prafulla, can assert herself in his defense, using to the full the capabilities she has developed as a result of the *anuśīlan* imposed on her by Bhabani Pathak (and Bankim, as articulated in the *DT*).

But there is another consideration that seems to be implicit here: Bankim's relationship with his own father, Jadabcandra, who had also worked under the British in the Bengal Civil Service (a division of the Indian Civil Service). Though a *bhadralok*—a man whose job entailed the use of English in the sphere of British influence—Jadabcandra also observed traditional ways in his household and this played a large part in Bankim's upbringing. Like Brajesvar, Bankim was in awe of his father. Jadabcandra was an imposing-looking man, with an imposing, headstrong personality. "He was a man of fair complexion, tall and powerful, with an aquiline nose and keen intellect, who exuded energy and practiced a selfless ethic. Jadabcandra's influence on Bankimchandra's life was far-reaching." (*BcJ*, 1991:18). Nevertheless, at the heart of the relationship between the two men lay a profound tension. On the one hand, Bankim expressed deep gratitude to his father for his training in the meaning and practice of *dharma*. This was articulated in no uncertain terms in Bankim's Dedication of *Debī Chaudhurāṇī*, which was made to his father. The Dedication was added when the novel was first published as a book in 1884 (three years after Jadabcandra's death).

"With loving devotion I offer this work at the revered lotus-feet of one from whom I first heard the teaching of selfless action (*niṣkām dharma*), who dedicated himself to its practice, and who by the fruit of virtue has now ascended to heaven," runs the Dedication.

On the other hand, circumstances led Bankim to feel the brunt of his father's actions in his life keenly, and to question the consequences of these actions. The bone of contention was the large debts his father incurred as the result of profligacy and the desire to keep up appearances, and which Bankim out of filial obligation felt under the pressure of discharging. Is it a coincidence that in the novel Brajesvar labors under a similar pressure? Here is an extract from a letter Bankim wrote in November 1874 to his older brother, Sanjibcandra; it was the inordinate expenses for the prospective wedding of Sanjibcandra's son, Jyotishcandra, that occasioned this deeply felt missive.

> I have written this letter in Bengali because if the need arises or if you think you should, then send it to father to read. [Father] has told you to incur a debt of Rs.1600 for Jyotish's wedding.... If you incur the debt, the 5000 rupees you owe presently will become Rs.7000.[28] Is it possible to clear this debt?... You've been in debt's grip for 20 years now, and except for the interest, you will never be able to pay it off.
>
> He who cannot clear a debt knows that by incurring it he is taking money by cheating another. If you borrow Rs.1600 now, then incurring this debt would have to be called deceitful. Rather than such deceit, it would be better to live as a beggar. You mustn't do this just to follow an instruction of father's or to increase his happiness. Rather than this immoral behaviour (*adharmācaraṇ*), you should transgress father's instruction.... There's no one in the world more miserable than someone who shoulders a debt, because however much he may earn he doesn't have the right to call even a single penny of it his own. You see me as an example of this. Ramesh Mitra [an acquaintance] is a High Court judge and I'm a minor official in Maldah—and the reason for this is nothing but father's debts.
>
> If he were to incur the debt, who would clear it? He'll say, "My sons." But among his sons [you] are incapable of clearing what you yourself owe, so there's no possibility of clearing even a penny of father's debt. Similarly for the youngest [their brother Purnacandra]; he just about manages to run his household with what he earns, so he couldn't pay off the debt. And there's no doubt that the eldest [their brother

[28]Bankim has rounded off the loan, or perhaps he included some interest; in any case, this was a large sum in those days.

> Syamacaran] won't give a single penny, so that leaves just me to bear the responsibility. So if [father] incurs a debt on account of Jyotish's wedding, it's to land it on my neck. Kindly explain to him how big an injustice that would be to me. (*BcJ*, 1991:326–7)

The frustration in these words is plain for all to see, and Bankim is prepared for his father to read them! Further, is this the way someone would write about his father being a model of selfless action (*niṣkām dharma*), as Bankim wrote a decade later in the Dedication to *Debī Chaudhurāṇī*? There is no doubt that Bankim experienced a deep tension in the memory of his relationship with his father. This was not the result of a single action or two on his father's part, but the imposition of a working lifetime so far as Bankim was concerned (cf. the bitterness in, "Ramesh Mitra is a High Court judge, and I'm a minor official in Maldah"). Was Brajesvar's helplessness in his devotion to his father, his strained attempts to free him of his ruinous debt, while performing other literary functions in the novel, also a way for Bankim to confront, or ease, or expunge a sense of guilt that he felt over his father? It would be surprising if this were not the case.[29]

We are now in a position to review the import of the variants in the development of the novel. Of course, the most substantial changes were made in the transition from the serial version to the first edition published as a book, in that the latter was completed by the addition of Part III. We can assume that Bankim had in mind more or less what he wanted to write when the serial version came to an end (for reasons extraneous to the writing of the novel).[30] Part III relates how Debi is reconciled with her husband, resourcefully evades capture by the British in spite of Haraballabh's deceitfulness, disbands her fighters and takes leave of her chief assistants, and returns home as Brajesvar's "new" and highly effective wife, with a number of interesting diversions *en route*. This Part demonstrates the culmination and effectiveness of Debi's training at Bhabani Pathak's hands after she escaped from her abductors in Part II.

But there are a number of lesser though quite significant changes over the various versions too. In general the Prafulla/Debi of the final edition is a somewhat more dignified, on occasion more obviously "Hindu," figure than her

---

[29]It was not unusual at the time for (Indian/Bengali) fathers to exercise dictatorial control over their households, and for their sons, "English-educated" though they might me, to be in thrall to them. Walsh (2004:70–1) recounts how the Bengali scholar, Sibnath (Sivanath) Sastri, who was later to become a member of the Brahmo Samaj, "was married at thirteen to a girl of ten. But when he was twenty, his father took a strong dislike to her family and sent her back to them. He then ordered Sivanath to take a second wife and a second marriage took place. 'I was old enough,' Sivanath writes in his autobiography, 'to form a strong opinion against bigamy but I was so used to unquestioning obedience to my father that I did not dare to speak out my mind to him' " (see also Kopf [1979:93], on the poignancy of this crisis for Sibnath).

[30]See footnote 2 of this Introduction.

earlier versions. Bankim tones down or omits some of her earlier actions that may cast her in an undignified or morally ambivalent light. Thus the passage at the end of ch.4 (Part I) of the serial version (when Prafulla and Nayantara—the rival co-wife—meet for the first time), viz.: "Then Prafulla and Nayantara eyed each other up and down. Just as the tiger and the hunter size each other up to see who will kill first, the two sized each other up. Each realized that the other was her chief enemy," is omitted in the book-editions. Similarly, the passage from Part III, ch.6 of the first book-edition (see under "Variants" in the Critical Apparatus), in which Debi might be seen to come across morally as a dissembler, is omitted in the final edition. As to her physical charms, Bankim trims his description of her voluptuousness somewhat in Part II, ch.3 of the book-editions (see Appendix B). Yet, significantly, in this chapter of the book-editions she plays a *vina* rather than a *sitar*. The *vina* is traditionally a more Hindu instrument in that it has been associated for centuries with Sarasvati, the Goddess of learning and fine art, to whom Debi is explicitly compared in this chapter (the *sitar,* on the other hand, can be seen as having Muslim associations).

Finally, in the serial version (and in the first book-edition) Bankim is authorially more free in his criticism of the corrosive effect on Hindu traditional ways of western education and codes of morality. At the end of ch.15 of Part I in the serial edition (which is ch.14, Part I, of the book-editions), he bewails, as we have seen earlier, the lack of respect shown toward their fathers by modern Bengali young men who have been influenced "by the deadly poison" (*halāhale*) of English education. Through this harmful influence, "Bengal's ancient code of practice (*prācīn dharma*) has been shattered. One's most revered, worshipful father, whose lotus feet one lacked the courage to touch in the past, has now become 'My dear father!' " When Brajesvar returns with the money Debi gave him to rescue his father from his ruinous debt, Bankim mocks (see earlier) the thinking of the "smart, refined, elegantly shod English-educated student of today" who, to obey the letter of English ethical codes enjoining avoidance of the "lie direct," would blithely violate the spirit of the traditional Hindu practice of filial devotion. We know, however, that Bankim was not unsusceptible to incorporating in his reconstruction of Hinduism scientific and rationalist ideas deriving from western sources; we have already noted the influence of Comte, Spencer, and others on his thought. Hence it is quite possible that some of the edge of these scornful authorial remarks was Bankim's way of letting off steam under cover of narratival license during a period of rapid and bewildering cultural change; he was not averse to changing old ways when this seemed called for.

Let us draw this Introduction to a close. *Debī Chaudhurāṇī* represents a development, in the direction of illustrating the kind of social activism that would serve society and country in the new India, of Bankim's vision of *dharma* expressed earlier in narrative form in *Ānandamaṭh,* and articulated more fully in the theoretical works mentioned above. It was followed by *Sītārām,* the third of the so-called *trayī* or loose trilogy of novels. To get down to brass tacks: what impact did it have in projecting Bankim's vision? As stated earlier, it achieved the popularity of being republished six times in book-form during Bankim's lifetime.[31]

But Bankim had wished for an even wider readership than his established Bengali clientele. There is record of a conversation held in 1891 in which Bankim revealed that he had himself translated *Debī Chaudhurāṇī* into English. "I can tell you," said Bankim to Sureshcandra Samajpati, "that a couple of my novels have been translated into English, but not to my satisfaction. So I decided to make the translations myself. I thought I would translate my last few novels in order to reveal the purpose with which I wrote them" (*BcJ*, p.751). This is interesting, for there is an indication here by the author himself that the last few novels (*āmār śeṣer upanyās kaykhānā*) were of a piece ideologically, and that Bankim was keen to disseminate what this was. The record goes on to say that Bankim opened a cupboard in his study in which the conversation was taking place and showed his interlocutor a large bound notebook which contained a translation of *Debī Chaudhurānī*. "Look how hard I've worked," continued Bankim. "I've made the translation. I've crossed and cut out and then made a fair copy. Then I've bound it and kept it aside." He added, "I've gone so far as to get an estimate from English publishers [as to how much it would cost him to get the book published]. In the end I decided there'd be no point in publishing. The English won't be able to appreciate my novel." When asked why, he answered, "Not only will they not like it, they'll revile me for

[31]One indication of the novel's sphere of influence emerges in Walsh's discussion (2004) of the popular Bengali household-management advice-manuals published in the last four decades of the nineteenth century. Walsh makes several references to the popularity of Bankim's writings. In a way, *Debī Chaudhurāṇī* is of a piece, didactically, with these manuals, providing a theoretical justification for a shift away from the social dominance of the old patriarchy to an incorporation of some of the ideals of the new, for example, education and a measure of independence for women within a more marked dyadic relationship with the husband, but in the context of a synthesis that granted even greater autonomy to the woman than was envisaged generally by the new patriarchy (hence our comment earlier that Bankim's vision in this novel might even be dubbed a "new matriarchy"). After noting that "Fiction by writers such as Bankimchandra Chatterji and Rabindranath Tagore produced plots revolving around romantic entanglements and explored romantic love within the context of the older arranged-marriage system" (2004:88), Walsh later considers the work of the female writer, Nagendrabala, whose advice-manual in Bengali, *Women's Dharma* (published in 1900), was in wide demand. *Women's Dharma* sits uneasily between affirmation of the old ways and of the new. However, as Walsh goes on to record (op.cit., 148), "Any and all of Bankim's novels are to be recommended, [Nagendrabala] says, because his works are 'seriously educational.'" When discussing Nagendrabala's Sanskrit references, Walsh mentions "The father is dharma, the father is *svarg* [heaven]" (150). Can it be a coincidence, in view of Nagendrabala's endorsement of Bankim's novels, that Nagendrabala quotes the very Sanskrit text Brajesvar learned by heart to combat his yearning for the (presumed) dead Prafulla? Walsh contends that Nagendrabala glossed this text to suit her own purposes, but its mention by Nagendrabala in her manual is an indication of *Debī Chaudhurāṇī*'s influence. How important *Debī Chaudhurāṇī* and other writings of Bankim were in shaping the trajectory of new patriarchy thought in general and of the (later) advice-manuals in particular merits further study.

it." "Revile you?" said Sureshcandra taken aback. "Yes," Bankim replied. "Take Debi, for instance. I've given it much thought. Do you think they'll be able to understand the matter of Brajesvar's marriages? 'Polygamy!' they'll cry! Foreigners won't be able to understand why I've given Brajesvar three marriages...." "That can be explained in a Preface to the book," said Sureshcandra. But Bankim wasn't convinced (ibid.). Times have changed, however, and in a world more adept at understanding cultural specificities of the past, Bankim's objections no longer hold water.

Only a few chapters of Bankim's English rendering survive. It is important to show what he tried to achieve. Below I give first an extract from my translation of the penultimate chapter of the novel, followed by Bankim's rendering of the same passage:

My translation

"Sagar looked for her co-wife and found her by the steps to the pond. Prafulla was scouring some dishes with her back to Sagar. Sagar went up behind her and said, "Hello, so you're the new wife of the house?"

"Who's that, Sagar?" said the new wife, turning round.

Sagar saw who it was. Astonished, she exclaimed, "Queen Debi?"

"Quiet!" said Prafulla. "Debi's dead."

"Then Prafulla?" said Sagar.

"Prafulla's dead too."

"Then who are you now?"

"The new wife."

"But how did this happen? Tell me, I want to know everything!"

Prafulla replied, "We can't talk here. I've been given a room. Let's go there and I'll tell you everything."

They locked the door, and thus secluded, started a conversation. When Prafulla had explained everything, Sagar asked, "Do you think you'll get used to housework now? After sitting on a silver throne wearing a crown of diamonds like a queen, will you be able to cope with washing the dishes and sweeping the rooms? Do you think you can put up with Grandaunt Brahma's fairy tales after those yoga treatises? Will someone who made two thousand men jump to her command enjoy ordering the maidservants about?"

"It's because I want to do those things that I'm here," said Prafulla. "For this is precisely the right life for a woman. Women aren't born to rule. It's the family life you've described that's a hard duty; there's no yoga harder than that. Just think how many illiterate, self-seeking, ignorant people we've constantly got to deal with. And our task is to see to it that none of them are put out, that each one is happy. Is there any form of renunciation more difficult than this? Any virtue greater than this? This is the kind of renunciation I want to embrace."

Sagar replied, "Well then, I'll stay with you for a while and follow your example."

✿ *Bankim's rendering* ✿

"Sagar found Prafulla on the steps leading to the tank situated within the premises. She found her seated on the steps, scouring some utensils of brass used in the kitchen. She was seated with her back toward the direction from which Sagar was coming. Somebody told Sagar that this was the new Bahu [wife]. Sagar approached and accosted her.

"Are you our new sister?"

Prafulla turned round. "Is it you, sister Sagar?" said she.

Sagar was thunderstruck. The last person she expected to see in the new rival was the very person she saw.

"Devi Rani!" she exclaimed in amazement.

"Hush," replied Devi Rani. "Devi Rani is dead. Come to my apartment, and I will explain all. This is not the place."

The two then left, each entwining the other's neck with her arm. They conversed in private for a long while, till all was explained. Sagar was delighted. Sagar could never think of Devi as a rival.

"But," said Sagar, "do you believe that this domestic life will suit you? After your throne of silver and diadem of gold, does this scouring of kitchen utensils suit you? Will the thorough adept in Yoga Philosophy patiently listen to Brahma Thakurani's lectures on the art of frying fish? Will the lady who commanded hosts submit to the dictation of foolish men and silly crones?

"I have come here," said Prafulla, "because I think that this life will suit me better than the other. This is the woman's proper sphere—woman was not made to reign. And this discipline—that which has to be acquired within the four walls of the family dwelling-house, is the highest and severest of all disciplines. Here you have to deal every day with a number of illiterate, often selfish, generally ignorant people; and it has to be made your object that you shall to the best of your ability, promote their happiness and welfare, very often in spite of themselves. And you have to do it, when you yourself are a subordinate, one of the ruled, not the ruler; when you have not the power to dispose of things in your own way—where you must expect every effort of yours for good opposed, thwarted, and often overruled. And it is only by inexhaustible patience, unflinching self-sacrifice, and only through passionate love of good that you can properly fulfill your destiny in the domestic life. It is much easier to rule a kingdom. It is much easier to give up the world, and to lead an ascetic life. True asceticism, true devotion to Him who has commanded us to act only for others and not for ourselves can be found only here, the station most difficult fitly to occupy. The grandest life, or the loftiest sphere is not that in which there is the most show and ostentation, but that which calls for the exercise of your highest gifts. I am ambitious, sister, of the highest station woman can occupy—that of the wife and mother, and therefore I am here."

"Let me see," said Sagar, "how you fulfil this lofty destiny."

It was the case of common sense striving to comprehend transcendent genius" (*BcJ*, pp.642–3).

This is not a translation, but an adaptation of the original, a paraphrase, with the addition of much new material.[32] In the process, Bankim is obviously trying to "reveal the purpose with which he wrote" the novel, as the conversation between him and Sureshcandra mentioned above records. It is almost as if Bankim the deputy magistrate, serving under the British, is speaking through Prafulla, and in the language appropriate to that profession! This is not good novel-writing; it is more like the lecture-giving Bankim claimed derived from the English education of the time, and which he deplored in several places in the novel! Further, the English is awkward and does a disservice to the directness of Bankim's Bengali idiom.[33]

To the best of my knowledge, the novel has been translated into English only once before—over 60 years ago, in fact. In an Appendix, Das (1984: 242–3) notes that Subodhcandra Mitra produced an English translation of *Debī Chaudhurāṇī,* published from Calcutta, in 1946. This translation has long been out of print and is difficult to procure (I know of no copy available in the United Kingdom); so far as I was concerned, it was proving elusive, and I had resigned myself to being unable to consult it. Then, at the last moment, when my own book was virtually complete, Rachel McDermott, who has written so illuminatingly about various features of earlier and later modern Bengali culture, came to the rescue. She kindly presented me with a photocopy of the work. Mitra's book is a translation of the sixth book-edition of the novel, as is mine. Except for a Glossary of Bengali expressions at the end, it lacks both an Introduction and a Critical Apparatus, and so does not provide variant translations of earlier editions of the novel, including the serial version, which I have sought to provide. Though Mitra's work is a reasonably faithful rendering on the whole, it tends toward paraphrase, and its somewhat unidiomatic English reflects the florid style of Mitra's time and context. Nevertheless, I readily acknowledge that I was glad to consult it, both to improve my own translation in places and to confirm

[32]For my understanding of the philosophy and objectives of translation, see *AM*(L):108–24, and more extensively, my "The truth(s) of translation," in Lipner (2005b).

[33]We may add here that it is not the task of the translator to try and "improve" on the original by recourse, say, to paraphrase or literary embellishment. The task of the translator is to be "faithful" to the original, to reflect not only its spirit but also its material form—the style of the language in which the original is written (see the article mentioned in the previous note). For all its pioneering innovations of idiom and style, *Debī Chaudhurāṇī* is not a literary masterpiece; there are deficiencies of plot and style which the translator cannot strive to remedy. But then Bankim was not particularly concerned about that. His greater aim was to convey a teaching through the instrument of writing a novel.

what I had done in others. Unsurprisingly, of course, at times we are both constrained to use the same or similar expressions when translating, though I have made it a point to reflect the directness of Bankim's generally crisp style (an innovation for his time). From time to time in the Critical Apparatus I refer to Mitra's translation where this has seemed called for.

To revert to our earlier question about the influence of the novel, one cannot view it in isolation, of course. From the wider point of view it was part of an intensifying trend of discussion among the Bengali intelligentsia, begun early in the nineteenth century, to attempt to come to terms first with modernity, and then with nationhood. "Internally," so to speak, it was part of a larger corpus of work serving this trend of one of the most significant intellectuals in the second half of the nineteenth century, not only of Bengal but also of the subcontinent as a whole. As such, the novel is part of the intellectual story of the development of India as a free and independent polity. In general, Bankim's vision toward this end is noble and powerful, demanding of its participants selfless service to a motherland that must take its proud place in the emerging world order. This vision had its shortcomings: it was somewhat triumphalist (not uncommon in other narratives of emergent nationhood[34]), and failed to spell out how other longstanding co-inhabitants of the land, for example, Muslims and Christians, might be equal and integrated partners in the new *dharma* of the new India.

This hiatus need not have occurred. In the *DT,* Bankim reasons as follows (the Guru is instructing the disciple):

> Love for one's country is not the furthest limit of love's development (*sphūrtti*). There is a step beyond that. Love for the whole world is the furthest limit of love's expression and that is true *dharma.* So long as love does not embrace the whole world, it remains incomplete, and *dharma* too remains incomplete. . . . The Christian God (*īśvar*) is independent of the world. No doubt he is Lord of the world, but just as the king of Germany or Russia is an individual separate from all Germans and Russians, the Christian God is likewise separate. He too, remaining separate like a mundane king, protects and governs his kingdom, chastising the wicked and protecting the virtuous, and like a policeman keeps track of what people do. To love him one must do what pleases Him just as in the case of a mundane king.
>
> The Hindu God is not like that. He pervades everything (*sarvabhūtamay*); it is He who is the inner Self (*antarātmā*) of all things. He is not the material world, being different from it, but the world exists in Him alone. Like the thread of a necklace, like wind in space, even so He exists in the world. No human being exists independently of Him; He is present in everyone. He is present in me. In

[34]See, for example, with respect to Mexico, David Brading's *Mexican Phoenix,* 2001.

> loving myself, I love Him, and in not loving Him, I fail to love myself. And in loving Him, I love every human being. In not loving every human being, I have failed to love Him and myself. In other words, love (*prīti*) cannot exist without love of the whole world. So long as I do not grasp the fact that the whole world is myself, that the universe is not different from me, I have not acquired knowledge, or *dharma,* or devotion (*bhakti*), or love (*prīti*). Therefore love for the world lies at the very root of Hindu *dharma,* and there can be no Hinduness (*hindutva*) without this indivisible, non-separate, universal love. (ch.21)

This declaration does not in principle rule out anyone from the ground plan of the love for one's country that Bankim was formulating, for the foundation of this love is a universal magnanimity. This included all non-Hindus. What Bankim failed to do was explicitly to incorporate love for non-Hindus in his recipe for patriotism. It could be argued that in the circumstances of the times, when his sights were fixed firmly on the alienating British presence in the land, he was speaking directly to his Hindu compatriots in the first instance. Perhaps, but this is not enough. Indian Muslim and Christian presence was significant and longstanding, and in the former case, had a troubled history in the subcontinent. It was necessary to address this issue explicitly in the shaping of a polity for the new era. This failure was to have fateful consequences, for it has been exploited in recent times by forces that have paid no heed to context in their opportunistic attempt to establish one form or other of exclusivist rule in the country, both politically and culturally.

At bottom, however, *Debī Chaudhurāṇī* is a story, not a philosophical treatise; so the reader is invited now to enter Bankim's world of glory and adventure and to follow the threads of the story as they unfold.

Debī Chaudhurāṇī, or *The Wife Who Came Home*

With loving devotion I offer this work at the revered lotus-feet of
one from whom I first heard the teaching of selfless action,
who dedicated himself to its practice,
and who by the fruit of virtue has now ascended to heaven.*

The Substance of Religion is Culture.
"The Fruit of it The Higher Life"
—*Natural Religion* by the Author of *Ecce Homo,* p.145.

"The General Law of Man's Progress, whatever the point of view
chosen, consists in this that Man becomes more and more
Religious"
—Auguste Comte, *Catechism of Positive Religion*, English
Translation by Congreve, 1st Edition, p.374.**

❂ *Notice* ❂

Only a portion of *Debi Chaudhurani* was published in *Bangadarsan.* The whole book is published here.

After *Anandamath* was published many wanted to know if there was any historical basis to that work. The *sannyasi*-revolt was historical no doubt, but there was no special need to make that known to the reader, and it was with this in mind that I said nothing about it. Since it was not my intention to write a historical novel, I made no pretense about historicity. Now, after all the publicity, I would like to provide some historical information about the *sannyasi*-revolt in a future edition of *Anandamath.*

Similarly, there's a slight historical basis to *Debi Chaudhurani.* Whoever wishes to be apprised of the facts can do so if they read the historical evidence pertaining to Rangpur District in the "Statistical Account" of Bengal collated by Mr Hunter and promulgated by the Government. There's not much in this respect, and there's very little connection between the historical Debi Chaudhurani and the book. The names Debi Chaudhurani, Bhabani Pathak, Mr Goodlad, and Lieutenant Brenan are historical, as indeed are the few facts that Debi lived in a boat, and that she had "fighters" and armies etc. But that is all. If the reader would be so kind as not to consider *Anandamath* or *Debi Chaudhurani* a "historical novel," I'd be most obliged.

*A dedication to the author's father. See Introduction for more on this point.

**These two statements appear in English. See endnotes for more information.

PART I

Chapter 1

"O Peee—Peepee—Prafulla—Wretch," mother called affectionately.

"Coming mother."

The daughter went up to her mother and said, "Yes, mother?"

"Why don't you go to the Ghosh's house and ask them for an eggplant?" asked her mother coaxingly.

Prafullamukhi said, "I can't. I feel ashamed to beg."

"Then what will you eat?" said her mother. "There's nothing in the house."

"We'll eat plain rice. How can we beg from people every day?"

"Because that's your lot!" was the reply. "There's no shame in begging if you're a pauper."

Prafulla said nothing. Her mother said, "All right then, you put up the rice, and I'll try and get some vegetables to cook."

"You eat my head!"[1] said Prafulla, "but don't go begging any more. There's rice in the house and salt, and green chillies on the plant—more than enough for us women."

Prafulla's mother had no option but to agree. Water for the rice was put up to boil, and Prafulla's mother went to wash the uncooked rice. She took the washing-basket in her hand,[2] and then put her other hand to her cheek. "There's no rice!" she said in dismay. She showed Prafulla—there was only half a handful of rice, not even enough to feed one.

Prafulla's mother went outside with the basket in her hand.

"Where are you going?" asked Prafulla.

"I'm going to borrow some rice" said her mother. "How else could even plain rice come our way?"

"We borrow so much rice from people" said Prafulla, "and we can't pay it back. Don't go borrowing any more."

"Wretched girl, what'll you eat? There's not a coin in the house."

"We'll fast."

"How long can you survive by fasting?"

"Till we die."

"You can do what you like when *I'm* dead" replied her mother, "But I can't stand by and watch you starve to death. I'll do what I can, and feed you by begging."

[1]A mild imprecation.

[2]*Dhucuni:* a wicker-basket used as a sieve to wash rice, fish etc.

"You don't have to beg" urged Prafulla. "People don't die from fasting for a day. Why don't we make some sacred threads today[3] and sell them tomorrow for a little money?"

"Where's the thread?" asked her mother.

"Why, we've got a spinning wheel."

"There's no cotton."

Then Prafullamukhi bowed her head and wept. Her mother took the washing-basket and prepared to go out again to borrow some rice, but Prafulla grabbed the basket from her and put it to one side.* "Mother, why should I live by begging and borrowing when I've everything I could want?" she said.

Wiping the tears from her daughter's eyes, her mother replied, "You've everything you could wish for, my dear, except the good fortune to use it."

"Why can't I use it, mother?" asked Prafulla. "What wrong have I done that I've nothing to eat when my father-in-law has plenty?"

"Born from a wretch like me—that's the wrong you've done!" said her mother, "And your bad luck! Otherwise, no one would have the right to take what's yours!"

"Listen mother," said Prafulla, "I've made up my mind today. If it's in my luck to eat what my father-in-law provides, I'll eat, otherwise I won't, and that will be that! Go get some food in the way you think best and eat it. Then take me to my in-laws' house and leave me there."

"How can that be, child!" exclaimed her mother. "That's impossible."

"Why impossible, mother?"

"Because unless they come to fetch you, you cannot go to your in-laws' house."

"Oh, I see," said Prafulla. "You can beg from strangers, but unless they come to fetch you, you can't go to your own in-laws' house!"

"But they don't even mention your name!"

"All right," replied the girl. "But that's no fault of mine. I'm doing no wrong to beg from those who are responsible for looking after me. I'm asking to eat what's mine—where's the shame in that?"

Her mother said nothing, but wept. Prafulla said, "I didn't want to leave you here alone and go on my own. I want to go with you in the hope that if you see my troubles solved, you'll be less miserable."

After mother and daughter had discussed the matter at great length, Prafulla's mother realized that what her daughter proposed was right.[4] She cooked whatever rice there was,* but Prafulla wouldn't eat a thing, so neither did her mother. Then Prafulla said, "What's the point of wasting more time? We've far to go."

---

[3]"Sacred threads": cotton threads worn in particular by Brahmin males after ritually coming of age; the thread hangs from the left shoulder in a loop across the chest down to the waist.

[4]By now the reader will have noticed that Prafulla's mother is not mentioned by name; this was customary with respect to older, married women. In fact, we will not learn Prafulla's mother's name, or what the names of other women in the novel in similar circumstances are.

*See the procedural note for the significance of an * in the body of the novel.

Her mother said, "Then let me tie your hair."

"No, leave it as it is," said Prafulla.*

Her mother thought, "Yes, leave it as it is. There's no need to dress up my daughter," while the daughter thought in turn, "Leave it be. Am I going there all dressed up to pull the wool over their eyes? Shame!"

Then both left the house, dressed as they were in their soiled clothes.

Chapter 2

There was a village called Bhutnath in Barendrabhumi, and it was there that Prafullamukhi's father-in-law had his residence. Whatever one may say of Prafulla's own circumstances, her father-in-law, Haraballabh-babu,[5] was a wealthy man. He had many estates, salons on both floors of his house, a private shrine, an assembly-hall, an office in which he stored files and records, and a rear garden and ponds, all surrounded by a wall. His residence was something over twelve miles away from where Prafullamukhi lived. Without eating anything, mother and daughter walked the twelve miles or so and, early in the afternoon, entered that rich man's house.

Yet, Prafulla's mother was reluctant to do so. Haraballabh-babu didn't despise Prafulla because she was a pauper's daughter. The truth was, there had been a misunderstanding after the wedding. Even though he knew Prafulla and her mother were destitute, Haraballabh had gone ahead with his son's marriage. The girl was so very beautiful that he'd found no one to compare with her—so he had agreed to the marriage, while for her part Prafulla's mother, heartened that her daughter had entered a rich man's house, spent all she owned on the wedding. And it was through that wedding that everything she had turned to ashes; it was from then on that they had become destitute.

For fate decreed that that desirable wedding produce undesirable results. Even though Prafulla's mother spent all she had—indeed, how much could that be?—widow as she was, she was unable to meet all her obligations. For the groom's party she made excellent arrangements with regard to the savoury and sweet dishes served, and in every other respect as to place, time, and person. But the bride's party got only flaked rice with curds.[6] The neighbors among the bride's party took offense at this and went away without eating. There was a quarrel with Prafulla's mother over this, and she rebuked them roundly. The neighbors exacted a heavy price in revenge.

On the day of the *paksparsa*, when the new bride feeds her husband's relatives for the first time, Haraballabh invited all the neighbors from the bride's side for the occasion. Not a single one attended. They sent an emissary to say that if

[5]babu: a suffix denoting a respectable man.

[6]In traditional wedding celebrations, such hospitality took place on separate occasions.

Haraballabh-babu must enter into a family-alliance with a woman who had lost caste, he could do so, of course—after all, the wealthy were immune from such things—but that they were poor folk for whom caste was their sole possession; *they* would not eat at the *paksparsa* of a girl whose mother had lost caste.

This news spread among the assembled company. Since Prafulla's mother lived alone as a widow with her daughter, and was rather young at that, the charge didn't seem impossible, especially as it occurred to Haraballabh that on the night of the wedding the neighbors didn't eat at the house where the wedding took place. In any case, why should the neighbors lie? Haraballabh believed them, and so did everyone in the gathering. All those who had been invited had something to eat, of course, but not one partook of the food touched by the new bride.

Next day, Haraballabh sent the bride back to her mother's house, and it was from then that Prafulla and her mother were renounced by Haraballabh. From then on he refused to keep in touch, and even forbade his son to do so. In fact, he married his son off to someone else. Once or twice, Prafulla's mother sent him something as a gift, but Haraballabh returned it. So it was that Prafulla's mother's legs trembled as she entered that house.

But now that they had come, there was no going back. Taking their courage in both hands, mother and daughter entered the house. At the time, the head of the house was engulfed in the bliss of his afternoon-nap somewhere in the inner apartments; his wife—Prafulla's mother-in-law—was having her grey hairs plucked, her legs stretched out in front of her. It was then that Prafulla and her mother appeared before her. Out of respect, Prafulla had almost fully covered her face with the end of her sari. She was now eighteen.

Seeing them, her mother-in-law said kindly, "Who are you two?"

Prafulla's mother heaved a deep sigh and said, "What can I say to introduce ourselves?"

"Why," asked the lady of the house, "What do people say to introduce themselves?"

Prafulla's mother said, "We're family."

"Family? What family?"

A maid, known as Tara's mother, was working nearby. She had been to Prafulla's house once or twice, soon after the marriage. She cried out, "My goodness, I recognize them! I recognize them! I know who that is—it's mother-in-law, isn't it?" (In those days, maidservants kept track of these relationships).

"Mother-in-law? What mother-in-law?" asked the lady of the house.

Tara's mother said, "The mother-in-law from Durgapur. Your eldest son's senior mother-in-law!"

Now her mistress understood. Her face darkened. "Sit down," she said. Her son's mother-in-law sat down, but Prafulla remained standing.

"And who is this girl?" asked the mistress of the house.

Prafulla's mother replied, "This is your eldest daughter-in-law."

The other was not very pleased; she said nothing. After a while she said, "Were you on your way somewhere?"

"We've come directly to your house," answered Prafulla's mother.

"Why is that?"

"Why not? Can't my daughter come to her father-in-law's house?"

"Of course she can come" was the reply, "but only when her in-laws ask for her. Does a girl from a good family come uninvited?"

"But if her in-laws ignore her completely?"

"Well, if they do that, then why has she come?"

"Who will feed her? I'm a penniless widow, how can I look after your son's wife?"

"If you can't even feed her, then why did you have her?"

"Did you conceive your son after working out whether you could feed and clothe him? In that case, couldn't you have included your future daughter-in-law's food and clothing as well?"

"To hell with you! I see the witch has come here to quarrel with me!" exclaimed the lady of the house.

"No, I haven't come here to quarrel," replied Prafulla's mother. "I brought your daughter-in-law here since she couldn't come alone. Now that she's here, I'll leave." And with that, Prafulla's mother left the house. Even then, the unfortunate woman had had nothing to eat.

Though her mother had gone, Prafulla stayed behind. She remained standing as before, with the edge of her sari across her face.

Her mother-in-law said, "Your mother's gone. You can go too."

Prafulla didn't move.

"You're not budging?" said her mother-in-law.

Prafulla still didn't move.

"How tiresome!" said the mistress of the house. "I must send someone to accompany you again, is that it?"

Prafulla removed the cloth from her face. It was such a beautiful face, with the tears streaming from her eyes. Her mother-in-law thought, "Pity I haven't had the chance to make a home with such a beautiful daughter-in-law." She softened a bit.

Prafulla murmured, "I've come here to stay."

"What can I do, dear?" said her mother-in-law. "Do you think I don't want to take you in? But people were talking. They said they'd outcaste me, so I've had to turn my back on you."

"Mother, who's ever turned their back on a child for fear they'll be outcasted?" answered Prafulla. "Aren't I your child?"

Her mother-in-law softened even more. "What can I do, dear" she replied, "It's this fear of losing caste."

Prafulla spoke timidly, as before. "I may be beyond the pale, but so many women of low caste serve in your house. There'd be no harm if I did the same."

The lady of the house could resist no longer. "Such a sweet girl," she said, "Both in looks and speech. I'll go and ask the head of the house and see what he says. Sit here, my dear, and wait."

Prafulla had sat down promptly when, from behind a door, a young girl—fourteen years old, and also beautiful, with her face half-covered*—beckoned to her with her hand.

"What can this be?" thought Prafulla as she rose and went up to the girl.

Chapter 3

By the time the lady of the house had waddled along to her husband's room, fiddling with the clasp of her bangle on the way, the master of the house had woken from sleep. He had splashed his hands and face with water and was just drying them. When she saw this, his wife tried to put him in a good mood by saying, "Who woke you up? I try so hard to keep people away, but no one listens."

The master of the house thought, "The chief disturber of my sleep is you. I expect she wants something today." But aloud he said, "No one woke me up. I slept very well. What is it?"

His wife put on a jovial face and said, "Such a strange thing happened today! I've come to tell you." After broaching the topic in this way and trying to charm her husband with a coquettish gesture or two—after all, she was still only forty five—she gave him a detailed description of Prafulla's and her mother's arrival and the conversation that ensued. With her daughter-in-law's beautiful face and sweet words in mind, she turned her account strongly in Prafulla's favor. But none of this scheming worked. Her husband's face darkened like rain-clouds in the month of Baisakh. "Such utter cheek!" he exclaimed. "That *Bagdi* girl dares enter my house![7] Go take a broom to her and send her packing this minute!"

"How awful!" said his wife. "That's not the way to talk. All said and done, she's your son's wife. And how has she become a *Bagdi*'s daughter? Just because people say she is?" She knew she was in a weak position, so she tried to bluster a bit. But it was to no avail; the order remained the same: "Take a broom to that *Bagdi* girl and get rid of her!"

At last his wife got annoyed and said, "Go take a broom to her yourself. I'm going to stay out of your household affairs from now on." She left the room grumbling angrily, but when she returned to where she had left Prafulla, she saw that Prafulla wasn't there.

The reader might recall where Prafulla had gone. From behind a door, a fourteen-year old girl, with the edge of her sari screening her face, had beckoned to her with her hand, and Prafulla had gone up to her. No sooner had Prafulla entered the room than the girl shut the door.

[7] *Bagdi:* a low-caste group that caught and dealt in fish.

"Why have you shut the door?" asked Prafulla.

"So that no one comes in," said the girl. "I want to have a little chat with you."

"What's your name, friend?" asked Prafulla.

"My name's Sagar, friend," was the reply.

"And who might you be, friend?" said Prafulla.

"I'm your co-wife, friend," the girl answered.[8]

"So you know who I am?" said Prafulla.

"Well, I heard everything from behind the door."

"So you're the bride of the house, the housewife. . . . ," said Prafulla.[9]

"No fear!" said the girl. "Do you think there's a curse on me? Why'd I want to be that? Do I have buckteeth, or am I dark to look at?"

"Who has buckteeth?" asked Prafulla bewildered.

"The bride of the house, the housewife," answered the girl.

"Who's that?" asked Prafulla.

"Don't you know? Well, how would you know! You've never been here. Do you know that we've got another co-wife?"

"I know there was another marriage other than mine. I thought that was you," said Prafulla.

"No, that was her," said the girl. "I got married three years ago."

"Is she very ugly?" asked Prafulla.

"Just looking at her makes me want to cry."

"Is that why he married you, then?"

"No, that's not why. I'll tell you why, but don't tell anyone else. (Sagar lowered her voice to a whisper). My father's very rich, and I'm the only child. So for the sake of the money. . . . "

"I see," said Prafulla. "Say no more. But you're beautiful. So how did the ugly one become the wife of the house?"

"I'm my father's only child," said Sagar, "So he doesn't want to send me here, and my father and father-in-law don't get on very well. So I don't really live here. He brings me here when there's some domestic need. I'll be here for a few days, and then I'm off."

Prafulla saw that Sagar was a sweet girl; she couldn't look askance at her even though she was a co-wife. She said, "Why did you call me?"

"Can I give you something to eat?" asked Sagar.

Prafulla laughed. She said, "Why do you say that?"

"Well, you look tired; you've come a long way, and you must be thirsty. No one's offered you anything to eat. That's why I called you."

---

[8]In the Bengali (Hindu) society of the time, polygamy was permitted, but not polyandry. These marriages usually occurred when the girl was still very young, though the bride was not generally expected to assume her domestic (and conjugal) responsibilities till well after puberty.

[9]The established daughter-in-law of the house. *DCM* has "the ruling wife" which makes the point.

Prafulla still hadn't had anything to eat, and she was dying of thirst. But she said, "Mother-in-law's gone to find out what father-in-law thinks. Without first knowing my fate, I shan't eat anything here. If it's to be the broom for me, then that's all I'll swallow, nothing else."

"No, no," said Sagar, "There's no need for you to eat anything from them. I've got some lovely *sandesh* from my father's house."[10]

She brought a few pieces and began to stuff them into Prafulla's mouth. Prafulla couldn't help but eat some. Then Sagar gave her some cool water to drink. Prafulla drank and felt refreshed. She said, "I'm feeling much better, but my mother will die if she doesn't have something to eat."

"Where's she gone?" asked Sagar.

"I've no idea. Perhaps she's waiting on the road outside."

"I know what I can do," said Sagar.

"What?"

"Shall I send Grandaunt Brahma to help her?"

"Who's she?"

"An aunt on my father-in-law's side who lives in this household."

"And what will she do?"

"She'll help your mother, give her something to eat."

"Mother will eat nothing in this house," said Prafulla.

"Of course not!" said Sagar with spirit. "That's not what I'm saying. I mean in some Brahmin's house."

"All right, do what you can," said Prafulla, "I can't bear any longer for mother to suffer."

Sagar shot off to Grandaunt Brahma and told her the whole story. Grandaunt Brahma said, "Is that so, my dear? She was made to go without food in a respectable house? That'll bring bad luck." She went out to look for Prafulla's mother. Sagar came back and gave Prafulla the news.

Prafulla said, "Now, friend, continue what you were saying before."

"There's nothing more to say," replied Sagar. "I don't live here, and I shan't get the chance to. My luck's like a mango made of clay: kept on the ledge, but never used as an offering to the god.[11] Still, now that you've come, try and stay. None of us can bear the sight of that Grisly Owl."[12]

"Well, I've come here to stay," said Prafulla, "I'll stay if they let me!"

"Even if our father-in-law doesn't agree, don't leave immediately," said Sagar.

"If I don't go, what would I do here? And why should I stay?* I'll stay only if. . . ."

[10]*sandesh:* a sweetmeat produced from milk.

[11]Fruit was one of the items used in domestic worship. The deity "enjoyed/consumed" the fruit offered. There is a pun here on "offering" and "god": both terms are used in reference to Sagar's husband, who as his wife's "god" (*debatā*), was free to enjoy—or not—his married state with her.

[12]The third co-wife!

"If what?" asked Sagar.

"If you can make my existence worth the while."

"How could I do that, friend?" asked Sagar.

Prafulla smiled. Then the smile vanished, and she began to cry. She said, "Don't you understand, friend?"

Then Sagar understood. She thought awhile, and then said with a deep sigh, "Come to this room when it's dark and sit here. You won't be able to see him during the day."

(The reader will recall that we are not writing about the shameless girls of today. Our story took place a hundred years ago. Even forty years ago young women never got to see their husbands during the day.)

Prafulla said, "Let me go and find out what's in store for me first. Then I'll come and meet you again. Whatever's in store, I want to see my husband before I go. I want to hear what he has to say."

Prafulla came out of the room and saw that her mother-in-law was looking for her. When she saw her, her mother-in-law said, "Where were you, my dear?"

"I was looking around the house," answered Prafulla.

"Really it's your house, my child, but what can I do? Your father-in-law simply won't agree."

The words hit Prafulla like a thunderbolt. She sat down with her head in her hands, but she didn't cry, she remained silent. Her mother-in-law felt extremely sorry for her and resolved to try again, this time more forcefully. But she kept that to herself. Instead, she asked, "Where will you go now? Stay here today, and you can leave tomorrow morning."

Prafulla raised her head and said, "All right, I'll stay, but I want you to ask my father-in-law something. My mother lives by the spinning wheel, but she can't make enough to provide even one meal a day for one person. Please ask him: how am I to survive? I may be a *Bagdi* or a *Muci,* but I'm his son's wife.[13] How is his son's wife supposed to survive?"

Her mother-in-law replied, "I'll certainly ask him that." Then Prafulla got up and left.

Chapter 4

After dark, Sagar and Prafulla were sitting in the room with the door closed, speaking in whispers, when someone knocked on the door.

"Who's that?" asked Sagar.

"It's me," was the reply.

---

[13] *Muci* (pronounced with a soft "c"). *Muci*s were a low-caste group who skinned, tanned, and worked in leather.

Sagar nudged Prafulla and said in a whisper, "Say nothing. It's the Grisly Owl."

"The other wife?" asked Prafulla.

"Yes. Quiet."

The newcomer said, "Who's inside? Why don't you speak? Isn't that Sagar-Bou's voice?"

"Who are you?" asked Sagar. "Isn't that the barber's wife's voice?"[14]

"What, damn it, am I like the barber's wife?"

"Then who are you?"

"Your co-wife! Your co-wife! I'm Nayan-Bou."

(Her real name was Nayantara, but people called her "Nayan-Bou," and Sagar, "Sagar-Bou"[15]).

Sagar said with feigned concern, "Who? *Didi*?[16] God forbid! How could you be like the barber's wife? She's a tad lighter-skinned."

"Damn it, so I'm darker than her? What a co-wife I've got! If you weren't just fourteen. . . . "

"So what if I'm fourteen? You're just seventeen, and I'm prettier and younger than you."

"Go take your youth and beauty to your father's house and enjoy them there! Since I'm stuck with you now, I've come to ask you something."

"What's that, *Didi?*"

"How can I say if you don't open the door? Why have you locked the door at this time of night?"

"Because I'm eating some *sandesh* on the quiet. You do the same, don't you?"

"Oh, I see," said Nayan. "All right then, keep eating." (She loved *sandesh* herself). She continued, "I'll tell you what I came to ask: I've heard someone else has come?"

"Someone else? What, another husband?"

"Damn it, is that possible!"

"Good if it happened," said Sagar, "We two could share them out. I'd give you the new one."

"How awful!" said Nayan. "Is that the way to talk!"

"So I'm only to think it then?"

"Do you think you can say anything you want to me?"

"Look," said Sagar, "Unless you speak clearly, how can I give you an answer?"

"What I want to ask is, has another daughter-in-law come to the house?"

"What daughter-in-law?"

---

[14]Barbers were of low caste.

[15]"Bou" means "wife," "daughter-in-law."

[16]"Elder sister": a term of affection or respect for an older sibling, relative, or acquaintance.

"The *Muci* one."

"*Muci?* No, I haven't heard," said Sagar.

"Well, if not *Muci* then *Bagdi?*"

"No," said Sagar, "Don't know about that either."

"Haven't you heard we've got a *Bagdi* co-wife?" asked Nayan.

"No, is that so?" said Sagar.

"You're really awful!" said Nayan. "The one who got married first?"

"That was a Brahmin's daughter."

"Right, Brahmin's daughter! Then why didn't they take her in?"

"So if they send you away tomorrow, and took me in instead, that'd make you a *Bagdi*'s daughter, would it?"

"How dare you insult me, you wretch!" cried Nayan.

"Then why do *you* insult someone else, you wretch!"

"Go to hell!" said Nayan. "I'm going to tell our mother-in-law you say what you like to me just because you're a big shot's daughter!"

Nayantara (aka "The Grisly Owl") was just departing with a clash of bangles when Sagar saw the danger of the situation. "*Didi,* come back!" she called, "I'm sorry. *Didi,* come back! I'm opening the door."

Nayantara was angry, and hardly inclined to return. But because she was a little curious to see how much *sandesh* Sagar was secretly eating, she came back. When she entered the room, she saw, no *sandesh,* but another person inside!

"Who's this?" she asked.

"Prafulla," said Sagar.

"And who might she be?"

"The *Muci* daughter-in-law."

"So good-looking!"

"But not more good-looking than you," replied Sagar.

"Stop it! Don't keep on at me" retorted Nayan. "But not more good-looking than *you!* "*

Chapter 5

Meanwhile, as the night was drawing in, the master of the house sat down to his evening meal.[17] The mistress of the house, with fan in hand, sat resplendent beside his eating-plate. There were no flies on the rice, of course, yet her duties as wife decreed that she was to drive them away. Alas, who are these vile men—lowest of the low!—who seek to destroy this most pleasant of duties? The lady of the house may have five* maidservants at her beck and call, but when it comes to serving her husband, who else but she is entitled to do this? Heaven, have

[17]This was done with the man squatting on a low stool or (on a mat) on the floor, with his wife in attendance.

you no thunderbolt for the heads of the villains who seek to do away with this duty?[18]

While he was at his meal, the master of the house asked, "Has that *Bagdi* girl gone?"

Still waving away the flies, his wife said with a toss of the head, "Where could she go at night? You don't drive away a guest who comes at night, and I'm supposed to drive away a daughter-in-law?"

Her husband answered, "If she's a guest, why can't she go to the guesthouse? Why here in the house?"[19]

"I've already told you I can't drive her away. If you want to get rid of her, you'll have to do it yourself. Such a good-looking girl....."

"You get the odd beauty in *Bagdi* houses," said her husband. "All right, I'll get rid of her." He turned to a maidservant and said, "Call Braja, will you."

Braja was the name of his son. A servant girl went and came back with Brajesvar. He was twenty-one or twenty-two, with good looks that couldn't be faulted. He came and stood meekly by his father's side, not daring to speak.

When he saw him, Haraballabh said, "Son, you know you've three wives?"

Braja didn't say a word.

"Do you remember the first one? A *Bagdi* girl?"

Braja remained silent. In those days a son of twenty-two, though he were as sharp as a diamond, wouldn't speak in his father's presence. Now, the greater the fool, the longer the speech he spouts.

Haraballabh continued, "That *Bagdi* girl's come here today. She's insisting on staying, so I told your mother to take the broom to her and get rid of her. But do you think one woman will lay a hand on another? That's your job. You've the right to do it. No one else can touch her. So take the broom to her and get rid of her tonight. Otherwise I shan't sleep a wink."

His wife said, "Shame! Don't raise your hand to a woman, dear. Must you always listen to your father? Don't I have a say in things? Whatever you do, tell her to go nicely."

Braja said, "As you say" to his father, and "Very well" to his mother. But as he didn't go at once, his mother took the opportunity to ask her husband, "Now that you're going to drive your daughter-in-law away, how is she going to provide for herself?"

"She can do what she wants—she can steal, become a bandit, beg."

His mother said to Brajesvar, "When you drive your wife away, make sure you tell her that. She asked."

Brajesvar left his father's presence and turned up in Grandaunt Brahma's quarters. He saw that she was engrossed in reciting her beads, and waving away mosquitoes.

---

[18]A dig at the social reformers of the time.

[19]Large residences of the time had separate guesthouses.

"Grandaunt!" said Brajesvar.

"Yes, dear?"

"Has something unusual happened today?"

"Unusual? You mean Sagar breaking my spinning wheel? She's only a child, so if it's broken, it's broken. She fancied using the wheel and..."

"No, no, not that," said Braja. "I mean, today hasn't something...."

"Don't tell her off," said Grandaunt Brahma. "Don't worry, so long as all of you are alive, I'll have plenty of spinning wheels. Still, I'm an old woman, so....."

"Will you listen to what I'm saying!"

"....an old woman. Who knows how long I'll last? So I spend my time spinning a sacred thread or two for the Brahmins. Well, anyway...."

"If you don't listen, it's me who'll break every spinning wheel you'll ever have!"

"Oh, so it's not about spinning wheels?"

"No—you know I have two Brahmin wives?"

"Brahmin wives? I tell you! Both those Brahmin wives of yours, Nayan-Bou and Sagar-bou, are just the same—they keep pestering me for fairy-tales! "Tell me a fairy-tale, tell me a fairy-tale!" Where am I to get so many fairy-tales, tell me, dear."

"Forget the fairy-tales...."

"*You* can say that, but do you think they'll leave me in peace? So I told them that fairy-tale about the male bird and the female bird. Do you know that one? Listen, I'll tell you. In a forest in a large silk-cotton tree, there lived a male bird and a female bird...."

"Good grief, Grandaunt, what are you on about? Fairy-tales, now? Listen to what I have to say!"

"What would *you* have to say?" retorted Grandaunt. "I'll do the talking since you've come to hear fairy tales. Don't you folk have anything else to do?"

Brajesvar thought, "Oh for the day these old women drop dead!" Aloud he said, "I have two Brahmin wives, and one who's a *Bagdi*. Has the *Bagdi* one come here today?"

"Heaven forbid!" said Grandaunt. "Why do you say *Bagdi?* She's a Brahmin's daughter."

"Well, is she here?"

"Yes."

"Where? Can I meet her?"

"You can, and if I let you I'm as good as poison in your parents' eyes! Instead, listen to the story of the male bird and the female bird......"

"Don't worry," interrupted Brajesvar. "My parents called me and told me to drive her away. But how can I do that unless I meet her? Since you're the aunt of the house, I've come here to find out where she is."

"Look, dear, I'm an old woman," said Grandaunt. "I say my beads to Krishna and eat sun-bleached rice. If you want to hear a fairy-tale, I can tell you. I know nothing about *Bagdi* and Brahmin wives."

"Really!" said Brajesvar, "I hope the bandits get you in your old age!"

"Oh, don't say that," cried Grandaunt in alarm, "We're all so terrified of bandits! You want to meet her?"

"Do you think I've come here to watch you recite your beads!"

"Then go to Sagar-Bou."

"Do co-wives introduce each other to their husband?"

"Just go," said Grandaunt. "Sagar's called for you. She's waiting for you in her room. You don't get girls like her any more."

"Because she's broken your spinning wheel?" said Braja. "Then I'll tell Nayan. Maybe she'll break a spinning wheel too."

"You're comparing the two?" said Grandaunt. "What an idea!"

"If I go," said Braja, "Will I get to see the *Bagdi* girl?"

"Why don't you listen to an old woman? This is such a nuisance! I've not finished reciting my beads yet. Your granduncle had sixty three wives, but when one called for him, whether she was fourteen or seventy four, he never said no!"

"May granduncle enjoy heaven forever," rejoined Braja. "I'm off to look for the fourteen-year old. When I return should I go looking for this seventy-four year old?"

"Get away!" cried Grandaunt. "My beads are all twisted up! I'm going to tell Nayantara you just lark about!"

"Yes, tell her," said Braja. "She'll be so pleased she'll send you a couple of fried lentil cakes."[20]

And with that Brajesvar went off in search of Sagar.

Chapter 6

When Sagar came to her father-in-law's house, she would be given two rooms, one downstairs and the other upstairs. In the room downstairs she would prepare *paan,* pass the time with others of her own age, and chat.[21] At night she would sleep in the room upstairs; if she felt sleepy during the day, she would go to the room upstairs and close the door. So it was that Brajesvar, shrugging off his irritation at Grandaunt's fairy-tales, went to the room upstairs.

But Sagar was not there; instead someone else was present, and it occurred to Braja that this was his first wife.

The consternation! Here they were—husband and wife—so closely related, one the other half of the other, the most intimate relationship in the world.

[20]See endnotes.

[21]*Paan:* the betel leaf folded around various ingredients such as small pieces of betel nut, quicklime paste, etc. This would then be inserted whole into the mouth and chewed, with the resulting juice, dark red in color, being spat out from time to time (analogous to tobacco being chewed in the West).

Yet they never met or spoke to one another! How should a conversation begin? Who should speak first,* especially since one had come there to be driven away, and the other had come to do the driving! We would like to ask the older lady-reader: how ought a conversation to begin?

Well, leaving aside what ought to happen, nothing happened as it ought. At first neither spoke for a long while. At last, Prafulla, smiling a little, drew the edge of her sari around her neck, went up to where Brajesvar stood and bent down and touched his feet.[22] Brajesvar was not like his father. He accepted Prafulla's obeisance embarrassedly, drew her up by the arm and seated her on the spacious bed. Then he sat down beside her.

Prafulla had drawn the edge of her sari slightly across her face (the girls of that time were not like the girls of today—a curse on today!). But as Prafulla was being seated on the bed that little screen across her face fell away, and Brajesvar saw that she was crying. Without taking stock of the situation—dear, dear, dear (a curse on being twenty two!)—without taking stock of the situation or thinking things through, just there—where a tear was gathering under one of those large eyes—(dear, dear, dear)—Brajesvar suddenly planted a kiss. Your author has got on in years—so he's not ashamed to write this—but he hopes that the younger reader of good taste will stop reading this book right here.

Now while Brajesvar himself was being tainted by this abominable crime (and became the cause of tainting the author with the very same crime)—and while the foolish Prafulla was thinking that perhaps never had anyone in this world done something so holy, so blessed as to plant such a kiss—someone poked her face round the door. Perhaps because the face laughed a little, or perhaps because the jewelry on its owner's hand made a little sound, Brajesvar cocked an ear in that direction. He turned to look, and saw that the face was a very pretty one. Glossy black curls ringed on one side by a kind of half-moon tiara (girls wore such tiaras then), with the edge of the sari slightly screening the face—and behind the screen, two large eyes like lotus-petals and two slim red lips smiling sweetly. Brajesvar saw that it was Sagar's face.

Sagar showed her husband a padlock and key. Sagar was still very young; she didn't speak much to her husband, so Braja didn't grasp what she intended. But it didn't take him long to catch on. Sagar closed the door from outside, latched the chain, turned the key in the padlock and ran off. When he heard the key turn, Brajesvar shouted, "Sagar! What are you doing!" But Sagar didn't listen; her ornaments jingling, she ran straight to Grandaunt Brahma's bed and threw herself upon it.

Grandaunt asked, "What is it, Sagar-Bou? What's happened, dear? Why are you lying here?"

Sagar didn't say a word.

"Has Braja sent you away?"

[22]The way a wife formally showed respect to her husband.

"Why else would I come to your place for shelter?" said Sagar. "I'll sleep here today."

"Very well, sleep here," said Grandaunt. "But he'll send for you again this very minute. Your granduncle used to send me away like this all the time, and then call for me immediately! Then I'd get more angry and wouldn't go. But since I had a woman's heart I couldn't stay away! You know, one day. . . ."

"Auntie, tell me a fairytale," said Sagar.

"Which one shall I tell you?" asked Grandaunt. "The one about the male bird and the female bird? Do you want to hear it by yourself? Where's the new wife? Why don't you call her? Both of you can listen to it."

"I can't go about looking for her now," said Sagar. "I'll listen to it on my own. Go on, tell it to me."

Then lying down by Sagar's side, Grandaunt began the story of the two birds. No sooner had she begun, than Sagar fell asleep. Unaware of this, Grandaunt continued with the story for a while, but when she realized that her listener was fast asleep, she sadly brought her story to an end in midstream.*

Next day, just when dawn was breaking, Sagar came, unlocked the padlock to the room, and went away. Then without saying a word to anyone, she took Grandaunt's broken spinning wheel and began to spin it noisily in the ear of the old lady who was sleeping soundly.

Prafulla and Brajesvar heard the sound of lock and chain being unfastened. Prafulla had been sitting down. She got up and said, "Sagar's undone the chain, so I'll go.* Whether you acknowledge me as your wife or not, remember me at least as your servant."

"Don't go now," said Braja. "Let me speak to my father again."

"Do you think he'll change his mind if you do?" asked Prafulla.

"Whether he does or not, I must do what I must" said Braja. "If I abandon you without reason, won't I be doing wrong?"

"You haven't abandoned me," said Prafulla, "You've accepted me. You've made room for me by your bed on one occasion. That's more than enough for me. I'm begging you, don't fall out with your father for the sake of a wretch like me. I won't be happy with that."

"At least let me see to his providing for you."

"He's turned his back on me," answered Prafulla. "I shan't beg from him. If you've got anything of your own, I can beg from you."

"I've nothing except this ring," said Brajesvar, "Take it with you. For the time being you can ward off some troubles for the price of the ring. Afterward, I'll do my best to earn a little money and look after you as best I can."

Brajesvar removed the expensive diamond ring from his finger and gave it to Prafulla. As she placed the ring on her finger, Prafulla said, "Suppose you forget me?"

"I can forget everyone else, never you."

"But if you're not able to recognize me later?"

"I'll never forget your face!"

"I shan't sell this ring. Even if I die from starvation, I'll never sell this ring. When you fail to recognize me, I'll show you this ring. Is there anything written on it?"

"My name's engraved on it," answered Brajesvar. Then drenched in their tears, they said goodbye to each other.

When she came downstairs, Prafulla met Sagar and Nayan. That wretch Nayan asked, "*Didi,* where did you sleep last night?"

"Friend," said Prafulla, "Those who've crossed to a holy place don't speak about it."

"What do you mean?" asked Nayan.

"Can't you understand?" said Sagar. "Yesterday after she saw me off she and our husband stayed on like Lakshmi and Vishnu on my bed. And out of love for her that fellow gave her a ring."[23]

Sagar showed Nayan the ring on Prafulla's hand. When she saw it, Nayantara was furious. She said, "*Didi,* have you heard how our father-in-law replied to your question?"

Prafulla, basking in the love Brajesvar had shown her, had forgotten about that. So she said, "Reply to what question?"

"You asked how you would survive."

"How could he answer that?" said Prafulla.

"Father-in-law said, tell her to survive by becoming a robber and a bandit."

"We'll see," said Prafulla shortly and took her leave.

Without saying another word to anyone, Prafulla marched straight out by the back gate, Sagar hurrying after her. Prafulla said to Sagar, "I'm leaving now, friend, and I'll never come to this house again. When you go back to your father's house, you'll meet me there."

"Do you know where my father lives?" asked Sagar.

"No, but I'll find out," said Prafulla.

"Will you really go to my father's house?"

"What have I left to be ashamed of?" said Prafulla.

"Your mother said she wants to see you. She's waiting for you," said Sagar. In fact, Prafulla's mother was waiting by the garden gate. Sagar pointed to her and Prafulla went up to her mother.

Chapter 7

Prafulla and her mother came back home. The journey there and back was a great strain physically for Prafulla's mother, but even more so mentally. After all, one cannot endure everything all of the time, so upon her return Prafulla's

[23]See endnotes.

mother fell into a fever. The fever was not much to begin with, but coming from a Bengali household as she did—and a Brahmin one at that—not to mention being a widow, Prafulla's mother didn't take the fever seriously. She carried on as before: she bathed twice a day and ate when food came her way. *She managed because from time to time the neighbors felt sorry for her and gave her something. Gradually the fever increased till Prafulla's mother had to take to her bed. There wasn't much medical expertise in the rural areas of the time, and widows rarely took recourse to medication; in particular there was no one whom Prafulla could send to summon a practitioner on her behalf. In any case, such physicians were hard to find in the area. So the fever increased and turned into delirium, till finally Prafulla's mother was released from all her troubles.

A number of people from the locality—the very people who had baselessly cast aspersions on her—came forward and performed Prafulla's mother's funeral rites. At times like this, Bengalis do not keep enmity: the Bengali race has this virtue.

Now Prafulla was alone. The same people came forward and told her that she was required to perform the rites of the fourth day after her mother's demise.[24] Prafulla replied that she wished to make the offerings but that she had no idea how to go about it. Her interlocutors said that she need do nothing, that they would see to it all. So some gave money, others contributed materials for the rite, and in this way both the rite and the meal for the Brahmins were arranged. It was the neighbors themselves who saw to everything.

*Then one of them said, "Something's occurred to me. Shouldn't your father-in-law be invited to your mother's funeral rite?" Prafulla replied, "But who will go to invite him?" Two of the local leaders (who suffered from the tendency to be the first to get involved in whatever was brewing) came forward. "But it was you," exclaimed Prafulla, "who spoke ill of us and turned that house against us!" They answered, "Don't worry about that; we'll put it to one side. Now that you're a girl without a protector, we have no further quarrel with you."

So Prafulla agreed. When the two men went to Haraballabh to invite him to the rite, he said to them, "Well sirs! It was you who ostracized my son's mother-in-law, saying that she had fallen from caste, and now you tell me the opposite!"

"You know how it is," the two Brahmins replied, "Misunderstandings like this happen among neighbors. It doesn't mean anything." But Haraballabh was a mercenary man. He thought, "This is all humbug. That *Bagdi* girl has bribed these fellows. *Now tell me, where did she get the money from?" As a result, not only did Haraballabh refuse to listen to them, he became even more hard-hearted and angry toward Prafulla. *Brajesvar, who heard this news, resolved to visit Prafulla secretly one night and return home that very night!

[24]Rites to be performed by a married daughter on the fourth day after the death of a parent.

The neighbors came back without achieving their goal. Prafulla duly performed her mother's funeral rite and with the help of the neighbors saw to it that the Brahmins were fed properly, *while for his part, Brajesvar looked for an opportunity to visit Prafulla.

❁ *Chapter 8* ❁

The home of Phulmani, the barber's wife, was close to that of Prafulla. From the time Prafulla lost her mother, she lived alone at home. Since she was young and beautiful, living alone was a cause for both fear and scandal; she needed another woman to sleep by her side at night. So Prafulla requested Phulmani to do this. Phulmani was a widow and except for a widowed sister, she had no one else to call her own. Both the sisters had been devoted to Prafulla's mother; this is why Prafulla had made her request to Phulmani, and Phulmani for her part was happy to agree. So it was that from the day Prafulla's mother passed away, Phulmani came regularly after dark to sleep in Prafulla's house.

But the naive Prafulla didn't really know what kind of person Phulmani was. Phulmani was ten years older than Prafulla. In looks and behavior she didn't come across badly, and she kept up a certain spruceness in her appearance. But being a woman of low caste who had been a child-widow, she had failed rather to maintain an unblemished character.

*The landlord of that village was Paran Chaudhuri. One of his rent-collectors, Durlabh Chakrabarti, would come from time to time to the village to hold court on behalf of his master. People gossiped that Phulmani was particularly favored by Durlabh, or rather that *he* was favored by her. It was not that Prafulla had never heard such rumors, but what could she do? There was no one else who was prepared to leave her home and come and sleep by her side. Indeed, Prafulla would say to herself: "She may be a bad lot, but if I'm not, who can make me bad?"

So Phulmani came and slept in Prafulla's house for a few days. On the day after the funeral rite, while Phulmani was making her way to Prafulla's house a little later than usual, she entered a thicket that lay under a mango tree. A man was waiting in that thicket—needless to say, it was Durlabhchandra himself.

As soon as Mr Chakrabarti saw Phulmani advancing to keep her tryst, dressed in a white sari with a crimson border and smiling broadly, her lips reddened by betel juice, he inquired, "Well now, will it be today?"

"Yes, today's good," Phulmani replied. "Come late at night with the palanquin and tap on the door, and I'll open it. But make sure there's no disturbance."

"Don't worry. But won't *she* cause a disturbance?"

"We'll have to see to that. I'll open the door quietly; you slip in and tie a cloth round her mouth whilst she's still sleeping. Then let her scream! Who can help her then!"

❁

"But if we take her forcibly like that, she's not likely to stay long."

Phulmani replied, "All we have to do is take her there. D'you think someone who's all alone and desperate for food won't stay once she's given food, clothing, jewelry, money, love? Leave that to me. But make sure I get my share of the jewelry and money."

When they had finished speaking, Durlabh returned to his place while Phulmani went on to Prafulla's. Of course, Prafulla hadn't the slightest inkling of the calamity that was to befall her. She lay down thinking of her mother, and weeping as one weeps for a mother, she fell asleep weeping as she did every day. When it was late at night, Durlabh came and tapped on the door. Phulmani opened it, and tying a cloth round Prafulla's mouth, Durlabh seized her and carried her to the palanquin. The bearers silently bore her away toward the landlord, Paran-babu's, leisure-room. Needless to say, Phulmani went with them. *Shortly after this happened, Brajesvar arrived at that empty house, looking for Prafulla. He had fled in the night, without telling anyone, but alas, when he arrived he found no one there!

I have said that the bearers bore Prafulla away in silence. Let no one think I made a blunder there: after all, it's in the nature of palanquin-bearers to make a noise. This time, however, they had been forbidden to make a sound. For if they had, there would have been a commotion. But there was something else. We've heard Grandaunt Brahma say how terrified people were of bandits. In fact, it's doubtful if folk had such a fear of brigands in any other place. The region had no proper ruler at that time: Muslim rule had passed, while British rule had not been properly established. Besides, a few years earlier the famine of '76 had devastated the land, on top of which Debisingh was in charge of exacting the revenue.[25] On the other side of the world, Edmund Burke had stood up in Westminster Hall and had made him immortal. With a fiery torrent of words resembling the flames bursting from a volcano, he had recorded Debisingh's depredations for posterity. Many women fainted from grief when they heard that stream of words issue from his lips, like a proclamation from on high, and even today, a hundred years later, the flesh creeps and the heart pounds when one reads that speech.

Those terrible deeds had overwhelmed Barendrabhumi. It was not only the case that a great many didn't get food to eat; they didn't even have a roof over their heads. Those who had no food seized from others so that they could eat. In consequence, there were bands of thieves and bandits in every village. Was anyone able to control this? Mr Goodlad, Rangpur's first Collector, was the person in charge of policing the area. He kept sending troops of sepoys to catch the bandits, but they were able to do nothing.

[25] "The famine of '76": that is, 1176 of the Bengali *San* era, corresponding to mid-April 1769 to mid-April 1770 of the Western calendar (since the *San* year begins in mid-April). The terrible famine of that time assumed legendary status in Bengali culture. About this famine and Debisingh, see further in endnotes.

So Durlabh was afraid that he who was carrying off Prafulla by an act of banditry might fall a victim to bandits himself, for it was possible that bandits might come if they saw the palanquin. It was for fear of that that the bearers were silent, and to avoid a commotion no one else was present except Durlabh himself and Phulmani. In this way, they fearfully covered a distance of about 8 miles.

Then they entered a dense jungle. The bearers were frightened to see two men approaching them. Since it was night, and there was only starlight to show the way, the men's shapes were indistinct; the bearers thought that the Lord of death himself was advancing in twofold form! One of the porters said to the others, "I'm not sure about those two!" Another said, "Can they be good folk if they're roaming about at night?" A third bearer said, "Those two men look very strong to me." A fourth said, "Aren't those staves they're carrying?" The first porter asked, "What do you say, Mr Charkrabarti? We'd better stop here or else we'll perish at the hands of bandits!"

Mr Chakrabarti said without more ado, "I quite agree—we're in real trouble! Just what I thought would happen!"

Just then, when they saw people on the path ahead, the two who were approaching called out, "Who goes there!"

There and then the porters dropped the palanquin on the ground and ran off into the jungle, crying out in fear. When he saw this, Mr Durlabh Chakrabarti was quick to follow suit, while Phulmani shouted, "Where are you going without me?" and dashed after him!

Those two advancing men—who had caused such fear in these ten people—were but travelers from North India, on their way to Dinajpur where they hoped to find some work in the service of the king. Very early in the morning, as dawn seemed to break, they had begun their journey. When they saw the porters run off they laughed heartily and continued on their way. But the porters—not to mention Phulmani and Mr Chakrabarti—didn't look back!

Prafulla had herself removed the gag from her mouth as soon as she had been placed in the palanquin. Unsure as to what would happen if she cried out so late at night, she had refrained from doing so. In any case, who would risk confronting bandits even if they did hear her cries! At first, out of fear she had been somewhat at a loss; then it became clear that if she didn't act bravely there'd be no chance of escape. When the bearers dropped the palanquin and ran off, Prafulla realized that some fresh danger had arisen. Very slowly she opened the door of the palanquin, and peeping out saw two men approaching. She slowly closed the door again and saw through a crack that the two men had gone away. Then she emerged from the palanquin and realized there was no one about.

Thinking that those who abducted her would surely return, Prafulla resolved to remain hiding in the jungle, for if she tried to take a path out, she might be caught. Later, when it was day, she could decide what to do. So Prafulla entered the jungle. Fortunately, since she didn't go in the direction in which the porters had run away, she met no one. She remained waiting in the jungle, and it wasn't long before dawn broke.

As soon as it was dawn, Prafulla began wandering in the jungle; she still lacked the courage to find a way out. Then she saw in one place the faint trail of a path leading into the forest. Surely the path meant that there must be people living in that direction—so she followed the path. She was afraid to return home lest the bandits abduct her again. Better to be eaten by bears and tigers, than to fall once more into the hands of bandits!

Prafulla followed the trail for a long time; the morning was getting on, and still she didn't come upon a village. Finally, the trail petered out, and the path came to an end. Then she saw an old brick or two and hope revived, for surely the bricks meant that people lived in the vicinity.

The number of bricks increased as she went further. The jungle became impenetrable, till finally deep in the jungle Prafulla saw the ruins of a huge mansion. She climbed onto a mound of bricks and looked carefully about her. Noticing that even now several rooms remained intact, she came to the conclusion that people could still be living there, so she entered each room to investigate. The door of every room was open, but there was no one there, though there were a few signs of human habitation. Then, after a while, Prafulla heard what sounded like the moans of an old man. She followed the sounds into a room and saw an old man lying there, groaning. He had an emaciated body, parched lips, his eyes were sunken, and his breath came in gasps. Prafulla realized that he was close to death; she went up and stood by his bed.

The old man said with a gasp, "Who are you, my dear? Are you some divine being, come to save me at the time of my death?"

"I've no one to care for me," said Prafulla. "I lost my way and came here. I see that you're alone too. Can I do anything to help?"

"You can be of great help right now," answered the old man. *"Victory to Lord Krishna, that I'm able to see a human face at this time! I'm dying of thirst—give me some water."

Prafulla saw that there was a jug with some water and a bowl in the old man's room, but no one to give him the water. She brought some water and fed it to him. After he had drunk, the old man recovered a little. Prafulla was filled with curiosity to see him in such a state, alone in this forest and about to die. But since he couldn't speak much at the time, Prafulla was unable to learn much about him. This is the gist of what he was able to say:

The old man was a Vaishnava. Except for a female companion—a Vaishnavi—he had no one to call his own. When the Vaishnavi saw that the old man was on the point of death, she had run away with all his possessions. Since the old man was a Vaishnava and could not be cremated, he wanted to be buried. Following the old man's instructions, the Vaishnavi had already dug a grave in the courtyard of the house. Perhaps a crowbar and spade lay there even now. The old man had this request to make of Prafulla: to drag him to the grave when he died and bury him there.

Prafulla agreed. Then the old man continued: he had some money which he had buried. The Vaishnavi didn't know about it, otherwise she would have taken it with her. If he didn't give the money to someone before he died, his spirit would not find release. If he died before giving the money away, he'd become a ghost wandering about near the money, unable to pass on. He had planned to give the money to the Vaishnavi, but she had deserted him. Now that he was unlikely to see another human being, he was giving the money to Prafulla before he departed. There was a square, wooden lid below his bed. On lifting the lid, she would see a tunnel with steps going straight down. She was to go down the steps with a light—there was nothing to fear. Below, inside the earth, she would see a room like this one, and there, if she searched in the northwestern corner, she'd find the money.

Prafulla remained there attending to the old man. He told her that the house had a cowshed with a cow in it, and asked her to milk the cow and bring him some milk, and then to have some herself, which Prafulla did. When she went to get the milk she noticed the open grave and the crowbar and spade lying there.

That afternoon, the old man breathed his last. Prafulla lifted him—she had the strength to do so since the old man's emaciated body was not heavy—took him to the grave, laid him inside and buried him. After this she bathed in a well nearby, drying her wet sari in the sun (wearing half while she dried the other half). Then taking the crowbar and spade she went in search of the old man's money. The old man had given her the money and gone, so she felt no qualms about taking it, for Prafulla was both destitute and wretched.

Chapter 9

Before she put the old man in his grave, Prafulla had taken his pallet and thrown it into the forest. She had seen that below the pallet there was indeed a trapdoor, about three foot square, flush with the ground. Now fetching the crowbar, she twisted the trapdoor open, and a dark cavity met her eyes. Gradually Prafulla could make out in the dark that, sure enough, there were steps leading down.

There is no lack of wood in a forest, and a few chopped logs were lying in the courtyard. Prafulla carried some and threw them into the hole. Then she went in search of flint and a match; after all, he was an old man—surely he smoked? Tell me, which old man—after the discovery made by Sir Walter Raleigh—has been able to see this mean, this transient, this cheerless and insufferable life through without smoking? I say freely, as the author of this book, that if ever there were such an old man, it'd be good if he didn't die—rather, let him live a little longer and suffer the intolerable woes of this world! After searching about Prafulla found flint, pith, and matches—the lot. Then she swept the cowshed and brought back some straw. She lit the straw with fire from the flint and climbed down the narrow stairway into the cavity below, having first thrown the spade and crowbar down before her. At the bottom she found that she was in a proper room. Now for the northwestern corner! She ascertained where that was and lit the logs she had thrown down with the burning straw. The smoke found a way out through the hole above. The room was lit up and Prafulla began to dig.

As she kept digging she heard a metallic clang. *The hairs of her body stood on end, for she realized that the crowbar had struck the side of some jar or small pot. But first let me tell you where this treasure came from and to whom it belonged.

The old man's name was Krishnagobind Das. Krishnagobind was a Kayastha;[26] he had lived happily on his own, but after many years he fell into the hands of a beautiful Vaishnavi, and selling his heart to the insignia of her faith—the marks on her forehead and her tambourine—he took up begging and set off with the Vaishnavi for Sri-Brindaban. When they arrived at Sri-Brindaban Krishnagobind's Vaishnavi lady, taken by the sweet songs of the poet Jayadeva that the local Vaishnavas sang, their learning in the *Srimadbhagavata*, and their well-nourished bodies,[27] promptly applied herself to the acquisition of virtue in the service of their lotus feet. When he saw this, Krishnagobind left Brindaban with the Vaishnavi and returned to Bengal. He was still poor, so he went to Murshidabad in search of a living. Krishnagobind found a job, but news reached the Nawab's residence that his Vaishnavi was a real beauty. An African eunuch began visiting her at home to see if she would become the Nawab's wife, and out of greed the Vaishnavi was ready to agree.

Once more seeing the danger, Krishnagobind Babaji[28] took the Vaishnavi and fled. But where should he go? It was not desirable, he thought, to live among people with this priceless treasure; someone might snatch her away some day. So the Babaji crossed the Padma river with the Vaishnavi and began looking for a lonely place. During his travels he came upon this ruined mansion and saw that it was the very place to hide his priceless jewel from the gaze of others. For who else except Death himself could find them there? So that's where they stayed. The Babaji would go out every week to the local market for provisions, and forbade the Vaishnavi from venturing out anywhere.

One day, as Krishnagobind was digging into the earth to prepare a clay oven in a room underground, he found an old *mohur*,[29] older even than those of his time. He dug further and came upon a clay pot full of money.

If he hadn't found this money, Krishnagobind would have had a hard time of it. As it was, the days began to pass easily, but now Krishnagobind had a new worry. After he had found the money, he remembered that many people had discovered a great deal of treasure buried in these old houses. He became convinced that there was more money here. From then on, Krishnagobind began to search daily for buried treasure. As he searched he discovered many tunnels, and many secret rooms below ground. Like one obsessed, Krishnagobind looked in all those places, but found nothing. After a year of such searchings, Krishnagobind reduced his efforts, but still he went looking from time to time in those secret

[26]The Kayasthas are a respectable caste of Bengal (see endnotes).

[27]All with erotic connotations; see endnotes for further details.

[28]A title given to Vaishnava ascetics (meaning something like "Respected Father").

[29]A gold coin.

chambers down below. One day, in the corner of a dark room, he saw something glinting. He ran forward to pick it up—and saw that it was a *mohur!* Rats had turned the soil, and had raised it with the earth.

Krishnagobind did nothing. He waited for the local market-day to come round. When the day came, he said to the Vaishnavi, "I'm feeling very unwell, so you do the marketing today." So she went in the morning to do the marketing. The Babaji knew that since she was given leave to go out that day, the Vaishnavi would not return in a hurry. He used this opportunity to dig in the corner, and twenty large jars of treasure came to light!

In the past, in northern Bengal, powerful kings used to reign who belonged to the dynasty of a ruler called Nildhvaj. The last king of that line was Nilambar Deb. Nilambar had many capital cities and he built numerous palaces in many towns. This was one of them, and he lived here every year for a week or two. It so happened that the Muslim ruler of Gaud dispatched an army against Nilambar to conquer northern Bengal. If the Pathans, thought Nilambar, attack and capture my capital city, the wealth accumulated by my ancestors will fall into their hands; better to take precautions. So before the battle Nilambar secretly brought all the wealth from his treasury to this place, and buried it with his own hands. No one else knew where the treasure lay. Nilambar was taken prisoner in the battle, and the Pathan General had him transported to Gaud. After that, no one ever saw him again, nor does anyone know how he met his end, for he never returned to his own land. From that time his wealth lay buried here, and it was this treasure that Krishnagobind found—gold, diamonds, pearls, and innumerable other treasures—an incalculable amount, no one could say how much there was. It was twenty large jars of this wealth that Krishnagobind discovered.

Krishnagobind kept the jars carefully buried. Not even for a day did he mention anything about this treasure to the Vaishnavi. He was so miserly that he never spent even a single *mohur* from this hoard; he treated it like the blood from his own body. It was from the money of the clay pot that he eked out his days, so it was the buried wealth that Prafulla obtained. After carefully burying the jars again, she returned and lay down to rest. After the whole day's labors, Prafulla was quickly overcome by sleep on a bed of the straw mentioned earlier.

Chapter 10

Now let me say a word about what happened to Phulmani. In making her escape Phulmani the barber's wife entrusted her life, as a doe does, to the creature that was fleetest of foot.[30] For fear of the bandits Durlabhchandra ran on ahead,

[30]That is, just as a deer when escaping with others singles out the fastest creatures to act as pacemakers, so Phulmani singled out the fleetest of foot when making her escape, viz. Durlabh.

while Phulmani dashed after him. But so bent was Durlabh on escaping that he became "scarce indeed" for his beloved who chased after him![31] However much Phulmani called out, "Oh, please wait for me! Please don't leave me behind!" Durlabh cried in turn, "Oh God! Oh, here they come!" Through thickets of thorns, jumping over ditches, rushing through the mire, Durlabh tore on, breathless. Dear me! The neat tuck at the back of his loincloth came undone, one of his fancy shoes came unstuck somewhere, while his shawl attached itself to a thicket and fluttered in the wind like a banner to his heroism. The lovely Phulmani cried out, "Hey you vile fellow! Deceiving a woman like that.... Is that the way to go, you rascal, leaving me to the bandits!" Durlabhchandra heard this and thought that the bandits had got her for sure, so without wasting words, he ran even faster, while Phulmani screamed after him, "Hey you vile fellow! You wretch! You monster! You good-for-nothing! Rascal! Rogue!" But by then Durlabh had disappeared. So Phulmani stopped shouting and began to cry, and in the process had a number of uncomplimentary things to say about Durlabh's parentage!*

Then Phulmani realized that there were no bandits after her. She stopped crying and paused to think—no bandits after her, and Durlabh nowhere to be seen. So she began to look for a way out of the jungle. It was not difficult for someone as sharp as Phulmani to find a path. She easily made her way out to the main street, and seeing no one about, headed for home, furious with Durlabh.

It was very late when Phulmani reached her house. She saw that her sister Alakmani was not at home—she had gone to take her bath.[32] Without saying a word to anyone Phulmani closed the door and lay down. Since she hadn't slept all night, no sooner did she lie down than she fell asleep.

Her older sister returned and woke her up, saying "So you've just come back?"

"What do you mean?" replied Phulmani, "Where do you think I've been?"

"Where indeed!" answered Alakmani. "You went off to sleep in the Brahmin's house, and since you didn't come back for ages, I'm asking you."

"You've gone blind, that's what!" said Phulmani. "I came back early in the morning and went to sleep right in front of you. Didn't you notice?"

"Oh really!" exclaimed Alakmani. "When I saw you were late, I went thrice to the Brahmin's house looking for you! I didn't see you there, nor anyone else either. So where's Prafulla gone today?"

"Quiet!" said Phulmani with a shiver. "*Didi,* be quiet! Don't speak about that!"

"Why not?" asked Alakmani fearfully, "What's happened?"

---

[31]"Durlabh" means "hard to get."

[32]In the local pond or river.

"Let's not speak about that."

"Why not?"

"We're nobody. What have we to do with those gods, the Brahmins?"

"What do you mean? What's Prafulla done?"

"Well, is Prafulla still alive!"

Alakmani (again fearfully), "What do you mean? What are you saying?"

Her sister mumbled, "Tell no one, but yesterday her mother came and took her away."

"What!" Alakmani began to tremble violently. Phulmani told her some wild tale about seeing Prafulla's mother seated on Prafulla's bed very late at night. In a moment a great storm had arisen in the room, and then—there was no one to be found! Phulmani had fainted, lying there with teeth clenched, etc. etc. When she finished her tale, Phulmani sternly warned her sister not to tell a soul.

"Promise me you won't," she insisted.

"Of course I won't," her sister replied. "How can I tell this to anyone!"

But then and there the said sister went out to make the rounds of the neighborhood, washing-basket in hand, on the pretext of having to clean the rice, and embroidering the story from house to house, warned everyone not to spread the news. Consequently it spread rapidly and reached Prafulla's father-in-law's house in an altered form. Altered in what way? I'll tell you later.

Chapter 11

When she rose very early in the morning Prafulla wondered what to do. Where could she go? This dense jungle was not the place to stay; in any case, how could she stay there alone? But where would she go? Should she return home? She'd be abducted by the bandits again. Besides, wherever she went how could she take this treasure with her? If she found people to carry it away for her, news would get around and robbers and bandits would snatch it away. And where would she get such people? Could anyone be trusted? How long would it be before they killed her and seized the money? Who could control their greed for this pile of wealth?

Prafulla thought it over for a long time. Finally she decided that whatever fate had in store for her, she couldn't bear the misery of poverty any longer. She would stay here, for what was the difference, so far as she was concerned, between Durgapur and the jungle?[33] The bandits had tried to kidnap her from there just as they might do from here.

Having made up her mind, Prafulla began to set up house. She cleaned the place and saw to the cow; finally she turned to preparing some food. But what

[33]Durgapur was the name of her village.

would she cook? Cooking pot, wood, rice, lentils—there was nothing in the place. So she took a *mohur* and set out in search of the local market. The reader will know well by now what extraordinary courage Prafulla had.

But where would a market be in this jungle? Prafulla decided to look for one. I said earlier that there was the trail of a path in the jungle. Prafulla began to follow that trail.

As she made her way, she came face to face with a Brahmin in the dense jungle. The names of God were impressed on his body,[34] he wore a mark on his forehead, and his head was shaven. He was of fair complexion, a most handsome-looking man, not very old. He was a bit taken aback to see Prafulla, and asked her kindly, "Where are you going?"

"To the market," said Prafulla.

"There's no market along this path," said the Brahmin.

"Then where should I go?" asked Prafulla.

"Where are you coming from?"

"From this jungle."

"You live in this jungle?"

"Yes."

"And you don't know the way to market?"

"I'm a newcomer here."

"No one comes to this forest of their own accord," said the Brahmin. "Why are you here?"

"Kindly tell me the way to the market," asked Prafulla.

"It's half a day's walk away," was the reply. "You won't be able to go alone. There's great danger from robbers and bandits. Do you have anyone to accompany you?"

"No one," said Prafulla.

The Brahmin stood looking at Prafulla for a long time. "This girl shows all the right signs," he thought, "Good, let's see what this is all about." Aloud he said, "Don't go on your own to the market, you'll fall into danger. I have a shop nearby, if you wish you can buy provisions from there."

"That would be good," answered Prafulla. "But you look like a learned Brahmin to me, not a shopkeeper."

"There are many kinds of learned Brahmin," said the Brahmin. "Come with me, my child."

As he led Prafulla into even denser jungle, she began to feel a little afraid, but then which part of this forest wasn't fearful? Then she saw a small hut, padlocked, with no one about. The Brahmin opened the lock and Prafulla saw that though it wasn't a shop it had plenty of cooking pots, jugs, rice, lentils, salt, oil, and so on. The Brahmin said, "You can take whatever you're able to carry by yourself."

---

[34]Or perhaps on a shawl he wore, a not uncommon practice among the religious-minded.

Prafulla took as much as she could. Then she asked, "How much do I owe you?"

"One anna," was the reply.[35]

"I don't have change," said Prafulla.

"Do you have a rupee?" asked the Brahmin. "I can give you change."

"I've no rupees either," said Prafulla.

"Then with what were you going to market?" asked the Brahmin.

"I have a *mohur.*"

"Let me see."

Prafulla showed him the *mohur*. The Brahmin inspected it and returned it to Prafulla. "I haven't change in rupees for a *mohur,*" he said. "Come on, I'll accompany you to your home and you can give me the money there."

"I haven't any change at home either," said Prafulla.

"Only *mohurs!*" exclaimed the Brahmin. "All right, come on, let's see where you live. When you get the change, you can give it to me. I'll come and get it."

Now Prafulla didn't like the sound of it when he said, "Only *mohurs!*" She was sure this crafty Brahmin believed that she was in possession of a great many *mohurs*, and that out of greed he wanted to see where she lived. Prafulla put back all the things she was carrying and said, "I think I'll have to go to the market, after all. I need to buy clothes and things."

The Brahmin laughed. He said, "Child, you're thinking that if I find out where you live, I'll rob you of your *mohurs!* Did you think that if you went to market you'd get rid of me? But if I don't leave you how can you leave me?"

Now all was lost! Prafulla began to tremble. The Brahmin continued, "I won't deceive you any longer. Whatever you think I am, learned Brahmin or no, I'm really a bandit-chief. My name is Bhabani Pathak."

Prafulla froze. She had heard of Bhabani Pathak even in Durgapur. He was a notorious brigand and Barendrabhumi trembled from fear of him. Prafulla was unable to speak. Bhabani said, "If you don't believe me, see for yourself."

He brought out a war-drum from inside the hut and beat it a few times. In a trice fifty or sixty young men appeared, looking as fierce as the Lord of death himself and carrying staves and spears. They said to Bhabani, "What is your command?"

Bhabani replied, "Take careful note of this young woman. I've called her 'mother'; each of you will do the same and regard her as a mother. None of you must harm her or allow anyone to do so. Now you can leave." No sooner had he spoken than the gang of bandits melted away.

Prafulla was astonished, stupefied. She knew perfectly well that she had no choice but to take refuge in this man, so she said, "Please come with me and I'll show you where I live." Picking up the various things she had put back, she walked on ahead, Bhabani Pathak following. When they reached the ruined

[35]Sixteen annas made the old rupee, a not inconsiderable sum in those days.

house, she put down her load and gave Bhabani Thakur[36] a small torn mat of kusha-grass to sit on. It had belonged to the old ascetic.

❁ *Chapter 12* ❁

Bhabani Pathak said, "So you found *mohurs* in this ruined house?"

"Yes sir."

"How many?"

"Plenty."

"Tell me exactly how many. If you prevaricate my men will come and dig up this house."

"Twenty large jars."

"And what will you do with this wealth?"

"I'll take it home."

"Will you be able to look after it?"

"If you help me, I can."

"I have full authority in this forest," answered Bhabani Pathak. "But outside it, I have no such power. If you take the treasure outside this forest, I shan't be able to protect it."

"Then I'll stay with the treasure in this forest," said Prafulla. "Will you protect it?"

"I will," replied Bhabani. "But what will you do with so much treasure?"

"What do people do with wealth?"

"They enjoy it."

"Then I'll enjoy it too."

Bhabani Thakur burst out laughing. Prafulla looked put out. When he saw this, Bhabani said, "Child, I laughed because you spoke like a foolish girl. You said you're all alone, so with whom will you enjoy this wealth? Can wealth be enjoyed by oneself?"

Prafulla bowed her head. Bhabani continued, "Listen. When people get wealth, some enjoy it, some build up merit,[37] while others clear the way to hell. You don't have the chance to enjoy it properly, because you're on your own. So you can build up merit or clear the way to hell. Which will you do?"

Prafulla was very bold. She said, "Bandit-chiefs don't talk like this."

"No," replied the Brahmin, "But then I'm not only a bandit-chief. So far as you're concerned I'm no longer a bandit-chief. Since I've called you "mother," I'll tell you only what's good for you from now on. The proper enjoyment of wealth is not for you because you're on your own. But you can acquire either great demerit or great merit by means of this wealth. Now which path will you take?"

[36]"Thakur": a term of respect.

[37]Viz. good karma, in contrast to demerit or bad karma; unexpended good or bad karma is generally experienced in a subsequent rebirth, generating pleasant or unpleasant circumstances respectively.

"Suppose I say it'll be demerit?"

"In that case" answered the Brahmin, "I'll send people to accompany you and your wealth out of this forest. I've plenty of followers in this forest who out of greed for your treasure would be willing to live a sinful life with you. So if that's your wish, I'd have no choice but to send you away right now, for this is my forest."

"If you send people to come away with me and my wealth, why would I object?" said Prafulla.

"But will you be able to look after it?" said Bhabani. "You're young and beautiful. You might escape from the grasp of bandits, but you won't escape from the grasp of youth and beauty. The treasure will go before the covetousness of sin does. However much wealth you have, it won't take long to finish it. And then, child?"

"And then what?" asked Prafulla.

"The path to hell becomes clear.[38] You may covet, but there's no way you can satisfy your coveting—then hell opens up before you. So will you build up merit?"

"Goodness!" exclaimed Prafulla. "I come from a respectable family! I've no experience of sin, so why should I take the path of sin? I'm so poor that if I have food and clothing it's enough for me. I have no desire for wealth, I just want to get by. You can take all the treasure, just see to it that I have something to eat without doing wrong."

Bhabani thanked Prafulla in his mind, but aloud he said, "The treasure is yours. I shan't take it."

Prafulla was surprised. Bhabani understood what she was thinking. He said, "You're thinking: he's a bandit, he seizes other people's wealth, so why is he trying to deceive me like this? There's no need to explain right now. But if you follow the path of sin, then I'd be free to rob you of your wealth. Now I won't. So I ask you again: what will you do with this wealth?"

Prafulla answered, "I can see you're a wise man, so please teach me what to do with it."

"It will take five to seven years to teach you," said Bhabani. "That is, if you want to learn, I can teach you. You must not touch the treasure during this period. You'll have no trouble so far as your upkeep is concerned. I'll send you whatever you need for food and clothing. But you must follow whatever I say without objection. Well, do you agree?"

"Where will I live?" asked Prafulla.

"Here," was the answer. "I'll see to it that some repairs are made."

"Must I live here alone?"

"No. I'll send two women to keep you company. There's nothing to fear. I'm the master of this forest. So long as I'm here no harm will befall you."

---

[38]"Hell": *narak,* here and elsewhere. The *Purāṇas* and other folkloric texts have graphic descriptions of *narak,* making it a vivid reality in the popular imagination.

"How will you instruct me?"

"Can you read and write?"

"No."

"Then first I'll teach you to read and write."

Prafulla agreed; she was overjoyed to have found a friend in this forest. After Bhabani Thakur took his leave and emerged from the ruined mansion, he saw that someone was waiting for him—a man of powerful build, with beard parted in the middle and turned upward, and clipped side-whiskers. Bhabani said, "Rangaraj! Why are you here?"

Rangaraj replied, "I came looking for you. What brings *you* here?"

"At last I've found what I've long been looking for."

"A king?" said Rangaraj.

"A queen."

"There's no need to look for king or queen," said Rangaraj. "Now the English are becoming king. I think there's an Englishman called Hostin[39] in Kolkata who's created a fine kingdom."

"I'm not looking for a king like that," said Bhabani. "You know what I'm looking for."

"And have you found it?"

"You can't find the finished article," answered Bhabani. "You must prepare it. God creates the iron, but man makes the chopper. I've found some good steel, now it will take five to seven years to mould and sharpen it. See to it that no other man except myself enters this house. The girl's young and beautiful."

"As you command," said Rangaraj. "The leaseholder's men have just looted Ranjanpur. That's why I came looking for you."

"Then come on," said Bhabani, "Let's go and loot the leaseholder's headquarters, and return the villagers' wealth to the villagers. Will the village folk help us?"

"Perhaps they will," said Rangaraj.

Chapter 13

Bhabani Thakur kept his promise* and sent two women, one to fetch and carry, the other to be a companion to Prafulla. The two were as different as can be. The one to fetch and carry was called Gobrar Ma.[40] She was seventy three years old, dark-skinned, and hard of hearing. If she were completely deaf, that would be fine: one could get by with signs and gestures. But she was not like that. Sometimes she caught bits of the conversation, and sometimes she didn't—and this gave rise to high confusion.

---

[39]The text has a footnote which says, "Warren Hastings."

[40]That is, "Gobra's Mother"; her personal name is not given (see footnote 4).

The one who came as a companion to Prafulla was a different woman in every respect. She was about six years older than Prafulla, with a glowing darkness of complexion like the fresh, soft leaves of the rainy season, and a beauty that radiated about her.

The two came together—like the full moon and new moon holding hands. Gobrar Ma respectfully touched Prafulla's feet. Prafulla said to her kindly, "What's your name?" Gobrar Ma didn't hear, so the other said, "She's a little hard of hearing. Everyone calls her Gobrar Ma."

Prafulla said, "Gobrar Ma! How many children do you have, tell me?"

"Before this, where would I be?" said Gobrar Ma. "I'd be at home, that's where."

Prafulla asked, "Which caste do you come from?"

"Oh, I'm very good at coming and going," said Gobrar Ma. "I'll go wherever you ask me to."

"I was asking about your folk."

"You'll need no other folk except me, dear! I'll do all the work you need. It's just one or two things I can't do."

"Well, what can't you do?"

Gobrar Ma heard clearly now. "What can't I do?" she said. "Well, I won't be able to fetch and carry water. I've no strength in my hips. As for washing clothes—perhaps you'll have to do that yourself, dear."

"I suppose you'll be able to do everything else?" asked Prafulla.

"Scouring the pots and pans—now if you could manage that yourself. . . . ?"

"You can't do that too? So what can you do?"

"There's not much else I can't do, though I'd find it difficult to sweep the room, swab it, and so on."

"So what can you do then?"

"Anything else you say! I'll roll wicks for burning, pour water, throw away the leaf I've eaten on, do the things I really need to do—I'll go to market."

"Can you do the daily accounts?" asked Prafulla.

"I'm an old person, dear, and quite deaf, so how could I do all that! But I'll spend all the money you give me to spend! You'll never be able to say your money's not been spent!"

"Well, my dear," said Prafulla at last, "It'd be a task to find someone of your qualities!"

"It's your own good qualities that make you say that, I'm sure" said Gobrar Ma.

Prafulla turned to the other woman and asked, "And what's your name?"

"I've no idea, friend," said the newly-arrived beauty.

"How's that?" asked Prafulla laughing, "Didn't your parents give you a name?"

"It's quite possible they did," replied the beauty, "But I was completely unacquainted with it."

"How's that?"

"Because before I knew anything I'd left my parents. I was abducted by kidnappers when I was very little."

"Indeed! Well, they must have given you a name?"

"Oh, various kinds," was the reply.

"Such as?"

"Such as Wretch, Miss Bad Luck, Miss Unfortunate, Miss Disaster..."

Thus far Gobrar Ma had lost her hearing again. But at the sound of these familiar and choice expressions her hearing perked up. "Whoever calls me 'wretch,'" she cried, "is a wretch herself! Whoever calls me 'Miss Disaster' is Miss Disaster herself! Whoever says I'm 'barren' is barren herself..."

Beauty said laughing, "I didn't say 'barren,' dear!"

"You said it, or at least you wanted to!" retorted Gobrar Ma. "But why d'you want to say it?"

"She didn't say it to you," said Prafulla laughing, "She was speaking to me."

Gobrar Ma breathed a sigh of relief and replied, "Good heavens, not to me? Then let her say it, dear, let her say it, don't get angry. That Brahmin's wife's got such a foul mouth, but you musn't get angry, dear."

The two young women were amused to see Gobrar Ma display such valor in her own defense but advocate restraint where another was concerned. Prafulla then inquired of her companion, "'Brahmin's wife'? You never mentioned this to me? I haven't paid you my respects." She touched the other's feet respectfully.

The older woman duly blessed her and said, "I've been told that I'm a Brahmin's daughter all right, but I'm not a Brahmin's wife."

"How's that?" asked Prafulla.

"Because I haven't got a Brahmin husband."

"Aren't you married? But how can that be?"[41]

"Do people who kidnap children marry them off?"

"So you've always lived with your kidnappers?"

"No. They sold me into an aristocratic family."

"And didn't *they* see that you married?"

"Well, the aristocrat's son was willing—but then the marriage wasn't a formal affair."

"So the son himself acted as the groom?"

"But it wasn't for long."

"Why, what happened?"

"When I saw what he was like, I ran away."

"And then?"

"Well, the aristocrat's wife had given me some jewelry and I ran away with the jewelry! Then I fell into the hands of some bandits whose leader was Bhabani

---

[41]In the normal course of events, a girl of her age would have been formally married for a considerable number of years.

Thakur. When he heard my story, he didn't take my jewelry away; in fact, he gave me some more and offered me shelter in his house! Now I'm a daughter to him and he's a father to me. He too gave me away as a bride, in a manner of speaking."

"What do you mean?" asked Prafulla.

"He gave me wholly to Sri Krishna."[42]

"In what way?"*

"My looks, my youth, my life," answered the older woman.

"So He's your husband?"

"Yes," said her companion. "For he who owns me completely is my husband and master."[43]

Prafulla heaved a deep sigh; then she said, "I don't know about that. You've never had a husband, so you're saying that. If you'd had a husband, your heart'd never be taken with Sri Krishna." (That fool Brajesvar never understood as much....)

The older woman replied, "Every girl's heart can be taken with Sri Krishna because he has beauty and youth and wealth and virtues without end."

This young woman was a disciple of Bhabani Thakur while Prafulla was uneducated—so Prafulla was unable to respond. But those who had shaped the Hindu way of life knew how to respond: "We know that God is unlimited, but we cannot fill the heart's tiny cage with what is unlimited. We can do this only with what is limited. So the unlimited Lord of the world becomes the limited Sri Krishna in the cage of the Hindu's heart! Now the husband is more obviously limited. Thus even though marital love is holy, the husband is the first step in one's ascent to God. This is why the husband of a Hindu girl is a deity. Every other society is inferior to Hindu society in this respect."

But Prafulla was an ignorant girl and could grasp none of this. So she said, "Friend, such talk is beyond me—and you still haven't told me your name."

The older woman replied, "Bhabani Thakur gave me the name "Nishi" or "Night"; I'm sister to Diba or "The Day." One day I'll introduce you to Diba. But now listen to what I was saying. God himself is our supreme husband and master. A woman's husband is her deity, but Sri Krishna is everyone's deity. Now tell me, why two deities? Are there two Gods? If you divide the paltry devotion of our paltry hearts into two how much would remain?"

"Enough of that!" exclaimed Prafulla. "Does a woman's devotion have any limits?"

"A woman's *love* has no limits," answered Nishi, "But devotion is one thing and love another."

---

[42]"Sri"—a prefix denoting reverence. According to some Vaishnava traditions, Krishna was the most important avatar or descent of the Supreme Being in human form.

[43]"Husband/master": two senses of the Bengali word, *swami*.

Prafulla replied, "I've known neither to this very day. Both are new to me." The tears began to stream from her eyes. Nishi said, "Sister, I understand now—you've suffered so much." Then she put her arm round Prafulla's neck and wiped the tears away. She said, "I had no idea." Then Nishi realized that the first step toward devotion to God is devotion to one's husband.

Chapter 14

It so happened that on the very night that Durlabh Chakrabarti abducted Prafulla, Brajesvar had arrived at her house in Durgapur. Brajesvar owned a horse and was an accomplished horseman. While everyone slept at his house, Brajesvar secretly mounted his horse and rode off in the dark to Durgapur. When he arrived at Prafulla's hut it was all empty and dark, for the bandits had taken her away, and he could find no one among the neighbors that night to ask where she might be. When he saw that Prafulla wasn't there, he thought that she had gone to some relative's house because she couldn't stay on her own. Brajesvar could delay no longer; since he was afraid of his father, he returned home right in the middle of the night.

Some days passed. Haraballabh's household carried on as before, with everyone going about their daily routines. Only Brajesvar's time* passed somewhat differently. At first, no one noticed. It was his mother who was the first to do so. She saw that the small bowl of milk lay untouched on her son's plate, that only the flesh from the shoulder of the fish-head was eaten. Braja would say, "The food's no good," and push the dish to one side. "The boy's lost his appetite" thought his mother. At first she tried various remedies like a digestive of pickled lime etc.; then there was talk of calling the Ayurvedic practitioner. Brajesvar laughed all this off. He could laugh off his mother, but not Grandaunt Brahma.

The old lady accosted him one day and said, "What's wrong, Braja, why do you have nothing to do with Nayan-Bou any more?"

Braja laughed and said, "For a start, her face is as black as the night of the new moon—with clouds and storms to boot, so I'm not keen to see her."

"All right," said Grandaunt, "That's for Nayan-Bou to see to, but why aren't you eating?"

"Because you're cooking," replied Braja.

"But I always cook like that," said Grandaunt.

"And your hand's well and truly set now," said Braja.

"And do I cook the milk as well? Is that the fault of the cooking too?"

"The cows are giving sour milk."

"What do you keep gawping and thinking about all the time?" persisted Grandaunt.

"About when I'm going to see to your funeral rites," answered Braja.

"Is that all?" said Grandaunt. "Many say that to my face! When it comes to it, you'll see me off under this *neem* tree—I shan't even get to see the *tulsi* tree![44] Don't worry about it. So you've been wasting away worrying about my death?"

"Is that a small worry?"

"When you went to take your bath yesterday, what were you thinking about, sitting there by the steps? Why were you crying?"

"I was thinking that I'd have to eat your cooking after I'd finished. The misery of it made me cry."

"Do you want Sagar to cook for you? Will you be able to eat then?"

"Why, didn't she cook every day she was here? Haven't you ever gone to her play-room? You'll see samples of her cooking made of sand, mud, and brick! Try them yourself and then ask me to eat her cooking."

"Do you want Prafulla to come and cook for you then?" asked Grandaunt.

Brajesvar's face lit up for an instant at the mention of Prafulla's name—just as a wayside hut in the dark lights up when someone walks by with a lamp, and then plunges into darkness again.

"But she's a *Bagdi,*" he said.

"She's not a *Bagdi,*" said Grandaunt. "Everyone knows that's a lie. It's just that your father's afraid of what society will say. But no society is more important than a child. Do you want me to raise the matter again?"

"No," said Brajesvar, "Father'll be disgraced socially because of me. That's not right."

Not much more was said that day. Even Grandaunt Brahma didn't understand fully, for it wasn't that simple. Prafulla was incomparably beautiful, and while it was true that it was by her beauty that she had captivated Brajesvar's heart, he also realized that day he'd met her that she was more beautiful and sweet within than outside. If Prafulla had, as his wife, lived with him in her own right, like Nayantara, then this intoxicating infatuation would have turned into the tenderest love. Infatuation for her beauty would have given way to infatuation for her virtues. But that didn't happen. The lightning that was Prafulla flashed but once, and then dissolved forever into the darkness, so that that intoxication multiplied a thousandfold. So much for the simplicity of the matter.

As to its complexity—there was an intense compassion to preside over it all! After that golden icon had been deprived of its rightful claim, and been insulted and falsely given a bad name, it had been cast out* forever. And it was now desperate for food. Perhaps it would die of starvation! Add to that deep attachment this profound compassion, and the measure was full. Brajesvar's heart was

---

[44]The *tulsi* or basil shrub, often kept domestically and venerated as sacred by Hindus in general and Vaishnavas in particular. Grandaunt means that when her time comes not only will she not be accorded the full funeral rites, but also that she will be disposed off most perfunctorily.

overwhelmed by Prafulla—there was room for nothing else. The old lady didn't understand as much.

A few days later the news of Prafulla's disappearance that Phulmani, the barber's wife, had put out reached Haraballabh's residence. The tale had changed in its passage from mouth to mouth. The news now reached his house as follows: Prafulla had died from an attack of rheumatic fever that had taken a turn for the worse, and before her death, she had seen her dead mother. Brajesvar heard the news too.

Haraballabh took the purificatory bath, but forbade the rites for the dead. "Do Brahmins perform such rites for a *Bagdi?*" he said. Nayantara took a bath too, and after drying her head remarked, "That's one sin seen to, now if I could take a bath for another, I'd be relieved!"[45]

Some days passed. Gradually Brajesvar wasted away and took to his bed. In fact, he wasn't seriously ill, there was only a mild fever, but Brajesvar became listless and confined to his bed. The local practitioner came to see him but the medication proved ineffective, and the sickness increased till at last Brajesvar hovered between life and death.

The real reason now could hardly remain hidden. The old lady understood first, followed by the lady of the house. (It's the women who understand such matters first). And because the latter realized what was going on, the master of the house did too. Haraballabh was pierced to the core; he wept bitterly and said, "For shame! What have I done! I've taken an axe to my own foot!" His wife promised that she would take poison if her son died, while Haraballabh promised in turn that if the deity spared Brajesvar he'd do nothing without first consulting his son.

Well, Brajesvar did survive. Slowly his health began to improve and he left his bed. One day, the annual rites to commemorate the death of Haraballabh's father came round. While Haraballabh was performing the rite, Brajesvar happened to be there for some task or other when he heard the priest make Haraballabh recite at the end: *A father is heaven, a father is duty, a father indeed is one's highest concern. All the gods are pleased when a father is satisfied.*

Brajesvar learned these words by heart, and whenever he felt like weeping for Prafulla, he'd console himself by saying: *A father is heaven, a father is duty, a father indeed is one's highest concern. All the gods are pleased when a father is satisfied.*

In this way Brajesvar tried to forget Prafulla. Whenever it struck him that it was his father who was the cause of Prafulla's death, he'd immediately bring to mind: *A father is heaven, a father is duty, a father indeed is one's highest concern.*

Prafulla had gone, but even then Brajesvar's devotion to his father remained unshaken.*

[45]See endnotes.

Chapter 15

Prafulla's Instruction now began. Mistress Nishi had learned to read and write first in the aristocrat's house and then from Bhabani Thakur, so Prafulla learned the alphabet, how to write and some basic arithmetic from her. Then Bhabani Thakur himself took on the role of teacher. He started Prafulla off on grammar—but within a few days of teaching her, her instructor was amazed, for Prafulla's mind was so sharp and her desire to study so strong that she began to learn very quickly indeed. Even Nishi was astonished at her efforts. Prafulla cooked, ate, and slept in the most perfunctory manner, for her mind was set on the rules of Sanskrit grammar alone. Nishi realized that it was to forget those "two new things" that Prafulla was trying to study so single-mindedly.[46] Within a few months she had mastered grammar. Then Prafulla negotiated the *Bhattikavya* as easily as swimming through water, mastering lexicology in the process. Poetical works such as the *Raghuvamsa*, *Kumarasambhava*, *Naishadha*, and *Sakuntala* were easily traversed in turn. Then her teacher taught her a little Samkhya philosophy, Vedanta, and traditional logic—but only a little. After introducing Prafulla to these philosophical systems, he occupied her in the detailed study of the Yoga texts. Finally, he made her study the *Srimad Bhagavad Gita*, the best of all works.[47] Her instruction was completed in five years.

But in the meantime Bhabani Thakur had been busy making arrangements to instruct Prafulla in other ways. Gobrar Ma did no work: all she did was go to market; Bhabani Thakur had been behind this too. Even Nishi had not been of much help—consequently, Prafulla had to do all the chores herself. But this didn't trouble Prafulla since in her mother's house it was she who had had to do all the work.

For the first year, Bhabani Thakur arranged for her to eat coarse rice seasoned with rock salt, *ghee*, and green bananas—nothing else.[48] Nishi had to eat the same food. But even this didn't worry Prafulla: she usually had less to eat in her mother's house. But in one matter Prafulla disobeyed Bhabani Thakur. On *ekadashi* day she would insist on eating fish. If Gobrar Ma did not bring fish home from the market on that day, Prafulla would sieve any ditch, pool, bog, or canal she could find and catch her own. As a result on *ekadashi* day Gobrar Ma no longer objected to bringing fish home from market.[49]

For the second year, the arrangements for Nishi's food remained the same, while for Prafulla it was only salt, finger-chillis, rice and, on *ekadashi* day, fish. She made no objection. For the third year, Nishi was told to eat curds, *sandesh*, *ghee*, butter, sweetened condensed milk, cream, fruit, root vegetables, and rice

[46] See the end of ch.13.

[47] For information on these texts and philosophical systems see endnotes.

[48] *Ghee* is a form of clarified butter, and the green bananas (*kackala*) would be cooked as a very basic ingredient.

[49] Since Bengali Hindu widows ate a strictly regulated diet on *ekadashi*, the eleventh day of the lunar fortnight, which excluded fish, Prafulla wants to show that she is *not* a widow; see also endnotes.

with various curries, to her heart's content, while Prafulla was to have only salt, finger-chillis, and rice. As Prafulla and Nishi sat down to eat together both would laugh, though Nishi didn't indulge too much in the delicacies—she'd give them to Gobrar Ma. Prafulla passed this test too.

For the fourth year,* Prafulla was told to eat palatable fare, so she complied, while for the fifth year she was told to eat whatever she wanted; she ate as she had done in the first year.

Where resting, clothes, bathing, and sleep were concerned, Bhabani Thakur put his disciple through the same discipline.* With regard to dress, for the first year she was allowed four items of clothing; for the second year, just two. During summer in the third year she had to wear a thick, coarse cloth; it was to be washed and dried while she was still wearing it. During winter she had to do the same with a thin piece of Dhaka cotton. For the fourth year, she had to wear a cloth of Dhaka silk, woven in the Shantipur style. Prafulla would first shorten these items by tearing strips off them before she wore them.[50] For the fifth year, she could wear whatever she wished: Prafulla continued with the thick, coarse cloth. From time to time she'd wash it in alkaline water.

The same applied with regard to doing her hair. For the first year, she was not allowed to use oil: she had to tie her hair unoiled. During the second year, she was not allowed even to tie her hair; day and night her dry tresses would hang disheveled. During the third year, in accordance with Bhabani Thakur's instructions, Prafulla shaved her head. In the fourth year, her hair grew again, and Bhabani Thakur ordered her to rub her hair with perfumed oil and keep it dressed continually. For the fifth year she was told to do as she pleased. That year, Prafulla never even touched her hair.

For the first year, Prafulla slept on a pillow and thin mattress made of cotton. For the second year, the bed and pillow were of paddy-straw, while during the third year the ground was her bed. For the fourth year her bedding was as soft as the froth of milk; for the fifth year she could do as she liked. That year, Prafulla lay down to sleep wherever she found room to do so. For the first year, she could sleep the whole night through; for the second, for only about six hours. During the third year, she had to stay awake all night after an interval of every two days, while in the fourth year, she could sleep even when she felt drowsy. During the fifth year, she could do as she pleased. Prafulla would stay awake all night, studying and copying manuscripts.

Prafulla began to inure her body against water, wind, sun, and fire. Bhabani Thakur ordered Prafulla to learn one other thing that I feel embarrassed to tell you, but unless I do so my account will remain incomplete. In the second year, Bhabani Thakur said to Prafulla, "Child, you must learn to wrestle." Prafulla looked down in embarrassment; finally she said, "Sir, whatever else you may ask me to learn I shall learn, but this I cannot do."

[50]As a mark of abnegation; the well-to-do tended to wear voluminous clothing. Prafulla wants to do the opposite to show that she discards this practice.

Bhabani Thakur answered, "If you don't, we can't proceed."

"But how can you say that, Sir?" asked Prafulla. "What would a woman gain by learning to wrestle?"

"This is to overcome the senses," replied Bhabani. "A weak body cannot overcome the senses. Without being trained in physical exercise, you cannot overcome the senses."

Prafulla said, "But who will teach me to wrestle, for I cannot learn to wrestle with a man."

"Nishi will teach you," replied Bhabani. "She's a girl who was abducted, and abductors will not keep boys or girls with them unless they're strong.[51] When she was young, Nishi learned physical exercises while staying in their group. It was only after thinking this whole matter through that I sent Nishi to you." So Prafulla learned to wrestle for four years.

For the first year Bhabani Thakur forbade any man from going to where Prafulla lived; he also forbade Prafulla from conversing with any man outside her residence. For the second year, the prohibition to converse with a man was lifted, but no man was allowed to go to her residence. Then during the third year, after Prafulla shaved her head, chosen male disciples would accompany Bhabani Thakur to Prafulla's place. With head shaven and face lowered, Prafulla would converse with them about religious texts. During the fourth year, Bhabani would come with *lathials* chosen from among his followers and order Prafulla to wrestle with them.[52] Prafulla would do so in his presence. In the fifth year no rule or prohibition remained in force. Prafulla would converse with men as the need arose, and when there was no need she refrained from doing so. When she talked to a member of the opposite sex she would regard him as she would a son. In this way, by dint of various tests and practices, Bhabani Thakur endeavored to make of Prafulla, the owner of incomparable riches, a person fit to make use of wealth. In five years, all her instructions came to an end.

But besides the eating of fish on *ekadashi* day, there was one other matter in which Prafulla resisted Bhabani Thakur. She would tell him nothing about herself. Even when he interrogated her, he was unable to learn anything.

Chapter 16

After he had finished teaching her for five years, Bhabani Thakur said to Prafulla, "It's been five years since your instruction began, and today it is over. Now you may spend your wealth as you please, I shan't prevent you. I'll offer advice,

[51]Here a footnote in the original says in Bengali: "Warren Hastings himself has written as much."

[52]*Lathial:* a henchman or hired hand skilled in the use of a staff (usually made of bamboo) as a weapon (from *lathi*, a staff, heavy stick).

which you can accept if you choose to. I'll provide food for you no longer*—you'll have to fend for yourself. But let me say a few things first. I've said this many times and I'll say it once more: which path will you follow now?"

Prafulla replied, "I'll pursue the path of action; meditation is not for a spiritual novice like me."

"Very good," said Bhabani, "I'm glad to hear it. But you'll have to pursue action in a detached way. Remember what the Lord has said: "*So you must pursue action, ever-detached, for the person who pursues action while detached attains the Goal.*"[53] You know what detachment is. Its first characteristic is control of the senses. I've taught you this these five years, and there's not much more to be said. The second characteristic is selflessness. Without selflessness you cannot follow the right path, for the Lord has said: "*Actions are always done by Nature's constituents, but the soul deluded by the ego thinks, 'I am the actor.'*" In other words, it is sheer egotism to think: "It is *I* who have done all these actions"—actions which have really been performed by the senses etc. You must never think that whatever you've done has been done by your power. If you do, your good actions become void. Finally, the third characteristic is to offer Sri Krishna the fruit of all your actions.* The Lord has said: "*Whatever you do, whatever you eat, whatever you offer in sacrifice, whatever you give, whatever penance you perform, Kaunteya, do it as an offering to Me.*" Now tell me, child, what will you do with all the treasure you have?"

Prafulla answered, "Well, in offering all my actions to Sri Krishna, I've offered all this wealth to him as well."

"All of it?" asked Bhabani.

"All of it," said Prafulla.

"In that case," replied Bhabani, "Your actions will not be detached, for if you must strive to feed yourself, attachment will arise. For either you will have to resort to begging, or else you will have to look after your body by making use of this wealth. But there's attachment even in begging! So, look after your body from this wealth, and offer the rest to Sri Krishna. Now how do you think this wealth will reach Sri Krishna's lotus-feet?"

Prafulla replied, "I have learned that He dwells in all beings. So I shall distribute this wealth among all beings."

"Very good," said Bhabani, "For the Lord himself has said:

> '*He who sees Me everywhere, and who sees all in Me,*
> *I am not lost to him, nor is he lost to Me.*
> *He who, based on oneness, loves Me as dwelling in all beings,*
> *Howsoever such a disciplined soul acts, he acts in Me.*

[53]The quotations in this chapter are all from the *Bhagavad Gita*. See endnotes for further comment and references.

> *He who sees everything as his own self—as the same—whether through pleasure or sorrow, Arjuna, I regard that disciplined soul as the very best.'*[54]

But there'll be call for many trials, much effort for this giving that embraces all beings. Will you be able to do it?"

"Well, what have I learned all this while?" said Prafulla.

"That's not the sort of trial I'm talking about," answered Bhabani. "From time to time we'll have to dissemble a bit, to put on a show with regard to the way we present ourselves and live. That'll be really hard. Will you be able to bear it?"

"How do you mean?"

"Well, I've already told you I live as a bandit."

"Well then, why don't you keep some of the wealth I've given to Sri Krishna? Take it and live a virtuous life and stay away from bad deeds."

"But I too have no need of wealth," replied Bhabani. "I have plenty of it. I don't engage in banditry for the sake of wealth."

"Then for what?" asked Prafulla.

"Because I act as a ruler."

"What kind of rule is banditry?"

"He who has the power to rule is king."

"On the contrary, it is the king who has the power to rule," answered Prafulla.

Bhabani said, "There's no king in this land. The Muslims have been eliminated and the British are coming in. They do not know how to govern, nor are they doing so. It is I who subdue the wicked and protect the virtuous."

"By banditry?"

"Now listen, let me explain it to you."

Then Bhabani Thakur began to speak, and Prafulla to listen. It was with a powerful succession of words that he explained the terrible state of the land. He described the intolerable wickedness of those who controlled the land: how the officers of the local courts looted the houses of those whose dues were in arrears, broke into their homes, digging up the floor in search of hidden wealth, and if they found it, how they'd take not just their dues but a thousand times that, and if they didn't find it, how they'd thrash, truss up, imprison, burn, hack, set fire to homes, and kill. He described how they'd throw away the sacred relics of Vishnu from their household thrones, grab infants by the leg and dash them, knead and crush the chests of young men with bamboo rods, fill old men's eyes with ants and their navels with insects and then bind up these parts; how they'd take young women to their courts and strip them naked in front of everyone, beat them, cut off their breasts, and—in the presence of everyone—inflict the final insult on womankind, the ultimate outrage. After describing, like the poets of

[54]A footnote here in the original has: "Srimad Bhagavadgita, ch.6:30–2." See endnotes for further comment.

old, this terrible situation with the most blazing combination of words, Bhabani Thakur said, "It is *I* who punish these evildoers, and protect the defenseless weak. Do you want to stay with me for a few days and see how I do this?"

Prafulla's heart had melted when she heard this harrowing tale of the people. She thanked Bhabani Thakur a thousand times and said, "Yes, I'll go with you. If I'm entitled to spend this wealth, then I'll take some of it with me, and give it to those who suffer."

Bhabani said, "I've said we'll need to dissemble to do this work. If you come with me, you'll have to dress up a bit. This job can't be done in the clothes of a renouncer."

"I have offered my actions to Sri Krishna," replied Prafulla. "So the actions are His, not mine, and the pleasure and pain that arise from getting the job done are His alone, not mine. I'll do whatever is necessary to get His work done." Bhabani Thakur was well-satisfied. When he set out as a bandit with his gang, Prafulla accompanied him with the jars of treasure, and Nishi went with them too.

Whatever his designs might be, Bhabani Thakur had need of a sharpened weapon. So after whetting Prafulla for five years, he was now taking her with him as his sharpened weapon. It would have been better if she were a man, but no man was available with the various qualities Prafulla possessed, in particular a man with so much wealth. And the sharpness of wealth is sharpness indeed! But Bhabani Thakur had made one big mistake: he would have done well to get to the bottom of Prafulla's insistence on eating fish on *ekadashi* day. Still, now that we've launched Prafulla on life's stream, let us slumber for another five years. Prafulla had learned various things but not how to put them into practice. So let's say that for these five years she learned how to put them into practice.

PART II

Chapter 1

So, in all, ten years passed—ten years from the day Haraballabh called Prafulla a *Bagdi*'s daughter and drove her away. But these ten years didn't go well for Haraballabh Ray. I have already spoken about the parlous state of the land—about the misdeeds of Debisingh the leaseholder, and about those of the bandits. On one occasion, after the bandits had looted a consignment of money on its way from an estate under Haraballabh's jurisdiction, Debisingh didn't receive his revenue, so he sold off one of Haraballabh's estates. Debisingh could hardly be criticized for the way he sold things off in this way; thanks to Mr Hastings and Gangagobind Singh every government officer did his bidding, so he could do whatever he wished in this respect. Debisingh himself bought up Haraballabh's estate worth Rs.10,000, for Rs.250. The outstanding revenue was hardly cleared by this, and the balance of what was due remained. Because of Debisingh's harassment and the fear of imprisonment, Haraballabh mortgaged another property and cleared the debt. All this led to a big fall in his income, but not to the slightest reduction in his expenditure: it's not easy to lower the fine lifestyle one's got used to! A day comes for nearly every individual when the Goddess of wealth makes her presence felt and says: "Either you give up your old ways or you give me up!" and many reply, "My dear, I'll have to give you up, for I cannot give up my ways." Haraballabh was one of these.

The great religious festivals of Krishna, Durga, and other deities, the domestic rites and rituals, the munificent gifts and observances of various kinds, the deployment of his *lathials* to enforce his authority—all continued as before. Rather, from the time the bandits looted that consignment, the costs for his *lathials* had increased somewhat. In fact, income could no longer keep up with demand. With every installment, his official dues fell into arrears. Whatever was left of his wealth and property was in danger of being sold off. Debt mounted upon debt; the interest now exceeded the original sum owing, till finally there was no more money available on credit.

The money he owed Debisingh fell into arrears by almost Rs. 50,000. There was no way Haraballabh could clear this debt. Eventually, a warrant was issued for Haraballabh Ray's arrest. In those days, there was not much call to take recourse to laws or regulations to issue warrants of arrest since there was no English law. It was a time when no laws were in place.

Chapter 2

There was a great buzz of excitement: Brajesvar had come to his father-in-law's house. (*Which* father-in-law's house, I need hardly say: Sagar's father's house, of course!). In those days the arrival of a son-in-law was not a straightforward matter; besides, Brajesvar rarely ever came to his father-in-law's house. There was much darting about among the fish in the village ponds, but they could ill survive the tyranny of the fishermen! The walking about of the fisherwomen made the pond-waters as black as ink,[1] and little boys played truant from school in the hope of pilfering a fish or two.

As for the milkman, the worry of orders for curd, milk, cream, cottage cheese, butter, and the milk's creamy layer put his head in a whirl; sometimes he'd mix three measures of water in the milk instead of one, and sometimes he'd end up mixing one measure of water instead of three. The clothier's legs ached from the coming and going he had to do with his load—it was so difficult to please everyone as they tried to decide which item of clothing to give the son-in-law. There was much agitation too among the women of the neighborhood. Those who possessed jewelry tried to make everything look new by mending, cleaning, and polishing, while those who had none went out and bought thin bangles of glass or lac or shell, and contrived to borrow items of silver or gold, and tried in one way or another to have the wherewithal to dress smartly—else how was one to go and see the son-in-law? Those known for their wit rehearsed a few old wisecracks in their minds, while those with no such reputation* prepared to pass off stolen ware.

But the fun with words would come later—first the fun with food! Committees were set up in one place after another to prepare for this. Many fake items of food and drink, of fruit and vegetables,* began to be prepared. So many sweet lips began to fill with sweet laughter and the popular dental powder that made the teeth sparkle![2]

But the person for whom so much trouble was being taken was not a happy man. Brajesvar had not come to his father-in-law's house to be fêted. A warrant had been issued for his father's arrest and there was no way to ward it off. No one wanted to lend him any money. But Brajesvar's father-in-law had money, and he could lend some of it to his father if he wished. This is why Brajesvar had come to his father-in-law's house.

---

[1]By walking about in the shallows to catch the fish, the women stirred up the dark mud underfoot. See endnotes for a further comment.

[2]It was a practice at the time, particularly in rural areas, to play jokes on the visiting son-in-law by solemnly offering him items of fake food (such as fruit and vegetables fashioned from clay and painted to look real), and then delighting in his embarrassment when he got taken in. The women of the family were especially keen on this. See endnotes.

But his father-in-law said to him, "My boy, in due course all my money will come to you alone. Do I have anyone else? But the money will stay with me so long as I live. If I give it to your father will it last? His creditors will eat it up. So why do you want to waste your own wealth?"

Brajesvar replied, "That may be, but I'm not keen to have the wealth. My first task is to save my father."

His father-in-law said curtly, "How does my daughter profit if your father is saved? If my daughter has money life will be easier for her. If your father is saved that won't happen."

Brajesvar was furious at these harsh words. "Then your daughter can keep the money!" he retorted. "It's obvious you've no need of a son-in-law. So I'll leave and have nothing to do with any of you again."

Enraged, Sagar's father berated Brajesvar at length, and Brajesvar answered harshly in turn. The outcome was that Brajesvar began to pack his bags. Sagar was thunderstruck when she heard this. Sagar's mother sent for Brajesvar and made a great effort to pacify him, but her son-in-law's anger remained unabated. Then it was Sagar's turn. In those days, it was easier for a bride to see her husband during the day when he visited her in her father's residence, than it was for her to see him when she came to her father-in-law's house. Sagar met Brajesvar secretly, fell at his feet and said, "Please stay one more day. I've done nothing wrong, have I?"

But Brajesvar was furious, so he pulled his leg away in anger. When one is angry bodily movements become exacerbated, and hands and legs don't move quite as one intended. You try to do one thing, but things take a turn for the worse. For this reason, and partly because of Sagar's eagerness, Brajesvar blundered in trying to remove his leg: his foot struck a little sharply against Sagar. Sagar thought that her husband had kicked her in anger. She released his foot and rose like an angry cobra.

"What!" she cried, "You dare kick me?"

In fact, Brajesvar had not intended to kick her, and if he had said so, the matter would have ended there. But he was enraged, while for her part Sagar stood there, face set defiantly. This made Brajesvar even more furious. "So what if I kicked you!" he said, "You may be a rich man's daughter, but this foot of mine—even your big shot father groveled before it once!"[3]

Sagar was beside herself with rage. "Then he made a big mistake," she cried, "And I'll make up for it."

"How?" said Brajesvar, "By kicking me in turn?"

"I'm not that low," replied Sagar,* "But upon my word as a Brahmin's daughter, you'll. . . ." Before she could finish, someone continued from the window behind her, ". . . . put my foot in your lap and massage it like a servant."

[3]A reference to the formal deference shown by the bride's father to the groom during the wedding ceremonies. See endnotes.

In fact, Sagar had intended to say something of the kind. So without more ado, she said those very words in her rage: "Put my foot in your lap and massage it like a servant."

"And I say the same to you," Brajesvar blindly shouted back in anger, "that until I massage your leg, I'll not set eyes on you again. And if I break this promise, *I'm* no Brahmin!"

Brajesvar stormed away, bursting with fury, while Sagar sat down to bawl, her legs thrust out in front of her.* Just then, curious to see the state Sagar was in after Brajesvar had left, a maidservant entered the room in which Sagar was crying on the pretext of doing some work. Sagar remembered that someone had spoken from the window. She said to the girl, "Did you say something from the window?"

"Not me," said the girl.

"Then see who's there," asked Sagar.

At that moment a woman who looked as beautiful and radiant as a Goddess, entered the room. "I was at the window," she said.

"Who are you?" asked Sagar in wonder.

The woman answered, "Don't any of you recognize me?"

"No," said Sagar, "Who are you?"

"I am Debi Chaudhurani," said the woman.

With a crash the tray with the betel-leaf fell to the ground from the maidservant's hand. She too sank to the floor, moaning and trembling, the cloth around her waist coming undone. Debi Chaudhurani turned to her and said, "Quiet, you miserable wretch! Stand up!"

Whimpering, the girl rose to her feet and stood as if paralyzed. Even Sagar broke into a sweat, unable to say a word, for who—young or old—hadn't heard the terrible name that had been uttered?

But a moment later Sagar burst out laughing—and then Debi Chaudhurani laughed too.

Chapter 3

It was a moonlit night in the rainy season. The moonlight wasn't very bright—the softest moonglow tinted with darkness, like some dreamy covering over the earth. The Teesta river had swollen its banks with the flood of the rains, and the rays of the moon glistened upon the currents and whirlpools, and at times the little waves of the fast-flowing waters. In some places there were soft sparkles of light where the water bubbled a little, in other places the river glittered as it lapped against a sandbank. The water had reached the foot of the trees on the bank and was pitch black in their shadows, the swift current running over the flowers, fruit and leaves of the trees in the darkness. The waters gurgled and lapped against the banks in the gloom, and in the gloom that mighty stream sped, swift as a bird, in search of the sea. The countless murmuring sounds of the water along the banks and the deep roar of the whirlpools, echoed by the roar of the checked current, rose as a single deep sound, filling the skies on all sides.

There, on the Teesta, a barge was moored not far from the bank. And not far from the barge, in the shade of a large tamarind tree, lay another boat in the darkness. About this boat later—first let me speak about the barge. The barge was painted in various colors—how many shapes and forms were drawn upon it! Its brass handles, bars etc. were plated with silver and gold. The prow was shaped like a sea-monster's head, also plated in gold. The whole place was clean, tidy, gleaming—yet silent. The deckhands lay under a sail on one side of the bamboo deck. There was no sign of anyone being awake—except for one person on the roof of the barge. In all, an amazing scene!

A small, rather thick rug,* very soft, with scenes of various kinds depicted upon it, lay spread on the roof. A woman was seated on the rug. It was hard to guess her age: one could never find so shapely a body in anyone under twenty-five, nor for that matter that bloom of youth in someone older than that. But whatever her age, there was no doubt that she was the most beautiful of women. Though this lovely woman was not slender, it would be a disservice to call her buxom. In fact, her figure was complete in every aspect. Just as the Teesta had now filled its banks, so did the fullness of her body reach its proper limits. Further, it was a body that was unusually tall and erect—and because it was so, we were unable to call her buxom. The flood-waters of youth's fullness were caught up in that lovely form without overwhelming it. Yet the waters that pushed at those banks heaved restlessly. The waters were restless though she who contained them was not; she was still and calm. Her beauty was restless, but she who bore that beauty was not so. She remained serene—calm, deep, tender yet full of joy, a fitting companion for that moonlit river. And like the river, that lovely woman was beautifully dressed.

Today cloth from Dhaka doesn't have the reputation it once had, though a hundred years ago its fine quality had the reputation it deserved. The woman was dressed in white, filmy Dhaka cloth, with a floral pattern woven into the fabric, and underneath she wore a bodice studded with glistening diamonds and pearls. Her shapely form, adorned with diamonds, emeralds, pearls, and gold, shone brightly in the moonlight, and her body glistened like the play of light on the waters of the river. Her lustrous clothes were like the still river-waters enraptured by the light of the moon, and just as the moonlight sparkled on the water from time to time, the diamonds and pearls of her clothes sparkled too. And like the shade of the wood along the river-bank her dark tresses fell disheveled upon her body. Her hair hung in clusters of curls twisted this way and that over her back, shoulders, arms, and breast. The moonlight played upon their soft, glossy splendor and the sky was filled with the fragrance of their crushed perfume.* A chaplet of white jasmine flowers encircled the back of her hair.

Having spread the rug on the roof of the barge, this bejeweled beauty, like an image of the Goddess Sarasvati herself, was absorbed in playing the *vina*.[4] Her complexion, like the moonglow, blended with the light of the moon, and with it mingled the sweet and plaintive sounds of the *vina*. Just as the rays of the moon played upon the waters and the moonlight played upon this lovely woman's rich attire, so the sounds of the *vina* played upon the currents of the air bathed in moonlight and fragrant with the scent of wild flowers. *Jhom jhom, chon chon, jhonon jhonon, chonon chonon, dom dom, drim drim*—I cannot describe the quality of sound and rhythm of the notes played on the *vina*. Now it wept, now it grew angry, now it danced or became tender, or rose to a crescendo—and as the woman played, she gave a little smile. Oh, how many sweet musical modes she played—the *jhinjhit, khambaj, sindhu;* how many serious ones—*kedar, hambir, behag;* so many displaying her virtuosity—the *kanara, sahana, bagisvari*.[5] Like a garland of flowers the sound floated away in the roar of the current. Then, adjusting a fret or two, this knowledgeable woman suddenly looked up and with renewed vigor struck the strings of the *vina* with great force. Her earrings, shaped like peepul leaves, swung to and fro, the mass of curls on her head began to dance like snakes, and the musical mode *nat* was heard on the *vina*.

Then one of those who seemed to be sleeping quietly in a corner wrapped in a sail, rose and came and stood silently by the woman—a tall, powerfully built man with a thick beard parted in the middle and turned upward. A sacred thread hung from around his neck. He came up close and asked, "What is it?"

The woman said, "Can't you see?"

"Nothing," was the reply. "Are they coming?"

A small spyglass lay on the rug. At the time the spyglass was a new arrival in India. Without a word the woman picked up the spyglass and handed it to the man. He put it to his eye and scanned the river with it. Finally, catching sight of another barge in a certain place, he said, "I've seen it—by the bend in the river. Is that it?"

"No other barge is expected on the river at present," the other replied.

The man once again began to peer into the distance with the spyglass.

Still playing the *vina*, the young woman said, "Rangaraj!"

"Yes?" said the other respectfully.

"What do you see?"

"I'm looking to see how many men there are."

"Well?"

"I can't make out. But not many. Shall I untie it?"

"Yes—untie the longboat and go silently upstream in the dark*."

Then Rangaraj called out, "Untie the longboat!"

[4]"Sarasvati": the Goddess of learning and the arts; *vina*: "a four-stringed musical instrument with a fretted finger-board and a gourd at each end": OED.

[5]See endnotes for explanations of these musical modes.

Chapter 4

I said earlier that close to the barge, in the shade of a tamarind tree, another boat lay hidden in the darkness. It was a longboat, about ninety feet long and little more than four feet broad. About fifty men had been huddled in it sleeping. As soon as they heard Rangaraj's call the fifty instantly awoke and sat up. Each lifted a bamboo plank and removed a spear and buckler, but without retaining these as weapons arranged them nearby on the plank. Then, still seated, each man took up a small paddle.

The men silently released the longboat and came up against the barge. Then Rangaraj, himself armed with five weapons, climbed into the longboat. The young woman called out to him and said, "Rangaraj, remember what I said earlier." "I remember," said Rangaraj as he climbed into the boat.

The longboat moved silently upstream along the bank. Meanwhile, the barge Rangaraj had seen earlier through the spyglass was approaching swiftly on the powerful current. The longboat didn't have to go very far upstream. As soon as the barge came close, the longboat left the bank and raced toward it. Fifty oars, yet not a sound!

There were eight Hindusthani guards on the roof of the barge. In those days, without so many men on board, no one had the nerve to travel by boat at night. Two from among the eight were armed, sitting on the roof and wearing red turbans; the other six were fast asleep, their black beards fluttering in the moonlight in the gentle southerly breeze. One of the guards caught sight of the longboat coming toward the barge. He called out, as was the custom, "Longboat! Keep your distance!"

"You keep your distance if you want," shouted Rangaraj in reply.

Seeing the danger of the situation, the guard fired a blank from his gun to frighten them off. But Rangaraj knew this was a blank, so he laughed and called out, "What's this, Pande Sir?[6] No bullets? Shall I lend you one?"

He raised his gun and aimed at the guard's head. Then lowering it, he said, "No, I won't kill you, I'll just send your red turban flying." No sooner had he said this than he put the gun down, took up a bow and arrow and released the arrow with force. The red turban flew off the guard's head. "O God! O God!" the guard wailed.

By now the longboat had come up behind the barge, and ten to twelve armed men from the boat instantly clambered aboard. The six Hindusthanis who had been asleep had woken at the sound of the gun, of course, but in trying to grope for their weapons while still groggy lost their chance. In a moment, their assailants had deftly trussed them up. The two who had been awake put up a fight but not for long. Their more numerous assailants quickly overcame

[6]Pande (and later, "Tewari"): names of northern Hindi-speaking Brahmin castes, members of which often adopted the profession of guard or soldier.

and disarmed them, and then bound them up as well. Then the men from the longboat got ready to enter the barge, but the door was locked.

Brajesvar was inside. He was returning home from his father-in-law's house—and now this calamity on the way! But it was only the result of his own audacity, for no one else would have been bold enough to take a barge out at night.

Rangaraj banged on the door and called out, "Sir! Please open the door!"

From inside, Brajesvar, who had just woken up, answered, "Who's that? Why all this fuss?"

"No fuss at all," said Rangaraj. "Bandits have attacked the barge."

For a while Brajesvar was nonplussed—then he called out to the guards, "Pande! Tewari! Ramsingh!"

Ramsingh called back from the roof in Hindi, "Virtue incarnate, these scoundrels have tied us all up!"

Brajesvar grinned; then he said, "I'm very sad to hear that! Instead of giving heroes like you something to eat, they've trussed you up! These bandits have made a big mistake. But don't worry, from tomorrow I'll increase your rations."

When he heard this, Rangaraj grinned too. He said, "I think you should. Now perhaps you'll kindly open the door."

"Who are you?" asked Brajesvar.

"Only a bandit," said Rangaraj. "All I ask is that you open the door."

"Why should I open the door?"

"So that we can loot everything you have," was the answer.

"Oh yes?" said Brajesvar, "Do you think you've got some Hindusthani nincompoop here? I've got a double-barreled gun in my hand. Get ready! Whoever comes into the room first, I'll kill him for sure."

"We won't come in one at a time," said Rangaraj. "How many will you kill? You're a Brahmin and I'm a Brahmin, so on one side or other there'll be a Brahmin killed. No point in killing a Brahmin uselessly."

"Well, maybe I'm the one who'll own up to that sin," retorted Brajesvar.

But hardly had he finished speaking when there was a splintering sound. Brajesvar saw that a bandit had smashed in a door in the side of the barge and entered the room; he reversed the gun in his hand and struck the bandit on the head with the butt. The man fell down senseless. Just then Rangaraj gave two hefty kicks to the outside door. The door broke open and Rangaraj entered the room. Again Brajesvar reversed the gun and was taking aim at Rangaraj when the latter snatched the gun from his hand. Though both men were equally strong Rangaraj was the quicker; before Brajesvar could get a proper hold on the gun, Rangaraj had snatched it away. At this Brajesvar clenched his fist and aimed a blow at Rangaraj's head with all his might, but Rangaraj grasped the fist in his hand.

There were many weapons hanging on one side of the barge; Brajesvar now snatched a sharp sword from among them and said smiling, "Now Sir, you'll see I'm not afraid to kill a Brahmin!" As he raised his sword to strike Rangaraj, four or five bandits entered the room through the open door, fell upon him and grabbed the upraised sword from his hand. Two of them held Brajesvar's hands while a third took a rope and said, "Do we have to tie you up?" "No, don't," said Brajesvar, "I admit defeat. Tell me what you want and I'll give it to you."

"We'll take everything you've got," said Rangaraj. "I could have left you something, but that fist you made would have smashed my head in had it landed. I'll not leave you a single coin."

"You can take everything in the barge," said Brajesvar, "I won't object any further."

But even before he had said this, the bandits had begun taking things from the barge to the longboat. By now about twenty-five men had climbed onto the barge. In fact, there wasn't much there, just a few things like the clothes Brajesvar would need and various items for daily worship. In a moment, they carried all this away to the longboat. Then Brajesvar said to Rangaraj, "You've got everything now, so why cause more trouble? Go back to where you came from."

"I'm going," said Rangaraj, "But you'll have to come with us too."

"What do you mean?" said Brajesvar, "Where are you taking me?"

"To see our Queen" was the reply.

"Which Queen is that?" asked Brajesvar.

"The Queen who rules over us."

"And who might that be? I've never heard of a bandit-Queen."

"Have you never heard of Queen Debi?"

"So that's it, you belong to Debi Chaudhurani's gang?"

"We're not members of some gang," answered Rangaraj, "We're followers of our gracious Queen."

"Like Queen like follower, I see," said Brajesvar, "Well, why should I go to see your Queen? Because you hope to get something by keeping me prisoner, I suppose?"

"Exactly. We've got nothing from the barge, but we might get something by detaining you."

"Well, I'd be glad to go with you," said Brajesvar. "I've heard that the Queen who rules over you is worth seeing. I expect she's a young woman?"

"She's a mother to us," said Rangaraj. "Children don't keep track of their mother's age."

"I hear she's very beautiful," continued Brajesvar.

"Our mother's like a Goddess," replied Rangaraj.

"Come on then," said Brajesvar, "Let's go see the Goddess."

Saying this, Brajesvar came out of the room with Rangaraj. He noticed that the helmsman of the barge and the other deckhands had jumped into the water through fear, and were hanging on to the hawser to stay afloat. He said to them, "You can climb back on to the barge now—there's nothing to fear! And when you do so, thank Allah," he continued in disdain, "For you've certainly kept your lives, your self-respect, your possessions and honor intact! How clever of you!" As they began to climb back onto the barge one by one, Brajesvar asked Rangaraj, "Can I untie my guards now?"

"I have no objection," said Rangaraj. "But if they attack us when they're free, please explain to them that we'll cut off your head instantly." Not only did Brajesvar explain that to them, but he also told them that he would speedily increase their food rations in proportion to the valor they had shown. As for his servants, he instructed them as follows: "Stay here with the barge without fear, and don't go anywhere or get up to anything. I'll be back soon." Then he got into the longboat with Rangaraj. The longboat departed, with the oarsmen shouting "Victory to Debi our Queen!"

Chapter 5

On their way Brajesvar asked Rangaraj, "How far are you taking me? Where does your royal lady live?"

Rangaraj replied, "Do you see that barge up ahead? It belongs to her."

"The one there? I thought that was an English ship on its way to loot Rangpur. Why is it so big?"

"A Queen must live like a Queen! It's got seven rooms."

"Who occupies so many rooms?"

"One is for holding court," answered Rangaraj. "Another is the Queen's bedroom. The women attendants stay in one and there's another for baths. And there's a galley and a jail. I expect you'll have to stay in that room today."

As they were speaking, the longboat came up beside the barge. Queen Debi (alias Debi Chaudhurani) was no longer on the roof. While her men had been engaged in their act of banditry, Debi had sat on the roof, still playing the *vina* in the moonlight,* but not so well now. Her mind had been elsewhere, and she played uncertainly, the music lacking tune and rhythm. As soon as the longboat returned, she descended from the roof and entered a room. Meanwhile, Rangaraj left the longboat and stood by the door of the room. "Victory to our gracious Queen!" he said. A silk curtain hung at the door so that it was impossible to see inside.

"What news?" asked Debi from within.

"All's well," said Rangaraj.

"Any wounded among you?"*

"No one."

"And they? Any dead?"

"No one. We followed your instructions."

"Any wounded among them?"

"Two Hindusthanis got a scratch or two—like thorn pricks."

"And the stuff on board?"

"We've brought everything. There wasn't much to bring."

"What about the man in charge?"

"We've brought him with us."

"Bring him here" said Debi.

Rangaraj motioned to Brajesvar. Brajesvar climbed on board and came and stood by the door.

"Who are you?" asked Debi; her voice sounded choked and rather unclear.

By now perhaps the reader will have realized what kind of person Brajesvar was. He had been a stranger to fear from boyhood. While northern Bengal trembled at Debi Chaudhurani's name, Brajesvar felt amused in her presence. He thought, "I've never heard of men being afraid of women! After all, women are meant to serve men." So he laughed and replied, "What's the point of knowing who I am? Now that you're all so well acquainted with my wealth, there'll be no money in my name!"

"Oh yes there will," said Debi. "Once we know what your standing is, we'll know how much money to go for." But her voice sounded strained.

"Is that why you brought me here?"

"We would not have brought you otherwise."

Debi was hidden behind the curtain; no one saw that she wiped her eyes as she spoke.

"Would you believe it if I said my name is Duhkhiram Chakrabartti?"

"No," said Debi.

"Then why ask?"

"To see if you'd tell me."

"My name is Krishnagobind Ghosal."

"No," said Debi.

"Dayaram Baksi."

"Not that too."

"Brajesvar Ray."

"That's possible" said Debi.

Just then another woman came up silently to Debi and sat down. She said, "Your voice sounds choked?" Debi could restrain her tears no longer. The tears had welled up in her eyes like flowers in bloom full of water during the rains, and just as the water in the flowers streams out when the branch is shaken, so her tears poured out when she shook her head. She whispered into the ear of her companion, "I can't keep up this game any longer. You carry on. You know everything, don't you?" Then she got up and went to another room.

The woman took Debi's seat and resumed the conversation with Brajesvar. The reader has already made her acquaintance: she was that Brahmin woman who lacked a Brahmin husband, Mistress Nishi!

Nishi said, "Now you've spoken the truth. Your name is Brajesvar Ray."

Brajesvar was a little confused. He could see nothing behind the curtain, yet when he heard the voice it occurred to him that this might not be the same person who spoke earlier. That voice had sounded very sweet—this one not quite so. Still, Brajesvar answered, "Now that you know who I am, fix a price, and I'll be getting back. What will it cost to let me go?"

"A tiny, worthless cowrie will do," said Nishi. "Do you have one with you? If so, give it to me and go on your way."[7]

"I don't have one on me right now" answered Brajesvar.

"Then please get one from your barge" said Nishi.

"Your attendants have brought back everything from the barge," said Brajesvar. "There's not even a tiny worthless cowrie left."

"Then borrow one from the deckhands."

"They don't keep worthless cowries," answered Brajesvar.

"Then stay on as prisoner till you bring the correct price," said Nishi.

Brajesvar then heard another person in the room—also a woman by the sound of her voice—addressing "Debi" as follows, "Your Majesty, if a tiny worthless cowrie is all this man's worth, then I'll pay it. Please sell him to me."

Brajesvar heard the Queen answer, "Well, what's the harm! But what will you do with him? He's a Brahmin. He can't fetch water or cut wood!"

Brajesvar heard the other woman reply, "I've no Brahmin to cook for me. He can do that."

Then Nishi said to Brajesvar, "Did you hear that? You've been sold, I've got my worthless cowrie. Please go with the person who's bought you. You'll have to work as a cook."

"Where is this person?" asked Brajesvar.

"She can't come out since she's a woman," answered Nishi, "So you'd better come on in."

Chapter 6

Now that he'd been given leave, Brajesvar lifted the curtain and entered the room. He was astonished at what he saw. The room had wooden walls on which a variety of beautiful pictures had been painted—the kind of pictures devotees commission for the canvas backdrop of the Goddess Durga's image when they want to worship her in the month of Asvin. Scenes of the battle of the Goddess with the demons Shumbha and Nishumbha, of her battle with the buffalo-demon, of the ten *avatar*s, the eight Nayikas, the seven Mothers, the ten Mahavidyas, of Mount Kailash, Brindaban, Lanka and Indra's Abode, of the Elephant made of nine women, and the Removal of the clothes—all were painted there.[8]

A thick rug—how many pictures on that too!—lay spread out in the room. On it stood a high throne—a divan of embroidered velvet, with bolsters done similarly in velvet, along three sides. There was a gold attar-pot with its

[7]At the time tiny cowrie shells acted as local currency. A well-to-do person was not likely to have such currency. See endnotes.

[8]See endnotes for information about these motifs.

gold rose-water spray, a gold container for betel-leaf, and a gold flower-platter with a heap of fragrant blossoms on it. There was a gold hubble-bubble with a smoking-pipe of clay, fired by cowdung;[9] a cluster of pearls hung from its golden mouthpiece. Tobacco, smelling fragrantly of musk, was arranged on top. On two sides stood two silver chandeliers, each with numerous fragrant lamps burning on a silver fairy's head. A small lamp hung by a gold chain from the ceiling. In each of the four corners of the room stood a silver statue holding a lamp in one hand.

A woman reclined on the throne, with a veil of very fine Dhaka cloth dotted with gold embroidery, across her face. Her face couldn't be seen clearly, yet it was the color of molten gold with tresses that appeared to be dark and curly. Her earrings shone from behind the cloth, yet the keen glances of those large eyes flashed even more brightly. The woman lay there reclining, but not asleep.

After he had entered the courtroom and observed the reclining beauty, Brajesvar said, "With what blessing must I greet your majesty?"[10]

"I am not her majesty," replied the woman.

Brajesvar realized that this was not the voice of the person with whom he had been conversing all this while. But it could well have been, for it was clear that the woman was masking her voice as she spoke. So Debi Chaudhurani is an impersonator, he thought, a sorceress; without knowing so many tricks could a woman engage in banditry? But openly he said, "Then where's the person with whom I was speaking?"

The beautiful woman answered, "After giving you permission to enter, she went away to rest. Why do you need the Queen?"

"Who are you?" asked Brajesvar.

"Your owner," said the woman.

"My owner?"

"Don't you know I've just bought you for a single worthless cowrie?"

"Very true" said Brajesvar, "Well then, with what blessing must I greet you?"

"Are there different kinds of blessing?"

"There are for women. One should bless a married woman in one way, a widow in another. For a woman who has a son. . . ."

"Well, bless me with 'Die soon,'" interrupted the woman.

"I don't bless anyone with that," rejoined Brajesvar, "May you live to be a hundred and three!"

"I'm twenty-five. Does that mean you'll cook for me for another seventy-eight years?"

"First let me do it for a day. If you can eat what I cook, maybe I'll do it for seventy-eight years."

---

[9]See endnotes.

[10]A benediction of courtesy from a Brahmin.

"Then sit down" said the woman, "and tell me how well you cook."

Brajesvar sat upon the soft rug. The beautiful woman asked, "What's your name?"

"It seems all of you know it already," answered Brajesvar. "My name's Brajesvar. What's your name? And why are you speaking so hoarsely? Do I know you?"

"I'm your owner. Speak to me with respect, using expressions like 'Madam' and 'By your leave'," said the beauty.

"By your leave, so be it," said Brajesvar. "What's your name, if you please?"

"My name's Pachkari. But since you're my servant, you can't use it. In fact, if you wish, I shan't use your name either."

"Then how will you address me so that I can reply with a 'By your leave'?" asked Brajesvar.

"I'll call you 'Ramdhan'," said the woman, "And you can call me 'Madam Owner.' Now tell me about yourself. Where do you live?"

"You've bought me for a cowrie," said Brajesvar, "Where's the need for so much information?"

"All right—I don't mind if you won't tell me. I can find out by asking Rangaraj. Are you a Rarhi or a Barendra, or a Baidik?"[11]

"You'll be eating what I cook whatever I am," answered Brajesvar.

"If your caste isn't compatible with mine,* I'll have to give you something else to do."

"Like what?" asked Brajesvar.

"You'll have to fetch water and cut wood. There's no shortage of work!"

"All right, I'm a Rarhi."

"Then you'll have to fetch water and cut wood. Because I'm a Barendra and you're a Rarhi. Are you a Kulin—the purest kind—or some lower type?"

"You need this information to arrange a marriage," answered Brajesvar. "Any chance of that here? I'm married already."

"Married already? How many wives do you have?"

"If I've got to fetch water, I'll fetch it," said Brajesvar, "I'm not going to tell you any more."

Then Pachkari called out to Queen Debi, "Your majesty! This Brahmin gentleman's very disobedient! He won't answer my questions!"

"Then cane him," called Nishi from the other room.*

One of Debi's maids came in with a very thin cane and with a swish or two threw it on Pachkari's divan and went away. Pachkari took the cane and gently biting her tender lip with her beautiful teeth behind the Dhaka cloth, beat the bed hard a couple of times with it. "See that?" she said to Brajesvar.

---

[11]Different Brahmin subcastes of Bengal.

Brajesvar laughed. "You people are capable of anything," he said. "All right, I'll tell you what you want to know."

"I don't really want to know about you," answered Pachkari. "It's of no use to me now, since I can't eat what you cook. Tell me, what else can you do?"

"Command me," said Brajesvar.

"Can you fetch water?"

"No."

"Can you cut wood?"

"No."

"Can you do the marketing?"

"After a fashion."

"After a fashion won't do. Do you know how to use the fan?"

"I do."

"Very well, then take this fly-whisk and fan me" ordered Pachkari.

Brajesvar took the fly-whisk and began to fan Pachkari. Then she asked, "Well now, can you do something else? Can you massage my feet?"

Unfortunately for Brajesvar, when he saw how cheeky "Pachkari" was, he thought he'd have a bit of fun; but he also hoped to win his freedom by humoring these women who led the bandits. So he replied, "What luck to massage the feet of beautiful women like you. . . . ."

"All right, do it then," said Pachkari and immediately placed a lac-painted foot on Brajesvar's thigh. Poor Brajesvar, what could he do? He himself had agreed to massage her feet! So he began to massage her foot with both hands. He thought, "This isn't going well at all.* I'll have to make amends for this. Now if only I can escape from here!"

Then the wicked Pachkari called out, "Your majesty, please come here for a moment."

Brajesvar heard Debi's footsteps approaching. He lowered Pachkari's foot. She laughed and said in her own voice now, "What's this? Why are you backing away?"

Astonished, Brajesvar blurted out, "What! I'm sure I know that voice." He plucked up courage and pulled the veil from Pachkari's face. Pachkari broke into a peal of laughter.

Stunned, Brajesvar said, "What on earth . . .? You're. . . . you're Sagar!"

"Yes I'm Sagar, the Ocean,"[12] replied Pachkari, "Not the Ganges, not the Jamuna, nor a marsh or canal, but the Ocean itself! Very bad luck for you, isn't it? When you thought it was some other woman, you were thrilled to massage her feet, but when as your wife I asked you to massage my feet, you stormed away in rage! Anyway, I've kept my word—you've massaged my foot. Now you can just gaze at my face, or you can leave me or you can look after me, I don't care! Now you know I'm truly a Brahmin's daughter!"*

---

[12]"Sagar" means "ocean" in Bengali.

❁ *Chapter 7* ❁

For a while Brajesvar was at a loss. At last he asked, "Sagar! Why are you here?"

Sagar replied, "Well, my husband, why are *you* here?"

"So that's it?" asked Brajesvar, "I'm a prisoner; are you a prisoner too? They brought me here by force. Did they bring you here by force as well?"

"I'm not a prisoner," said Sagar. "No one brought me here forcibly. I took Queen Debi's help willingly. I've been living in Queen Debi's domain so that I could get you to massage my feet!"

Nishi came in. When Brajesvar saw the finery of her clothes he thought she was Debi Chaudhurani, so he rose to show respect.

Nishi said, "Even when a woman becomes a bandit, she shouldn't be shown so much respect. Please sit down. So now you know why we attacked your barge! Now that Sagar's redeemed her pledge, we've no further need of you. If you wish to return to your barge no one will stop you, nor will anyone take the smallest item of your possessions, we'll send everything back to your barge. But this tiny item here, this wretch Sagar—what will happen to her? Must she return to her father's house, or will you take her with you? Remember, you're her bondsman for a cowrie."

Wonder upon wonder! Brajesvar was nonplussed. Then all this banditry was false; these were not bandits after all. Brajesvar thought for a while and said at last,* "You've all made a fool out of me. I thought Debi Chaudhurani's gang had attacked my barge to rob it!"

"But this really is Debi Chaudhurani's barge," answered Nishi. "And Queen Debi really is a bandit."

She had barely finished speaking when Brajesvar repeated, " 'Queen Debi really is a bandit'—then you're not Queen Debi?"

"No, I'm not Debi," said Nishi. "However, if you wish to see Her Majesty, she may grant your request. But first listen to what I was saying. We really are bandits, but so far as you were concerned the sole aim of our banditry was to help Sagar keep her promise. Now that she's kept her promise, how will she get home?"

"How did she come here?" asked Brajesvar.

"She came with Her Majesty."

"But I too went to Sagar's father's house," said Brajesvar. "That's where I'm coming from. I didn't see Her Majesty there?"

"Her Majesty went there later," answered Nishi.

"Then how did she return here before me?"

"Haven't you seen our longboat? We've fifty oarsmen."

"Well then, why don't you take Sagar back with you in the longboat?"

"There's a small obstacle there," said Nishi. "Sagar came with the Queen without telling anyone. If she returns in the longboat with people who are not her folk, everyone will ask her where she's been. But if she returns with you it'd be easy to give an answer."

❁

"Very well, then," said Brajesvar. "Please give instructions to the longboat." Saying that she would do so right away, Nishi left the room.

Now that Sagar was alone with him, Brajesvar said, "Sagar! Whyever did you make such a promise?" Covering her face with as much of the edge of her sari as came to hand—not the Dhaka cloth now—Sagar wept. Dabbing her face, shoulders heaving, that same impudent Sagar sobbed away silently—silently, lest Debi hear.

When the sobbing ceased, Brajesvar said, "Sagar, why didn't you call for me? If you'd called, everything would have been all right."

Controlling her tears with an effort and wiping her eyes, Sagar answered, "My bad luck! But since I didn't call for you, why didn't *you* come?"

"You sent me away," said Brajesvar, "How could I come unless you called?"

When this topic of conversation had run its course, Brajesvar asked, "Sagar, why did you come here with bandits?"

Sagar replied, "I knew that Debi was related to me by marriage. After you left she came to my father's house, and when she saw me crying she said, "Why are you crying, friend? I'll capture your beloved and bring him back to you! Why don't you stay with me for a couple of days!" So I came. I've reason to trust Debi implicitly. I told my maid that I was running away with you. I've arranged this hubble-bubble with its pipe etc. for you. So just make use of it once, and then you can leave."

Brajesvar replied, "How can I, since the owner of this place hasn't given me permission?"

Sagar sent for Debi, but Debi didn't come. Nishi came instead.

When he saw that it was Nishi, Brajesvar said, "If you've given instructions to the longboat, we can leave."

"The longboat's yours," said Nishi. Then she continued, "But see, you're the Queen's brother-in-law; here you are as a relative and we've not treated you well. All we've done is insult you, for which we're very sorry. Just because we're bandits doesn't mean we don't observe Hindu customs properly."

"So what must I do?" said Brajesvar.

"To begin with, sit more comfortably," said Nishi. She pointed to the throne-like dais, for Brajesvar had only been sitting on the carpet. He replied, "But I'm quite comfortable where I am."

Nishi turned to Sagar and said, "Take what's yours, friend, and make him sit properly! You know we don't touch other people's property. Except for silver and gold," she added, laughing.

"So I've fallen into the category of brass and bell-metal?" said Brajesvar.

"That's what I think," answered Nishi. "Men are part of women's utensils. We need them to make a home, but they easily get soiled, and all the scrubbing, polishing, and washing it takes to make them usable again is exhausting work! Go on, Sagar, keep your little pot-thing apart. Who knows, it may be soiled!"

"First I'm brass or bell-metal—then a little pot-thing! Aren't I worthy to be counted among the jars and pitchers?" asked Brajesvar.

"I'm just a Vaishnavi, friend," rejoined Nishi, "I have nothing to do with household utensils. Clay vessels are our limit! If you want to know about household utensils ask Sagar."

"I know the answer!" exclaimed Sagar. "Where utensils are concerned, men are jugs. Always empty! And because we women are so talented, we make them worthwhile by filling them with water to the brim."

"Well said," said Nishi, "That's why women drown in life's ocean with these objects tied to their necks! Go on then, take your jug and put it on its stand."

"The jug's going there of its own accord while its dignity is still intact," said Brajesvar rising and then sitting on the throne by himself. Immediately, from two sides, two maids—both young, beautiful women adorned with expensive clothes and jewelry—came and stood on either side of Brajesvar, with gold-plated fly-whisks in their hands. Without being ordered to do so, they began to fan him.

Then Nishi said to Sagar, "Now go and prepare the tobacco for your husband with your own hands and bring it to him." Without delay Sagar took the bowl from the top of the hubble-bubble, quickly prepared the tobacco with its fragrant odor of musk, and returned and placed it on the hubble-bubble.

"I'd rather you gave me the tobacco in a hookah with a new pipe," said Brajesvar.[13]

"Don't worry," said Nishi, "That hubble-bubble's not been used. No one's smoked it before, and none of us smoke."

"Really!" said Brajesvar surprised, "Then why is it here?"

"Well, it's part of Debi's regal display. . . ." replied Nishi.

"That may be, but the tobacco had been prepared when I came. Who had been smoking it?"

"No one," said Nishi, "That too is for show."

In fact, the hubble-bubble had been taken out that very day, and the tobacco had been bought that day too, seeing that Sagar's husband was expected. Brajesvar examined the mouthpiece, saw that it seemed to be unused, and then became engrossed in the ineffable pleasure of smoking. Nishi said to Sagar, "Why are you standing there, you useless thing! Once a man's put a hookah's pipe to his mouth do you think he's got time for wife or family? Go on, prepare a few pieces of *paan* for him. Take care to prepare it yourself; don't bring someone else's handiwork. Now win him over, if you can."

Sagar replied, "Well, all this was prepared by me! If I knew how to win him over, would I be in this mess?"

[13]The smoking-pipe of the hubble-bubble may already have been used by someone else, and he didn't wish to incur ritual pollution by then using it himself.

After saying this, Sagar fetched a gold vessel heaped with *paan* pieces rendered fragrant by a mixture of sandalpaste, camphor, perfume, and rosewater. Then Nishi said, "You've scolded your husband a lot. Now bring him something to eat."

"Heaven forbid!" said Brajesvar in consternation, "Food so late! Please, spare me that."

But no one listened. Sagar quickly swept clean another room, sprinkled it with water and wiped it, laid out a very thick mat, and arranged various items of food on four or five silver dishes. She also put out some excellent fragrant, cool water in a gold vessel. When Nishi knew that everything was ready, she called to Brajesvar, "Your place is ready. Please get up." Brajesvar stole a look, joined his palms together and said, "By banditry you brought me here as a prisoner by force, and I've put up with that. But so late at night, I can't put up with this. Please.....".

But the women wouldn't listen to any excuses, so Brajesvar was forced to eat something. Then Sagar said to Nishi, "After you've fed a Brahmin, it's customary to give him a gift."

Nishi replied, "The Queen herself will give him the gift. (Then to Brajesvar:) Come along, friend, the Queen will see you now." Then Nishi led Brajesvar to another room.

Chapter 8

Nishi took Brajesvar to Debi's bed-chamber. Brajesvar saw that it had been marvelously decorated, similar to Debi's meeting-room, though what stood out was a small divan, adorned with gold and fringed with pearls. But Brajesvar had no eyes for any of that: he wanted to see the famous Debi, the owner of such power and wealth. What he saw was a woman half-veiled and seated on an item of unadorned wood. There was nothing of that agitation about her that he had noticed in Nishi and Sagar. She was composed and calm, demure, with eyes cast down. Nishi and Sagar, especially Nishi, had been decked out with jewels all over, dressed in very expensive attire, but this woman had nothing of that. We've seen before that in the expectation of meeting Brajesvar Debi had been adorned with very expensive clothes and jewelry. But when the time came to see him she had put all that aside, and awaited him dressed in plain clothes, with a single simple ornament on her hand. Before—on Nishi's advice—Debi had made a mistake. But later, when she realized this, she rebuked herself saying, "Shame, what have I done! Trying to trap him with wealth!"—hence the change of clothing.

After taking Brajesvar to the room, Nishi went away. When Brajesvar entered, Debi rose and paid him obeisance. Brajesvar was even more amazed—what was this! No one else had paid him obeisance! When Debi stood up in front of Brajesvar,[14] Brajesvar saw that she really did look like a Goddess. Had he ever seen the like before? Yes, Braja had seen someone just like this once before, someone who had been softer—because the image of the Goddess had been more like that of a girl—when Brajesvar himself was in the first flush of youth. Alas, if only this were she! As he gazed on the face before him, Brajesvar thought of the other, but he saw that they were not the same. Was there nothing of the one in the other? Yes, there was a resemblance. Brajesvar gazed on in amazement. "But the other died long ago," he thought. "Still, one person sometimes so looks like another that when you see one the other comes to mind." "Isn't that what's happening here, Braja?" he asked himself.

Thus Braja reflected. But through the very resemblance his heart filled over, and the tears came to his eyes—but did not fall, so Debi didn't see them. If she had, then events would have taken an unexpected turn, for here were two clouds—and both charged with lightning!

Having paid obeisance, Debi began to speak with eyes lowered, "I've given you much trouble today by bringing you here against your will. You have heard why I did this bad deed. Please excuse me."

"On the contrary, you've done me a good turn," replied Brajesvar. He didn't have the strength to say much more.

Debi continued, "You've been kind enough to take some refreshment here which has greatly enhanced my standing. You're a Kulin, a ritually pure Brahmin, so it's my duty to maintain your standing too. You are also my relative. So please accept what I am about to give you for this purpose."

Brajesvar answered, "What wealth can compare to a wife? And that is what you have given me.[15] What more could you give?"

O Brajesvar! What have you said? There's no wealth to compare with a wife? Then why did you two, father and son, get together and drive Prafulla away?

There was a silver jar beside the divan. Pulling it clear and placing it next to Brajesvar, Debi said, "You must accept this."

Brajesvar said, "There's so much gold and silver about your barge, that if I were to refuse, Sagar would rebuke me. Yet, may I ask...."

Debi understood what he wished to say. She replied, "I swear to you that this has not been stolen or looted. You may have heard that I have some wealth of my own. So please have no doubts about accepting."

Brajesvar agreed (neither the scion of a Kulin nor a Brahmin priest has ever been loath to accept "parting gifts" or "tokens of esteem"—no doubt the same applies today!). The jar felt very heavy and Brajesvar was unable to lift it easily. He said in surprise, "The jar's not empty then?"

---

[14]Apparently no longer veiled, as we shall see.

[15]That is, Sagar.

Debi said, "When I pulled at it there was a sound from inside, so it can't be empty."

"I see? Well then, what's inside?" asked Brajesvar. He thrust his hand into the jar and pulled out—*mohur*s! The jar was filled with *mohur*s!

Brajesvar said, "Into what should I pour these out?"

"Why should you pour them out?" was the answer. "It's all for you."

"What!"

"Why not?"

"How many *mohur*s are there?"

"Thirty three hundred"

"Thirty three hundred *mohur*s is more than fifty thousand Rupees! Has Sagar spoken to you about money?"

"Sagar told me that you are in particular need of fifty thousand Rupees."

"Is that why you're giving them to me?"

"The money doesn't belong to me," replied Debi, "So I don't have the right to give it. The money belongs to God. As money in the service of God, it's in my care. So I'm lending it to you from my wealth, which is reserved for God's service."

"I'm in desperate need of this money," answered Brajesvar. "Even if I'd amassed it by stealing or banditry, perhaps that wouldn't be wrong, because without it my father would lose caste. So I'll take the money. But when must I pay it back?"

Debi said, "It belongs to God, so if God gets it back, that'll do. When you hear that I've died, spend the principal and an interest of one *mohur* in God's service."

"Which would be spending the money on what *I* want to do," answered Brajesvar. "And that would be to deceive you. I don't agree to this."

"Well then, pay it back in the way you wish."

"When I manage to collect the money, I'll send it to you."

"None of your people must come to me, nor will they be able to."

"I'll bring the money myself then."

"But where will you come? I don't stay in one place."

"Wherever you say."

"If you can fix a day, I can name a place."

"I can collect the money by March or thereabouts. But it would be better to have some time in hand. I'll give you the money by mid-May."

"Then bring the money to this mooring-place on the seventh night of the bright half of May. I'll wait here till the moon sets on the seventh night. If you come after that you won't find me."

Brajesvar agreed. Debi gave her maids orders to carry the jar of *mohur*s to the longboat, which they did. Then Brajesvar gave Debi the customary blessing and was on his way to the longboat when Debi stopped him and said, "There's one other thing. All I've given you is a loan—not a token of my esteem."

"Well, the jar is the token," said Brajesvar.

"That's not worthy of you," said Debi. "Let me do my best to show you my esteem."

She removed a ring from her finger, and Brajesvar, smiling, extended his hand to receive it. But instead of just giving him the ring, Debi took hold of his hand to put the ring on herself. Brajesvar was in control of his senses, but the inner confusion that now ensued, the self-controlled Brajesvar couldn't understand; his skin prickled all over and a torrent of nectar raced within! Brajesvar, the man in control of his senses, forgot to withdraw his hand! From time to time Providence creates such obstacles that one can't help forgetting what one ought to do!

So it was during that moment of human turmoil that Debi began lingeringly to put the ring on Brajesvar's finger. And it was then that a couple of hot tear-drops fell on Brajesvar's hand. Brajesvar saw that Debi's face was streaming with tears. What exactly happened after that I cannot say. After all, Brajesvar was in control of his senses. Nevertheless, there was turmoil within. Also, that other face came to mind; perhaps that face too had streamed with tears in the same way that night, and perhaps he remembered how he had wiped the tears away. In his confusion the two faces seemed to fuse, and without realising what was happening—why, I do not know—Brajesvar put one hand on Debi's shoulder and with the other lifted her face. Perhaps he thought it looked like Prafulla's face. Overwhelmed, bewildered—there on those gloriously red tear-drenched lips.....O Brajesvar, shame! Not again!

The heavens seemed to crash upon his head. What had he done! This wasn't Prafulla! She'd been dead ten years! Without even taking Sagar with him, Brajesvar ran with all his might straight to the longboat and climbed in.

Shouting "Catch the culprit, he's escaping!" Sagar ran after him and got into the longboat too. The longboat was untied and Brajesvar and his two treasures—Sagar and the jar—were deposited in Brajesvar's boat.

Meanwhile, Nishi had entered Debi's bedroom and saw that Debi had thrown herself, weeping, on the floor. Nishi lifted her up, made her sit down, and wiping her tears calmed her down. Then she said gently, "So this is your selfless duty, your life of detachment? Where are the Lord's teachings now, dear?"

Debi was silent. Nishi continued, "Such vows are not for women. If a woman must walk that path then she must become like me. I've no Brajesvar to make me cry. My Brajesvar and the Lord in heaven are one and the same."

Debi wiped her eyes and said, "Go to hell!"

"I'd have no objection," replied Nishi, "But hell has no power over me.* Give up your life of detachment and go home."

Debi answered, "If that path were open to me, I'd not have followed this one. Now tell them to release the barge. Raise all four sails!"

Then that huge ship-like barge spread its four sails, and like a bird, flew gracefully away.

❁ *Chapter 9* ❁

Brajesvar returned to his boat and sat down sombrely. He did not speak with Sagar. He saw that Debi's barge had spread its sails and flown away gracefully like a bird. He asked Sagar, "Where's the barge gone?"

Sagar answered, "Only Debi knows. She tells no one else such things."

"Who's Debi?"

"Debi's Debi."

"What's she to you?"

"A sister."

"What kind of sister?"

"Through family."

Brajesvar said nothing again. He called the deckhands. "Can you keep up with the big barge?" he asked. "How can we?" they replied. "It's shot off like a meteor!" Brajesvar was silent again. Sagar went to sleep. When it was dawn, Brajesvar had the barge untied and continued on his journey. As soon as the sun rose, Sagar came and sat next to him.

Brajesvar asked, "Is Debi a bandit?"

Sagar said, "What do you think?"

"What I saw certainly gave that impression," answered Brajesvar. "It occurred to me that she could well be a bandit. Yet I don't believe she is."

"Why not?" asked Sagar.

"I don't know" said Brajesvar. "Yet if she isn't a bandit, where did she get so much wealth?"

"Some say Debi got so much wealth as a favor from God," said Sagar, "Others say she found buried treasure, and yet others say Debi knows how to make gold."

"And what does Debi say?"

"Debi says that not even the tiniest coin of it is hers, that everything belongs to another."

"Well, where did she get so much wealth that belongs to another?"

"That I don't know."

"That wealth belongs to another and she lives in such grand style? Doesn't the other object?"

"Debi doesn't live in grand style. She eats the broken fragments of rice-grains, she sleeps on the ground, and she wears clothes made of coarse cloth. What you saw yesterday was just for your and my benefit—just for show. What's that on your hand?" Sagar had seen the new ring on Brajesvar's finger.

Brajesvar replied, "Debi gave me this ring as a token of esteem because I ate something on her boat yesterday."

"Let's see," said Sagar. Brajesvar removed the ring and gave it to Sagar to inspect. Turning it around in her hand, Sagar said, "It's got Debi Chaudhurani's name written on it."

"Where?" asked Brajesvar.

"Inside—in Farsi."

"What's this!" said Brajesvar in amazement, as he read the inscription, "This is my name! Does this ring belong to me? Sagar! I swear to you, if you don't tell me the truth.... Who's Debi, tell me!"

"It's not my fault if you couldn't recognize her," protested Sagar. "I recognized her at once!"

"Who? Who? Who is Debi?" cried Brajesvar.

"Prafulla."

Brajesvar did not speak again. Sagar saw that at first the skin prickled on his body, then there were signs of an unspeakable happiness—a pervasive joy seemed to course through his body. His face glowed, his eyes though brimming with tears glistened, his body was erect, its beauty radiant. Then everything seemed to die down instantly. A profound sadness seemed to come upon and overpower that glowing beauty. Brajesvar remained silent, motionless, unblinking. Slowly he stared into Sagar's face and then closed his eyes. His body sank down, and placing his head in Sagar's lap he lay still. Anguished, Sagar questioned him many times but received no answer. At last Brajesvar said, "Prafulla's a bandit! Shame!"*

Chapter 10

After Brajesvar and Sagar had left, Debi Chaudhurani.... Alas! What happened to Debi? That elegant attire, the Dhaka sari, the gold jewelry, the diamonds, pearls, and emeralds—what happened to all of that? Debi got rid of everything; she put everything away. She dressed in a single coarse cloth, and on her wrist wore only the lacquered iron band signifying that she was a married woman. In a corner, she spread a piece of sackcloth on the plain floor of the barge and lay down. Whether she slept or not, I cannot tell.

At dawn when she saw that the barge was moored at the desired place, she descended and bathed in the waters of the river. After bathing, she remained in her wet attire—a sari as thick as that piece of sackcloth. When she smeared some Ganges mud on her forehead and breast, and loosed her wet unkempt hair, the beauty that was now revealed had been absent in the finery and glamour, the glow of diamonds and pearls, the pomp of a Queen of the night before. Yesterday Debi had appeared in the guise of some bejeweled empress, today, in her garb of Ganges clay, she looked like a deity. Tell me, why do the beautiful forsake the clay only to put on diamonds?

Debi did not return to the barge. Dressed incomparably in this fashion, and with only one woman to act as companion, she walked along the bank. After walking a great distance in this way, she entered a jungle. We've often referred to jungles and bandits; from this the reader musn't think that we tend to exaggerate or that we have a penchant for such things! We speak of a time when that region was covered in jungle. Even now there are dreadful jungles in many places, some of which I've been and seen with my own eyes. As for bandits—let's not talk about them! Perhaps the reader will remember that before the Punjab Wars, there was no greater war-effort the Marquess of Hastings was called upon to make than that required to subdue India's bandits. In those lawless times, banditry was the business of the resourceful! It was the weak or feckless who were the "good sort." There was no blame or shame attached to banditry then.

Debi continued to make her way deep into the jungle she had entered. Finally, she arrived under a tree and said to her companion, "Diba, sit down here. I'll be back. There are very few tigers or bears in this forest, and even if they come near you've nothing to fear. There are guards nearby to protect you." Debi then went into a more dense part of the jungle. In the very depths there was a tunnel with a stone stairway. In the darkness, at the bottom of the stairs, was a stone room. Perhaps in the past this had been a shrine; now, since with the passage of time the earth had caved in, it had been necessary to construct that stairway. Debi climbed down in the gloom.

In the light of a flickering lamp in that underground temple, a Siva linga was visible.[16] A Brahmin was seated in front of it performing a ritual of worship. After paying obeisance to the Shiva linga, Debi went and sat down some distance away from him. Seeing her, the Brahmin completed his worship, performed the ritual ablution, and then began a conversation.

"Child!" he said, "What did you do last night? Did you engage in banditry?"

"What do you think?" asked Debi.

"How would I know?" was the reply. The Brahmin, of course, was no other than Bhabani Thakur whom we have met before.

" 'How would I know?' Master!" exclaimed Debi. "Don't you know me yet? I've roamed about with this band of brigands for ten years now. Everyone thinks it is I who carry out all the banditry that takes place. Yet you well know that I haven't done this work even for a day. And you say, 'How would I know?'!"

"Why are you angry?" said Bhabani. "The reason we do this banditry leads us to believe we're not doing wrong. Otherwise we wouldn't do it even for a day. I suppose even you don't think it's bad, else why for these ten years....."

"I'm having second thoughts about that," replied Debi. "I've been fooled by your words all this while, but no longer. If it's not bad to take other people's property by force then what would you call a great sin? I want to have nothing more to do with any of you."

"I see!" said Bhabani. "Must I explain to you again what I've explained all this while? If I kept even a single cowrie of the wealth that came from all this banditry that would be a great sin indeed. But you know very well that I act as a bandit only to give to others. Neither Rangaraj nor I have ever taken a single

[16]The Shiva linga is a tubular stone of various heights set in an ovoid base with a rim, worshipped as embodying the divine creativity. For more information see endnotes.

coin from someone who's honest, who acquires wealth by following the right path, or who would be hard put to it to make ends meet if they lost their wealth. We rob only those who are swindlers or frauds, who take other people's wealth by force or deceit. And when we do so, we don't keep a single coin. We give to those whom others have swindled. Surely you know all this? There's no law in the land, no king to keep things in check; the wicked go unpunished, and anyone who wants can live by robbing from others. So we've made you Queen, and govern the land. In your name we chastise the wicked and protect the good. Is this unrighteous?"

"Well, make anyone you wish king or queen and carry on," answered Debi, "But release me now. I've no mind for this queen business."

"This reign will suit no one else," said Bhabani. "No one else has your incomparable wealth. Everyone's beholden to you because of the wealth you bestow. . . ."

"I hereby give all my wealth to you," answered Debi. "Please spend the money in the way I've been doing. I've decided to go and live in Kashi."[17]

Bhabani replied, "Do you think it's only because of your wealth that everyone's obliged to you? Both beauty and virtue make you a truly great Queen. Many look upon you as the Goddess herself, for you've given up everything, and like our Mother the Goddess seek the welfare of others, bestow your wealth generously, and indeed appear as lovely as the Goddess herself. This is why we're able to rule the country in your name, otherwise who'd take us seriously?"

"And this is why folk know me for a bandit!" retorted Debi. "Even when I die this infamy will stick."

"How infamy?" asked Bhabani. "Is there anyone in Barendrabhumi today who's ashamed of your name? In any case, when one pursues duty does the question of fame or infamy arise? If you want fame can your actions be selfless? And if you're afraid of infamy you'll look to your own interests and forget about others. How can you renounce self then?"

"I shan't get the better of you in argument," answered Debi. "You're a great scholar. I say what I think as a woman. I just want to stop this acting like a queen. I don't like it any more."

"If you don't like it any more then why did you send Rangaraj to engage in banditry yesterday? I was informed about this, and it's important that you give me an explanation."

"Well if you were informed about it then you must also know that Rangaraj didn't engage in banditry yesterday. He only pretended to do so."

"Why? That's what I don't know, and that's why I'm asking."

"I wanted him to bring back a certain man."

"Which man?"

[17]Kashi: the traditional Sanskrit name for the holy city of Benares/Varanasi. See endnotes.

Debi was reluctant to mention the name, but she had no option; one couldn't prevaricate with Bhabani. So she was constrained to say, "His name is Brajesvar Ray."

"I know him well," said Bhabani. "What need did you have of him?"

"I needed to give him something. His father was going to be imprisoned by the leaseholder of his estates, so I gave something and preserved the caste of a Brahmin."

"You did wrong," said Bhabani. "Haraballabh Ray is an utter villain. He destroyed the caste of his son's mother-in-law for no good reason, so it would have been good if his own caste was lost."

Debi shivered. She asked, "What happened?"

"One of his son's wives had no one but a widowed mother. Haraballabh branded the penniless woman a *Bagdi* and drove the young wife out of his house. The girl's mother died from grief."

"What happened to the girl?" asked Debi.

"I heard that she died from starvation."

"What's that got to do with us?" replied Debi. "We've taken a vow to do good to others. When we see someone suffer, we must free them from sorrow."

Bhabani said, "No harm in that. But right now many folk are in the grip of poverty. All their possessions have been lost through the wickedness of the leaseholder. If you give them a little money, they can get something to eat and regain their strength. Then they can take up staves and get back what's theirs. So quickly rescue them by holding court one day."

"Then kindly announce that I'll hold court here next Monday."

"No," said Bhabani. "You can't stay here any longer. The English have discovered that you're in this region, and they're coming for you with five hundred sepoys. So you can't hold court here. I've announced that you'll hold court in the jungle area of Baikunthapur, and arranged it for Monday. The sepoys won't dare to enter that jungle, and if they do they'll be killed. So take as much money as you want and make for Baikunthapur's jungle today."

"I'll start at once," said Debi. "But I doubt if I'll continue with this work. I've no mind for it any more."

With this Debi rose, made her way through the jungle once more and returned to the barge. When she had embarked she summoned Rangaraj and secretly informed him that she would hold court the following Monday in Baikunthapur's jungle. He was to untie the barge immediately and proceed in that direction. Her fighters were to be informed that they should go via Debigarh, for she would pick up some money there since she didn't have enough with her.

In an instant, three or four white sails, large and small, began to swell in the breeze on the masts of the barge; the longboat came to the front of the barge and was tied to it. In it sat sixty strong men with short oars. Shouting "Victory to our Queen!" they began to paddle and the barge sped off like that boat with the speed of an arrow. On the shore, many men on foot—men of fine bearing who worked in the local markets—were seen running alongside the barge through the jungle. Each carried only a staff (though inside the barge there were plenty of shields, spears, and guns). These were Debi's private army of "fighters."

When Debi saw that everything was in order, she went into the galley to cook some rice and leaf-vegetables for herself with her own hands. Really, Debi, what a life of renunciation you lead!

Chapter 11

On the following Monday, in the heart of a dense forest lit up by the rising sun, Queen Debi held court or sat in judgment—but no "due process" or lawsuits took place in those courts. There was only one action in the royal business—giving liberally. It was a dense jungle, yet about a hundred acres had been cleared within. Notwithstanding the clearing, large trees had not been felled for it was in their shade that folk would stand. About ten thousand people had gathered in that cleared land, and Queen Debi held court in their midst. A large marquee, suspended from the branches of trees, had been erected. Underneath, fringed with pearls, hung a brocaded canopy on tall, thick poles of silver.* A large, thick rug had been spread on a sandalwood dais within, and on the rug stood a smallish silver throne surmounted by a cushion also fringed with pearls.

Debi's attire was particularly gorgeous today.* She wore a floral sari with diamonds set between the flowers. Her body was adorned with precious stones; from time to time its fair radiant complexion was visible through the gaps. So many pearl necklaces hung from her neck that they completely covered the clothing on her breast, and with her bejeweled crown Debi looked today like the image of the autumnal Goddess herself.

This is how Debi enacted the role of Queen! On both sides she was fanned by four beautifully dressed young women with gold-encrusted fly-whisks. Numerous resplendently-dressed mace and sceptre-bearers, supporting the large silver rods on their shoulders, stood in front and on the sides. Splendor everywhere, with rows of Debi's fighters! About five hundred fighters lined both flanks of her throne. Each was grandly dressed, with a red turban and jacket, a red loincloth tucked in tightly at the waist, red pointed shoes, and holding a buckler and spear. On all sides red pennants stood planted in the ground.

Debi was seated on the throne. After the ten thousand people gathered there cried out in praise once, "Victory to Queen Debi!" ten young men, smartly dressed, came forward and sweetly sang a song in praise of Debi. Then, one by one from among those ten thousand poor, Rangaraj began to bring the petitioners forward to Debi's throne. When they came up each devoutly made a full prostration. Even the old and those who were Brahmins did so because many believed that Debi was a portion of the Goddess who had come down to rescue people. This is why no one ever informed the English of her whereabouts or helped to procure her arrest. Debi addressed each one kindly, and asked to know their particular circumstances. After she had done so, she gave to each in accordance with their situation. The jars were arranged nearby, laden with money.

In this way from dawn till dusk, Debi dispensed her wealth to the poor. The giving came to an end when dusk turned to the first quarter of night. Until then Debi had not had even a drink of water. This is what Debi's banditry consisted of—this and nothing else!

Within a few days the news reached Mr Goodlad in Rangpur that Debi Chaudhurani's group of bandits had gathered in countless numbers in the jungles of Baikunthapur. It was also rumored that many bandits were returning home carrying large quantities of money, so there could be no doubt that they had engaged in much banditry. In fact, all those who had received wealth from Debi and were taking it home, dissembled, claiming that they had no money. They did this because they were afraid that if the leaseholder's foot-soldiers heard what had really happened they would seize it all. Nevertheless, Debi's beneficiaries now began to meet their expenses—so everyone concluded that on this occasion Debi Chaudhurani had plundered a great deal.

Chapter 12

In due course Brajesvar appeared before his father and made obeisance at his feet.* After some pleasantries, Haraballabh asked, "Now tell me the real news! What about the money?"

When Brajesvar replied that his father-in-law had been unable to give any money, Haraballabh was thunderstruck. "So you didn't get the money?" he cried.

"Well, it's true my father-in-law was unable to give any money," Brajesvar answered, "But I got it from another source..."

"So you got it! What took you so long to tell me? By Durga, I'm saved!"

"But I'm not sure," continued Brajesvar, "whether I should have accepted the money from where I got it."

"Who gave it to you?" asked Haraballabh.

Scratching his head and looking down, Brajesvar mumbled, "Can't think of her name now.... you know, that woman who's a bandit?"

"Who, Debi Chaudhurani?"

"Yes."

"How did you get the money off her?"

In the ancient ethical codes known to Brajesvar it was written that it's not wrong to prevaricate with one's father in such circumstances, so he said, "It came to hand rather conveniently...."

"Bad folk's money!" returned his father. "How was the money accounted for?"

"That wasn't necessary," said Brajesvar, "Since it sort of came to hand rather conveniently....." But so that his father wouldn't inquire into what happened more closely, Brajesvar immediately sought to suppress the matter by saying, "Whoever accepts sinful money also partakes of the sin, so I don't think we should accept it."

Incensed, Haraballabh replied, "Do you want me to go to jail if I don't take the money? I'll borrow it—irrespective of whether it's good money or bad. Who'd give me sainted money anyway? There's no point in making such objections. My real objection is this: the money belongs to bandits and it wasn't formally accounted for. My fear is that if I'm late in paying it back they'll redeem it by looting the house!"

Brajesvar said nothing.

Haraballabh asked, "How long before I've got to pay it back?"

"We've got till the moon sets on the seventh night of the bright half of May."

"And she's a bandit to boot," continued Haraballabh. "Where will she be so that I can send her the money?"

"After evening that day, she'll be waiting in her barge at Kalsaji pier in Sandhanpur. It'll be all right if the money gets to her there."

"Very well," said Haraballabh, "Then we'll send her the money there on that day."

After Brajesvar had left, Haraballabh turned the matter over carefully in his mind. Finally he came to the following conclusion: "We'll pay that girl back her money, all right! If we get the sepoys to catch her all my problems will be solved! On the night of May the seventh if the English Captain doesn't board her barge with his platoon of troops, my name's not Haraballabh! That'll see to her taking any money off me after that!" But Haraballabh kept this pious design to himself—he didn't trust Brajesvar to tell him about it.

Meanwhile, Sagar went to Grandaunt Brahma and spun her a tale about Brajesvar going off to the barge of some great Queen and marrying the lady: Sagar had warned him repeatedly not to do so, but he didn't listen. That wretch of a woman, continued Sagar, was a Kaibartta by caste, who had married twice already, so Brajesvar himself had lost caste. Accordingly Sagar had solemnly resolved not to share food with him any more. When Grandaunt Brahma tackled Brajesvar about all this he admitted his offense and said, "In fact, from the point of view of her caste, the Queen's all right; she's father's paternal aunt. As for marriage, well, I had three, and now so has she!"

Grandaunt Brahma knew none of this was true, but Sagar wanted her to tell the story to Nayantara. And this was done without a moment's delay. In any case, Nayantara was vexed to see Sagar, and when she heard that her husband had married some old woman, she was incandescent. So for a few days Brajesvar kept out of Nayantara's way and frequented the accommodation reserved for Sagar.

This is exactly what Sagar wanted. But Nayantara continued to cause trouble; finally, she complained to the lady of the house. Her mother-in-law said,

"Child, you're off your head! Tell me, does a Brahmin's son marry a Kaibartta? Everyone has a go at you, and you allow them to."

Even then Nayan Bou wasn't convinced. She said, "But supposing he really has married her?" "If he really has," replied her mother-in-law, "then I'll formally take the girl in. I can't turn away my son's wife again." Just then Brajesvar came by, and Nayan Bou, of course, made herself scarce. When Brajesvar asked his mother what she had been saying to her, she replied, "This: that if you marry again, we'll be glad to take your wife in." Without making any reply, Brajesvar went away thoughtfully.

That evening, as the lady of the house was fanning her lord and master, she tactfully put the matter to him. "What do you think?" he asked her.

"I think," she answered, "that of the wives, Sagar is not ready to settle down, and Nayan is not a wife fit for the boy. So if Braja finds someone suitable and marries her and settles down in the proper way, I'll be happy."

"Well, if you see that's what the boy has in mind, let me know," said her husband. "I'll summon the matchmaker and finalize the negotiations."

"Good," said his wife. "I'll see what he wants."

The task of seeing what Brajesvar wanted fell to Grandaunt Brahma. So she told him many stories about princes who were lovelorn or eager to marry, but none of this helped to reveal what Brajesvar was thinking. Finally she began to question him openly—but still she learnt nothing from him. All he said was, "Whatever my parents tell me to do, I'll do."

And that's where the matter was more or less laid to rest.[18]

---

[18]And here the novel in its original (serial) version was laid to rest too. Part III which follows, with revisions to Parts I and II, was added and published in book form later.

PART III

Chapter 1

The seventh day of the bright half of May had come, but no effort had been made to pay the debt owed to Queen Debi. Haraballabh himself was now clear of debt. If he had wanted he could easily have collected the money to pay Debi off, but he was quite unconcerned about that. When Brajesvar saw that Haraballabh had done nothing at all about the matter, he raised the topic several times but each time Haraballabh had stopped him with some excuse. The seventh day of the bright half of May was almost upon them—there were only a few days left. When Brajesvar began to press his father about the money, Haraballabh replied, "All right, don't worry. I'm off to get the money. I'll be back on the sixth day." So Haraballabh set off from home in a sedan-chair, with a Brahmin cook, retainers and two *lathials* (or guards) in tow.

Haraballabh went off to procure some money, no doubt—but not quite as envisaged. He went straight to Rangpur and met the British Collector there. In those days, the Collector was also a keeper of the peace. Haraballabh said to him, "Give me some sepoys and I'll catch Debi Chaudhurani for you. And if I can manage that, tell me, what reward will you give me?"

When he heard this, the Collector was delighted, for he knew that Debi Chaudhurani was the leader of the bandits. If he could catch *her,* all the others would be caught too. He had made many attempts to apprehend Debi, but without any success. So when he heard Haraballabh offer to catch that fearful ogress, he was pleased and agreed to give him a reward. Haraballabh asked that an order be given for five hundred sepoys to accompany him, which the Collector did. A lieutenant Brenan in command of five hundred sepoys, accompanied by Haraballabh, proceeded to apprehend Debi.

Haraballabh had heard precisely from Brajesvar at which pier he would find Debi. Because Debi might be on her barge, Lieutenant Brenan took some troops with him by longboat. In fact he set out to surround Debi's barge by traveling downstream with five longboats. The Lieutenant also dispatched another army of sepoys secretly through the woods along the banks. Haraballabh had said where Debi's barge would be, so that's where he hid his troops in the forest by the banks. In this way, if Debi, attacked by the longboats, tried to flee by some route on the bank, he could catch her by surrounding her with these troops.

But this left one other escape route. His longboats would come downstream. Debi might spy them from afar and be able to escape downstream too. So Lieutenant Brenan sent his remaining sepoys about four miles downstream and placed them in a particular spot where it would be easy to cross the Teesta river on foot in this dry season. The sepoys would remain there hidden on the banks, and as soon as they caught sight of the barge they could surround it by wading into the water.

So this was the huge fuss they made to catch a woman who was a renouncer! Nevertheless, those in charge did not consider such fuss to be unnecessary. For the British knew that renouncer or not, Debi had a thousand soldiers at her disposal, soldiers whom she called her "fighters," and word had spread that on many occasions the Company's sepoys had been put to flight by the blows of these fighters' staves.

Alas, O Staff, your day has gone! No doubt you derive from the lowly bamboo, but in a trained hand what was it you couldn't do! How many swords have you broken in two, how many bucklers and falchions smashed to pieces! Alas! A blow from you made gun and bayonet slip from a fighter's grasp, the fighter running away with a broken hand. Staff! It was you who preserved the honor of our women, our self-respect, our rice-harvest, our wealth and people, our peace of mind. For fear of you the Muslim shrank in terror, the threat of you frightened the bandit, fear of you stopped the indigo-planter in his tracks.

You were the Penal Code of the time, and like the Penal Code you chastised the wicked and restrained even the good—and also like the Penal Code you broke one skull for the offense of another! Yet you had this advantage over the Penal Code: no one could go above you and appeal! Alas, that glory is gone! Now the Penal Code has pushed you out, grabbed your place and taken over the task of ruling society, and you, Staff, you're the Rod no longer—just a piece of bamboo! Now you've become a walking stick and adorn the hands of babus frightened by jackals and dogs. But just let a dog bark and you slip from the hands of those dandies! Your glory-days have gone. They say that in times past you were the most excellent of remedies: the best doctors of troubles of the mind would say: "The Staff is the remedy for fools!" Today's remedy for the fool is to cluck "Son!" "Child!"—and even then the sickness doesn't get better!

The qualities of many of your far-flung ancestors and family shine brightly in this world—from crossbeam to slat, from stake to peg—not to mention the charming flute of Nanda's Son.[1] I value the virtues of them all. But Staff, there's none to compare with you! And now you've left us! I trust it's to the imperishable heavens that you've gone, where you prop up the flower-laden branches of the Amaranth in Indra's pleasure-groves, and where with a blow or two from you divine maidens knock down the fruits of virtue, wealth, love, and salvation from the tree that yields one's every wish. Oh, may but one half of such fruit roll down to earth!

[1]The God Krishna.

❁ *Chapter 2* ❁

But she for fear of whose staves so many sepoys had gathered had not even a single staff with her—nor even a *lathial* by her side. Debi was at the pier, the very pier to which her barge was moored when she had Brajesvar brought there as prisoner. It was just past dusk. The barge looked exactly like before—yet not quite. The longboat was no longer there, nor were the fifty *lathials* who had occupied it. Further, there wasn't a single man on the barge—helmsman, deckhand, Rangaraj, no one. Yet the masts were up and the four sails were raised, though for lack of wind these hung loose about the masts. Nor had the barge's anchor been cast; the barge lay there tied by just two hawsers to posts on the bank.

Lastly, Debi was not dressed in costly clothes or adorned with jewelry as before, yet in another way there was still a splendor about her. Her forehead, cheeks, arms, breast, all her limbs, were smeared with fragrant sandalwood paste, and there was a garland of sweet-smelling flowers encircling that sandal-smeared forehead and augmenting the particular radiance of her head and face. She had circlets of flowers on her arms, otherwise she wore no other ornament, and she was dressed in the same thick sari she had worn before. Nor was Debi sitting alone on the roof of the barge today. Two other women sat beside her; one was Nishi, the other was Diba. There'd be no harm if I took up the threads from the midst of the conversation these three were having.

Diba was saying—the reader must remember that Diba was uneducated—she was saying, "So you think we can see the supreme deity directly?"

"No," said Prafulla, "the deity cannot be seen directly. But I was not talking about *seeing* directly, I was talking about *perceiving* directly. There are six kinds of perception. When you spoke of seeing directly, you were talking of visual perception, 'perceiving' with the eyes. You can hear the sound of my voice—that's aural perception, we're talking here of 'perceiving' with the ears. Can you smell the fragrance of the flowers on my arms?"

"Yes," said Diba.

"That's olfactory perception. If I were to give you a slap on the cheek then you'd 'perceive' my hand; that's tactile perception. And if Nishi were to eat your head right now then she'd have gustatory perception of your brain."

"That wouldn't be a bad perception," answered Diba. "But one can neither see, hear, smell, touch nor eat the supreme deity, so how would one perceive him?"

"Well, that's seen to five kinds of perception," said Nishi. "But we've spoken of six kinds; don't you know there's one other organ of knowledge besides the eyes, ears, nose, taste, and touch?"

"What?" said Diba, "The teeth?"

"Be off, you wretch!" exclaimed Nishi. "I feel like breaking the neat rows of that 'sense' of yours with a good slap!"

Laughing, Debi said, "The eyes etc. are the five organs of knowledge, and the hands, feet and so on are the five organs of action, while the internal sense or *manas* which rules the senses is of both kinds, that is, the *manas* is an organ of knowledge as well as an organ of action. And in so far as the *manas* is an organ of knowledge, the mind also can perceive. This is known as mental perception. God is the object of mental perception."

"Because there is no reliable way of doing so, you cannot prove God's existence," said Nishi quoting in Sanskrit.

Anyone who has studied the *Samkhya-Pravacana-Sutras* and its commentaries will understand the gist of Nishi's cynical remark.[2] In a manner of speaking, she had been a fellow-student with Prafulla.

Prafulla replied, also speaking in Sanskrit: "But the author of the *Sutras* says: Because both kinds of external organs are deficient, God's existence cannot be proved by them—not because there is no reliable way of doing so."

Diba (who did not know Sanskrit) said, "Keep that high-flown nonsense to yourselves! I've never been able to see the supreme deity through my mind!"

"Again talk of 'seeing'?" said Prafulla. "Only visual perception is 'seeing.' Perceiving in any other way is not 'seeing,' and that includes mental perception. The object of visual perception is form—external objects—while the objects of mental perception are internal. God can be perceived directly through the mind, but you can't 'see' God."

"But I've never perceived God in my mind in any way," replied Diba.

"The natural power of humans to perceive is small," Prafulla answered. "Without help or some prop they cannot perceive every perceivable object."

"What kind of help would you need to perceive?" asked Diba. "Look, I can see all this—the river, water, trees, vegetation, stars—without any help."

"Not everything," said Prafulla, smiling. "Shall I give you an example of what I mean?"

When she saw the smile Prafulla gave, Nishi asked, "What is it?"

Prafulla said, "Both of you know the English have sent sepoys to catch me today?"

"Yes, I know," said Diba sighing deeply.

"Well, have you perceived them?"

"No. But I will when they arrive."

"Well, I'm saying they've arrived, but without help we can't perceive them. Here's some help for you." Prafulla handed Diba the spyglass and showed her exactly where to look. When Diba looked, Debi asked her, "What have you seen?"

"A longboat," was the answer. "And yes, I can see many men in it."

"Those are sepoys," said Debi. "Now see another one." In this way, she showed Diba the five longboats, each in a different place. Nishi observed them too. She asked, "I can see the longboats moored to the sandbank, but if they're

[2]See endnotes for an explanation.

here to catch us why don't they come after us instead of being tied to the bank?"

"Perhaps it's because the sepoys who are due to come by land haven't arrived yet," replied Debi. "The sepoys in the longboats are waiting for them. If they were to come on ahead before the land-sepoys, I might escape by land. For fear of this they're hanging back."

"But we can see them," said Diba. "We can escape whenever we want!"

"They don't know that," Debi replied. "They don't know we have a spyglass."

"Sister!" said Nishi. "If we save our lives now you'll be able to see your husband some other time. Let's escape today by land. Since the sepoys who are supposed to come by land haven't arrived, we still have a chance to save ourselves that way."

Debi said, "If I was so anxious about my life why would I come here in the full knowledge of what's happening? And having come here why have I told everyone to go away? I've a thousand fighters. Why have I sent them all to another place?"

"Well, if we'd known earlier," said Diba, "We wouldn't have let you do such a thing."

"Do you think that's in your power, Diba?" asked Debi. "Whatever I've made up my mind to do, I'll do! I'll see my husband today, take his permission and make a wish to be his in my next birth, and then surrender my life in this one! Now listen, Diba and Nishi. When my husband comes, I want you to get on his boat and return with him. I'll be the one who's caught and hung, no one else. That's why I sent everyone else away from the barge, but the two of you refused to go. All I ask is that you get into my husband's boat and escape."

"So long as there's life in my body, I shan't leave you," exclaimed Nishi. "If we're going to die, let's die together."

Prafulla replied, "There's no time for all that now. Let me finish what I was saying. Just as you needed the help of a spyglass to perceive what you couldn't perceive otherwise, I need a spyglass to perceive God mentally."

"What's the spyglass for the mind?" asked Diba puzzled.

"Yoga" was the reply.

"What, all those exercises of focusing, special breathing, the mumbo-jumbo, tricks..."

"That's not yoga," said Prafulla. "Yoga is nothing but practice, but not every practice is yoga. If it's your practice to drink milk and eat *ghee*, that's not yoga.[3] I call three kinds of practice 'yoga.'"

"Which three?"

"Knowledge, action, and devotion," answered Prafulla. "There's the yoga of knowledge, the yoga of action, and the yoga of devotion"—all this while Nishi

[3] *Ghee*: a form of clarified butter.

had been looking around with the spyglass. Finally Nishi said, catching sight of something, "And now we've got the yoga of complication."

"What do you mean?" asked Prafulla. "What's the yoga of complication?"

Nishi replied, "There's a pinnace coming. Probably spying for the English."

Prafulla took the spyglass from Nishi and observed the pinnace. "That's my yoga of opportunity," she said. "That's him coming.[4] You two go down below."

Diba and Nishi descended from the roof and went into the room below. The pinnace came up alongside slowly and bumped against the side of the barge. Brajesvar was inside. He jumped on board the barge and gave orders for the pinnace to be secured separately. The man in charge of the pinnace complied.

When Brajesvar came up, Prafulla rose, bowed her head, and made obeisance by touching his feet. Both then sat down and Brajesvar said, "I haven't been able to bring the money today. Perhaps I'll be able to do so in a few days. I want to know when and where I can meet you then."

For shame, Brajesvar! Is that all you could say to Prafulla after ten whole years?

Debi replied, "You shan't be able to meet me any more. . . ." But even as she spoke her voice choked. Wiping her eyes, she continued, "You won't see me again, but there's another way to clear your debt. When you can, give the money away to the poor and needy. That would be as good as giving it to me."

Brajesvar caught hold of Debi's hand. He said, "Prafulla, your money. . . ."

Useless money! Brajesvar couldn't finish—the words caught in his throat. No sooner did he say "Prafulla" and hold her hand, than Prafulla's dam—pent-up for ten years—burst open and the tears poured out. All talk of Brajesvar's worthless money was swept away in that flood, and Queen Debi—the spirited Queen Debi—wept like a little child. Thus far, Brajesvar had regarded the situation as highly unpleasant. He had thought: this sinful woman survives through banditry: I shan't waste a single tear on her. But tears are not very aware of such restrictions, and so, unbidden, they came and filled Brajesvar's eyes. If I lift my hand and wipe them, she'll know, thought Brajesvar. So he didn't wipe his eyes, and because he didn't the well overflowed and the tears trickled down his cheeks and fell on Prafulla's hand.

Then his own fragile defenses broke down. Brajesvar had come with the intention of rebuking Prafulla heavily for her banditry; he'd call her a sinful woman, berate her some more, and then leave her, never to return. But how can you berate someone when your tears fall and wet their hand?

Wiping his eyes, Brajesvar said, "Look Prafulla, since your money is my money why should I be anxious to repay it? But I've been very anxious about it. For these last ten years all I've thought of is you. Though I have two other

[4]Prafulla's husband, Brajesvar. As a respectful wife, she wouldn't utter his name.

wives, I haven't regarded them as such for these ten years: I know only you as my wife. I doubt if I can explain to you why. I'd heard that you'd died, but you hadn't died to me. In my mind only you remained my wife, no one else could take your place. I won't say I'd actually decided... well, there's no harm in saying it: when I heard that you'd died, I wanted to die too. Now I think perhaps it would have been best if I *had* died, or perhaps it would have been best if you had, but because you didn't, it would have been better if it had been me—then I wouldn't have to hear and know what I've heard and known. I've got you back today—the treasure I'd lost for ten years—and I should be happier than if I had gone to heaven. Instead, now that I've got you, Prafulla, there's only extreme sorrow." Brajesvar paused, swallowed a little, held his head in his hands and continued, "I'd built a golden icon in the temple of my mind. Now that Prafulla of mine—I can hardly say it—that Prafulla does this for a living."

"What?" said Prafulla, "Banditry?"

Brajesvar said, "Well, don't you?"

Prafulla could well have answered in a certain way. She could have said that when Brajesvar's father had driven her out of the house, turning his back on her forever, and Prafulla, grief-stricken, had asked her father-in-law how she, who needed food so desperately, could survive now that they'd got rid of her, her father-in-law had answered that she could do so by robbery or banditry. Prafulla was no fool—she hadn't forgotten his words. Those were not words one could forget. Now when Brajesvar had accused Prafulla of being a bandit, she could have given this reply. She could have said, "Well, yes, I'm a bandit, but why all these accusations? It was you lot who told me to survive by robbery and banditry. I'm just following what my elders told me to do." Just to check this reply would be merit enough, and Prafulla gained this merit. She never uttered the words. Instead, she joined her palms together and said to her husband, "I'm not a bandit. I swear to you, I have never engaged in banditry. Nor have I ever taken the smallest coin by banditry. You are my god. I learnt to pay homage to other gods but I couldn't put that into practice. You have taken the place of every other god to me. You alone are my god. I swear to you, I'm no bandit. But I'm aware people call me one, and I know why. Now you must hear from me why this is so. That's the reason I came here today. If you don't hear it today, you'll never hear it, so listen while I speak."

Then, without dissimulation, Prafulla told Brajesvar her whole story from the day she was turned out of her father-in-law's house to the present. Brajesvar was amazed, ashamed, yet much gladdened, and somewhat humbled to hear it from such a noble wife. When she had finished, Prafulla asked, "Do you believe what you've heard?"

There was no room for disbelief. Every word of Prafulla's had penetrated to Brajesvar's very bones. He was unable to make an answer, but when she saw how overjoyed and radiant he looked, she knew that he believed her. Prafulla continued, "Now give me the dust of your feet and leave me forever. Delay here no longer; there's danger ahead. I've got you after these ten years and here I am begging you to leave me at once! You'll know from this that the danger's considerable. I've two companions on this boat. They're very good girls, and I love them dearly. Take them with you in your boat, and when you get home send them wherever they wish to go. Remember me the way you've kept me in mind, and don't let Sagar forget me too."

Brajesvar thought for a while in silence. Then he said, "Prafulla, I've no idea what's going on. Please explain. You've so many men at your disposal, but there's no one here, not even the barge's deckhands. Just two women, and you want them to leave too. You say there's danger ahead, you don't want me to stay, and then you say we'll never meet again. What's all this about? If you don't tell me what danger we're facing, I won't go, and even if you do tell me I can't say whether I'll stay or go."

"That's not for you to hear," said Prafulla.

"Then do I mean nothing to you?"

Just then they heard a gun go off.

Chapter 3

When they heard the report of the gun, the words died in Brajesvar's mouth, and, startled, both stared straight ahead. They saw five longboats advancing in the distance, the water shimmering in the twilight at the strokes of the paddles. On closer scrutiny they could see that the five longboats were filled with sepoys. The report of the gun was the signal that the land-sepoys had arrived. As soon as they heard it, the five longboats had set off. When she saw this, Prafulla said, "Don't delay a moment longer. Quick, get on your boat and go."

"But why?" asked Brajesvar. "Whose longboats are these—and the gun?"

"You won't go if I don't tell you?"

"Certainly not."

"The Company's sepoys are in those boats, and the Company's sepoys on land fired the gun."

"Why are all these sepoys coming here?" asked Brajesvar, "To catch you?"

Prafulla was silent. Brajesvar continued, "I sense from your words that you knew all along?"

"Yes, I knew," said Prafulla. "My spies are everywhere."

"Did you know after arriving at this pier, or did you know before?"

"I knew before."

"Then if you knew why did you come here?"

"To see you one last time."

"Where are your men?"

"I've sent them away. Why should they die because of me?"

"So you've made up your mind to be caught?"

"Well, what's the point of surviving now?" said Prafulla. "I've seen you, told you everything I wanted to say, and heard that you still love me. I've also distributed all the wealth I had left. If I survive what is there left to do or accomplish? There's no point in carrying on."

"If you survive," answered Brajesvar, "you'll come to my house and make a home with me."

"Do you mean that?" said Prafulla.

"You've given me your word, and now I'm giving you mine. If you save your life today, I'll make you the wife of my house."

"But what will my father-in-law say?" asked Prafulla.

Brajesvar replied, "I'll square things with my father."

"What a pity I didn't hear this yesterday!"

"Why, what would you have done?"

"No one would have been able to catch me today!"

"But now?" asked Brajesvar.

"Now there's no hope. Call your pinnace, take Nishi and Diba with you and go quickly."

Brajesvar summoned the pinnace. When the man in charge had brought it up, Brajesvar said, "Escape quickly, look, there comes the longboat with the Company's sepoys. If they see you they'll force you to work for them without pay, so get away at once. I'm not going, I'll stay here."

Without another word, the man in charge of the pinnace untied it at once and made off. He was not worried about his money, since Brajesvar was known to him.

When she saw the pinnace leaving, Prafulla said, "You didn't go?"

"Why," said Brajesvar, "Do you think only you know how to die, and I don't? In so far as you're my wife, I'm entitled to forsake you a hundred times over. But as your husband, by rights it's I who must protect you in danger. If I can't save you, does that mean I'll desert you in time of danger?"

Prafulla answered, "So I'll admit now that if there's any chance of surviving, I'll be the one to bring it about." She glanced at the horizon as she spoke, and seemed to find some sign of hope there. But immediately she said despondently, "But there's another disadvantage to my remaining alive."

"What?"

"I didn't want to say," said Prafulla, "But I've no option now. My father-in-law's with those sepoys. If I'm not caught, he could be in trouble."

The hairs rose on Brajesvar. He struck his forehead and said, "So *he's* the informer?" Prafulla remained silent. Now Brajesvar understood everything. It was from Brajesvar that Haraballabh had heard that Debi Chaudhurani would be present here this night; Brajesvar had told no one else. Besides, no one else could know Debi's private conversation with him. Further, there could be no doubt that the Company's sepoys had left Rangpur before Debi reached this pier, else they would not have arrived by now. And in the meantime where had Haraballabh gone off without informing anyone, making such a long journey and still away from home? It didn't take Brajesvar long to understand what was going on. So this is why Haraballabh had made no effort to repay the debt. Yet Brajesvar still remembered that *a father is heaven, a father is duty, a father indeed is one's highest concern. All the gods are pleased when a father is satisfied.*

He said to Prafulla, "There'd be no harm if I died. If you died that would be much more serious, but I wouldn't be here to see it. But we must protect my father even before you save yourself or my own worthless life."

"Don't worry about that," said Prafulla. "I shan't escape, so he has nothing to fear, and he can protect you if he wants. But let me say this for your peace of mind—whether you had told me to or not, I'd do nothing to save myself so long as he might be in trouble. Rest assured of that."

Debi said this from the heart. Haraballabh had destroyed Prafulla, and now Haraballabh was bent on destroying Debi; still Debi wished him well. This was because Prafulla was selfless. Whoever follows a code of selfless virtue is not concerned with whose good they seek; it is enough if the good is done.

Just then, from the depths of the woods on the bank, the deep sound of a drum was heard. Both Debi and Brajesvar started in response.

Chapter 4

Debi called out to Nishi who came up on the roof.

"Who beat that drum?" asked Debi.

"Perhaps that religious fellow with the beard," answered Nishi.

"Rangaraj?"

"Sounds like it."

"How can that be?" said Debi. "I sent Rangaraj away at dawn to Debigarh."

"Well, perhaps he's come back."

"Summon Rangaraj," ordered Debi.

Brajesvar said, "The drum sounded from far off. He won't be able to hear us call from here. I'll get down and find the drummer and bring him here."

"No need for that," said Debi. "Just climb down and see how clever Nishi is." Nishi and Braja went down. Nishi went inside and took out a pipe. She was skilled in vocal and instrumental music which she had learnt in the rich man's house. It was Nishi who had taught Debi to play the *vina*. She blew into the pipe, playing a few notes in the musical mode *Mallar*. Before long Rangaraj had climbed onto the barge and greeted Debi with a blessing.

Then Brajesvar said to Nishi, "Go onto the roof. Perhaps they won't keep anything from you. Find out what they're saying and then come and tell me everything." Agreeing, Nishi went out of the room but then returned and asked Brajesvar to come out and take a look. Brajesvar stuck his head out and saw countless men emerging from the depths of the jungle. He asked Nishi, "Who are they—sepoys?"

"Probably our fighters. Rangaraj must have brought them," answered Nishi.

It was while Debi was also observing the lines of men that Rangaraj came up and greeted her with a blessing. "Rangaraj, why are you here?" asked Debi.

At first, Rangaraj made no reply. Debi said to him again, "I had sent you to Debigarh this morning. Why didn't you go? Why have you disregarded what I said?"

Rangaraj replied, "I was going to Debigarh but I met Thakur-ji on the way."

"Bhabani Thakur?"

"He told me that the Company's sepoys were coming to arrest you, so we've gathered the fighters and come. I hid the fighters in the jungle and waited on the bank. When I saw the longboats coming I sounded the drum as a signal."

"Are there sepoys in the jungle as well?"

"We've got them surrounded."

"And where is Thakur-ji?"

"He's leading the fighters out."

"How many fighters have you two brought?"

"There'll be about a thousand."

"And how many sepoys are there?"

"Five hundred, I hear."

"When these fifteen hundred men fight, how many will die?"

"Well, about two to four hundred might die."

"Go and tell Thakur-ji that what both of you have done today has upset me terribly," exclaimed Debi.

"But why?"

"Because you two have been prepared to kill so many men for the sake of one woman's life. Do neither of you have any idea as to what is right? My days are coming to an end, so only I must die; why should four hundred men die on my account? Do both of you have such a low opinion of me that you think I'm prepared to destroy the lives of so many men to save my own?"

"But if you live the lives of many will be saved," expostulated Rangaraj.

"For shame!" cried Debi, overwhelmed with anger and disgust. Rangaraj hung his head at the rebuke, wishing the earth would part and swallow him up.

Debi continued, eyes wide open and lips quivering with uncontrolled disgust, "Listen, Rangaraj! Go and tell Thakur-ji to take all the fighters away this instant! If he delays for even a moment, I'll jump into this water and die and none of you will be able to save me!"

Rangaraj seemed to shrink visibly. He said, "I'm going; I'll tell all this to Thakur-ji. He'll do what he thinks is best. As for me, I obey both of you." With that he left.

Nishi, who was standing on the roof, had heard everything. As soon as Rangaraj had gone, she said to Debi, "Fine, you can do what you like with your life, and no one has the right to stop you. But your husband is with you today. Haven't you thought of him too?"

"I have, sister!" replied Debi. "And there's nothing I can do. The Lord of the world alone is our hope, and whatever will be will be. But whatever may happen, Nishi, the point is that I have no right to destroy the lives of so many men to save my husband's. My husband may be very dear to me, but who is he to them?"

Nishi blessed Debi in her mind, thinking, "She really has imbibed this selfless code of practice. It would be a joy even to die with her." She went and told Brajesvar everything. No longer could Brajesvar think of Prafulla as a wife. "Truly, she's a real Goddess," he thought. "And I'm the lowest of the low. And here was I ready to rebuke her as a bandit!"

Meanwhile, the five longboats had come up close to the barge and surrounded it, but Prafulla didn't even glance in their direction. She remained sitting motionless as a stone statue upon the roof. In fact, Prafulla was looking neither at the longboats nor at her fighters; she was gazing at the horizon. There in the distance was a small cloud which had been visible for a long time. While she stared at it, it occurred to Prafulla that it had grown bigger. Then saying, "Conquer, O Lord of the world!" she went down from the roof.

When she saw Prafulla coming inside, Nishi asked, "What will you do now?"

"I'll save my husband," Prafulla replied.

"What about you?"

"Don't ask about me now," answered Debi. "Just pay close attention to what I say and do. Whatever may be in store for you and me, our task is to save my husband, Diba, and my father-in-law." She picked up a conch-shell and blew into it. "Very well," said Nishi.

"Well or bad, you be the judge," said Debi. "I'll tell you what to do. Everything depends on you now."

Chapter 5

Like columns of ants, the army of fighters began to emerge from the forests on the banks of the Teesta, with red turbans, loincloths tucked in at the waist, and bare feet. No one brought shoes, since they'd have to fight in the water. Everyone carried bucklers and spears; some had guns, but their numbers were small. Each had a staff tied to his back—the weapon typical of Bengal. The Bengali once knew its proper use; it was when he abandoned the staff that he lost his spirit.

When the fighters saw that the longboats had come up and were about to surround the barge, they ran forward shouting "Victory to our Queen!" so as to encircle it first. After they had surrounded the barge, the longboats took up positions around them, and just when the conch sounded some of the fighters mounted the barge. These were the barge's helmsman and deckhands; they worked on the boat and used staves and spears only when the need arose. But for the time being they showed no inclination to engage in battle. Each sat in his place by oar or helm, or grasped the rope of a sail, or a pole to push off with. Many more fighters climbed on to the barge, while three to four hundred remained on the banks and began to throw their spears from there at the longboats. Some of the sepoys got down from their longboats, fixed bayonets to their guns, and attacked the fighters on the banks. The remaining sepoys fell upon the fighters who had surrounded the barge.[5] Hand-to-hand fighting broke out everywhere. There was a tremendous uproar with the fighting and the killing and shouting, the roar of guns and the clashing of staves; none could hear what anyone else was saying, or was able to stay in one place for long.

The *lathial*s who fought from a distance had no prospect of surviving for long against the sepoys, since staves cannot be used from afar, while for their part the sepoys who remained in the longboats were at a disadvantage. The sepoys who climbed the banks and fought started to repel the *lathial*s with the points of their bayonets, but those who fought in the water began to suffer broken hands and legs and heads from the staves and spears of the fighters.

All this started shortly after Prafulla had descended from the roof of the barge. She thought that word of what she wanted either had not reached Bhabani Thakur, or that he had refused to follow it; he couldn't believe she would kill herself. Very well, now he'd see how she would respond!

Debi had developed a number of remarkable qualities in her role as Queen; one of these was that she'd keep handy any item that might be needed later on. We've had plenty of evidence of this quality. So now a white banner was found. Debi emerged with it and held it up in her hand.

No sooner did she display it than everybody stopped fighting. Everyone remained standing silently just where he was, grasping his weapon. It was as if a tempest had suddenly subsided or a turbulent sea had in an instant been transformed into a tranquil lake.

Debi saw Brajesvar standing nearby, for when he saw her going out during the battle he had followed her. "Hold the banner up like this," she instructed, "I'm going inside to confer with Nishi and Diba. If Rangaraj comes, tell him to take my orders from the door."

She gave him the banner and left, and Brajesvar stood there with the banner held high. Meanwhile, Rangaraj came up; when he saw the white banner in Brajesvar's hand, he glared at Brajesvar and said, "By whose order do you show this white flag?"

"By order of the Queen."

"The Queen? And who are you?"

"Can't you recognize me?"

Rangaraj peered at him and said, "Now I do. Aren't you Brajesvar-babu? What do you think you're doing here? Both father and son up to the same thing, no doubt! Someone tie him up!"

---

[5]The reader will recall that the water was low at this point in the river.

Rangaraj thought that Brajesvar, like his father, wanted Debi to be captured and had entered the barge on some pretext. At his command, two men came forward to tie Brajesvar up. Brajesvar made no objection, but said, "Bind me if you wish, no harm in that, but tell me first why both sides stopped fighting when they saw the white banner?"

"What are you, a little boy?" sneered Rangaraj. "Don't you know the English have to stop fighting when you show the white flag?"

"No, I didn't know," answered Brajesvar. "But regardless of whether I knew or not, why don't you go and find out if I've shown the white flag at the Queen's command? And there's an order for you too—to take the Queen's commands from the door." Rangaraj went straight to the room of the barge, and seeing the door closed, called out, "Your Majesty!"

From inside came the reply, "Who's that? Rangaraj?"

"By your leave, it is," said Rangaraj. "A white flag has been shown from our barge and the fighting has stopped."

"It's what I ordered," said Debi. "Now take that white flag, go to the English Lieutenant in charge and tell him there's no need to fight, I'm surrendering."

"Never, whilst I'm alive!" cried Rangaraj.

"You can't save me, even if you die."

"Still, I'll give up my life!"

"Listen, don't act like a fool," said Debi. "None of you can save me by sacrificing your lives. What good can staves and cudgels do in the face of the sepoys' guns?"

"We can still succeed!"

"Perhaps you can, but I'll die before one more drop of blood is shed—I'll go and stand in front of the guns: you'll not be able to save me then. Rather, if I give myself up now, there's hope of escape later. Save your own lives now and try when you can to set me free. I've plenty of money and all the Company's people are slaves to wealth, so don't worry about my getting away."

But not for an instant did Debi envisage escaping through bribes, nor did she wish to escape that way. This was just to deceive Rangaraj, and because he was incapable of grasping the subtle plot she had devised, she didn't explain it to him. She had decided to give herself up without prevarication. She knew that the English would squander their chances. She had decided not to harm them; rather she'd provoke them into action so that she could do what was necessary to rescue her husband, her father-in-law, and two companions. She could see everything that would happen as if in a mirror.

Rangaraj said, "But the stuff you need to control the Company's people with lies in this barge! If you surrender, the English will take the barge too!"

"You must stop that happening," answered Debi. "Tell them I'll give myself up but not the barge. I'll give up nothing that's in the barge. Nor can the Lieutenant arrest anyone else in the barge. On that condition, I agree to surrender."

"But if the English refuse, and seek to plunder the barge?" persisted Rangaraj.

"Stop them from coming to the barge, from even touching it," said Debi. "Say that in that case there'll be danger for the English. If they enter the barge, I won't surrender. The moment the Englishman enters the barge, our battle will start again. If he agrees to my terms, none of them need come here. I'll get into his longboat myself."

Rangaraj realized that a subtle plan lay behind all this, so he agreed to act as messenger. Then Debi asked, "Where's Bhabani Thakur?"

"He was on the bank, fighting in command of his men. He refused to listen to me. He's probably there right now."

"Then go to him first. He's to take our fighters back along the banks and instruct them to return to their homes. Tell him that if he leaves my boatmen behind that will be enough. And tell him there's no need to do battle to save me—the Lord has found a way to do that. If he objects, ask him to look up at the sky—he'll understand."

Rangaraj himself looked at the sky and saw that it had grown dark with a garland of fresh Baisakhi rain-clouds.[6] He said with familiar respect to Debi, "I ask you to issue one more command. Haraballabh Ray was the informer today. I've seen his son Brajesvar on the boat. He's up to no good, I'm sure of it. I want to have him tied up."

When they heard this, Nishi and Diba broke into peals of laughter. Debi said, "No, don't tie him up. Tell him to go up secretly on the roof and to remain sitting there. Later, when Diba tells him to do so, he must come down."

So, as instructed, Rangaraj got Brajesvar to sit on the roof, and then went off to Bhabani Thakur and told him what Debi had said to tell him. Rangaraj pointed to the clouds. When Bhabani looked at them, he made no further objection but gathered all the fighters from the banks and the water and encouraged them to return to their homes, along the banks of the Teesta.

Meanwhile, Diba and Nishi took the opportunity to come out and whisper something to the oarsmen disguised as fighters.

Chapter 6

For his part, after he had taken leave of Bhabani Thakur, Rangaraj carried the white banner in his hand, entered the water and made his way to Lieutenant Brenan's longboat. Seeing the white banner, nobody stopped him. When he had climbed into the longboat, the Englishman asked him, "You've shown the white flag. Will you surrender?"

"Do you really think we'll surrender!" answered Rangaraj, "I've come here to tell you that only the woman you're here to capture will give herself up."

[6]Baisakhi: pertaining to Baisakh, the first month of the Bengali calendar (mid-April to mid-May), when the first rains come prior to the monsoon in June.

"Debi Chaudhurani will surrender?"

"She will. She's sent me to tell you that."

"What about the rest of you?"

"Whom do you mean?"

"Debi Chaudhurani's gang."

"We won't surrender."

"But I'm here to capture the whole gang!"

"And who might they be?' answered Rangaraj. "How can you tell among these thousand fighters who belongs to the gang and who doesn't?"

Bhabani Thakur still hadn't left with his army of fighters during this conversation; he was preparing to do so. The Englishman said, "All of these thousand fighters are bandits! They must be bandits to be fighting against the government."

"But they won't fight," replied Rangaraj, "Look, they're going away."

The Englishman saw that the army of fighters was preparing to escape. "What's this?" he cried in rage, "You're escaping under the pretext of the white flag?"

"Sir," said Rangaraj, "So long as I've held the flag, none of us have escaped. Even now no one's getting away. Capture them if you can; I'll get rid of the white flag." So saying he threw the white flag away, but without an order from their commander none of the sepoys moved.

The Englishman realized that it would be a waste of time to go after them. If he followed them, they'd enter the dense jungle. To begin with, it was night, and the skies were overcast; there was no doubt that the jungle would be steeped in darkness, and his sepoys didn't know the way whereas the fighters did. There was no chance of his sepoys catching the fighters. So he abandoned this idea and said, "Very well, I've no need of them. Let's come back to what we were saying. Will all of you here give yourselves up?"

"Except for Queen Debi, not a single one of us will surrender," replied Rangaraj.

"Pish!" said the Englishman with contempt, "Who's here to resist? Will the few of you be able to carry on fighting against five hundred sepoys? I notice that your army of fighters has disappeared into the jungle!"

Rangaraj saw that in fact Bhabani Thakur's army had entered the jungle. He replied, "I know nothing about that. I'm telling you what our mistress told me to say. You're not to have the barge, or its wealth, or any of us. All you'll get is Queen Debi."

"And why is that?"

"That I don't know," said Rangaraj.

"Well, whether you know or not," replied the Englishman, "The barge is now mine, and I'm taking possession of it."

"Sir," warned Rangaraj, "Do not board the barge or touch it. You'll be in danger."

"Pooh!" was the reply. "Danger from a few of you when I've got five hundred sepoys!"

With that he disposed of the white banner and ordered his sepoys to surround the barge. The sepoys and the five longboats surrounded the barge. Then the Englishman ordered, "Board the barge and seize all the fighters' weapons!" This was said in a loud voice which reached Debi's ears. She too commanded in a loud voice: "All those on the barge with weapons in their hands—throw them into the water!" As soon as they heard this, all those on the barge with weapons in hand threw them into the water. Rangaraj also flung all his weapons into the water. When he saw this, the Englishman was satisfied, and said, "Now let's board the barge and see what's there!"

"Sir," said Rangaraj, "You're boarding the barge by force. I'm not to blame."

"How can any blame attach to you?" was the reply.

With this the Englishman took a single sepoy with him and, armed, boarded the barge. There was nothing particularly brave about this since everyone on board had disposed of their weapons. What the Englishman didn't realize was that Debi's sure mind was itself a sharp and powerful weapon; she had need of no other.

As soon as the Englishman and Rangaraj came up to the door of the barge, it was thrown open, and they went inside. They were amazed at what they saw when they entered. The room was decorated in the same charming fashion as on the day Brajesvar had first entered as prisoner: the same delightful pictures on the walls, the beautiful carpet laid out as before, the same attar-pot and rose-water spray, the same gold flower-dish full of blossoms as before, and the gold hubble-bubble dressed with its fragrant musky tobacco. The silver statues and chandeliers were still there as was the gold lamp hanging from its gold chain. But today instead of one throne there were two, each with a beautiful woman upon it supported by pillows overlaid with gold. They were dressed in rich clothing, every limb adorned with expensive jewelry. The Englishman did not know them, but Rangaraj did; he recognized one as Nishi and the other as Diba.

The Englishman sat down on a silver chair that had been placed there for him. Rangaraj began to look for Debi; where could she be? Then he saw her standing in a corner of the room, dressed simply in her thick cloth, with only an iron bracelet on her wrist, her hair undressed, and lacking all finery.

The Englishman asked, "Who is Debi Chaudhurani? With whom should I speak?"

"I'm Debi, speak to me," answered Nishi.

Diba laughed at this and said to Nishi, "Up to tricks when you see an Englishman? Is this the time for tricks? Lieutenant Sir, my sister inclines to fun and games, but this isn't the time for it. Please speak with me. I'm Debi Chaudhurani."

"To hell with you!" said Nishi. "So you want to hang in my place, do you?" Turning to the Englishman, she continued, "Sir, it seems this sister of mine is deceiving you, because out of fondness for me she wants to save my life! But how could I save myself by telling lies and handing her over to death? Life's such a trivial thing. We Bengali girls can give it up without any difficulty. Come on, I'm ready to accompany you wherever you want. *I'm* Queen Debi."

But Diba cried, "Sir, the curse of Jesus Christ on you if you arrest an innocent woman! It's me who's Debi."

Angered, the Englishman turned to Rangaraj and said, "What's all this about? Tell me which is the real Debi Chaudhurani."

Rangaraj was at a loss, but he realized that some stratagem was afoot, so recovering his wits he pointed to Nishi and with palms joined said, "Sir! Th. . . . is is the real Queen Debi."

Then Debi herself spoke for the first time. "It's very wrong of me to interrupt here," she said, "But I speak because for all I know everybody may die if you discover later that they've been lying. What this person says is not true." Then she pointed to Nishi and continued, "She's not Debi. It's because the one who's identified her as Debi reveres his Queen and is devoted to her as a mother that he's pointed to another to save his Queen."

"Then who's Debi?" asked the Englishman.

"I'm Debi," said Debi.*

As soon as Debi said this there was mayhem between Nishi, Diba, Rangaraj, and Debi. "I'm Debi," cried Nishi; "No, I'm Debi," said Diba; "She's Debi," cried Rangaraj pointing to Nishi; "But I'm Debi," said Debi herself. Complete confusion!

Realizing that he had to get to the bottom of this tomfoolery, the English Lieutenant addressed Nishi and Diba, "One of you two is Debi Chaudhurani for sure—*she's* just a servant, she's not Debi. Which of you two is that evil woman, you're hiding from me by trickery. But you won't succeed. I'm going to arrest both of you, and whoever can be proved to be Debi Chaudhurani beyond doubt, will be the one to hang. And if this can't be cleared up by proof, then you'll both hang."

Nishi and Diba replied, "But why all this confusion? Don't you have an informer with you? If he's around, just call him. He'll be able to say who the real Debi Chaudhurani is."

Debi's main objective was to bring Haraballabh to the barge, for she had resolved to take no steps to save herself without making provision to save him. And the only way to ensure Haraballabh's safety was to bring him to the barge.

Thinking that he had been given good advice, the Englishman ordered the sepoy who had accompanied him to summon the informer. The sepoy called for a *jamadar*[7] from one of the longboats and ordered him to call the informer. Fresh confusion ensued, for no one knew where the informer was or who he might be, while the summons rang out in all directions.

[7]An officer holding the lowest commissioned rank in the Company army.

Chapter 7

Mr Haraballabh Ray in fact was right there on the battlefield, but through force of circumstance—not because he wished to be there. At first he had kept his distance. With Canakya's sound advice in mind not to trust "horned beasts, people with weapons in their hands" etc., he hadn't got into any of the sepoys' longboats. He had stayed apart in a dinghy,[8] pointed the barge out to the English Lieutenant, and fleeing about a mile away, preserved both life and dinghy. Then noticing how overcast the sky was, he thought there'd be a storm and that his boat would sink at once, and that he'd lose his life for having come there out of greed for money—why, he wouldn't even have the proper funeral rites! So Mr Ray disembarked onto the bank. But when he saw no one about, he was gripped with fear—fear of snakes, of tigers, of robbers and bandits, even of ghosts. "Oh, why ever did I get into such a mess!" he thought. Haraballabh wanted to cry.

Just then the reports of the guns and the clamor of the sepoys and fighters came to a sudden stop. Haraballabh was sure that the sepoys had won and that that wretch of a bandit-woman had been apprehended, else why had the fighting come to an end? Gaining in confidence he began to move in the direction of the battlefield. But how could he move forward when it was nearly nightfall—in the dark, in these woods and jungles?

He said to the dinghy's oarsman, "Listen old chap, can you tell me how to get over there?"

"What's the worry?" said the oarsman, "Get into the boat, and I'll take you. Are you sure the sepoys won't kill or capture us? Suppose the fighting starts again?"

"The sepoys will leave us alone," answered Haraballabh. "And the fighting won't start again. All the bandits have been captured. But from the clouds you can see there's a storm brewing. Will it be safe to get into the boat?"

"No chance of a dinghy sinking in the storm," said the oarsman.

Haraballabh was loath to believe this, but in the end he had no choice but to get into the boat. He instructed the oarsman to go along the bank, and the oarsman complied. The dinghy quickly came up against the barge. Since Haraballabh knew the sepoys' password, none of them objected. Just then the shouting to summon the informer was heard. Haraballabh mounted the barge and said to the orderly who stood facing him, "You're looking for the informer? Here I am."

The orderly said, "The Lieutenant in charge has summoned you."

"Where is he?"

"In the room. Go inside."

When she learnt that Haraballabh was on his way, Debi started making preparations for departure. "Let me see to some refreshments for the Lieutenant,"

[8] A small boat propelled by oars.

she said and went into an inner apartment. Meanwhile Haraballabh approached the *durbar* room. Standing at the door he was astonished when he saw its trappings and opulence, and the beauty and attire of Diba and Nishi. In his confusion, instead of making a salaam to the Englishman, he salaamed Nishi instead. Nishi laughed and replied, "My humble salutations to you, Khan Sir. I trust you're in good spirits?"

"Humble salutations, Khan Sir!" exclaimed Diba, "And no greeting for me! I'm their Queen!"

The English Lieutenant said to Haraballabh, "These two are up to tricks, each one saying she's Debi Chaudhurani. Because I don't know which one is Debi Chaudhurani, I've summoned you. Who's Debi?"

Haraballabh was in a quandary. Neither he nor fourteen generations of ancestors had ever met Debi, so what could he do? Casting about, he pointed at Nishi. She broke into a peal of laughter. Disconcerted, and saying, "I've made a mistake," Haraballabh now pointed to Diba. Diba burst into a roar of laughter. With sinking heart, Haraballabh pointed at Nishi again. Infuriated, the Englishman said to Haraballabh (in the most appalling Hindusthani), "You vile fellow! Swine! Can't you recognize her?"

Diba intervened, "Sir, don't lose your temper, he can't tell. But his son can. His son's sitting on the roof of the barge. Fetch him, and he'll tell you."

Haraballabh came crashing to earth. "My son!" he exclaimed.

"So I've heard," said Diba.

"Brajesvar?"

"The very same."

"Where?"

"Up on the roof."

"Braja here? Why?"

"He can tell you himself."

The Englishman ordered, "Bring him here." Diba motioned to Rangaraj. Rangaraj went up on the roof and said to Brajesvar, "Mistress Diba orders you to come down."

Brajesvar descended and entered the room, for as Debi had given instructions earlier, he was to come down when Diba gave the order. It was Debi who had made this arrangement.

The Englishman asked Brajesvar, "Would you recognize Debi Chaudhurani?"

"I would," was the reply.

"Is Debi here?"

"No."

Blind with rage the Englishman shouted, "What! Neither of these is Debi Chaudhurani?"

"These are her maids," answered Brajesvar.

"Eh? But you'd recognize Debi?"

"Very well indeed."

"Well, if neither of these is Debi," said the Englishman, "Debi is certainly hiding somewhere on the barge. Perhaps she was that servant-girl. I'm going to search the barge, and you're going to identify her. Come on."

"Mister" said Brajesvar, "If you wish to search your barge, you can do so, but why should I identify anyone here?"

Amazed, the Englishman roared, "Why? You low fellow! Aren't you an informer too?"

"I'm not," answered Brajesvar, and he dealt the Englishman an almighty slap on the cheek.

"Oh, what have you done, what have you done? You've finished us!" wailed Haraballabh.

"Sir! A storm's up," cried the *jamadar* from outside. They could hear the wind coming from the horizon, howling and hissing with tremendous force. Just then—at the very moment that Brajesvar struck the Englishman on the cheek—they heard the conch-shell again from inside: two blasts this time!

The barge's anchor had not been cast. I said earlier that hawsers had been tied to bamboo posts. Two deckhands were sitting near the posts. As soon as the conch sounded they loosed the hawsers and jumped on to the barge. The sepoys who had encircled the barge on the bank raised their bayonets to kill them, but their guns remained stuck to their hands, for in the blink of an eye something extraordinary happened, and by a stratagem of Debi's, in an instant those five hundred Company sepoys were vanquished!

I noted earlier that from the very beginning the barge's four sails had been unfurled, and I also mentioned that in the meantime Nishi and Diba had approached the deckhands and given them some instructions. It was in accordance with those instructions that the men had been sitting by the posts and that four deckhands had been waiting by the ropes attached to the sails. As soon as they heard the conch they gripped the ropes while the helmsman engaged the wheel. Just then that huge driving gale filled the sails. The barge wheeled round, and the two sepoys who had raised their bayonets found no time to lower them—the prow of the barge had already moved about seventy-five feet away. The barge swung round, and with its sails billowing in the force of the storm, listed to the point of capsizing.

Though it's taken so long to write about them, these events occurred in the space of an instant. The Englishman had just raised his fist to return Brajesvar's slap when all this happened. The fist remained suspended, and just when the barge listed, the Englishman tipped over and with hand still clenched fell sprawling at the lovely Diba's feet while Brajesvar toppled on to his neck and Rangaraj collapsed upon Brajesvar. At first Haraballabh fell against the back of Mistress Nishi's neck; when she pushed him away he went rolling and was stopped by Rangaraj's pointed shoes. "The ship's sinking," he thought, "And we're all going to die. What's the point in invoking the Goddess now?"

But the ship didn't sink. It righted itself and sped like lightning with the wind at its stern. Those who had fallen stood up again, and the Englishman once more raised his fist. Meanwhile the ship bore down on the Englishman's forces, that is, on those who had been standing in the water. Many ducked underwater and saved their lives; some seeing the barge swing round from a distance, moved away quickly and escaped, while others were injured. But no one died. The longboats were run over by the barge and sank, but because the water there was not very deep and the current was weak, everyone survived.

However, no one got to see the barge any more. Flying like a shooting-star it disappeared into the storm and no one caught sight of it again. The sepoy army had been completely routed, vanquished by Debi. She sped away, full sail, with the Englishman and Haraballabh as her captives. In an instant the battle had been won. So Debi could point to the heavens and say, "It's the Lord who's finding a way to save me."

Chapter 8

Breaking through the waves and rocking from side to side, the barge sped away as swiftly as a shooting star. The noise was terrific—the roar of the waves as the prow cut through them and the clamor of the storm! But the barge had been incomparably well built and the skill and expertise of the sailors were well-known. Opening its four sails in the direction of the storm, the barge made unhindered progress. As for its passengers, after first rolling about like pumpkins, everyone stood up in his or her own place. Mr Haraballabh Ray twisted his sacred thread around his thumb and began to mutter Durga's name again and again lest they sink, and just as the English Lieutenant raised his hand once more in an effort to deliver that postponed punch Brajesvar grasped it firmly. "What are you doing?" Haraballabh cried to his son in rebuke. "Raising your hand to an Englishman!"

"Was it I who raised my hand to him, or did *he* raise his hand to me first?" asked Brajesvar.

"Master," said Haraballabh to the Englishman, "He's just a boy, he still hasn't learnt to think straight. Please don't be offended. Forgive him."

"He's a big scoundrel!" retorted the Englishman, "But if he joins his palms together and begs for forgiveness, I might forgive him."

"Braja, do it," said his father. "Join your palms together and ask the gentleman to forgive you."

Brajesvar said, "Sir, we're Hindus and we never disobey a father's command. So I join my palms together and beg you for forgiveness."

When the Englishman saw Brajesvar's devotion to his father, he was pleased and forgave him, and grasping his hand, shook it warmly. Brajesvar, who had not the least idea what shaking hands meant, was a little taken aback. "Perhaps he wants to start fighting again," he thought, so he went outside and sat down. Though the storm raged on, it wasn't raining much, so he didn't get drenched.

Rangaraj came out too, and shutting the door of the room, sat with his back against the door, thus guarding both the way in and the way out. It was best to be specially vigilant at this time outside since the barge was traveling at great speed and it was quite possible that some sudden danger might arise.

Since there was no longer any need to remain where the men were, Diba got up and went to Debi. Nishi stayed where she was; she had a plan in mind. As she had offered everything to Sri Krishna, she had unbounded courage.

The Englishman went and planted himself on the silver chair again and began to wonder how he might escape from the bandits' hands. "I've been captured by the very person I came to arrest," he thought. "And women have got the better of me. How can I show my face among my own people now? Best if I stay here!"

Because he had no place to sit down, Haraballabh went and sat near the beautiful Nishi's throne.

Seeing him there, Nishi said, "Why don't you get some rest?"

"How can I rest today?" said Haraballabh.

"If you don't rest today you won't get another chance."

"What do you mean?"

"Well, when will you get the chance to rest again?"

"Why not?"

"Didn't you come here to see Debi captured?"

"Well, er... you know......"

"Do you know what would have happened if Debi was captured?"

"Well, er...."

"Well, er, nothing! She'd be hanged!"

"Well, you know.... I mean...."

"Debi did you no harm," went on Nishi. "On the contrary, she did you a very good turn. When you were about to lose caste and your life, she gave you fifty thousand rupees in cash and saved you. And in return you tried to get her hanged! What punishment do you think you deserve?"

Haraballabh said nothing.

Nishi continued, "That's why I said, rest now. You'll not see the night through. Do you know where we're going?"

Haraballabh didn't have the strength to speak.

"There's a huge cremation ground called *Dakinir Smasan,*" said Nishi. "When we want to finish someone off, we take them there and kill them. That's where the barge is going. The Queen's given orders that as soon as we get there the Englishman will hang. Do you know what she's ordered for you?"

Haraballabh began to cry. He joined his palms together and begged, "Save me!"

Nishi continued, "Do you think anyone's such a base scoundrel as to want to save you? She's given orders that you be impaled on a stake!"

Haraballabh began to wail. The storm was raging outside, so Brajesvar didn't hear him bawl. Nor did Debi. But the Englishman heard (he hadn't heard the conversation, but he heard Haraballabh crying). "Stop blubbering, you fool!" he said angrily in bad Hindusthani, "We've all got to die some day!"

The old Brahmin shut his ears to this and joining his palms together to Nishi began to cry again. "Oh, please" he sobbed, "Can no one save me?"

"Who'll incur the sin of saving a lowlife like you?" said Nishi again. "We have a merciful Queen, but none of us will plead with her to show you mercy."

"I'll give you a lakh of rupees."[9]

"Don't you feel ashamed to speak like that?" replied Nishi. "For the sake of fifty thousand rupees you've behaved like an ingrate, and now you rant about a lakh?"

"Then I'll do whatever you want me to," wailed Haraballabh.

"Could someone like you ever carry out what I ask?"

"Even an insignificant person can do a good turn. Please tell me what you want and I'll do it with all my heart, just save me."

"Well," said Nishi pretending to think, "Even you could do me a favor, I suppose, but perhaps it's best if it didn't get done by someone like you."

"I beg you with palms joined," cried Haraballabh, "Look, I'll hold your hand and…" Beside himself, Haraballabh almost grabbed hold of Nishi's shapely, braceleted hand, but the adroit Nishi removed it in time. "Watch it!" she said, "That hand's been taken by Sri Krishna. But I don't need you to hold my hands or feet. Since you're so miserable, I'm prepared to do what's necessary to save you. But I can hardly believe you'll do what I say. You're a cheat, an ungrateful scoundrel, telling and informing on others—who can trust you?"

"I'll swear on whatever you want me to."

"An oath from you! What will you swear on?"

"Give me Ganges water, copper, and *tulsi* leaves—I'll touch them and swear."[10]

"Will you put your hand on Brajesvar's head and swear?"

Haraballabh started shouting. "Do what you want then!" he cried, "That I can't do!"

But this show of spirit was momentary. Haraballabh immediately began to wring his hands; he said, "I'll make any other oath you want, just save me."

"All right," said Nishi, "You don't have to take an oath. After all, you're our prisoner. Now listen, I come from a very strict *kulin* family, and we're under pressure to find suitable husbands. One's been found for me—(all lies, as the reader knows)—but not for my younger sister. She's still unmarried."

"How old is she?" asked Haraballabh.

"She'll be twenty five, thirty."

"There are many *kulin* girls like her."

---

[9]A lakh is a hundred thousand—a huge sum in those days.

[10]See endnotes.

"There are, but if she doesn't get married soon she'll have to marry beneath her station. And that prospect looms. You have the same caste status as my father. If you marry my sister, my father's family honor will be saved. I'll inform our Queen about it, plead with her on your behalf and win back your life."

A mountain had fallen off Haraballabh's head! So what was another marriage? That wasn't a problem for a *kulin*, however old the girl might be. Haraballabh gave the very answer Nishi was hoping for. He replied, "This isn't a big matter. After all, it's a *kulin*'s job to safeguard the family honor of *kulins*. But I've grown too old to marry again. Will it be all right if my son does the marrying?"

"Will he agree?" asked Nishi.

"If I tell him to, he'll agree."

"Then before you leave early tomorrow morning, please tell him to do so. After that, I'll call for a palanquin and bearers and send you back home. You can go on ahead and prepare for the *boubhat*.[11] We'll get the boy married and send him back with the bride."

Haraballabh was in seventh heaven! Where was being impaled on a stake and where the pomp and circumstance of a *boubhat!* Haraballabh said at once, "Then please go and inform the Queen about this."

"Right away," said Nishi and went into the inner room. After she had gone, the Englishman asked Haraballabh, "What was that woman saying?"

"Nothing much."

"Then why were you blubbering?"

"Blubbering? I wasn't blubbering."

"It's true. Bengalis are such liars."

When Nishi came in, Debi said to her, "What were you talking about with my father-in-law for so long?"

"I wanted to see if I could play your mother-in-law's role with him!" answered Nishi.

"Mistress Nishi!" exclaimed Debi, "I see you've offered your mind, your heart, your life and youth, everything, to Sri Krishna—except for the small matter of your deceit! That you've kept for your own use."

"Well, you must give only the good things to God—not the bad."

"You'll end up rotting in hell!"

Chapter 9

The storm stopped, and so did the boat. Debi could see from the barge's window that dawn was breaking. She called out, "Nishi! It's a fine morning."

"So I'll bring good luck today?" answered Nishi.

[11] Same as *paksparsa* (see Part I, ch.2): the ceremony during which the new wife feeds her husband's relatives for the first time. This signifies that she has come to the husband's home to stay.

"You'll be the end of us," said Diba, "I'll bring the good luck."

"The day I'm finished," was Nishi's response, "I'll say good luck! But there's no end to this darkness. Still, I see there'll be good luck for Debi today, for this is the day Debi Chaudhurani comes to an end."[12]

"What are you saying, horrorface!" said Diba.

"The right thing. Debi has died; Prafulla will go to her father-in-law's house."

Now Debi spoke. "There's time enough for that," she said. "First let's see if you can do what I say. Let's see if you can tell them to moor the barge."

Nishi gave the order and the boatmen moored the barge to the bank.

Then Debi said, "Ask Rangaraj where we've come. How far is Rangpur, and how far Bhutnath?"

Rangaraj gave the answer that in one night they had traveled four days' distance. Rangpur was many days' journey from where they were, but by land Bhutnath could be reached in a day. When asked if a palanquin and its porters could be procured, he replied that if he tried they could get everything they needed.

Debi said to Nishi, "Then see to it that my father-in-law is allowed to take his ritual bath in the river."

"Why the hurry?" asked Diba.

It was Nishi who answered. "Remember, her father-in-law's son's spent the whole night sitting outside. Don't you see the boy's unable to cross the sea and reach Lanka?"[13]

Nishi then summoned Rangaraj and said in Haraballabh's presence, "The Englishman will have to hang, but there's no need now to skewer the Brahmin. Send him under guard to take his ritual bath."

When Haraballabh asked if any instruction had been given concerning him, Nishi winked and said, "My request's been granted. Perform your ritual bath and come back here." Then she whispered in Rangaraj's ear, "By guards I mean men who belong to the right caste so that they don't obstruct the ritual." Rangaraj made the necessary arrangements and sent Haraballabh to perform his ritual bath.

Debi said to Nishi, "Order them to release the Englishman, and tell him to return to Rangpur. Since Rangpur is so far away give him a hundred *mohurs* for his journey's expenses, otherwise how will he travel so far?"

Nishi took a hundred gold coins and gave them to Rangaraj, telling him what to do in a low voice, but she added something to the instructions Debi had given. Then accompanied by two fighters Rangaraj went and apprehended the Englishman. "Get up!" he said.

---

[12]The reader must remember that "Nishi" means "night," and "Diba," "day"; further, *suprabhāt*, "fine morning," can also refer to good luck or to a person bringing good fortune. So there is word-play here. Nishi ("night") wants to end so that a fine day can dawn bringing her good luck. Diba ("day") has a dig at her sister and claims to be the fine morning that brings good luck.

[13]See endnotes for an explanation.

"Where are we going?"

"You're a prisoner. Who are you to ask?"

Without another word the Englishman followed Rangaraj, flanked by the two fighters. They passed by the landing point at which Haraballabh was bathing.

Haraballabh asked, "Where are you taking the Englishman?"

"Into the jungle," answered Rangaraj.

"Why?"

"When we're in the jungle we'll hang him."

Haraballabh shivered; he forgot all the invocations for his ritual bath, which didn't go well at all.

When they had gone into the jungle, Rangaraj said to the Englishman, "We hang nobody. Go back to your own home and leave us alone. You're free to go."

At first the Englishman was quite astonished; then he thought, "Well, how could a Bengali ever think to hang an Englishman!"

Rangaraj continued, "Mister, Rangpur is far away. How will you get there?"

"As best I can," was the reply.

"Well, you could hire a boat," said Rangaraj, "Or go to some village and buy a horse, or go by palanquin. Our Queen has given you a hundred *mohurs* for your journey's expenses." He began to count out the *mohurs*, but the Englishman took five of the gold coins and left the rest. "These will do," he said, "I'll take them on loan."

"Very well," replied Rangaraj, "You can pay us back if we come to collect. Also, if any of your sepoys have been injured send them to us, and send on the heirs of any who have died."

"Why?" asked the Englishman.

"Because our Queen makes some contribution to such people."

The Englishman didn't believe him, but without another word, good or bad, he departed.

As for Rangaraj, he went in search of a palanquin and some porters, for, as we know, he also had instructions to follow in that regard.

Chapter 10

Meanwhile, when he saw that the path was clear, Brajesvar discreetly made his way to Debi and sat down.

"I'm glad you came to meet me," she said. "Today wouldn't have happened if it hadn't been for what you said. You ordered me to save my life, and I did. Debi has died; Debi Chaudhurani is no more. But Prafulla still exists. Should Prafulla live, or die with Debi?"

Brajesvar kissed Prafulla lovingly on the lips. He said, "Come home with me. It will brighten up the house. If you don't go, neither will I."

"But what will my father-in-law say if I come home?"

"Leave that to me," said Brajesvar. "Make ready to send him off first, we'll follow."

"They've gone to fetch a palanquin and some porters."

These arrived speedily. Haraballabh too cut short his ritual bath and returned to the barge. He saw Mistress Nishi arranging sweet condensed milk, some cottage cheese, butter, and well-ripened fruits including mangoes and bananas for his meal. Obsequiously, she invited him to sit down and said, "You're family now. If you don't take some refreshment you won't be allowed to leave."

But Haraballabh was not ready to start. "Where's Brajesvar?" he asked. "Last night he went outside and I haven't seen him since."

"Now that he's going to be my brother-in-law, don't worry about him. He's around somewhere. Please sit down to eat, I'll send for him. Before you go, tell him what we've agreed to do."

Haraballabh sat down to eat, and Nishi went and fetched Brajesvar. Both Haraballabh and Brajesvar were embarrassed when Brajesvar emerged from the inner room. "These witches lost their heads when they saw my handsome boy," thought Haraballabh. "Good!"

He said to Brajesvar, "My boy, how you got here is still beyond me, but we'll talk about that later, not now. Right now, a request has been made of me which I feel obliged to honor. This lady here comes from a good *kulin* family—her father has the same ritual status as us. She has an unmarried sister and they can't find a suitable groom. They're in danger of losing their family honor. *Kulin*s must protect the honor of *kulin*s—the lower castes can't do it, can they? And both your mother and I are keen that you marry again. In fact, we've been a little anxious about this ever since our eldest daughter-in-law passed away. That's why I was saying, when pressed by this request I felt it necessary to comply. So I'm giving you permission to marry this lady's sister."

Brajesvar considered and then said, "As you command."

Nishi wanted to laugh out loud, but she restrained herself. Haraballabh continued, "My palanquin and its porters have arrived. I'll go on ahead and prepare for the *boubhat.* You get married in the proper way and come home with your wife."

"As you command," said Brajesvar again.

"What more is there to say," went on Haraballabh, "You're not a child. Think the matter through from the point of view of honor, virtue, caste, social standing etc. before you marry. . . . (then lowering his voice). . . . and don't forget what's rightfully our due by way of dowry. . . . ."

"As you command," said Brajesvar.

Haraballabh finished his meal and took his leave. After Braja and Nishi respectfully touched his feet, he mounted the palanquin, muttered Durga's name, and heaved a sigh of relief. "The boy's still in those witches' clutches," he thought, "but I'm not worried. He knows how to make his way. Good looks conquer everywhere!"

When he had gone, Brajesvar asked Nishi, "Now what trick is this? Who's this younger sister of yours?"

"Don't you know? Her name's Prafulla."

"Oh ho, so that's it! And how did you get my father to agree to this marriage?"

"Women have so many ways," answered Nishi. "If I didn't need to play mother-in-law for my 'younger sister,' I'd have made him agree to another marriage instead!"

"To hell with you!" cried Diba incensed. "Haven't you any shame? How can you talk to a man like that?"

"Where's the man?" said Nishi in surprise. "Brajesvar? But you saw yesterday who was the man, and who the woman!"

"And you'll see today as well," answered Brajesvar. "At least *you're* a woman since you've acted as stupidly as one! You've made a mess of things."

"What do you mean?" said Nishi.

"Do you think it's right of me to deceive my father? To throw sand in his eyes and live with my wife at home on the basis of a lie? If I can deceive my own father who else is there on earth to stop me from lying and cheating?"

Nishi was taken aback; she admitted to herself that Brajesvar was indeed a man. She realized that it was not only by wielding staves that one became a man.

"Is there a way out?" she asked.

"There is," said Brajesvar. "First, let me take Prafulla home. There I'll explain everything to my father. I'll hide nothing."

"If you do that," said Nishi, "Do you think your father will let Debi Chaudhurani stay in the house?"

Debi spoke. "Who's Debi Chaudhurani? Debi Chaudhurani is dead; don't even mention her name again. Now speak of Prafulla."

"Well then, will he let *Prafulla* stay in the house?" said Nishi.

"I've told you," replied Brajesvar, "to leave that task to me."

Prafulla was content, for she knew that Brajesvar was not the man to undertake a task he couldn't carry out.

Chapter 11

Preparations were now made to leave for Bhutnath. It was decided to take leave of Rangaraj from where they were, for on one occasion Brajesvar's guards had felt the brunt of Rangaraj's staff in Bhutnath and if they spotted him there they'd recognize him. Rangaraj was summoned and the matter explained to him, partly by Nishi and partly by Prafulla herself. Weeping, Rangaraj replied, "I had no idea, Ma,[14] that you would leave us."

[14]"Ma": see endnotes.

Everyone gathered round to comfort him. Prafulla had a residence and property in Debigarh which she had dedicated to the deity there. She made everything over to Rangaraj and said, "Go and reside there, and live off the offerings made to the deity in the temple. And do not take up the staff again. What you call doing good to others is really a form of oppression. You can't benefit others by means of sticks and staves. If the king does not chastise the wicked, then God will do so—who are you and I to do it? Take on the task of protecting the virtuous, but leave it to God to chastise the wicked. Kindly convey all this to Bhabani Thakur on my behalf, and tell him I send him countless obeisances."

Rangaraj departed, weeping profusely. Diba and Nishi accompanied Prafulla to the pier at Bhutnath. It was agreed that they would return to Debigarh in the barge and reside there, living off the offerings made to the deity and singing Hari's praises. The reader has seen that all Debi's trappings as Queen, which were worth a lot of money, lay in the barge. Prafulla gave everything to Diba and Nishi and said, "Sell everything and make use of whatever you need. Give the rest to the poor. None of it belongs to me and I won't take any of it." With this Prafulla gave her expensive clothing and jewelry to Nishi and Diba.

"Ma!" exclaimed Nishi, "Will you go to your in-laws' house without ornaments?"

Prafulla pointed to Brajesvar and said, "This is a woman's prize ornament! What need of any other, Ma?"

Nishi replied, "Well, you are going today for the first time to stay in your in-laws' house, and I want to bless you with a dowry gift for the occasion, so don't say no. This is the last thing I'll ask of you and you must agree." So saying, Nishi began to deck Prafulla with some very expensive jewelry.

The reader may recall that when Nishi had stayed with the grandee's wife at an earlier stage, the lady had given her many ornaments. These were the ornaments, and because Debi had presented her with new jewelry, she didn't wear the other. Now, seeing Debi without ornaments, she dressed her with the jewelry she had received earlier.

After this, since there was nothing else to do, the three of them proceeded to weep. Nishi had started them off while putting the jewelry on Prafulla; then and there Diba took up the refrain, after which the sobbing continued in earnest. Prafulla too: how could she do otherwise? The three of them loved each other dearly. Yet since Prafulla's heart was filled with joy, her sobbing was much restrained, and because Nishi noticed how happy Prafulla was in herself and rejoiced in her happiness, she too restrained her tears; so it was left to Mistress Diba to make up for their deficiencies in this respect.

In due course, the barge reached the pier at Bhutnath. There Prafulla took the dust of Diba and Nishi's feet and bade them farewell. Weeping copiously they made their way in the barge back to Debigarh. They paid the fighter-deckhands what was owing to them and sent them away. The barge itself could not be kept since it was easily recognizable. Prafulla had told them to get rid of it, so Nishi reduced it to firewood and took two years to burn it all.

And with these pieces of wood as a parting gift, let our readers duly take their leave of Mistress Nishi.

✿ *Chapter 12* ✿

No sooner had Prafulla's barge docked at Bhutnath than word spread throughout the village (how, I couldn't say) that Brajesvar had brought home another wife—and quite an old one at that! So every woman who could—young or old, the one-eyed and the lame—wherever she happened to be, hurried to catch a glimpse of her. Those who were busy cooking abandoned their cooking pots and dashed off; those who were slicing fish for a meal covered the fish in a wicker basket and hurried away, while those who were taking a bath dashed off with sodden clothes. Those who had sat down to a meal ate only the half of it; those who were quarreling made up with their adversaries then and there. The little boy being whipped by his wretch of a mother was spared this ordeal; he was whisked off in her arms to see the old bride!

Here was someone's husband in the midst of a meal: the lentils and vegetables had already been served on the eating-leaf, and the fish-gravy dish was about to descend, when news about the bride arrived—and as luck would have it, the husband missed out on fish that day! There was an old woman querulously telling her granddaughter to "hold my hand. If you don't, how can I get to the landing at the pond?" when there was a commotion the bride had arrived. There and then granddaughter abandoned Granny and ran off to see the bride (and Granny somehow managed to turn up too). Or take the young girl being scolded by her mother: "But I swear I never go out…," she says in reply. Just then news about the bride arrives. She's off in the direction of the bride's house without ever completing her protestations!

Mothers leave their infants and dash off, and the infants run after them bawling. Husband and elder brother-in-law are sitting together, and without so much as a by-your-leave, husband's wife screens her face and walks off under their noses! The young women's clothes come askew in their haste, and they don't have the time to adjust them; with hair falling about and no time to do it up, they fumble with their clothing in an effort to tidy themselves. What a hullabaloo! The Goddess of modesty flees in shame!

The bride and groom were standing on the *piri*[15] and the lady of the house was ceremonially welcoming them. People kept craning to see the bride's face but she played her part well, pulling the edge of her sari right across her face so that no one could see. Once, during the welcome ceremony her mother-in-law lifted the veil and looked at her face. She started a little but said nothing except to remark, "A fine bride," and a few tears came to her eyes.

[15]*piri*: a small, wooden platform, a few inches from ground-level.

When the ceremony was over, mother-in-law took the bride indoors and said to all the neighbors who had gathered, "Dear friends, my son and his wife have come from a great distance, and they must be hungry and thirsty. So let me see to that now. The bride's here to stay and you'll be able to see her whenever you want. So now please have some refreshments and go home."

None too pleased at these words, the neighbors went home grumbling. The fault lay with the lady of the house, but the bride got most of the blame since they didn't get a good look at her face! Everyone expressed disgust at the fact that she was quite old. "These things usually happen in a *kulin*'s house," they said. Then whoever had seen an older bride in a *kulin* household started gossiping about it: Gobind Mukherji had married a girl of fifty-five! Hari Chatterji had brought home an unmarried woman of seventy, while Manu Barua had actually gone and married some old woman during her last rites! They began to tell each other such stories—duly embroidered—along the way. So it was that after much agitation the village gradually calmed down.

When the commotion was over, the lady of the house summoned Brajesvar in private.

"What is it, mother?"

"My son, where did you get this wife?" his mother asked.

"She's not a new bride, mother!" he replied.

"So where did you find this lost treasure, dear?" his mother continued, tears falling from her eyes.

"Mother, in his mercy the all-Provider gave her back to me. But say nothing to father now. When I catch him alone I'll explain everything to him."

"You don't have to say a word, dear," said his mother. "I'll tell him what's to be said. But first let the *boubhat* be over. Now don't you worry, and don't say a word to anyone."

Brajesvar agreed. His mother had taken this heavy burden upon herself, and he felt relieved, so he said nothing to anyone. The *boubhat* passed off without a hitch. It wasn't a grand affair; Haraballabh just invited relatives from both sides of his family and concluded the matter.

After the *boubhat* Brajesvar's mother explained to Haraballabh what had happened; she told him that Brajesvar had not married again but that it was the same elder wife as before.

"What!" cried Haraballabh startled—it was as if a sleeping tiger had been pierced by an arrow—"The same elder wife? How do you know?"

"I recognized her" was the answer, "And Brajesvar told me so."

"But she died ten years ago!"

"Do the dead come back to life?"

"But where and with whom was the girl all this time?"

"I've not asked Brajesvar that, and I shan't do so. Since he's brought her home, he must have gone into that."

"Well, I'll ask him," said the father.

"You eat my head, but don't you say a word!" snapped his wife. "The last time you said something, the result was that I nearly lost my son—my only son. Don't you dare say a word! If you do, I'll hang myself!"

Abashed, Haraballabh never said a word. All he said was, "Then we'll tell everyone this is a new bride."

"So be it," said his wife.

Later, the lady of the house gave Brajesvar the good news. "I've told your father," she said, "And he won't say another word. There's no point in raking the matter up again." With a happy heart, Braja gave Prafulla the news. We must admit that the lady of the house discharged her responsibility as a housewife very well. No one suffers in a household where the housewife knows her job. If the helmsman knows how to wield the tiller, is there any fear for the boat?

Chapter 13

Prafulla wanted to see Sagar again, so when Brajesvar gave his mother the nod, his mother sent for Sagar, for she too wanted the three wives to live under one roof.

The man who went to fetch Sagar informed her that her husband had married again and brought home another wife, who was quite old. Sagar was outraged. "Shame!" she said in fury. "An old wife? So he's married again? Why, aren't we his wives? Pity the Creator didn't make me a poor man's daughter," she continued sorrowfully. "If I'd lived with my husband, perhaps he wouldn't have married again."

So, alternately angry and mortified, Sagar came to her father-in-law's house. As soon as she arrived, she went straight to Nayan-bou. Each was like poison in the eye of the other, but today they were as one, for both were in the same predicament. It was with this in mind that Sagar went first to Nayantara.

Just as a snake stuffed into a pot keeps hissing away, so had Nayantara fumed after Prafulla's arrival. She had met Brajesvar only once since then, but the sting of her abuse had driven him away and he hadn't returned. Prafulla too had gone to make friends, but she met with the same fate. Husband and (co-)wife apart, even the neighbors hadn't been able to get on with Nayantara these last few days. Nayantara had had a couple of children but their situation was worse, for she had been thrashing them mercilessly all the while.

It was in the gracious temple of this goddess that Sagar presented herself first. When she saw her, Nayantara said, "Come in, come in—why are you staying away? Is there anyone else to share our lot?"

"Well!" said Sagar in consternation. "Has he really married again?"

"Who knows whether he had a proper marriage or hitched up with some Muslim woman?" replied Nayantara, "How would I know what happened?"

"How could he 'hitch up' with a Brahmin's daughter?"

"Do you think I've been to see whether it's a Brahmin or a Shudra or a Muslim?"

"Don't speak like that," remonstrated Sagar. "People keep a sense of dignity when they speak."

"How can you keep your dignity in a house where an old bride's just arrived?'

"How old is she? Our age?"

"More like your mother's!"

"Does she have grey hair?"

"Well if she didn't would the wretch wander about day and night with her face and head covered?"

"Has she got any teeth?"

"If her hair's grey, her teeth must have fallen out."

"So you think she's older than our husband!"

"What do you think!"

"Can such things happen?"

"Such things happen in a *kulin*'s house."

"What does she look like?"

"A paragon of beauty, no doubt! With pudgy cheeks like Gobind's mother!"

"Didn't you say anything to our husband?"

"D'you think I get to see him? If I did, I'd say something. I've kept the rough end of the broom ready for that!"

"Well, let me go and have a look at this golden icon."

"Go on then, and make your life worth living."

Sagar looked for her co-wife and found her by the steps to the pond. Prafulla was scouring some dishes with her back to Sagar. Sagar went up behind her and said, "Hello, so you're the new wife of the house?"

"Who's that, Sagar?" said the new wife, turning round.

Sagar saw who it was. Astonished, she exclaimed, "Queen Debi?"

"Quiet!" said Prafulla. "Debi's dead."

"Then Prafulla?" said Sagar.

"Prafulla's dead too."

"Then who are you now?"

"The new wife."

"But how did this happen? Tell me, I want to know everything!"

Prafulla replied, "We can't talk here. I've been given a room. Let's go there and I'll tell you everything."

They locked the door, and thus secluded, started a conversation. When Prafulla had explained everything, Sagar asked, "Do you think you'll get used to housework now? After sitting on a silver throne wearing a crown of diamonds like a queen, will you be able to cope with washing the dishes and sweeping the rooms? Do you think you can put up with Grandaunt Brahma's fairy tales after those yoga treatises? Will someone who made two thousand men jump to her command enjoy ordering the maidservants about?"

"It's because I want to do those things that I'm here," said Prafulla. "For this is precisely the right life for a woman. Women aren't born to rule. It's the family life you've described that's a hard duty; there's no yoga harder than that.[16] Just think how many illiterate, self-seeking, ignorant people we've constantly got to deal with. And our task is to see to it that none of them are put out, that each one is happy. Is there any form of renunciation more difficult than this? Any virtue greater than this? This is the kind of renunciation I want to embrace."

Sagar replied, "Well then, I'll stay with you for a while and follow your example."

It was while Prafulla and Sagar were having this conversation that Brajesvar sat down to eat in the presence of Grandaunt Brahma. She asked him, "Bej, how do I cook now?" She remembered the conversation they had had a decade earlier. Their words had been of significance then, so both remembered them.

"Fine," answered Braja.

"How's the cows' milk now? Gone sour?"

"No, the milk's fine."

"And look, ten years have passed, and you still haven't seen to my death rites."

"Forgot."

"Because you haven't done so, you're a *Bagdi*!"

"Auntie, quiet! Don't speak like that!"

"Anyway, do it. If you get the chance, see to it that I'm disposed of properly. I won't object. But I hope, dear, that from now on nobody will break my spinning wheel or any of my other things."

Chapter 14

After a few months, Sagar saw that Prafulla accomplished what she had said she would do. She made everyone in the household happy. Her mother-in-law became so content after her arrival that, after handing over the responsibility of running the household to her, all she would do was roam about with Sagar's son in her arms! Gradually her father-in-law too learned to appreciate her qualities. So much so that in the end he had no time for anything that Prafulla did not set her hand to. Her in-laws relied on her judgment to such an extent that they did nothing without consulting her first.

[16]See endnotes for the Bengali terminology of this passage.

Grandaunt Brahma too put her in charge of the kitchen. The old lady found it difficult to cook much now, so the three wives did the cooking. But the day Prafulla didn't prepare a dish or two, no one had a liking for what was cooked. And if Prafulla wasn't present while a member of the family was eating, he or she didn't derive full satisfaction from the meal. In the end, Nayan-bou too was won over. No longer did she come to quarrel with Prafulla; rather, for fear of upsetting Prafulla she didn't have the courage to row with anyone else! She did nothing without consulting Prafulla, for she saw that she herself was unable to care for her children in the way Prafulla did. So she put her children in Prafulla's care and remained content. As for Sagar, she was unable to stay for any length of time in her father's house; she kept coming back since she couldn't be happy anywhere else in the way she was in Prafulla's company.

All this might seem strange, no doubt, with respect to someone else, but not so where Prafulla was concerned, for she had practiced the path of selfless action. It was after she came into the family that she became a true renouncer. She had no selfish desires; all she sought was to engage in work. The goal of selfish desire is to seek one's own happiness, while work's goal is to seek the happiness of others. Prafulla was selfless, that is, intent on work; so she was a true renouncer. This is why whatever Prafulla touched would turn to gold. As Bhabani Thakur's sharpened weapon, she easily cut through the entanglements of family life.

Yet no one in Haraballabh's household could guess that Prafulla was this sharpened weapon. Leave aside the fact that she had been the disciple of a great teacher who was second to none, and that she herself was a most learned person—no one guessed that she was even literate. Amidst household duties, there is no call to display knowledge. No doubt the learned can accomplish household duties well, but this is not the place to display knowledge. Whoever flaunts knowledge where it ought not to be displayed is really a fool, whereas the person who does not display knowledge in such circumstances is the truly learned one.

When Prafulla did have disagreements it was with Brajesvar. Prafulla would tell him, "I am not your only wife. Just as you belong to me, you belong to Sagar, and to Nayan-bou also. I shan't see to your needs by myself. A woman's husband is her god; so why shouldn't they get the chance to serve you too?" But Brajesvar wouldn't listen. Brajesvar's heart was filled with Prafulla alone. She would say, "If you don't love them as you love me, your love for me will remain incomplete. For they are one with me." But Brajesvar couldn't understand that.

Because of her shrewdness, sharpness of intellect and sound judgment, Prafulla was put in charge of household affairs. The work of managing the estates was conducted externally of course, but if there was the slightest need for consultation, the head of the house, her father-in-law, would come to her mother-in-law and ask, "Let me know what the new wife thinks about this." Because everything was done on Prafulla's advice, the family's wealth and prosperity grew with each passing day.

In due course, encompassed by wealth, family, friends, and every happiness, Haraballabh died, and the property came to Brajesvar. Thanks to Prafulla, new estates accrued to him so that a great deal of ready money was accumulated. Then Prafulla said, "Now redeem the Rs.50,000 I lent you."

"Why, what will you do with it?" asked Brajesvar.

"It's not for myself," replied Prafulla. "The money isn't mine. It belongs to Sri Krishna, to the poor and needy. It must go to the poor and needy."

"And how will you do that?"

"You must build a hostel with the 50,000 rupees," answered Prafulla.

So that is what Brajesvar did. They installed an image of the Goddess Annapurna in the hostel, and called the hostel, *Debinibas*: "Debi's Home."

In due course, surrounded by her children and grandchildren, Prafulla died, and the people of the region felt that they had lost a mother.

Rangaraj, Diba, and Nishi, after spending their days in Debigarh in Sri Krishna's service, passed away too. However, with Bhabani Thakur things took a different turn. The English assumed the task of ruling the kingdom, and they ruled it well, thus Bhabani Thakur's work became unnecessary. The rulers now chastised the wicked, so Bhabani Thakur ceased his activities as a bandit. Deciding that he must now do penance, he surrendered himself to the English, confessed to all he had done as a bandit and petitioned for punishment. The English ordered that he be transported for life to a distant island, and that is where he went, keeping both joy and Prafulla in his heart.

So come now, Prafulla! Return to our world once more and let us behold you. Why don't you confront this society of ours and say: "I am not something new; I go back in time. For I am that very same Voice of the past. How often have I come to you, and you have forgotten me, and so I have come again. "*To protect the good, to destroy the wicked, and to establish right order, I take birth in every age.*"

Critical Apparatus

The Dedication

NOTES

"With loving devotion": *bhaktibhābe.*

"the teaching of selfless action": *niṣkām dharma.* This is a major theme of the novel, and has been discussed in the Introduction.

"by the fruit of virtue": *puṇyaphale.*

"heaven": *svarga.*

For a comment on Bankim's father and the influence he had on Bankim and this novel, see the Introduction.

Epigraphs

"The Substance of Religion . . . by the author of *Ecce Homo*": the author here is John Robert Seeley (1834–95), educationist, political theorist, classicist, and historian, who after a period as Professor of Latin at University College, London, became Regius Professor of Modern History at the University of Cambridge. His two major books on religion, *Ecce Homo* and *Natural Religion*, influenced Bankim by the way they interpreted religion through a Positivist filter. "All Seeley's work in theology belongs to the period when he worked in London. The influence of his Positivist friends on him is most marked in his first study of religion in society, *Ecce Homo*. In this survey of Christ's life and mission, he sought to reconcile the Positivist faith in science and the conception of a Church of Humanity with Christianity seen as an international ethical society. . . . In *Natural Religion* he argued that, to be true to itself, Christianity should be allied with all those elements in society which recognize non-material goals, however far removed they might be from the institutional churches. He believed that Christianity could learn from a neo-religion which, he thought, was peculiarly well adapted to the intellectual needs of his society, [that is] Christianity must appropriate the best aspects of Positivism, respect for science and thorough humanism" (Wormell 1980:22, 29).

As in the case of his assessment of other Western thinkers like Comte, John Stuart Mill, and Spencer, Bankim's use of Seeley was eclectic. He sought to integrate aspects of these thinkers' views into the new Hindu religio-cultural position he was constructing. He could never be called, simply, "a Spencerian" or "a Comtean" as some other Bengali intellectuals of the time might be. It appears that explicit reference to Seeley in the context of Bankim's work is considerably later than reference to Comte. The first issue of the journal *Nabajīban* in July 1884 carried a substantial article by Bankim on *dharma* in which reference to Seeley (and other Western thinkers) is made. *BcJ* points out that Bankim's lengthy *Nabajīban* contributions on *dharma* were reformulated later in his work, *Dharmatattva* (op.cit., p.647). The *DT* explicitly refers to Seeley's work (see ch.4 of that text and especially an extract taken from Bankim's *Nabajīban* article referred to earlier, included toward the end of the second Appendix of the *DT*).

"The General Law of Man's Progress...": Auguste Comte (1798–1857) was a French philosopher who founded the school of Positivism. According to Comte each branch of human knowledge passes through three successive phases of development. In the first—the theological state—the human mind "represents...phenomena as being produced by the direct and continuous action of more or less numerous supernatural agents, whose arbitrary intervention explains all the apparent anomalies of the universe.

In the metaphysical state... the supernatural agents are replaced by abstract forces, real entities, or personified abstractions, inherent in the different beings in the world. These entities are looked upon as capable of giving rise by themselves to all the phenomena observed.

Finally, in the positive state, the human mind...gives up the search after the origin and hidden causes of the universe and a knowledge of the final causes of phenomena. It endeavors now only to discover, by a well-combined use of reasoning and observation, the actual laws of phenomena—that is to say, their invariable relations of success and likeness" (A. Comte 1988:2). Thus according to Positivism, knowledge proper is based on universal laws which are ultimately humanly demonstrable, not on some species of faith. According to Comte, human relationships inside and outside the family are also subject to fixed laws which can be discerned and demonstrated ("Sociology"), though not easily. Comtean ethics is expressed in terms of human social relations. "The aim, both in public and private life, is to secure to the utmost possible extent the victory of the social feeling over self-love, or Altruism over Egoism" (*Encyclopaedia Britannica,* 1910–11, Vol.VI:820b–821a). But it was not as straightforward as that. Comte complicated his system in various ways, introducing hierarchical and cultural notions borrowed from his Catholic upbringing. The *Catechism* was published in 1852.

Comte's thought was one of Bankim's prime Western intellectual influences. Bankim's interest in Comte has relatively early literary pedigree. The fourth issue of *Baṅgadarśan* (1279 Śrāban, July 1872) has an unsigned article summarizing Comte's philosophy, which *BcJ* opines, on the basis of the writing-style, was Bankim's work (*BcJ*, pp.144–5); there are several references to Comte in the *DT*. Bankim may not have made a deep study of Comte's work. "Bankimchandra and Krishnakamal Bhattacarja were close friends for a long time. In his book *Purātan Prasaṅga,* Krishnakamal observes: '[Bankim] would occasionally come to my house in Howrah when he was staying at Alipur as Deputy Magistrate. And when he was in Howrah, I often used to practice as a pleader at his court.

Even now I remember well how one day the two of us travelled together in a horse-drawn carriage to Jogendrababu's house (i.e., Jogendracandra Ghosh, an ardent student of Comte and Bankimchandra's friend). On the way we talked a bit about Comte. 'I don't think,' I said, 'that even now the time has come in our country to discuss Comte's thought; the time is not ripe for it.' 'Why not?' answered Bankimbabu. 'There's no right or wrong time for truth.' I'm quite sure Bankimbabu hadn't studied Comte deeply, but I got the impression then that he said exactly what he believed' " (*BcJ*, p.563). Nevertheless, Comte, in so far as Bankim assimilated him, was an important influence on Bankim's thinking, in particular with reference to Comte's views on religion and society and, not least, on the place of women in a progressive social order.

The Notice

"Only a portion": in fact, Parts I and II. Though the story line remained more or less the same, the serial version in *Baṅgadarśan* deviated considerably in places from the material in the book-editions (including that of the sixth edition translated here). All the noteworthy changes are given under "Variants" and in the Appendices. As I point out in the Introduction, some of these changes are significant in various ways for understanding the novel and its author's intentions. The serial version was published in *Baṅgadarśan* from Pauṣ B.E. 1289 (viz. December 1882) through Māgh B.E. 1290 (January 1884).

"After *Anandamath* was published": for a detailed analysis of the writing of the novel, its implications, and the so-called *sannyasi*-revolt, see the Introduction in Lipner (2005a).

"a slight historical basis": for a discussion of this, with reference to Hunter's account, see the Introduction.

"the Rangpur District": now in northern Bangladesh; at the time it was a part of British India and greater Bengal. Hunter (1876:Vol.VII) describes it as follows: "Rangpur [is] a frontier District bordering on Nepāl, Bhutān, Kuch Behar, and Assam (158)....The District is one vast plain, without natural elevations of any kind....The general inclination of the surface is from north-west to south-east, as indicated by the flow of the great rivers, the Brahmaputra, Tīstā, Karātoyā, and Dharlā. Besides these main channels, the whole District is intersected by a network of water-courses, forming cross lines of communication between the great rivers. The District contains, also, numerous *jhils,* or small stagnant sheets of water or marshes, found either in the deserted channels of streams, or formed by the overflowing of springs (161)." See map.

"Mr Hunter": *hanṭar sāheb.* Sir William Wilson Hunter (1840–1900) was a noted civil servant and India-expert in the latter half of the nineteenth century.

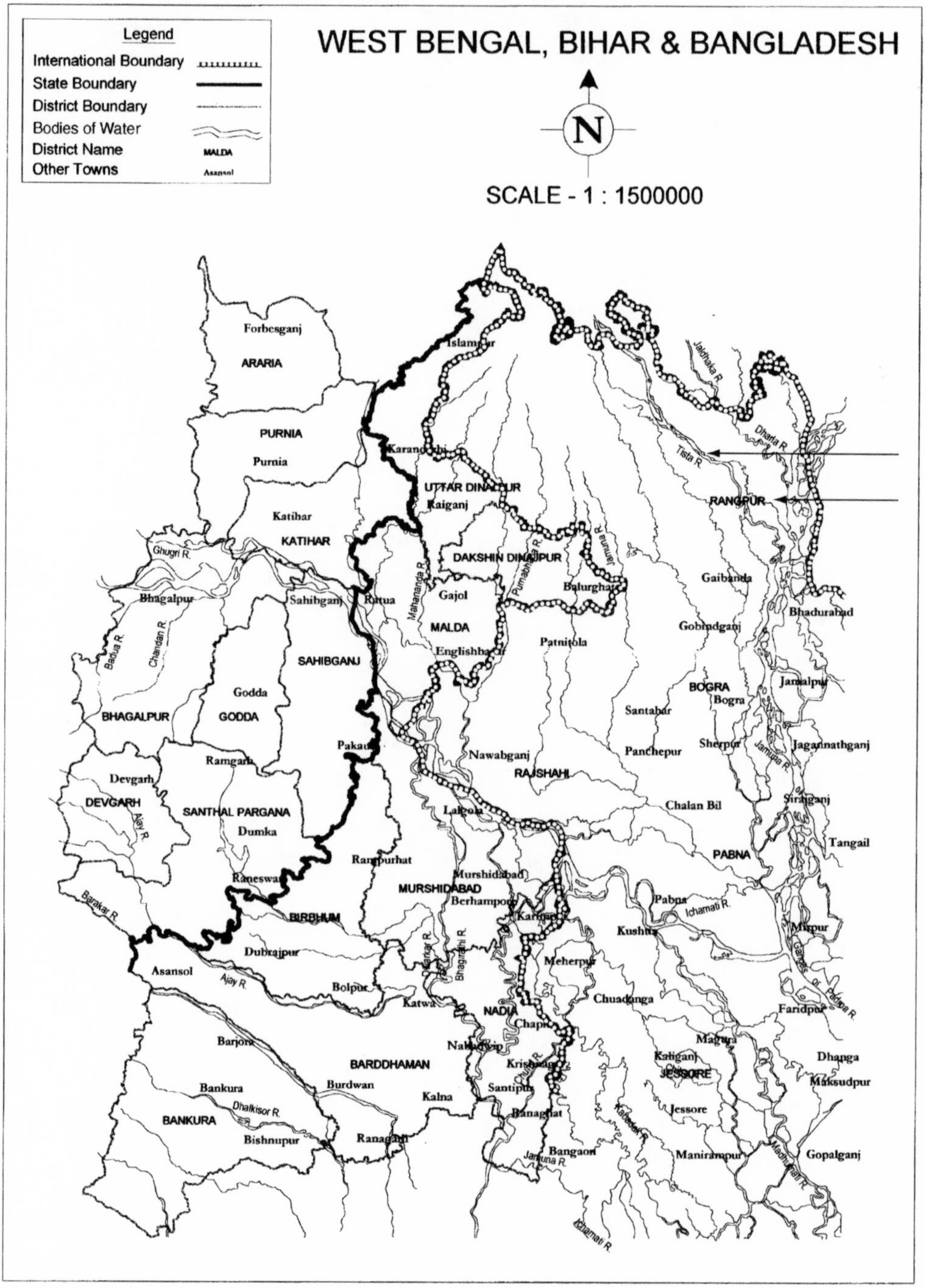

MAP I

West Bengal, Bihar, and Bangladesh.
Courtesy of Riddhi Management Services, Kolkata.

MAP 2 (*facing page*)

West Bengal, Bihar, and Bangladesh.
Courtesy of Riddhi Management Services, Kolkata.

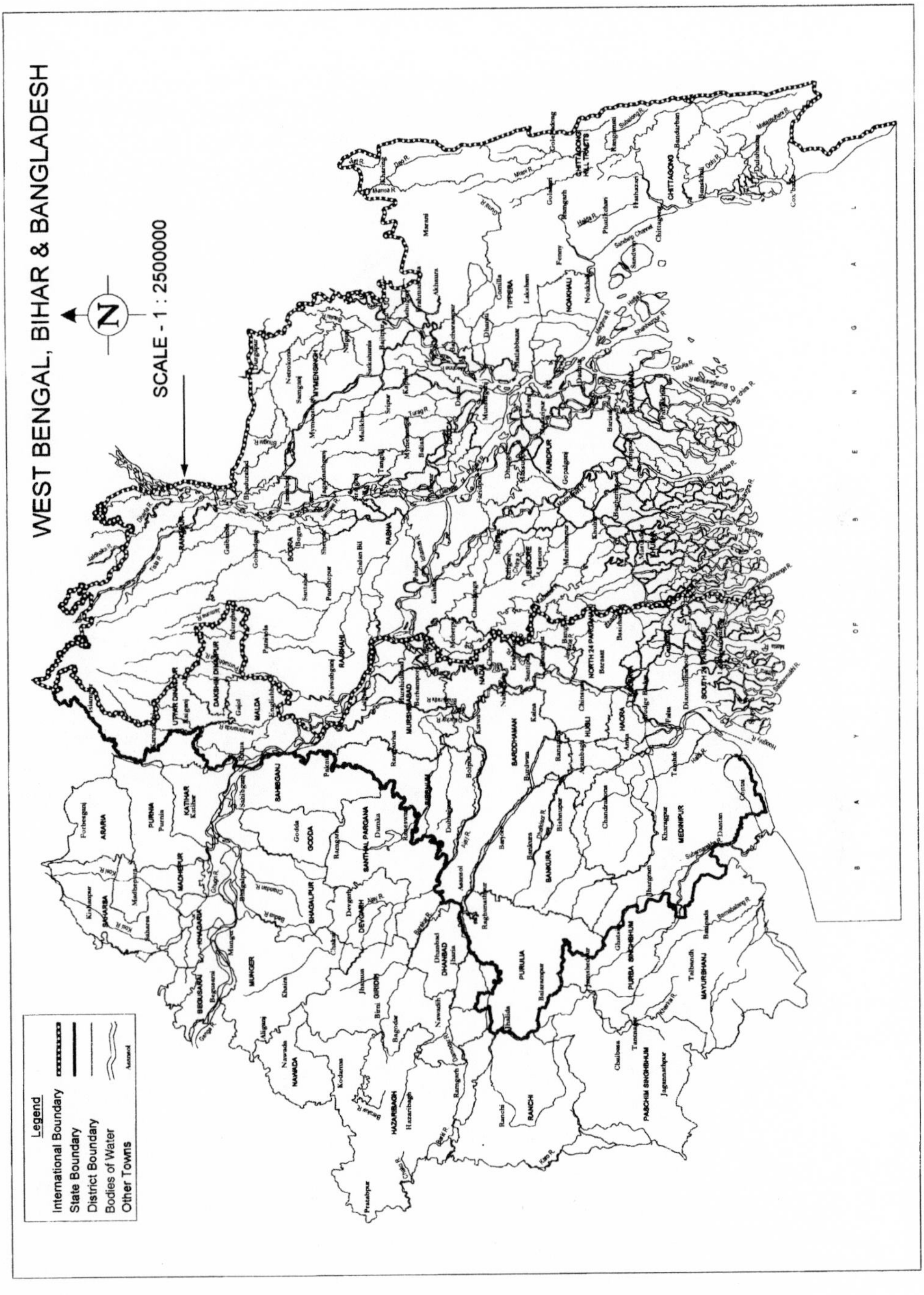
WEST BENGAL, BIHAR & BANGLADESH
N
SCALE - 1 : 2500000
Legend
International Boundary
State Boundary
District Boundary
Bodies of Water
Other Towns
Asansol
B A Y   O F   B E N G A L

After he passed his Civil Service examination in 1862, he was "posted in the remote district of Birbhum in the lower provinces of Bengal [where] he began collecting local traditions and records, which formed the materials for his novel and suggestive publication, entitled *The Annals of Rural Bengal*," a work well known by Bankim. Besides overseeing or producing a number of other publications related to his work or experience in India, he "undertook the supervision of the statistical accounts of Bengal (20 vols., 1875–7) and of Assam (2 vols., 1879)," was elected vice-chancellor of the University of Calcutta in 1886, and in 1887 retired from the Civil Service to Oaken Holt, near Oxford, where he died of a severe attack of influenza in February 1900 (cf. *The Encyclopaedia Britannica*, 11th edition, 1910–11, Vol.XIII, p.945).

—PART I—

Chapter 1

VARIANTS

"Peepee": *DCsv* has "Pip" instead.

* "but Prafulla grabbed the basket…": *DCsv* has instead: "but Prafulla took the basket from her and threw away the little rice that remained. Astonished, her mother asked, "What are you doing? You've thrown away even the little we had?" Her mother wiped the tears from her eyes and said, "You've everything you could wish for, my dear" etc.

* "She cooked whatever rice there was…": *DCsv* has instead: "Then she borrowed some rice and cooked it, but Prafulla wouldn't eat a thing" etc.

* " 'No, leave it as it is,' said Prafulla": *DCsv* adds: "Let them see the state they've kept me in," then concludes with the last sentence of the standard text: "Then both left the house" etc.

NOTES

"Wretch": *poḍārmukhī:* analogous to the way people in the West affectionately call their children, "madcap," "scamp," "tearaway" etc. This was and is a common practice in Bengal, though precise appellations may have changed with time. *DCM* retains the Bengali expression and explains it in a Glossary at the end.

"eggplant" (or "brinjal"): *begun:* the *Solanum melongena,* a familiar item of Bengali cuisine, more familiarly known in the English-speaking West as the aubergine.

"Because that's your lot": *jeman adṛṣṭa kare esechili.*

"There's no cotton": *pāj* is cotton for carding and spinning.

"And your bad luck": *ār tomār kapāl.*

"Then let me tie your hair": Prafulla's mother wanted to keep up appearances; unkempt hair in public was a sign of wretchedness.

❂ *Chapter 2* ❂

VARIANTS

* "and also beautiful . . . half-covered": this phrase does not occur in *DCsv.*

NOTES

"Barendrabhumi": a large tract of (central-)northern Bengal of the time, and a favored location of Bankim's narratives (see map). "The stretch of land from the east bank of the Mahananda river to the west bank of the Kartoar. Some parts of present-day north Bengal, that is, Rajsahi, Rangpur, Pabna, Bagura, Dinajpur, Maldaha, and Jalpaiguri, and parts of Murshidabad and Maymansingh, are known by the name of Barendra" (*DCB:* Notes, p.9).

"estates": *jamidārī:* tracts of land over which the landholder had jurisdictional and revenue rights.

"salons on both floors of his house": *dotālā baiṭhakkhānā. DCM* has "high floored drawing rooms and parlors" (p.6). Perhaps he means "high-ceilinged. . . ." In any case, the idea is to indicate that this was a large mansion.

"salons on both floors . . . all surrounded by a wall": *dotālā baiṭhakkhānā, ṭhākurbāḍī, nāṭmandir, daptarkhānā, khiḍkite bāgān, pukur prācīre beḍā.* The trappings of success and power.

"something over twelve miles": *chay kroś.* A *kroś* is little more than two miles.

"had gone ahead with his son's marriage": these were arranged marriages, when the girl was still very young, and they were intended to conform strictly to the caste-codes of the time (see also footnote 8 of text).

"caste was their sole possession": *jāt-i āmāder sambal.*

"with a woman who had lost caste": *je kulṭā jātibhraṣṭā. . . .* If they accepted food from such a source, they implied, they would lose caste too.

"In fact, he married his son off to someone else": it was not unusual for sons of respectable Brahmin households at the time to have multiple marriages. The domestic arrangements for co-wives could vary and the reader will see how matters were conducted in this family (see also footnote 8).

"had almost fully covered her face...end of her sari": *prafulla mukhe ādh hāt ghomṭā ṭāniyā diyāchila. DCM:* "Prafulla had her veil drawn fully over her face" (p.8). Hindu Bengali women did not have a separate veil to show modesty or respect. When occasion demanded, they used the free end of their saris, otherwise draped over their shoulders, to act as a veil (=*ghomṭā*).

"it's mother-in-law": *behān.*

"Does a girl from a good family come uninvited?": there were strict rules about this; brides could not take living in or even occasional visits to their in-laws' house for granted.

"Did you conceive your son...?": the author has already said that Prafulla's mother had quarrelled with her neighbors, which led to them turning against her with disastrous consequences; here is another example of her feisty nature.

"the witch": *māgī.*
"They said they'd outcaste me": *ekghare karbe bale.*
"I may be beyond the pale...of low caste": *halem jena āmi ajāti—kata śūdra...DCM* has "I may be a class lower than yours," but *ajāti* is stronger than this. The *śūdra* is not an untouchable, but belongs to the lowest of the four traditional caste-orders (*caturvarṇa*). The function of the *śūdra* was to serve the higher castes, especially Brahmins (though not all servants were Shudras). This was a Brahmin household. The reader will note that servants of the time, Shudras or otherwise, could act with familiarity toward their betters (e.g., Tara's mother). Nevertheless, for a daughter-in-law to occupy the position of a servant was hardly acceptable.

Chapter 3

VARIANTS

* "And why should I stay?": *DCsv* and the first edition now continue as follows: 'Sagar said, "Don't you want a meeting?"

> "With whom?" asked Prafulla. "You?"
>
> "Of course not!" exclaimed Sagar. "Don't be silly! Do you think you must see only your co-wives when you come to your father-in-law's house and not someone else?"'

Prafulla smiled, but then the smile vanished. She said. "I don't understand, friend. Do you mean our husband? Will I be lucky enough for that to happen?"

Sagar replied, "I'll make it happen. Come to this room...."' etc.

[The first instalment in *DCsv* ends here: *Baṅgadarśan,* Pauṣ 1289 B.E. (Dec.1882)].

NOTES

"month of Baisakh": Baisakh is the first month of the Bengali calendar, viz. mid-April to mid-May, when rains fall for the first harvest of the year. *DCM:* "like the gathering clouds in the eastern sky" (p.13).

"am I dark to look at?": a light, 'wheatish' complexion (to use a popular description) was the ideal.

"in this household": *ei saṅgsāre.*

"I mean in some Brahmin's house": to preserve the rules of caste. Sagar knows Prafulla's mother is not a *Bagdi.*

"respectable house": *gṛhasthabāḍī:* that is, the home of a twice-born man in the householder stage of life. Hospitality is the mark of such a house.

"Grisly Owl": thus *kālpecā:* a species of dark-colored screech-owl, regarded as a bird of ill omen; the term is used derogatorily to express revulsion.

"If you can make my existence...": the wife existed to fulfill her husband's needs and duties. If she could never have contact with him, her life was hardly worth living. For an account of the traditional Hindu wife's duties, see Leslie (1989); also Leslie (1991).

"more forcefully": *nathnāḍā diyā.*

Chapter 4

VARIANTS

* "But not more good-looking than *you!*": *DCsv* adds here: "Then Prafulla and Nayantara eyed each other up and down. Just as the tiger and the hunter size each other up to see who will kill first, the two sized each other up. Each realized that the other was her chief enemy."

NOTES

"Brahmin's daughter" *bāmaner meye.*

"mother-in-law" *ṭhākuruṇ.*

"big shot": *baḍa mānuṣ.*

"I'm sorry": *ghāṭ hayeche.*

Chapter 5

VARIANTS

* "five maidservants": *DCsv* gives "ten."

NOTES

"guesthouse": *atithiśālā. DCM:* "in some way-side inn." But large country mansions often had separate accommodation, sometimes attached to the main residence, sometimes close by in the grounds, for guests.

"That's your job": It would be highly unlikely for a girl's father-in-law, or the *kartā* or master of the house (in this case the same person), to deal/speak directly with a daughter-in-law. He was too exalted in the domestic hierarchy.

"Grandaunt Brahma's quarters": *nikuñje* for "quarters." *Nikuñja* is a "bower," a "retreat": that is, Grandaunt was probably not living in the main body of the house, but in an outhouse or annex of some kind.

"Both those Brahmin wives...": *duiṭi brāhmaṇī.*

"I...eat sun-bleached rice": *ālo cāl khāi. Ālo-cāl (=ātap-cāl)* are rice-grains prepared for cooking by being bleached in the sun rather than by undergoing a process of boiling and then drying so as to make them more "refined." Hence *ālo cāl* is considered ritually more pure; the refined rice, on the other hand, is the kind generally bought in the shops. Grandaunt means that she observes the austere lifestyle traditionally expected of a widow.

"May granduncle enjoy heaven forever": Braja is talking of karmic heavens (*svarga*), which come to an end when the enjoyer's good karma runs out. Braja is being very generous to granduncle.

"this seventy-four year old?": that is, Grandaunt Brahma!

"...you just lark about!": *tui baḍa ceṅgḍā hayechis.*

"a couple of fried lentil cakes": *cholā bhājā*. These were hard and crusty—not easy for an old woman to eat if she lacked teeth...*DCM* paraphrases: "Probably she will make you a present of some hard parched gram to chew with your toothless gum" (p.30).

Chapter 6

VARIANTS

* "Who should speak first...": after this sentence, *DCsv* continues with "Well, leaving aside what ought to happen" etc as in the standard text.

* "to an end in midstream": Here *DCsv* adds: "Now Nayantara knew that her husband was in Sagar's room, and wanted to eavesdrop on him. When she arrived at the room, Sagar had already locked it and run off. As she listened, Nayantara realized that the *Bagdi* wife was in the room. "You monkey, Sagar!" she thought furiously, "You can go to hell, you wretch! Vile thing! Can't lie with him herself so she summons an ogress!" Then carefully instructing a servant-girl, she sent her off to her father-in-law. The girl, under some pretext of work, went to the head of the house and informed him that the *Muci* wife (from a *Bagdi* Prafulla had now become a *Muci*) was spending the night in Brajesvar's room. The head of the house gave orders that early the very next morning his daughter-in-law, Nayantara, was to take a broom to the offender with her own hand and send her packing. As for Brajesvar, his lot would be a heap of rebukes stored up by his father." *DCsv* now continues as in the standard text.

* "So I'll go": In *DCsv,* the narrative differs from here to the end of the chapter (as follows):

[Prafulla is still speaking]: ' "Will you remember what's happened?"

"Which part could I forget?" replied Brajesvar.

"Everything" answered Prafulla, "Because *I'm* a thing to be forgotten. But I beg you to remember for ever what's happened. I have a special reason for this, so let me ask you properly. First, have you really abandoned me?"

"Why do you say that?" said Brajesvar. "I'll never abandon you. Whoever abandons his wife is a great sinner (*mahāpātakī*). But so long as my father is alive, you and I cannot see each other. I can never disobey my father—how could I do that? But when he's no longer with us...."

Prafulla said, "In other words, you'll take me in when we're both old! All right, but how am I to survive till then? What my father-in-law's bluntly replied to that you've told me yourself, but is that what you think too? That I'm to survive by stealing, banditry, begging? Is that your view?"

Brajesvar bowed his head. Then he said, "I possess nothing of my own. But I'll collect something as best I can and send it to you."

" 'Collect something...'—you mean by taking your father's money in some way. I'll not survive on a single penny of your father's money! Can't you get an income of your own and support me?"

"I'm dependent on my father," replied Brajesvar, "It's not that I'm incapable of making a living—I haven't had the chance, but it's useless to do anything now."

"Then there's no point in taking anything from you. If I can I'll survive by stealing, banditry or begging; if not, I'll die."

"Don't speak like that," said Brajesvar. "I have a ring—worth a lot of money—take it and go, it'll last you for some time. After that. . . ."

"Where could I go to sell the ring? Still, give it to me. My life's been made worthwhile by this one night we've spent together. From time to time I'll look at this ring and think of it. But won't I be taken for a thief if someone sees me with this ring? Do you have anything else . . . ?"

"My name's engraved on the ring, so have no fear about taking it."

Brajesvar brought the ring and showed it to her; inside, on the back, his name was engraved in Farsi. Prafulla took the ring.

"Now tell me where and how we can meet again" asked Brajesvar.

"That responsibility is yours," said Prafulla. "I've done as much as I could. I can't come here again. Will you come to our house?"

Again Brajesvar bowed his head. He said, "Our enemies will outcaste us."

"Then we can't see each other any more," said Prafulla. "If we meet again somewhere. . . ."

" 'If we meet again somewhere'—then what?" asked Brajesvar. "Why have you kept quiet?"

"Will you recognize me then? I'll be much older."

"I shan't forget."

"You will."

With this Prafulla removed the brass bangle from one hand and smashed it into two. "You keep one half," she said, "And I'll keep the other. When the two halves meet, we'll recognize each other. Now I'm leaving. But remember, you've abandoned me through no fault of my own."

She opened the door and went out. Brajesvar was left standing there, wondering what to do.

When she opened the door, Prafulla saw Nayantara standing there with a broom in her hand. As soon as she saw Prafulla, Nayantara said, "Get away, you wretch! I'm going to sweep your poison away with this broom!"

Prafulla laughed and said, "So you're the house sweeper, are you?"

Nayantara was incandescent with rage. She raised the broom to strike but Prafulla didn't move. Brajesvar saw what was happening from inside the room. Before the broom could fall on the back of Prafulla's neck he snatched it away from Nayantara's hand. Again Prafulla laughed and said to Nayantara, "Don't be disappointed, *Didi*. As far as I'm concerned, the broom struck me. All my life I'll think that. So remember—you've struck me with the broom and driven me from this house."

Without saying another word, Prafulla went straight out the back entrance and saw Sagar picking flowers in the enclosed garden for Grandaunt Brahma's morning worship (*pūjā*). Prafulla went up to the garden and said to Sagar, "My friend, I'm leaving now. I shan't come to this house again. When you go to your father's house, I'll meet you there."

"Do you know where that is?" asked Sagar.

"I'll find out," was the reply.

"You'll go to my father's house?"

"What have I left to 0be ashamed of? I'm no longer a wife of this family—that's been taken away from me."

"Nonsense," said Sagar. "Don't speak like that. Your mother said she wants to see you. She's waiting for you." In fact, Prafulla's mother was waiting by the garden gate. Sagar pointed her out and Prafulla went up to her mother. Thanks to Grandaunt Brahma, Prafulla's mother hadn't had to endure the misery of going without food and shelter. When mother and daughter met each gave the other her news. Then Prafulla's mother said, "Now I'm satisfied. Come on, let's go home." '

Note: There is no follow-up in this or other editions of the novel to the idea of matching the two halves of the bangle when Brajesvar and Prafulla meet again later in life.

[This installment in *DCsv* ends here: *Baṅgadarśan,* Māgh 1289 B.E. (Jan.1883)].

NOTES

"Here they were—husband and wife...": this statement describing the relationship between husband and wife surely intimates the author's own view of how a marriage should be. For how this might link into the distinction between the so-called old patriarchy and the new in Bankim's thought, see the Introduction.

"the most intimate relationship in the world": *pṛthibīr madhye sarbbāpekṣā ghaniṣṭha sambandha*. See previous note and Introduction.

"Then he sat down beside her": a significant act of intimacy in the developing Bengali culture between a man and a woman.

"will stop reading this book right here": *DCM:* "will not cease reading the book" (p.33)—evidently an oversight. Bankim, of course, is writing sarcastically.

"a kind of half-moon tiara": *jhāpṭā*. Rarely in evidence today.

"Those who've crossed to a holy place": *keha tīrtha karile.... Tīrtha* is generally translated as "ford," a holy crossing-point, a meeting-place between the sacred and mundane. Bankim wishes to emphasize the sanctity of marriage by such references. This night together, between husband and wife, sealed their love and what up to then was a ritual bond.

"stayed on like Lakshmi and Vishnu on my bed": *āmār pālaṅke, biṣṇur lakṣmī haiyāchen. Pālaṅka* is a large, often ornate bed. Husband and wife being together is compared by Sagar to the God Vishnu and his wife Lakshmi, the goddess of prosperity, meeting—a highly auspicious occasion. Prafulla became Lakshmi to Brajesvar's Vishnu. But then Sagar being Sagar, she goes on to say irreverently about their husband, "... that fellow...": *minse.*

"What have I left to be ashamed of?": It would be unusual, and demeaning, for a senior co-wife to visit, on her own, a more junior co-wife in the latter's own home.

Chapter 7

VARIANTS

* "She managed...": this sentence does not occur in *DCsv.*

* "Then one of [the neighbors] said...": *DCsv* has: 'Then Prafulla said, "Something's occurred to me. Shouldn't my father-in-law be invited to my mother's funeral rite?" The neighbors replied, "Certainly he should.,"' etc.

* "Now tell me... money from?": after this sentence, *DCsv* adds, "There's no doubt she's a bad character (*niścit tāhār caritra manda*)." That is, she's a woman with loose morals. This explains why Haraballabh became more set against Prafulla.

* "Brajesvar... that very night": this sentence does not occur in *DCsv.*

* "while for his part... to visit Prafulla": this sentence does not occur in *DCsv.*

NOTES

"a practitioner": *kabirāj,* a practitioner of Ayurvedic or indigenous herbal remedies.

"the Bengali race": *bāṅgālī jāti.*

"the rites of the fourth day...": *caturther śrāddha:* that is, the rites that a married woman must perform on the fourth day after the death of a parent. This involves making offerings of food, and feeding a number of Brahmin males (*brāhmaṇ-bhojan*)—a costly ritual for Brahmins generally.

"that she wished to make the offerings": *icchā piṇḍadān kari.*

"a girl without a protector": *anāthā bālikā.*

Chapter 8

VARIANTS

* "The landlord...Paran Chaudhuri": After this sentence, *DCsv* adds, "His house was about sixteen miles (*prāy āṭ kroś*) away."

* "Shortly after this happened...found no one there": This passage does not occur in *DCsv.*

* "Victory to Lord Krishna...": *DCsv* has instead, "Victory to the Lord of the world!" (*jay jagadīśvar!*).

NOTES

"Since she was young...by her side at night": an indication of the status of women and the strict norms to which they were expected to conform in rural Bengali society at the time.

"naive": *chelemānuṣ.*

"a woman of low caste": *itar jātir meye. DCM* has "Born of an uncultured family" (43). *DCM* has a tendency to be somewhat euphemistic with regard to references about birth in a low caste.

"she had failed rather...unblemished character": *caritraṭā baḍa se khāṭi rākhite pāre nāi.*

"to hold court on behalf of his master": *kāchāri karita.*

"a white sari with a crimson border": *rāṅgāpeḍe śāḍīparā*; "white" because Phulmani was a widow and it was the custom for widows to wear white; "crimson" because rather than being a retiring person, Phulmani wished to flaunt her independence and *joie de vivre*. After all, it was rumored that she had a special relationship with Durlabh, indicated by the use of the term *kṛtābhisārā*, "advancing to keep her tryst."

"leisure-room": *bihār-mandir*. A male preserve in palatial residences.

"it's in the nature... to make a noise": grunts, rhythmic panting etc. to keep moving in step, calling out to change pace or indicate obstacles on the way and so on.

"bandits/brigands": *ḍākāt/dasyu.*

"Muslim rule had passed... British rule...": as the text goes on to say, the Great Famine of 1770 had occurred a few years earlier. Bankim was influenced by the description of the catastrophe given in Sir William Wilson Hunter's *Annals of Rural Bengal*: "All through the stifling summer of 1770 the people went on dying. The husbandmen sold their cattle; they sold their implements of agriculture; they devoued their seed-grain; they sold their sons and daughters, till at length no buyer of children could be found; they ate the leaves of trees and the grass of the field.... At an early period of the year pestilence had broken out" (1897, seventh edition, pp.26–7). Thus the events of *Debī Chaudhurāṇī* took place, say, in the mid-1770s. There was no established political power in the Bengal region of the time. Marshall (1987:89) notes: "[B]y 1765 an independent government of Bengal had virtually no existence. The Nawabs and their ministers were appointed by the [East India] Company. The Company had disbanded much of the Nawab's army, while accepting for itself exclusive responsibility for the defence of the provinces and exercising the right to appropriate the lion's share of the resources of Bengal for its own use."

"Debisingh was in charge...": Debīsiṅgh's ancestors came from Panipath in northern India. He arrived in the Bengal region in 1756 and in 1781 the British East India Company awarded him the rights of collecting revenue on their behalf in the districts of Purnia, Edbakpur, Rangpur, and Dinajpur. He acquired a reputation for rapacity, and in January 1783 cultivators in Rangpur rioted against him. He died in April 1805. Over a decade separates the beginning of the Great Famine from the start of his tenure in Rangpur; thus, it is not clear how historically precise Bankim wishes to be in locating the events of this chapter—whether the "few/some years" (*bachar kata haila*) that he says had elapsed since the Famine is meant to span a decade or less. Bankim often sits lightly to geo-political precision in his so-called historical novels, so it is likely, as stated above, that the events of this chapter occurred in the mid-1770s.

"Edmund Burke" etc.: parliamentarian, orator, and polemicist of Irish descent (1729–97). Burke was famous for the eloquence and power of his speeches. He had been interested in the activities of the East India Company for a number of years, and outraged by the reports he had heard about its administration, led the impeachment of the Company's first governor-general, Warren Hastings, at Westminster in 1786. This was a protracted process, and Hastings was eventually acquitted in 1795. The speech referred to, which relentlessly and graphically lists the cruelties allegedly perpetrated by Debisingh and condoned by Hastings, was delivered on 18th February, 1788 (see P. Langford/P. J. Marshall [1991:408–27]).

"Barendrabhumi": see endnotes under chapter 2 (thus Barendrabhumi would have been included in the territory under Debisingh's jurisdiction).

"Mr Goodlad . . . policing the area": As we have noted in the Introduction, Richard Goodlad was a historical figure, though he seems to have left before Debi and her followers disappear from the historical record. The job of a Collector at the time was multifarious. In his *The Indian Empire,* Hunter writes of the Collector's responsibilities as follows: "[T]he unit of administration is the District. . . . The District officer, whether known as Collector-Magistrate or as Deputy Commissioner, is the responsible head of his jurisdiction. . . . His own special duties are so numerous and so various as to bewilder the outsider. . . . He is not a mere subordinate of a central bureau, who takes his color from his chief, and represents the political parties or the permanent officialism of the capital. . . . He is a fiscal officer, charged with the collection of the revenue from the land and other sources; he also is a revenue and criminal judge, both of first instance and in appeal. . . . Police, jails, education, municipalities, roads, sanitation, dispensaries, the local taxation, and the imperial revenues of his District, are to him matters of daily concern": Hunter (1886:436).

"sepoy": *sipāhī.* Indian soldiers in British employ.

"the Lord of death himself": *kālāntak jam.* A distinguishing attribute in the iconography of Yama (Bengali: *jam* (pronounced "jom") = the Lord of death) is a large stick or staff (*daṇḍa*) which he carries in his hand. A porter will say that he thinks he sees the approaching figures carrying large staves.

"North India": *hindusthānī.* Hindi speakers.

"Dinajpur": a town/region north of Rajsahi and west of Rangpur.

"When they saw the porters . . . continued on their way": without going up to investigate the palanquin! Unlikely.

"bears" *bhāluke. DCM,* unaccountably, "wolves" (p.50)!

"huge mansion": *bṛhat aṭṭālikā.* These were truly large, imposing brick-built buildings, more than one storey high, with numerous rooms, out-buildings, and courtyards—the homes of local rulers or grandees. Haraballabh seems to have lived in one.

"divine being": *debatā. DCM,* less accurately, "angel" (p.51).

"Lord Krishna": thus *nandadulāl,* an epithet of Krishna Vāsudeva: literally, "Darling son of Nanda (Krishna's foster father)."

"A Vaishnava": as the context indicates, the old man followed a form of Vaishnava practice based on mendicancy and the (sexual) association of a female companion (a Vaishnavi). For a good account of the kind of life this might entail, see J. Openshaw (2002).

"spirit": *prāṇ,* or life-force.

"ghost": *yakṣa.*

"be unable to pass on": *āmār gati haibe nā,* that is, he would be unable to pass on either to his next rebirth or, indeed, to heaven.

"After this she bathed...": because (as a Brahmin) she was ritually impure by contact with a dead body.

"wearing half while she dried the other half": that is, half the sari preserved her modesty while the other half was laid open to dry—a common practice in rural Bengal.

Chapter 9

VARIANTS

* "The hairs of her body...small pot": After this sentence, the story in *DCsv* takes a different turn (with substantial sharing of text) till the end of this and the next issue of *Baṅgadarśan,* viz. Phālgun and Caitra 1289 B.E. (February and March 1883); thereafter, the journal was temporarily discontinued. After some months, the journal was started up again and so was the novel, but the journal finally came to an end soon after that, leaving the novel stranded at the end of Part II (Bankim completed and published the novel in book-form in 1884). For the translation of the major text changes of the novel in its serial form (*DCsv*) from this point in ch.9 till the end of Part I, see Appendix A.

NOTES

"pallet": *śajyā.*

"flint and a match": *cakmaki diyāśalāi.* The "match" here would not be a version of the modern safety-match, of course, but some material (e.g., cloth or wood) dipped or coated with a combustible material which would burn when sparks were struck from the flint, and which could then be used to light tobacco, a fire etc.

"Sir Walter Raleigh": An English grandee and adventurer (1552–1618), who is supposed to have introduced smoking as a leisure activity in Europe. As the passage that follows indicates, Bankim enjoyed a good smoke.

"Kayastha": though the Kayasthas are a respectable caste in Bengal, their position in the caste-hierarchy is disputed. For some authorities they do not belong to the twice-born orders, being placed high up among the Śūdras; for other authorities they are on a level with Kṣatriyas, and are accorded twice-born status. Traditionally they functioned as scribes, clerks, and accountants.

"to the insignia of her faith . . . tambourine": thus, *raskali o khañjanite citta bikrīta kariyā*. "*Raskali*" is the vertical mark of colored paste drawn upward from the bridge of the nose to the forehead by Vaishnava devotees, as a sign of Vaishnava commitment and identity. The tambourine (*khañjani*) is likewise carried about and played by female ascetics of some Vaishnava sects. It has small cymbals around the rim that jangle when the tambourine is struck.

"he took up begging": *bhek laiyā*, that is, he dressed like a Vaishnava ascetic and began the formal practice of seeking alms.

"Sri-Brindaban": Brindaban (*Bṛndāban* in Bengali and *Vṛndāvana* in Sanskrit) is an important centre of pilgrimage and devotion for Vaishnavas, situated in northern India, south of Delhi—the place where many incidents of the God Krishna's youth were enacted. "Sri" is a term of respect (with the connotation of beauty, graciousness, and wealth).

"the sweet songs of the poet Jayadeva": Jayadeva (12th century) came from the Birbhum region of Bengal and composed a long erotic work in Sanskrit verse, the *Gītagovinda*, which became famous. The "sweet songs" were no doubt taken from there. The *Gītagovinda* graphically depicts the love-play between Krishna and his favorite milkmaid-companion, Rādhā. There are a number of English translations with Introduction, Notes etc.; see, for example, Lee Siegel (1990) and Barbara Stoler Miller (1977).

"*Srimadbhagavata*": The *Śrīmad-bhāgavata Purāṇa* is a lengthy ninth-century Sanskrit devotional text and a favorite among many Vaishnavas; a highlight is the depiction of the amorous exploits of Krishna with the milkmaids of Brindaban. Thus, reference to these two texts and the "well-nourished bodies" of the local Vaishnava ascetics clearly implies that Krishnagobind's Vaishnavi felt their sexual allure.

"Murshidabad": the capital of a kingdom in Barendrabhumi (in Bengal) under a Muslim ruler, or *nawab*, at the time. The main part of the kingdom was south of the Padma river, adjoining the region of Birbhum.

"An African eunuch": *ek jan hābsī (*sic*) khojā. "Hābsī/-śī"* denoted "an Abyssinian" (viz.Ethiopian), and was often used as a generic term for Africans, who were regular visitors and travellers to Muslim courts in India at the time. *DCM* has: "An Abyssinian eunuch was seen frequenting her house, presumably with a proposal to convert her into a *Begum*." But this doesn't make clear whose *Begum* or wife the Vaishnavi would be.

"the Padma river": the large river separating India and Bangladesh today in the area of northern Murshidabad district and Rajsahi respectively. It plays a significant literary and historical role in the Bengali imagination.

"local market": *hāṭ*. The *hāṭ* is held regularly on a particular day (or days) in an area.

"clay oven": *culā,* in which wood, coke, or coal would be burned as fuel.

"large jar": *ghaḍā.*

"belonged to the dynasty of a ruler called Nildhvaj": *nīldhvajbaṅśīya.* We have a clue as to what Bankim might mean. Hunter (1876:Vol.VII) quotes from a Report on the history of Rangpur District made by one of its Collectors, a Mr. Glazier, much earlier in the century. Glazier himself is recounting from local folklore about the succession of dynasties in the region from a period before "the close of the fifteenth century." After mentioning earlier groups of rulers, Glazier writes: "The next dynasty had three Rajas [kings],—Niladwaj, Chakradwaj, and Nilambar.... The third king of this dynasty, Nilambar, attained to great power.... Several isolated forts scattered over the District are called by Nilambar's name. The fall of this monarch is attributed to the vengeance of his prime minister, a Brahman named Sochi Patra. He had ordered the son of this man to be killed for some misconduct, and part of his flesh to be cooked, of which he contrived that the father should partake. The Brahman went to the court of the Afghan kings at Gaur, and procured the invasion of Rangpur by the Muhammadans, which is their first appearance in this direction. The Muhammadan commander gave out that he despaired of taking the place, and proposed a peace. He asked and obtained permission for Musalman [viz. Muslim] ladies to go and pay their respects to the Hindu queen; but in the litters armed men were concealed, who captured the town. Nilambar was taken prisoner, and put into an iron cage to be carried to Gaur; but he escaped by the way, and has ever since remained concealed.... The Afghan king who made this conquest is supposed to be Husain Shah, who reigned A.D. 1497–1521" (pp.314–15).

"This was one of them...": Apparently isolated in the middle of a dense forest, with little or no sign of the ruins (and clearings) that would have been marked by dwellings associated with a royal court! A good example of narratival license.

"Gaud" (or Gaur): a kingdom more or less in middle-Bengal at the time, but "north" for the Bengalis of the Gangetic basin which was the cultural centre of Bengal. "Northern" Bengal properly speaking would include the regions of Darjeeling, Jalpaiguri, and Coochbehar (Kuch Behar).

"Pathans": Muslims from the region of northwestern India and Afghanistan; they had a reputation for being a hardy people who were ruthless warriors.

Chapter 10

VARIANTS

* "Durlabh's parentage": the first edition (and *DCsv*—see under ch.12 of Appendix A) has "Durlabh's ancestry," viz. *baṃśāvalī.*

NOTES

"entrusted her life": *prāṇ samarpan kariyāchila.*

"The neat tuck at the back of his loincloth": *kāchā*. The tuck in the front is called *kõcā*.

"fancy shoes": *nāgrā jutā*. Shoes with pointed toes and without laces.

"You've gone blind": *tui chokher māthā kheyechis.*

Didi: older sister.

"We're nobody. What have we... those gods, the Brahmins?": *āmrā choṭo lok—āmāder debatā bāmuner kathāy kāj ki*. Bankim has said earlier that Phulmani came from a low caste.

❂ *Chapter 11* ❂

NOTES

"fate": *adṛṣṭa:* literally, the "unseen" (power).

"the misery of poverty": *dāridrya-duḥkha,* reading this compound as a *tatpuruṣa* rather than a *dvandva*.

"Cooking pot": *hāḍī*. A pot with a bulge in the middle, made of clay or metal.

"local market": *hāṭ* (see under Notes for ch.9).

"The names of God... body": *gāye nāmābali*. As noted earlier, probably on a shawl. All the features of this description—the divine names, the mark on the forehead, the shaven head—indicate that he was a religious-minded Brahmin who studied the texts, probably a Vaishnava.

"and asked her kindly": that is, he said, *kothā jaibe, mā* (literally, "Where are you going, mother"?). *Mā* ("mother") can be used as a term of kindly respect or familiarity for young girls or women. It helps to bar the possibility, in the mind of the reader, of an erotic/sexual relationship developing between the speaker and Prafulla (even though we are told that the Brahmin was not very old).

"It's half a day's walk away": *hāṭ ek belār path*. There were no watches in such circumstances, and it was the rural practice to measure time by the passage of the sun and moon, how long it took to walk/travel certain distances, and so on.

"This girl shows all the right signs": *e bālikā sakal sulakṣaṇjuktā*.

"learned Brahmin": *brāhmaṇpaṇḍit*. A Brahmin familiar with the textual tradition and its interpretations.

❂

"child": *bāchā*. A term reinforcing the lack of an erotic relationship.

"jug": *kalasī,* that is, pitcher-shaped, with a lip and handle, and a rounded body, viz. urceolate.

"One anna": This form of currency (which underwent many changes with the passage of time) was discontinued only in 1957.

mohur: mohar. Though they were made of gold, the size and hence value of *mohars* could vary from region to region, kingdom to kingdom.

"Child, you're thinking . . .": here *mā*, literally "mother" (see earlier).

"a war-drum": *nāgrā bā dāmāmā*. A drum with two faces.

"looking as fierce as the Lord of death himself": *kālāntak jamer mata*. The *Padma Purāṇa* says that Yama appears to virtuous people benignly and to sinners in terrible form (see S. Sarkar [2003:444b]). In his *The Development of Hindu Iconography,* J. Banerjea notes: "Yama, the guardian of the south, is described in the *Bṛhatsaṃhitā* simply as 'having a staff in his hand and riding on a buffalo' (*daṇḍī Yamo mahiṣago*; Ch.57, v.57). The *Viṣṇudharmottara* gives an elaborate description of the four-armed god seated on a buffalo with his consort Dhumrorṇā on his left lap, his right hands holding a staff and a sword and the left ones a trident with flames and a rosary, a face with flames issuing from it being shown on the top of the staff. . . . Citragupta dressed as a Northener (*udīcyaveśa*) holding a pen and a leaf in his hands on his right, and the fierce-looking Kāla (Time, the destroyer) holding a noose in his hand on his left, are his characteristic attendants. . . ." (1956:525).

"a small torn mat of kusha-grass": *cheḍā kuśāsan*. Kusha (*kuśa*), a grass with long, pointed stalks, has been used in Hindu ritual from ancient times. "Grass, especially *kuśa* (*poa cynosuroides*) and tufts or bunches of it ([called] *darbha*), is very often used for sacrificial purposes including lustration, apotropaeic [viz. protective] rites etc. It is regarded as pure [*śuddha/medhya*] and hence as a means of purification" (Gonda, 1980:114). It is also thought to have strengthening properties (Gonda, 1980:passim). Thus ascetics often used mats made of kusha-grass to signify but also to effectuate their ascetic state.

"old ascetic": *bairāgī*—a Vaishnava ascetic.

Chapter 12

NOTES

"Yes sir": *ājñā hā̃*.

"I'll take it home": *deśe laiyā jaiba*, that is, to my own place (village) where I live/grew up.

"full authority": *pūrṇa adhikār.*

"They enjoy it": *bhog kare.*

"Child": *mā,* viz. "Mother" (see under Notes for ch.11).

"some build up merit": *keha puṇyasañcay kare.* Merit (*puṇya*)/demerit (*pāpa*) tend to be spoken of as balances in a bank, which can be in credit or deficit according to circumstances. For a semantic treatment of these terms in the Sanskritic tradition, see Hara (1967–8:382–411). In this respect, "merit/demerit" are analogous to *tapas* or "ascetic energy." On the expenditure of *tapas* also see Hara (1997:226–48). *DCM:* "Wealth is a source of enjoyment to some, to others it is means to earn bliss..." (p.72). But this translation does not really convey the meaning of *puṇyasañcay.*

"clear the way to hell": *naraker path sāph kare.*

"great demerit or great merit": *bistar pāp athabā bistar puṇya.*

"covetousness of sin": *pāper lālasā.*

"I come from a respectable family!": *āmi gṛhasther meye.*

"I've no experience of sin": *kakhano pāp jāni nā.*

"without doing wrong": *niṣpāpe.*

"a wise man": *jñānī.*

"It will take five to seven years to teach you": *DCB* makes a perceptive observation here: "Bankimchandra was influenced by the thought of the famous philosopher Auguste Comte, and the influence of Comte's five-year plan is noticeable with regard to the arrangement envisaged for Prafulla's instruction" (Notes, p.30). Even so, Hindu tradition frequently speaks of the need for disciplined preparation before a special task or way of life is embarked upon (see, e.g., the famous story of Prajāpati, Virocana, and Indra in *Chāndogya Upanishad* 8.7.1 f., and the *Bhagavadgītā*'s constant reference to the practice (*abhyāsa*) of *yoga* of various kinds as a requisite for special tasks).

"with beard parted...clipped side-whiskers": *caugōppā o chāṭā gālpāṭṭā.*

"Hostin": Warren Hastings (1732–1818); he became the first governor-general (chief administrator) of British India under the East India Company in 1773. This office was based in Kolkata (Calcutta), the administrative centre of British-controlled India at the time, and quite far away from the scene of action.

"I'm not looking for a king like that....You know...": we don't really, and it's never made clear. Perhaps the real point is that authorially Bankim doesn't wish to give the impression to his British political masters that he is writing subversively.

"leaseholder": *ijārādār*, the man who leases villages/land from the *jamidār* or landowner, and is responsible for paying the latter a portion of the revenue and/or rent accruing from his leasehold. *DCM*, oddly: "The British have recently raided Ranjanpur."

"headquarters": *kāchāri*, where the governing administrator holds court as it were.

Chapter 13

VARIANTS

*"Bhabani Thakur kept his promise": *DCsv* begins the chapter (ch.14 of *DCsv*) as follows: "When Prafulla asked Bhabani Thakur how she could live alone in that forest unless a woman came to stay with her, he sent her not one but two women, one to fetch and carry, the other to be a companion to her" etc. as in the standard text.

*"In what way?": instead of this sentence, *DCsv* has the following: " 'Like me?' The older woman replied, 'You've offered only your wealth to Sri Krishna. I've given everything to Sri Krishna.' " Then the text continues as in the standard version.

NOTES

"one to fetch and carry": *ekjan hāṭe ghāṭe jāibe.*

"with a glowing darkness … radiated about her": *ujjval śyāmabarṇa—barśākāler kaci pātār mata rang. rūp uchaliyā paḍiteche.*

"Prafulla said, "Gobrar Ma! How many children …" etc.: Now follows one of those passages translators view with dismay, viz. passages containing wordplay that lies embedded in the host-language. Because Gobrar Ma is hard of hearing, she mishears words and speaks out of context. *DCM* makes heavy weather of this section. He places the initial exchange with word-play (till Gobrar Ma's full hearing returns) between asterisks, with a footnote remarking: "The portion between the asterisk lines is changed from the original, but the spirit is intact." This is followed by some reference to word-play, but without a faithful rendering of the text (e.g., " "What caste do you belong to?" asked Prafulla. "No, there was no cast-iron hurry about it, but I feared I might miss marketing," said Gobra's mother" etc. There is no reference to "cast-iron hurry" and "marketing" in the text here; p.78).

"caste": *jāt.*

"throw away the leaf I've eaten on": *āmār eṭo pātā phelbo*. "*Eṭo*" refers to the leavings of something eaten, fit only to be thrown away as ritually impure. The use of crockery was not traditional practice, for this implied reusing *eṭo* plates etc., however much these might be washed. Food was generally eaten on broad, flat leaves (squares of banana leaf were the favorite), which could then simply be thrown away after a meal. In time, westernized, middle-class, generally urbanized Hindus used crockery, but this took some getting used to. The reader must recall that the story takes place in the latter half of the eighteenth century in a rural context, where traditional practices were prevalent.

"Brahmin's wife": *bāmanī.* A Brahmin woman married to a Brahmin.

"aristocratic family": *rājār bāḍī. "Rājā"* here refers to a leading man of a region or district, a grandee and a man of high caste.

"the marriage wasn't a formal affair": thus *bibāhaṭā gāndharbbamata.* The Gandharva form of marriage, which consisted of a stable union between individuals on the basis of sexual attraction, was recognized as valid (after a fashion) in the ancient law-codes. The well-known *Manu Smṛti* (200 B.C.E.–200 C.E.?) describes it thus: "The mutual union of bride and groom through choice is known as the Gāndharva [marriage]; it must be understood as pertaining to sexual union, that is, as based on sexual desire" (*icchayānyonyasaṃyogaḥ kanyāyāś ca varasya ca/ gāndharvaḥ sa tu vijñeyo maithunyaḥ kāmasaṃbhavaḥ,* 3.32). There were other (similar) descriptions, however, some putting the onus of choice on the girl, others describing the relationship more or less as a marriage of convenience for lovers. Religious ritual seemed not to be involved. No doubt Prafulla's companion was speaking euphemistically here, and the impression is given that pressure for this relationship came from the boy's side on a woman who had few options. In the socio-religiously rigid Bengali society of the time "Gandharva-marriages" could hardly be accepted or tolerated.

"He too gave me away... in a manner of speaking": *tinio āmāke ek prakār sampradān kariyāchen.*

"husband": *svāmī.*

"For he who owns me completely... husband and master": *jini sampūrṇarūpe āmār adhikārī, tini āmār svāmī.*

"But those who had shaped the Hindu way of life": *hindudharmmapraṇetārā.*

"God": *īśvar.*

"marital love": thus *prem. Prem* is sensual love, but not necessarily carnal. In some traditions, for example, Gauḍīya Vaiṣṇavism, it is directed to the deity embodied as Krishna.

"deity": *debatā.*

"Diba": Diba will appear later in the story.

"A woman's husband is her deity": *strīloker patii debatā.*

"devotion": *bhakti.*

"love": *bhālobāsā.*

"the first step toward devotion to God is devotion to one's husband": Bankim is saying through this rather obscure philosophical digression that the Hindu woman has access to God in a special manner: through devotion to her husband. In other words, she ought so to love her husband that this love leads wholeheartedly to an encompassing devotion to God (this seems to be the point of the distinction between the use of "love" (*bhālobāsā*) and "devotion" (*bhakti*) toward the end of the passage). Thus God becomes all in all. This, says the passage, is how the ancients who shaped Hindu society recommended that a woman love her husband (rather than through a selfish, carnal love—though Bankim gives no evidence to back this up). But in his role as a modern guide, Bankim does not go on to point out here that the Hindu husband ought to reciprocate this love so that both loves, that of wife for husband and of husband for wife, become two sides of the same coin. A more balanced equation occurs in the *DT.* For further discussion on this, see the Introduction. For the concept of a woman's husband being her "god" according to developing notions of domesticity in Bengal in the second half of the nineteenth century, though not necessarily in the context of Bankim's thought, see Walsh (2004, esp.ch.7).

❁ *Chapter 14* ❁

VARIANTS

* "It so happened… to ask where she might be": This section is omitted from the first edition.

* "When he saw that Prafulla wasn't there": the first edition adds, "that night."

* "Only Brajesvar's time": *DCsv* has instead, "Only a particular person's time" etc.

* "had been cast out": *DCsv* has, "had been cast out of the house" etc.

* "remained unshaken": *DCsv* continues as follows, giving a different ending to the chapter (viz. ch.15 of *DCsv*):

> Aryan devotion to one's father (*ārya pitṛbhakti*) no longer exists in the land of Bengal. Through the deadly poison (*halāhale*) of English education, Bengal's ancient code of practice (*pracīn dharma*) has been shattered. One's most revered, worshipful father, whose lotus feet one lacked the courage to touch in the past, has now become "My dear father"! He is no longer the object (*pātra*) of devotion

> (*bhakti*), only of reproach (*anujog*). And the Bengali who doesn't refer to him as "the old man" is now reckoned a virtuous son. Perhaps this society is making progress and not going to ruin, now that the Bengali has learnt to give speeches! Instead of our traditional code of practice (*dharma*), we've now got lectures—what great gains we've made!

In context, this is an important passage in so far as it indicates Bankim's ambivalent attitude toward his own father (see Introduction). The same idea is expressed in Bankim's *Dharmatattva* (ch.10): "Nowadays proper respect (*bhakti*) has completely disappeared among the English-educated and half-educated. Without being able to understand the true meaning of Western egalitarianism (*pāścātya sāmyabād*), they've arrived at the perverse notion that humans are equal everywhere and in every possible way. There's no need to show anyone proper respect (*bhakti*)....One's father is now "my dear father," or "the old man" (*buḍo beṭā*), one's mother is one's Dad's wife, an older brother is just a relative" and so on.

NOTES

"bandits": *dasyu*.

"since he was afraid of his father": the traditional relationship of son to father had become one of awe rather than of familiar affection, a relationship that to some extent Bankim experienced with regard to his own father. "Respectful distance, rather than great warmth, appears to have been the true nature of Bankim's feelings for his father. But the fact of great deference and a strong sense of filial duty are not in doubt....Evidently, both in terms of inherited values and his own emotional responses, his relationship with his father had a certain centrality in his life experience. Yet his own awareness of this relationship was torn by mutually contradictory feelings—deference, a sense of duty, impatience and resentment" (Raychaudhuri [1988:108]). Perhaps Brajesvar's almost slavish deference to his father (which will grow in evidence as the novel unfolds) is the projection of an ideal scenario that Bankim could never enact, or is it an ironic depiction of how such a relationship could ruin a family? For more on this, see the Introduction.

"that only the flesh from the shoulder of the fish-head...": the fish-head is a Bengali delicacy and the careful removal of the flesh from its bones—by sucking etc.—was (and is) generally relished. But Brajesvar was not up to this labor of love; he only picked at the most accessible portion of the dish.

"push the dish to one side": *byañjan ṭheliyā rākhe.*

"The boy's lost his appetite": *cheler mandāgni haiyāche.*

"a digestive of pickled lime etc.": *jārak lebu prabhṛti.*

"the Ayurvedic practitioner": *kabirāj.*

"*Neem* tree:" or the Margosa tree, the *azadirachta indica:* a tall tree with rich foliage and "feathery leaves, toothed leaflets, curved like a sickle," thought to have medicinal properties. "Its leaves repel insects and its mere presence is believed to keep an area free from malaria. Neem-oil is efficacious against pyorrhea and is used in toothpaste" (R. E. Hawkins, ed., 1986:407). It is regarded as a shade-giving tree.

"*Tulsi* tree": skr. *tulasī*, the Basil plant (*Ocimum sanctum*), which can grow to the size of a tree. Though now favoured by the God Vishnu and his surrogates (e.g., Krishna) and their devotees, the Vaishnavas, it is sacred to Hindus more generally. Sacred plants are often believed by Hindus to contain the essence of the deities favoring them, and so become objects of worship in themselves. The *tulsi* is believed to have curative properties and to be able to purify the air (e.g., of mosquitoes and other pests) and even ward off Yama, the Lord of death, and his messengers. Many Hindu homes have a sprig of *tulsi* or a *tulsi* plant on the premises. The *tulsi* is often used as an ingredient of the funeral pyre. See Stutley (1977:306).

"sitting there by the steps": *rāṇāy base*; that is, sitting there on the brickwork surmounting or adjoining the steps/small jetty near a body of water.

"samples of her cooking... brick": the "dishes" are named, viz. *dhūlā-caḍcaḍī, kādār sūkta, iṭer ghaṇṭa*, that is, "sand-*caḍcaḍī*, mud-*sūkta*, and brick-*ghaṇṭa*." *Caḍcaḍī* was a dry dish of vegetables cooked in oil with some seasoning, *sūkta* was a thick-gravy dish containing bitter vegetables, while *ghaṇṭa* was another dry dish of cooked, seasoned, diced vegetables. For more information about these and other examples of Bengali cuisine in the context of Bengali culture, see the excellent C. Banerji (1997).

"intoxicating infatuation... tenderest love": *unmādakar moha... susnigdha sneha.*

"an intense compassion": *dāruṇ karuṇā.*

"golden icon" etc.: *sonār pratimā*. Like a golden icon, Prafulla had been enshrined in Brajesvar's heart, but the irony of it was that in actual fact she had been rejected without cause, and was desperate for food and shelter—she was without a proper home or shrine. Religious images (*pratimā*) could not be cast out from their shrines without due cause.

"rheumatic fever... worse": *bāt-śleṣma-bikāre. DCM*, less convincingly: "Prafulla had died of pneumonia" (p.89).

"purificatory bath... rites for the dead": *śauca snān... śrāddha.*

"That's one sin seen to... relieved": the "sin" (*pāp*) of ritual impurity cleansed by the bath, but more importantly the bane that was the favored co-wife, Prafulla; the other "sin" would be the other co-wife, Sagar. She would be greatly relieved to take the prescribed ritual bath in the aftermath of the second death too!

"local practitioner": *vaidya:* skilled in Ayurvedic or herbal remedies.

"deity": *debatā.*

"*A father is heaven... a father is satisfied*": *pitā svargaḥ pitā dharmaḥ pitā hi paramaṃ tapaḥ/ pitari prītim āpanne prīyante sarvadevatāḥ//* A Sanskrit verse, found in the *Mahābhārata* (see Poona edition, 12.258.20, with only slight changes, though retaining the same meaning, viz. *paramakaṃ tapaḥ* for *paramaṃ tapaḥ,* and *sarvāḥ prīyante devatāḥ* for *prīyante sarvadevatāḥ*). The context in which this verse occurs is interesting. The eldest Pāṇḍava brother, Yudhiṣṭhira, asks the wise Bhiṣma how one should respond to a problematic task: should one carry it out with despatch or take one's time over it (*śīghraṃ vātha cireṇa vā*)? Bhiṣma replies with a cautionary tale about the youth Cirakārī ("He who takes his time"), son of the sage Gautama. Gautama had become furious with his wife, and in his rage, before leaving his hermitage on a journey, ordered Cirakārī to kill her (that is, Cirakārī's mother). True to his name, Cirakārī procrastinated and kept turning the matter over in his mind. His dilemma was summed up as follows: on the one hand, a father must be obeyed because "A father is heaven, a father is duty, for a father indeed is one's highest concern (*tapaḥ,* in the sense of 'chief observance imposed by one's state in life')"; on the other hand, "There is no shelter like a mother, no refuge like a mother, no protection like a mother's, no recourse like a mother" (12.258.29: *nāsti mātṛsamā chāyā nāsti mātṛsamā gatiḥ/ nāsti mātṛsamaṃ trāṇaṃ nāsti mātṛsamā prapā//*). Cirakārī was still pondering the matter when his father Gautama returned, repenting of his rash order and hardly daring to hope that his son had lived up to his name and stayed his hand. The relief and joy when he found that this was the case! Both father and son eventually attained heaven, the moral of the story being, "One who takes his time to act is a wise person who does not default in deeds" (12.158.3). Note that in effect the text lauds Cirakārī for disobeying his father. I am grateful to Pradip Bhattacharya for directing me to this passage.

"devotion": *bhakti.* In light of Nishi's distinction toward the end of the preceding chapter, viz. "But devotion (*bhakti*) [to God] is one thing and love (*bhālobāsā*) [for a husband] another," it may be no accident that the author describes Brajesvar's commitment to his father as "devotion." This turned out to be an overriding, potentially destructive devotion that was finally rendered harmless only because Prafulla, as a loyal and resourceful wife, was able to make it serve the family's ends without dishonoring it.

Chapter 15

VARIANTS

* "For the fourth year": after this, *DCsv* proceeds as follows: "Prafulla was instructed to eat whatever she wanted. Prafulla ate only salt, finger-chillies, and rice. For the fifth year she was told to follow what she ate in the first year; in

addition Bhabani Thakur gave her permission to have milk and *Mug dal*. He said, 'Since we need strength in your body now, you must eat food that builds you up.' " Then the text continues with "Where resting, clothes, bathing and sleep...," as in the standard edition.

* "through the same discipline": after this, *DCsv* continues as follows, condensing the text: "Except for himself, he allowed no other man to come to their residence. He had tremendous power in this forest, and what he did not permit, no one could do. There was no bar to Prafulla going out herself. She would wander here and there from time to time, but when she did so she would never speak to any man. She was unaware that his spies would accompany her about. In this way, by dint of various tests and practices" etc. as in the standard edition.

NOTES

"Mistress Nishi": *niśi ṭhākurāṇī*. Bankim is being somewhat sarcastic.

"basic arithmetic": *śubhaṅkarī āk*. Śubhaṅkar or rather Bhuguram Das, a Bengali from Bankura district, composed a well-known text giving the basic rules of arithmethic for the performance of everyday tasks; this work was called the *Śubaṅkarī*. As we shall see later, Prafulla didn't advance very far in this knowledge.

"teacher": *adhyāpak*, and later "instructor."

"*Bhattikavya... Bhagavad Gita*": all the works mentioned in this passage represent high points in the tradition of Sanskrit grammar, literature, and thought. The *Bhaṭṭikāvya* is a poem, possibly of the fifth–seventh century C.E., ascribed to the savant Bhaṭṭi. "Originally called the Rāvaṇa-vadha," this poem is characterized by "celebrating the exploits of Rāma and illustrating Sanskrit grammar by the systematic application of all possible forms and constructions" (Monier-Williams [1970:745]). The *Raghuvaṃśa*, *Kumārasambhava*, and *Śakuntalā* are long poetical works by the famous classical poet, Kālidāsa (*c*.5th century C.E.). The *Naiṣadha* is an epic poem by Śrī Harṣa. These are all works that call for a mastery of Sanskrit grammar and literature.

Sāṃkhya is an ancient Indian philosophical system whose conceptual categories describing self and world assumed crucial importance in the Sanskritic tradition. The "Vedānta" represents various philosophical–theological schools based largely on the Upanishads, the final section of the Sanskrit canonical scriptures, the Vedas. In Bankim's day, "Vedānta" on its own usually stood for one of these schools, the highly influential monistic system of Advaita whose chief thinker was Śaṃkara (*c*.8th century C.E.). "Traditional logic" (*nyāya*) is a reference to the great logical tradition developed in Sanskrit over two millennia, and for which Bengal was a famous centre (especially at the time in which the novel is set). Prafulla was made to undertake a detailed study of Yoga because she was to become for all practical purposes a yogi by disciplining her senses and womanly desires (see further below). Finally, the *Śrīmad Bhagavad Gītā* ("Revered Song of the Lord"; *c.*2nd century C.E.) refers to the discourse in 700 verses about the supreme being's relationship to the world and the individual, that took place between Krishna, the embodied form (*avatāra*) of the deity, and his friend, Arjuna, just before the beginning of a great battle described in the Sanskrit epic, the *Mahābhārata.*

This chapter of the novel is particularly important for three reasons: first, it shows the normative role the Sanskrit tradition played in Bankim's estimation of Hindu culture. One could not be properly educated as a Hindu without a good grasp of Sanskrit. In other words, traditional Sanskrit paradigms of thought and language provide the normative framework for a Hindu approach to life. (Thus Bankim is not being particularly "historicist" here, that is, he is not defining Prafulla's education solely in terms of the norms in force at the time the novel is set—a century or so before Bankim wrote. So far as Bankim was concerned, the normative Sanskritic framework for constructing a modern approach was to be implemented even in his own time. Prafulla's education was but a throwback of contemporary needs.) Second, for Bankim, the *Gītā* is "the best of all works" (*sarbbagranthaśreṣṭha*) in this normative framework. This is not necessarily the case because of the *Gītā*'s particular theology, but rather because of its ethic, its advocacy of a way of life that prioritizes *engagement* with the world by means of selfless action (*niṣkāma karma*), viz. action performed without regard for gainful fruit, over a life of meditative non-action etc. This ideal will become clearer in the next chapter. Finally, this chapter illustrates the kind of ascesis that endorses this ethical outlook of the *Gītā:* a self-mastery that renders one impervious to pain and pleasure, to what would otherwise be the seductions of this world. Prepared in these three ways, the individual, or yogi-in-action, is ready to lead India, especially Hindus—for these are the attributes of a Hindu leader—into the new age of cultural dialogue with the westerner. Note that Bankim is prepared to devolve these attributes upon a woman, for in Sanskritic tradition the land is personified as female. As such, in Bankim's previous novel, *Ānandamaṭh,* the land of India becomes the Motherland, iconized as the Mother Goddess (is it a coincidence that in her new life, Prafulla will be renamed *Debī,* "Goddess"?). There is a presumption in all this that a new form of Hindu belief and practice, rooted in the Sanskritic traditions of the past, must dominate the new order, and it is no accident that the British—the dialogue-partner of this new form of Hinduism—will duly appear as a significant feature of the novel's cultural landscape. See also the Introduction.

"coarse rice": *moṭā cāul.*

"On *ekadashi* day ... insist on eating fish": skr. *ekādaśī. DCB* points out: "It is a practice for the Bengali woman whose husband is alive to eat at least some fish on *ekadashi* day, even though no harm is done if fish is not eaten on other days" (Notes, p.37). This practice was intended to bring about the wellbeing of the husband who was living a householder's life. In fact, more generally in Hindu tradition, keeping special observances, dietary and otherwise, on *ekādaśī*, goes back to ancient times. There is a huge literature on this, incorporating the Purāṇas and medieval digests, that both records and prescribes a wide range of practices. Our text but highlights a cultural specificity of Bengal (*deśācār*). For traditional textual information on *ekādaśī*, see Kane (1974:95–121). *DCM* provides a paragraph of explanation between asterisks in the body of the translation explaining what is meant by reference to *ekādaśī*: "One may feel curious to know why of all days this particular eleventh day of the moon was taken a fancy to.... On that day no [Bengali] Hindu widow, young or old, rich or poor, of whatever caste or creed, whether Vaishnav or Sakta touches fish at all, by way of penance in memory of her departed husband. So long as one's husband is alive the idea of... adopting a widow's mode of living is shocking to every Hindu woman. Prafulla too could not get rid of that sentiment" (p.94).

"discipline": *abhyās*.

"woven in the Shantipur style": *kalkādār śāntipure*. A distinctive and pleasing floral pattern.

"in alkaline water": *kṣāre*: treatment reserved for cloth that was not fine or valued.

"not allowed to use oil": rubbing with oil was a stage in dressing the hair. This was done to make the hair (especially a woman's hair) thick and glossy—a mark of health and beauty.

"perfumed oil": *gandha-tail dvārā*.

"on a thin mattress made of cotton": *tūlār toṣake*.

"sleep the whole night through": *trijām nidrā*. A *jām* is a period of about three hours. So *trijām nidrā* is sleep of approximately 3×3=nine hours. Similarly, for "about six hours" subsequently.

"you must learn to wrestle": *mallajuddha śikhite haibe*.

"Sir": *ṭhākur*, or "Master."

"overcome the senses": *indriyajay*.

"physical exercise": *byāyām*.

"abductors will not keep... they're strong," with reference to Warren Hastings (see footnote 51 in text). Perhaps Bankim had a passage in a letter of Hastings to Josias Dupre (March 9th, 1773) in mind (Hastings is speaking about roving bands of so-called ascetics or "Senassies" (*saṃnyāsīs*) and some of their practices): "The history of this people is curious.... They go mostly naked. They have neither towns, houses, nor families, but rove continually from place to place, recruiting their numbers with the healthiest children they can steal in the countries through which they pass. Thus they are the stoutest and most active men in India" (recorded in G. R. Gleig [1841:303–4]. Bankim gives an extract from this letter, which includes this passage, in an Appendix entitled "History of the Sannyasi Rebellion" in the fifth edition of his earlier novel, *Ānandamaṭh*; see Lipner [2005:293]).

"For the first year Bhabani Thakur forbade any man from going to where Prafulla lived...": *DCM* first provides an explanation before translating: "How to appear before the public with an amount of grace and decency is no mean problem to one accustomed to seclusion. Prafulla was gradually initiated in this art. During the first year of her training no male person was allowed..." etc. (p.98). But this does not seem to be the right explanation. It seems that Bhabani Thakur implemented this training to make Prafulla indifferent to male company in particular.

"converse...about religious texts": *śāstrīya ālāp*.

❂ *Chapter 16* ❂

VARIANTS

* "I'll provide food...no longer": For changes in *DCsv*, see under ch. 17 of Appendix A.

* "the fruit of all your actions": the first edition adds here: "Do not desire to arrogate to yourself the good fruit (*śubha phal*) of any action."

NOTES

"action": the word used is *karma*, but this can also mean "job/work," viz. purposeful action, and I have used these translations for the same word in what follows.

"meditation...spiritual novice": *jñān... āmār mata asiddha*.

"in a detached way": *asakta haiyā*. The explanation will follow.

"*So you must pursue action... the Goal*": Bhabani Thakur quotes in Sanskrit from *Gītā* 3.19. We shall now understand better how important the *Gītā*'s ethical philosophy was for Bankim's project of creating a new social order in the India that was to emerge from colonial domination.

"detachment": *anāsakti*.

"control of the senses": *indriya-saṃjam*; this is more or less synonymous with the *indriya-jay* ("overcoming of the senses") of the previous chapter: a crucial part of the ethics of the *Gītā*.

❂

"selflessness... follow the right path": *nirahaṃkār byatīta dharmācaraṇ nāi. Ahaṃkār* (literally, "I-making") refers to the ego, to the self-absorbed tendency of I-making. Here *dharma* also implies *sva-dharma* or what one ought to do personally, an important teaching of the *Gītā,* cf. 3.35: "Better to perform one's own *dharma* though inadequate, than that of another; better to die in one's own *dharma.* The *dharma* of others is perilous": a verse occurring in the same chapter of the *Gītā* in which the first two quotations occur, and to which commentators in general have attached great significance. *DCM* translates *dharmācaraṇ* by "any religious life" (p.101), which is not quite what is meant.

"*Actions are always done... thinks, 'I am the actor'*": quoted from *Gītā* 3.27. "Nature" or *prakṛti* is the psycho-physical (as opposed to spiritual) basis of our selves and of the world in which we live. In the conscious individual, it is responsible for developing into psychical and physical states. Its fundamental constituents (*guṇas*) have an inexorable tendency to predispose to action in certain ways, giving the lie to common notions of complete and spontaneous autonomy. But this is not a fully deterministic notion in the context of *Gītā* teaching as a whole, otherwise Krishna would not try to *persuade* Arjuna to follow a certain course of action, rather than to simply *explain* what he must do. Although one is predisposed to act in certain ways by the *guṇas*, one is still able to act generally out of a core of moral autonomy. There are a number of verses in the *Gītā* that presuppose freedom of action (e.g., 18.63, where Krishna says: "Thus have I given you this knowledge, more mysterious than the mysterious. After thinking it through, do what you will": *iti te jñānam ākhyātaṃ guhyād guhyataraṃ mayā/ vimṛśyaitad aśeṣena yathecchaṣi tathā kuru*). Indeed, the basic ethical teaching of the *Gītā,* that one ought to act in accordance with one's duty, presupposes freedom of the will. This is reflected in Bhabani Thakur's asking Prafulla, after her initial instruction of five years, what she intends to do.

"has been done by your power": *tomār guṇe tāhā haila.*

"your good actions become void": *puṇya karma akarmatva prāpta hay.*

"*Whatever you do... do it as an offering to Me*": see *Gītā* 9.27. A teaching of total dedication to the Lord, compatible with the ethic of selfless action (*niṣkāma karma*).

"attachment will arise": *āsakti janmibe.*

"He dwells in all beings": *sarbbabhūtasthita.*

"*He who see Me everywhere... I regard that disciplined soul as the very best*": characteristic *Gītā* teaching of what we may call "participative theology." By this mutual indwelling of deity and self, our actions become, as it were, joint action with God, non-appropriative and hence efficacious. Like God, we act with equanimity toward all, transcending the vagaries of the world. Such an agent is the best kind of "disciplined soul" or *yogī.*

"we'll have to dissemble a bit": *kichu dokāndāri cāi,* that is, put on a display as shopkeepers do.

"a virtuous life/bad deeds": *dharmācaraṇ/duṣkarma.*

"the power to rule": *rājdaṇḍa,* the staff (*daṇḍa*) of royal authority, the rod of punishment. On the royal *daṇḍa* and its symbolism in traditional context, see Gonda (1966:22–3), and Glucklich, 1994:ch.9.

"Muslims": *musalmān.*

"British": *iṅgrej,* or "English," though often in the language of the time, *iṅgrej* also meant "British."

"It is I who . . . the virtuous": *āmi duṣṭer daman, śiṣṭer pālan kari,* taking his cue from *Gītā* 4.8, where Krishna justifies his periodic descent in human form (*avatāra*) as a coming to protect the virtuous (*sādhu*) and destroy the evil-doer (*duṣkṛt*).

"the intolerable wickedness": Bankim refers here implicitly to the excesses described by Edmund Burke in his speech of February 18th, 1788 during his impeachment of Warren Hastings (see under endnotes for ch.8). The list of cruelties enumerated by Bhabani Pathak matches those graphically recounted by Burke in his speech.

"those who owned the land": *bhūmyadhikārī*: those who had entitlement over land and over those who live and work on it, viz. landowners, leaseholders, and their officers.

"the sacred relics of Vishnu from their household thrones": *siṃhāsan haite śālgrām.* The *śāl(a)grām* is a sacred ovoid or tubular stone made of or containing fossil ammonite, said to harbor the presence of the God Vishnu. It is installed in the home on a small pedestal, as if on a throne, to symbolize Vishnu's rule in the house. For more information on the *śalgrām,* see Gonda (1954:94–5). Desecration of the *śālgrām* is a characteristic sign of degenerate times for Bankim (see, e.g., *Ānandamaṭh,* Part I, ch.10, where the same point is made: Lipner 2005:147).

"Prafulla's heart had melted . . .": Bhabani Thakur's fiery speech was the seal to Prafulla's decision to embark on a new life.

"harrowing tale of the people": *prajābarger duḥkher kāhinī*; that is, the "people" who are subject to rule (*prajā*).

"in the clothes of a renouncer": *sannyāsinībeśe.*

"But Bhabani Thakur had made one big mistake": that is, he had failed to appreciate how steadfastly Prafulla valued her status as a married woman. This is why throughout her training she had insisted on eating fish on *ekadashi* day. She was ready to go along with Bhabani's schemes to benefit the oppressed, but not at the expense of this commitment.

"Prafulla had learned various things but...": *prafuller anya śikṣā haiyāche. karmmaśikṣā hay nāi.* That is, Prafulla had learned *what* to do to comply with the *Gītā*'s teachings of selfless action, but not *how* to implement them in following Bhabani's scheme (*karmaśikṣā*). Now for five more years, which the author does not record, she learns how to implement her instruction at Bhabani's hands. Thus, ten years pass as Bhabani's disciple, from the time she was rumored to have died to the time her full instruction came to an end. She has now been transformed from Prafulla into Debi Chaudhurani; the next part of the narrative takes up the story from after this transformation.

—PART II—

Chapter 1

NOTES

"the leaseholder": *ijārādār.* (from the Persian word, *izārā,* meaning "lease"). Haraballabh didn't pay his dues directly to the government. His estates were leased to him by Debisingh, who allegedly extorted a large proportion of the revenue they yielded, only to pay a proportion of this himself to his political masters. This was often the practice at the time. Burke referred to this practice in his speech of February 18th, 1788 (see endnotes under ch.8, Part I). Mr. Kumud Ranjan Biswas, a retired Indian Administrative Service officer who is an expert on the history of land tenure, writes (private communication, 12.07.2007): "[In Bengal, toward the end of the Mughal emperor, Aurangzeb's reign in the early 1700s] land was settled with different kinds of people. Some chieftains held it directly under the central authority, calling themselves Rajas, and others held it on izara (a Persian word meaning lease) from the provincial governor. These izaradars often sub-leased parts of their holdings to people who came to be known as talukdars and by various other names. Debi Chaudhurani's father-in-law, Haraballabh, must have been one such talukdar under one of the most infamous and oppressive izaradars, Debi Singh. There were disputes among these people over the extent of their geographical jurisdictions, each one trying to encroach upon the others' holdings. This was because their boundaries were not precisely demarcated. Moreover, the izaradars and talukdars had their own private armies called paiks and barkandazes. Taking advantage of the lawlessness of the time, these landholders, both superior and subordinate, committed widespread depredations.... [At that time] the Permanent Settlement of 1793 was yet to be introduced [by the British]. So the izaradars, zamindars [Bengali: jamidar] and talukdars were not the zamindars under the Permanent Settlement Regulation. After the Permanent Settlement came into force all landholders immediately under the government were uniformly called zamindars. There were sublease-holders under them called by various names—talukdars, pattanidars etc." Bankim does not clarify these time-bound distinctions.

"Mr. Hastings and Gangagobind Singh": that is, the Governor-General, Warren Hastings, appointed by the East India Company to supervise their interests. Gangagobind was a well-known protégé of Hastings', famous for lavish expenditure on various projects of his own. Gangagobind came from a Rarhi Kayastha family in the Murshidabad district. At the beginning of the 1770s, he became Warren Hastings' *dewan* (chief revenue officer). His fortunes fluctuated somewhat in tandem with Hastings', but in time he struck various lucrative financial deals and soon became one of the most powerful Indians in the region. His job came to an end when Hastings returned to England (*SBA*:455–6). On the status of British rule in Bengal at the time, represented by the East India Company, see the Marshall quote (1987:89) under ch.8, Part I, above.

"the fine lifestyle one's got used to": *buniādi cāl.*

"the Goddess of wealth": *lakṣmī.* The Goddess who presides over wealth and prosperity. Once Lakshmi leaves the home, the family is ruined.

"My dear": *mā*, literally "Mother." But here the tone is one of dismissive familiarity, hence "My dear."

"The great religious festivals of Krishna, Durga...": *dol durgotsab; dol* or *dol jātrā* is a festival during the full-moon day of Phālgun (mid-February to mid-March); the child Krishna is celebrated with his image being rocked in a cradle. *Durgā Pūjā* is perhaps the most important festival of Hindu Bengal; it is celebrated with great festivity for ten days in the autumn and commemorates the Goddess Durga's annual visit to her parental home on vacation from her father-in-law's house. These festivals could be the occasion of lavish expenditure.

"The domestic rites and rituals... observances of various kinds": *kriyā karmma, dān dhyān.* Throughout the year, there was occasion to perform many ceremonies, such as everyday worship, rites of passage and so on, in a Bengali Hindu household, which entailed the giving of stipends and fees to the officiants, and all this could be done with great pomp by a wealthy householder. Thus Gangagobind Singh is reputed to have spent Rs. 20 lakhs—a lakh is 100,000—on the funeral rites of his own mother: a fabulous sum in those days. On another occasion, for the *annaprāśana* (the ceremony when solid food is given for the first time to an infant) of his grandson, the invitations to the Brahmins were engraved on gold plates (see *SBA* [456]). It was almost *de rigueur* for the rich to display their wealth in these ways. Such practices have not entirely disappeared. The Indian industrialist, Mr Lakshmi Mittal, is said to have spent about £30 million on the wedding celebrations of his daughter in 2004 (for a report see cover story of *India Today* (International edition), July 05, 2004).

"the deployment of his *lathials* to enforce his authority": thus *lāṭhālāṭhi,* literally, "fighting with, the violent use of, *lathi*s (or staves)."

"official dues": *sarkāri khājānā.*

"Rs.50,000": a large sum.

"Haraballabh Ray's arrest": "Ray" pronounced as "Rai."

"since there was no English law . . . no laws were in place": Bankim was not necessarily being ironical. Elsewhere, for example, in the novel *Ānandamaṭh* (Part I, ch.13; see Lipner [2005:158]), he also refers to the lawlessness of the land before the British imposed their authority. The reader must remember that Bankim earned his livelihood as a district magistrate under the British, and was in a position to appreciate the contrast between the regimes of law and lawlessness.

✧ *Chapter 2* ✧

VARIANTS

* "while those with no such reputation": after this, *DCsv* has, "began to think how they might acquire one," etc.

* "fruit and vegetables": *DCsv* has "fruit and flowers."

* "I'm not that low": after these words, Sagar continues in *DCsv* as follows: "But I'll make you serve at my feet, otherwise I'm no Brahmin's daughter." Then the text continues with Brajesvar saying, "And I say the same to you: that until I massage your leg," etc.

* "thrust out in front of her": *DCsv* continues as follows: "Just then, without saying a word, a woman entered the room in which Sagar was crying and stood at the door. Sagar, who was preoccupied with weeping, didn't notice her. But a maidservant, curious to see the state Sagar was in after Brajesvar had left, had entered the room and was engaged in a task or two on the pretext of doing some work. She spotted the woman and inquired, "Who are you?"

Then Sagar also looked at her and asked the same question. The woman answered, "Don't any of you recognize me?"

"No," said Sagar, "Who are you?"

"I am Debi Chaudhurani," said the woman.

With a crash the tray with the betel-leaf fell to the ground from the maidservant's hand. She too sank to the floor, moaning and trembling, the cloth around her waist coming undone. Even Sagar broke into a sweat, unable to say a word, for who—young or old—hadn't heard the terrible name that had been uttered?"

In *DCsv* the chapter ends here.

✧

NOTES

"There was a great buzz of excitement": *baḍa dhum paḍiāche.*

"There was much darting about...the tyranny of the fisherman": *pukure pukure māchmahale bhāri huṭāhuṭi chuṭāchuṭi paḍiyā gela. jeler daurātmye prāṇ ār rakṣā hay nā. DCM* gives the second sentence another interpretation: "The noise fishermen made, made the place too hot for others to live in the neighborhood" (p.111). This is strained both as to style and meaning; it seems clear that Bankim is talking about the chances of survival of the fish, not of what the neighborhood has to endure from the persistence of the fisherfolk. The whole first paragraph trades on the Bengali's reputation for his/her love of fish, not least on such special occasions.

"curd, milk, cream...milk's creamy layer": *dai, dudh, nanī, chānā, sar, mākhan* (I have translated the last two items in inverse order): this phrase indicates the importance of milk as a base for the preparation of the wide range of Bengali sweets available. Traditional Bengali sweets are largely milk-based, and continue to proliferate and remain widely popular today.

"three measures/one measure": that is, three *sers*/one *ser* of water. The *Concise Oxford Dictionary* defines a "seer" (=*ser*) as "an Indian (varying) measure of weight (about one kilogram) or liquid measure (about one litre)." It was commonly believed (with some justification) that the milkman regularly adulterated the milk with water. In our household during my childhood, a family servant was sent daily to the milkman to ensure that he did not adulterate our milk.

"which item of clothing...": *dhuti cādar.* A *dhuti* is a voluminous wrap of cotton (occasionally silk) worn around the waist of Bengali men, its end-piece drawn up between the legs and tucked in at the waist behind. A *cādar* is a kind of shawl, an upper-body cloth.

"thin bangles of glass or lac or shell": *cuḍi kiniyā, śākhā kiniyā. Cuḍi*s could be made of various materials, but here possibly silver or gold is not meant, since these metals are mentioned separately.

"Those known for their wit...in their minds": *jāhāder rasikatār janya pasār āche—tāhārā dui cāriṭā prācīn tāmāśā mane mane jhālāiyā rākhilen.* The Bengali has an excellent, often dry or ironical, sense of humor.

"The fun with words...the fun with food": *kathār tāmāśā.... khābār tāmāśā;* a *tāmāśā* is a display, a spectacle.

"Many fake items of food and drink...": "Even not so long ago, it was customary to tease the new son-in-law publicly in various ways. Items of fake food would be placed in front of the son-in-law, and when he tried to eat these, thinking them to be genuine, the womenfolk of the family (from the side of the sister(s)-in-law or grandmothers) would find it highly amusing.... However, occasionally the joke went too far" (*DCB*, Notes, p.45).

"So many sweet lips . . . teeth sparkle!": *madhur adharguli madhur hāsite o sādher miśite bhariyā jāite lāgila. Miśi* (also *misi*) was a blackish dentifrice, which after rinsing left the teeth sparkling white. The term is used here to indicate the zest of anticipated fun.

Though Bankim's classic cameo of the fuss made over the visiting son-in-law or *jāmāi* applies in some details to an earlier age, the Bengali *jāmāi* continues to be the object of similar attention even today: there is even a special feast—*jāmāi-ṣaśṭhī*—in his honor (on the sixth day of the bright half of the month *jyaiṣṭha*, viz. mid-May to mid-June).

"My boy": *bāpu he.*

"So I'll leave . . . any of you again": this is the threat of a final farewell by Brajesvar, and if carried out would have momentous consequences: no longer taking Sagar in as a bride in her in-laws' house, with its repercussions, viz. no children by Sagar, and her being ostracized as a wife (like Prafulla). No wonder Sagar was "thunderstruck" when she heard what had happened.

"In those days, it was easier for a bride . . . father-in-law's house": Husbands and wives did not consort familiarly or show intimacy during the domestic routine of daytime.

"an angry cobra": *kupita phaṇinī*, that is, a female cobra.

"Even your bigshot father . . . before it once": *tomār baḍamānuṣ bāp-o e pā ek din pūjā kariyāchilen.* As the author of *DCB* points out: "During the wedding, the bride's father ceremoniously touches the groom's knee. This is called worshipping the foot (*pā-pūjā*)" (*DCB*, Notes, p.45).

"I'll make up for it": *āmi tār prāyaścitta kariba; prāyaścitta* is formal reparation.

"Upon my word as a Brahmin's daughter . . .": the reader will notice the social and religious power invested, in everyday discourse (and no doubt in Bankim's mind), in the status of being a Brahmin as the story unfolds. This is one such example. A Brahmin's word uttered with serious intent by way of imprecation or blessing would tend to come true.

"*I'm* no Brahmin": the ultimate imprecation for a Brahmin, for this means falling from the highest rung of the religious hierarchy, that is, being outcasted.

"as a Goddess": *sākṣāt bhagabatīr mata. Bhagabatī* is the feminine form, grammatically, of *bhagabān*, the Lord, or God. At intervals in the narrative, Debi (which also means "Goddess") is compared to a Goddess; we have discussed this in the Introduction. There is also a Goddess Bhagabatī, who is a specific form of Kālī, though she is not particularly prominent in Bengal. For an account of this Goddess, but in the context of her worship in Kerala, see S. Caldwell (1996:195–226). *DCM* prefers this interpretation: "Almost as stately as the goddess *Bhagavati*" (p.115).

Chapter 3

VARIANTS

* "a small, rather thick rug": from here enough significant textual differences occur in *DCsv* to warrant a separate translation of the serial version. For this, see Appendix B, chapter 3. The first edition (and *DCsv*) has, "a small but thick rug": that is, "four fingers thick" (*cāri āṅgul puru*), rather than the "two fingers thick" of the sixth edition.

* "of their crushed perfume": the first edition (and *DCsv*) has, "their perfumed oil."

* "in the dark": the first edition (and *DCsv*) adds, "Approach from the rear."

NOTES

"the rainy season": *barṣākāl*: an evocative time in Hindu literature. The scorching heat of summer is over, the air is cooler, and the parched earth is rejuvenated by the warm and copious rainfall. This gives rise to tropes of erotic love—plaintive, unrequited, or fulfilled. In the fulsome description that follows, with its parallels between the (obviously) full moon, the swollen river heaving at its banks, and the voluptuous Debi, the reader will notice a running tension between images of fullness and awaited fulfillment all converging in the figure of Debi (and her unfulfilled relationship with Brajesvar). An underlying theme of this description is the way Debi symbolizes the nurturing land, that is, the motherland. The description of Debi's beauty blends a number of tropes of classical Sanskrit literature (the full moon and its light, the heaving waters etc.) with specific regional/Bengali imagery, viz. the sounds and scenes of the Teesta swollen by the rains, aspects of Debi's rich attire, the musical modes (*rāgas/ rāgiṇīs*) played, and so on. This is typical of Bankim's style. All his young principal women are beauties, and he often lingers over their description.

"The Teesta river....": *trisrotā nadī*. In ch.5, a reference will be made to the town of Rangpur as being in the vicinity of the unfolding action. This sets the scene for ensuing events. The Teesta is a major river which flows from the kingdom of Sikkim, in the foothills of the Himalayas, through the northern reaches of what was then the Bengal Presidency (but is part of Bangladesh today), into the much larger Brahmaputra which eventually wends its way into the Bay of Bengal. It has a number of sandbanks, and becomes considerably swollen with the rains of the monsoons. Hunter (1876:Vol.VII) makes the following comments about the Teesta (Tista) of the time in which the novel is set: "The Tista (Trisrota) is the second river in importance [in the Rangpur District, after the Brahmaputra]... [it] runs across the District from north-west to south-east, till it falls into the Brahmaputra a few miles to the south-west of Chilmari police station in Bhawaniganj Subdivision; its length is estimated at about a hundred and ten miles within Rangpur District.... [At the time of a Survey after the turn of the eighteenth century] the main stream of the Tista flowed south instead of south-east as at present, joined the Atrai river in Dinajpur, and finally fell into the Padma or Ganges. In the destructive floods of 1194 B.S., or 1787 A.D., which form an epoch in the history of Rangpur, the stream suddenly forsook its channel, and turned its waters into a small branch marking an ancient bed of the same river; running south-east into the Brahmaputra, it forced its way through the fields and over the country in every direction. . . ." (164–5).

Rivers are an important part of the Bengali rural landscape for Bankim. Anyone familiar with large rivers in rural Bengal will warm to this description of a swollen, fast-flowing river. At 16 Bankim was admitted to Hooghly College and he had to cross the Hooghly river daily to attend the College. His brother Purnacandra describes this phase of Bankim's life as follows: "Hooghly College was on the other side of the river from our village, and for about seven or eight years Bankimchandra took a boat to get to the College. During the holidays, at the beginning of Baisakh [April–May], the sky would sometimes be covered with clouds. Bankimchandra would ask the boatman, 'Well now, will you untie the boat?' The boatman . . . would never say 'no,' and he'd untie the boat. On some days, before the storm broke, the boat would reach the other side, but on other days it would barely reach the middle of the river when the black clouds would make the whole horizon dark. The waters of the river would become black and within a short time a storm would arise with great force. The foam from the crests of the waves all round looked just like bubbles of cotton-effluent on the surface of the water. Those who have been in the middle of a river during a storm will know what an impressive sight this is. Bankimchandra would take in the whole scene" (*BcJ*, p.49). Thus Bankim experienced the moods and reality of river-waters first-hand. This made it possible for rivers to function as a salient literary device for him, reflecting the various moods (and principal women) in his narratives.

There has always been a close association between rivers (the noun *nadī:* river, is feminine) and females, in human or divine form, in Hindu tradition. The Goddess often personifies, or emerges from, or returns to the river, quintessentially represented, as the tradition developed, by the Goddess Gaṅgā (Ganges), the chief river of Hindu religious sentiment in post-Vedic times (see D. Eck [1996:137–53]). Bankim uses this established association of river and Goddess to good effect in his writings. Here, in the novel, for the first time Debi Chaudhurani is intimately associated with the river: she lives on the river and is at home on it. In a way, she is the Goddess of the river (hence *Debi* which means "goddess"), and a representative of Bengal. As such, her actions of "banditry" are legitimated, as she is engaged, in the dire circumstances of the time, in liberating Bengal from the oppressions of poverty, the rigidities of custom (a Comtean idea), and misrule. She will help bring the new Bengal, and by extension a new India, into being. The reader will see this idea develop as the novel progresses.

"barge": *bajrā:* a large vessel, often fitted with sails, with living quarters under a flat roof. Though Debi's barge was propelled by sails, some varieties of these flat-bottomed boats (also called "flats") could be pulled by a steamer, though perhaps this took place at a later date (see Eden [2003: xi, 3] for descriptions pertaining to her up-country travels in India in 1837).

"how many shapes and forms were drawn upon it!": *tāhāte kata rakam murad ākā āche.*

"sea-monster" *hāṅgar*—a shark, but really a sea-monster of sorts particularly associated iconographically with the Ganges.

"so shapely a body": *teman pūrṇāyata deha.*

"slender . . . buxom": *kṛśāṅgī . . . sthūlāṅgī.*

"unusually tall and erect": *bilakṣaṇ unnata deha.*

"The flood-waters of youth's fulness . . . without overwhelming it": *jauban-barśār cāri poyā banyār jal, se kamanīya ādhāre dhariyāche—chāpāy nāi.*

"though she who contained them": thus *nadī.* The metaphor of likening Debi to a full-bodied river and her qualities to its waters continues.

"Dhaka": the capital city of eastern Bengal at the time, and now of Bangladesh.

"white, filmy Dhaka cloth . . . woven into the fabric": *pariṣkār mihi ḍhākāi, tāte jarir phul.*

"bodice": *kâcali.* It was not the custom for Hindu women to wear "blouses" in those days—that was to come later. Hence this was an ornate bodice of some kind.

"dark tresses fell disheveled": in appropriate context the disheveled (*ālulāyita*) hair of a young woman is regarded as sexually alluring.

"fragrance of her crushed perfume" *sugandhi-cūrṇa-gandha*: perhaps containing sandalwood paste or powder.

"like an image of the Goddess Sarasvati herself": *mūrttimatī sarasvatīr nyāy.* The whole description has been converging toward this point. Sarasvatī is the Goddess of learning, creativity, and inspiration. She is an ancient figure in Hindu tradition. In Vedic times she was identified with a great river, apparently flowing south of the Indus into the Arabian Sea, but now no longer extant. At the same time she was regarded as the physical manifestation of purifying, life-giving celestial waters. There are references in the *Ṛg Veda* to sacred rites being performed by the "Aryans" along her banks, and to her identification with the Goddess of speech, or Vāc. This latter attribute probably gave rise in later tradition to a new and enduring emphasis on her power to inspire learning and the creative arts. In Hindu iconography, Sarasvatī is associated with the *viṇā* (as representative of the fine arts), and is usually depicted or described as beautiful and fair-skinned, in white, shining attire (see Kinsley [1987:10–11, 55–64]). The radiant beauty seated on the barge is also described as playing expertly on the *viṇā*, in white, shining bejeweled attire—she is a veritable Sarasvatī.

There is a further point worth considering. The identification of the woman—Prafulla, now transformed into Debi Chaudhurani—with the river not only harks back to a traditional Hindu motif that feminizes and sacralizes the land (land = woman = Goddess), but also indicates the kind of transformation envisaged for both Prafulla personally, and the land and its culture that she represents. "A particularly Indian association with rivers is the imagery of crossing from the world of ignorance or bondage to the far shore, which represents the world of enlightenment or freedom.... The river in this metaphor represents the state of transition, the period of rebirth, in which the spiritual sojourner undergoes a crucial metamorphosis" (Kinsley, 1987:56–7). We saw earlier in the novel how Prafulla underwent a transforming discipline to become Debi Chaudhurani. Now that her home is the river, she represents the transition to the neo-Hinduism that must characterize the new order envisaged by Bankim. That it is a woman who symbolizes this transformation is interesting, but it is by no means at odds with the Bengali (and one may say, by extension, Hindu) psyche. Of course, it is a neo-conservative man who is fashioning this reborn woman.

"was absorbed in playing the *vina*": *bīṇābādane nijuktā*. Note that in the serial version of the novel, Debi was playing the *sitar* (*setār*). The *vīṇā* is more appropriate for the image of the Goddess Sarasvatī to which she has been likened, since iconographically Sarasvatī is associated with the *vīṇā*. Also, the *vīṇā* is a more "Hindu" instrument; the *sitar* has historic associations with Islamic culture.

"*jhinjhit, khambaj, sindhu... kedar, hambir, behag... kanara, sahana, bagisvari*": In a personal e-mail (21.05.2007), Richard Widdess, Professor of Musicology at the School of Oriental and African Studies, University of London, writes as follows: "The comments below are based on my own experience plus Bhatkhande's comments in *Kramik Pustak-mālikā*. Most of these rāgas are relatively recent in origin and therefore do not have a specific iconography. They would no doubt have been well-known to cultivated readers in the late nineteenth century, as most still would be today.

What seems clear is that there is a musical logic to the sequence of rāgas. There are three groups of three rāgas each, plus one at the end. Within each group the three rāgas are related by scale and by mood; successive groups become more serious in tone, while the final rāga Naṭ seems to make a contrast. This final rāga is not well known today, so its musical character is not clear to me, but its iconography suggests a very different ethos from that of the other rāgas.

The sequence of rāgas is strikingly contrary to what a sitārist would normally play in a formal concert today, where one would start with the most serious rāgas and introduce lighter ones toward the end. The impression is given of a lone player moving from rāga to rāga in accordance with her changing mood.

The scales of the rāgas are such that a sitārist would need to adjust his/her frets between each group and the next, as mentioned in the text for the last rāga. On the vīṇā the frets are usually fixed and not adjusted by the player.

Group 1 [*Jhinjhit, Khāmbāj, Sindhu*]

These rāgas would all be considered "light" rāgas today, and would normally be used for short metrical pieces rather than for extended *ālāp* [detailed exposition of a rāga]. They all use the Khamāj [Khāmbāj] scale and would be performed in the evening. There is no consensus about the *rasa* [mood, sentiment] of rāgas but I would suggest *śṛṅgār* [erotic love] is likely for all three.

Jhinjoṭī [Jhinjhit]: A minor (*kṣudra*) rāga suitable for short pieces; second prahar [watch, period: a prahar is equivalent to 3 hours] of the night. Its form is "very direct and clear" according to Bhatkhande.

Khamāj [Khāmbāj]: An important but not a very serious rāga; second prahar of the night. Same scale as Jhinjhoṭī.

Sindh/Sindhu: A minor rāga, not well-known today except in the combination Sindhu-Bhairavī. Similar scale to Jhinjhoṭī and Khamāj. Can be sung at any time. Iconography features a vīṇā player, sometimes female, sometimes male.

Group 2 [*Kedār, Hambīr, Behāg*]

These rāgas are all major, well-known rāgas, suitable for extended musical development, for example in *ālāp*. They all use the Bilāval scale plus an extra sharpened fourth: the use of both fourths is sometimes said to mark a mood of uncertainty or transition, but I would say that all three rāgas have a confident, assertive character: *rasa*s seem to be *vīra* [heroic] and/or *śānta* [peaceful].

Kedār: A major rāga, suitable for elaborate development. First prahar of the night. A different scale from the foregoing: a sitārist would need to adjust one or two frets at this point in the sequence. The iconography usually features a sage playing or listening to a vīṇā.

Hamīr [Hambīr]: A less common rāga having the same scale as Kedār, and also sung in the first prahar of the night.

Bihāg [Behāg]: Another very important rāga in present practice. Same scalar material as Kedār and Hamīr. Second prahar of the night.

Group 3 [*Kānarā, Sāhānā, Bāgīśvarī*]

These rāgas mark another change of mood. They are among the most serious rāgas in the repertoire, and would display the artist's technical and aesthetic skill to the full, for example, in an extended *ālāp* or *dhrupad* performance [*dhrupad*: an old, serious style of vocal music associated with temples and the Mughal court]. They share scales with flattened third and seventh (and sixth in Darbārī, if that is the "Kānaḍā" intended), and a mood suggesting *karuṇa rasa* [compassion, fellow-feeling] These rāgas would be played later in the evening than Groups 1 and 2.

Kānaḍā: Originally a single, ancient rāga, the name now applies to a large and important family of rāgas, having many varieties. Today the leading variety is Darbārī Kānaḍā, described by Bhatkhande as "serious" (*gambhīr*) and attributed by him to the middle of the night. In keeping with its serious character, the melody is predominantly in the lower register, and features unusually heavy oscillations on certain notes. The scale is very different from that of the previous three rāgas in the sequence, and would need adjustment of three frets on the sitār if following Bihāg. Iconography for Kānaḍā is variable: sometimes a male hero on horseback.

Śahānā [Sāhānā]: A rāga of the Kānaḍā family, having a similar scale to Darbārī but a somewhat lighter mood. Third prahar of the night.

Bāgeśrī [Bāgīśvarī]: A serious rāga. Middle of the night. Same scale as Śahānā." Debi's musical expertise here is a manifestation of what Bankim in the *DT* has called the *cittarañjinī* or aesthetic capabilities (see note 18 of the Introduction). This has also been part of Bhabani Pathak's training.

"adjusting a fret or two": *dui ekṭā pardā uṭhāiyā nāmāiyā laiyā*. Since *vīṇā*s at the time would be unlikely to have adjustable frets, this doesn't make much sense; it would, though, if the instrument were a *sitar,* and in fact in the original serial version, as we have seen, the instrument Debi is playing is a *sitar*.

"the musical mode *nat*": *naṭ-rāgiṇī*. Widdess comments: "An ancient rāga-name but not a common rāga today (except as an element in certain mixed rāgas). An evening rāga. The scale is very different from that of the previous three rāgas: the sitārist would have to adjust two frets following Bāgeśrī. The iconography usually depicts a scene of carnage with a sword-wielding hero riding a horse, suggesting *vīr* or even *raudra* [fierce] as the *rasa*" (ibid.). *DCB* says: "The *rāgiṇī Naṭ* has the capacity, as it were, to rouse an individual to daredevil action. Hence, as soon as this *rāgiṇī* sounded on Queen Debi's *vīṇā* Rangaraj was alerted to the situation" (Notes, p.47). This is why Debi "suddenly looked up" and "struck the strings of the *vina* with great force."

"A sacred thread hung": *yajñopabīt*. The mark of an upper-caste Hindu, usually a Brahmin (soon we will learn that Rangaraj is a Brahmin). Bankim's agents of change—Bhabani Pathak, Debi Chaudhurani, etc.—are of a high ritual and social status—once again a Comtean idea.

"spyglass": *dūrbīn*. These were a "new arrival" (*nūtan āmdānī*). Bankim's leaders are not averse to making use of modern technology to accomplish their ends.

"India": *bhāratbarśa*. Bankim uses a word now commonly used in Bengali for India.

"the longboat": *chip*.

DCM takes many liberties in his translation of this chapter.

Chapter 4

NOTES

"about ninety feet long...": literally, "about sixty 'hands' (*hāt*) long." A *hāt* is the length from the elbow to the tips of the fingers, that is, about a foot and a half. Thus "sixty hands" would be about ninety feet: an uncommonly long longboat! The oarsmen would be sitting in single-file, each on alternate sides of the boat.

"paddle": *"boṭe."*

"Rangraj...armed with five weapons": *pañca hātiyār bâdhiyā:* a stock expression to signify the following five traditional weapons: buckler, sword, bow and arrow, and spear. *DCB* updates with the following suggestion: "staff, buckler, spear, bow and arrow, and gun" (Notes, p.48). *DCM* omits to translate this expression.

"Hindusthani guards": Hindi-speaking Hindu or Muslim men from northern India, often incorporated into the armed forces of local or regional authorities, would act as guards on river-traffic in Bengal.

"wearing red turbans": *māthāy lāl pāgḍi*. The mark of their profession.

"in the gentle southerly breeze": *madhur dakṣiṇ bātāse*. The breeze from the south is supposed to be particularly gentle and fragrant, having passed through the sandalwood forests of the eastern ghats.

"fired a blank from his gun": *banduke ekṭā phākā āo(y)āj karila*. The generic term *banduk* ("gun") is used here and elsewhere in this chapter. But in the period of the story, these would have been some kind of musket. For more information on the firearms used at the time, see Lipner (2005:237).

"Pande Sir": *pâḍe ṭhākur*. See footnote in text. So much for the view that Brahmins could function only as priests.

"O God, O God!": literally, *Rām, Rām. Rām* often designates the supreme being—who descended to earth in some traditions as Rāma Dāśaratha, king of Ayodhya—for Hindus in north India. "[I]n North India today the word *Rām* is the most commonly used nonsectarian designation for the Supreme Being" (Lutgendorf 1991:4).

"Pande…Ramsingh": "Pande" (*pâḍe*; see above) and "Tewari" (*teowāri*) are Brahmin caste-names; Ramsingh is a personal name.

"Sir!": *mahāśay*.

"called back…in Hindi": Bankim formulates a sentence in Hindi patois in Bengali script: (*dharmābatār!*) *śalā lok sab koiko bâdhke rākkhā*.

"Virtue incarnate": *dharmābatār*. A standard appellation of deference at the time.

"Brajesvar grinned…" etc.: the sarcasm that follows has a subtext. The north-Indian guards who performed such duties were supposed to be able and martial, but Bankim takes this opportunity to undermine this perception, not least in contrast to the Bengali protagonists of the unfolding drama: the bandits on one side, and Brajesvar, in charge of the assailed barge, on the other. Bengalis could be martial too.

"Hindusthani nincompoop": *hindusthānī bheḍīo(y)ālā*. See preceding comment.

"double-barrelled gun": *donalā*. A pistol-like firearm with a heavy gourd-like handle, which when reversed in the hand could be used as a club. See further.

"there'll be a Brahmin killed": *brahmahatyā haibe*. According to traditional Hindu codes, killing a Brahmin (*brahmahatyā*) was one of the greatest sins. One could be outcasted as a result (not to mention acquire really bad karma…).

"that sin": *se pāpṭā*.

"gracious Queen": *rāṇīji*. the suffix *-ji* indicates respect, reverence.

"Goddess": *bhagabatī:* see note at the end of ch.2.

"Let's go see the Goddess": *cala, tabe bhagabatī-darśane jāi*. A pun on *darśan: darśan* implies standing in the presence of a revered person or the deity (in the latter context, a sanctified "viewing"), and also "seeing" something.

"the helmsman…deckhands": *mājhimāllā*. These were usually Muslims.

"food rations": *ḍālruṭir barādda*.

"Victory to Debi our Queen!": *debī rāṇī-ki jay*. A stock Hindusthani slogan.

Chapter 5

VARIANTS

* "*vina*": *DCsv* has *sitar*.

* "Any wounded…": *DCsv* and the first edition continue as follows:

Debi: "Any dead among you?"
"No," replied Rangaraj.
"Any wounded?" etc. as in the standard edition.

NOTES

"royal lady": *rāṇīji.*

"Rangpur": a northern town in Rangpur District in the Bengal of Bankim's time (now in Bangladesh), about thirty-five kilometers to the south-west of the Teesta and fifty kilometers or so from where the Teesta joins the Brahmaputra. See map.

"One is for holding court": *darbār*. A *darbar* is a room or hall where rulers formally met visitors and/or their subjects and displayed and exercised authority.

"the Queen's bedroom": *śayanghar*: a boudoir.

"One is for holding court...and a jail": only six rooms, even though Rangaraj says earlier that there are seven!

"lacked tune and rhythm": *besur, betāl.*

"the man in charge": *bābu*, that is, Brajesvar, the patron of the journey.

"After all, women are meant to serve men": *meyemānuṣ ta puruṣer bâdī.* Brajesvar will have to eat his words. The reader will note that Bankim laces the narrative with these chauvinist comments so that he can undermine them as the story unfolds; this is part of his project to depict wives as fitting partners for their husbands in the regenerated Bengali society he envisaged. But, as we have seen in the Introduction, the new woman must ideally fulfill her role in a domestic context.

"what your standing is": *āpni ki darer lok*; viz. your socio-ritual status. Among Hindus, this could generally be deduced from the name.

"Duhkhiram Chakrabartti": Cakrabarttī is a Brahmin name.

"Krishnagobind Ghosal": The Ghoṣāls belonged to a clan of Rarhi Brahmins.

"Dayaram Baksi": "Baksī" could be a Brahmin name.

"this game": *e raṅga. DCM*: "farce."

"Mistress Nishi": *niśi ṭhākurāṇī.* An element of sarcasm/jest here.

"A tiny, worthless cowrie": *ek kaḍā kāṇā kaḍi. Kāṇā/kānā* means "one-eyed," "with a hole," that is, a cowrie with a hole: a useless cowrie, worth nothing.

"Your majesty": *rāṇīji.*

"He's a Brahmin...or cut wood": a dig at Brahmin men.

"I've no Brahmin to cook for me": For reasons of ritual purity, Brahmin households sought Brahmins of the appropriate ritual status to act as cooks.

❁ *Chapter 6* ❁

VARIANTS

* "isn't compatible with mine": after this *DCsv* has, "then you won't be able to cook for me. In that case" etc. as in the standard edition.

* "Then cane him...": *DCsv* has instead: '"Then cane him," said Nishi of her own accord."'

* "This isn't going well at all.": *DCsv* has instead, "He thought, 'This isn't turning out well, is it?'," then continues with, "Then the wicked Pachkari" etc. as in the standard text.

* "a Brahmin's daughter": *DCsv* concludes the chapter with the words, "Well and truly a woman of her word! Do you believe me now?"

NOTES

"He was astonished at what he saw... holding a lamp in one hand": this was part of the *dokāndāri,* the worldly display or apparent compromise with the world, that Bhabani Pathak warned Prafulla would be necessary to keep up appearances if she lived as a bandit (see Part I, ch.16). Whether it can be adjudged to be strictly necessary is another matter.

"canvas backdrop": *cāl*; canvas was the usual material for this kind of backdrop.

"the Goddess Durga in the month of Asvin": that is, "the ten-armed image (*daśbhujā pratimā*)" of the Goddess Durgā worshipped in the month of Asvin (*āśvin māse*), the sixth month of the Bengali (lunar) year (running from mid-September to mid-October in the Western calendar).

"Scenes of:

'the battle of the Goddess... Shumbha and Nishumba': lit. *śumbhaniśumbher juddha.* A *dvandva*-compound naming the demons (*asur*) Śumbha and Niśumbha. These two brothers terrorized and took control of the heavenly realms. When the gods asked the Goddess Bhagabatī/Durgā for succor, the Goddess herself appeared in her mode as Kālī, confronting and slaying the demons on the battlefield. This incident is described in the *Devī-māhātmya* section of the *Mārkaṇḍeya Purāṇa* (for more information, see D. Kinsley [1987:chs.7 and 8]).

'her battle with the buffalo-demon': *mahiṣāsurer juddha.* Perhaps the most famous exploit of the Goddess and described in various Purāṇas. The Goddess kills the demon on the battlefield and asserts her cosmic supremacy (see Kinsley [1987:ch.7]).

'the ten *avatars*': though the texts speak of numerous *avatars* or physical descents to earth of the God Vishnu, a list of ten is well known (though one or two names on this list vary). A standard list of the ten *avatars* might consist of (i) the fish (*matsya*), (ii) the turtle (*kūrma*), (iii) the boar (*varāha*), (iv) the man-lion (*nṛsiṃha*), (v) the dwarf (*vāmana*), and the human *avatars* Paraśurāma, Rāmacandra, Krishna (or sometimes his brother, Balarāma), the Buddha, and Kalkin (vi–x). The first nine have descended to earth; the tenth is still to come. Each descent has its own iconographic representations.

'the eight Nayikas': *aṣṭa-nāyikā*. These are (female) forms or personifications of either the Goddess, or some human quality or emotion. Lists vary, and it is not clear which set is meant. Examples include two lists of eight forms or powers of the Goddess Durgā: (i) Ugracaṇḍā, Pracaṇḍā, Caṇḍogrā, Caṇḍanāyikā, Aticaṇḍā, Cāmuṇḍā, Caṇḍā, and Caṇḍabatī; or (ii) Maṅgalā, Bijayā, Bhadrā, Jayantī, Aparājitā, Nandinī, Nārasiṅghī, and Kaumārī.

However, the Nāyikās can also be personifications of illicit sexual love, viz. Balinī, Kāmeśvarī, Bimalā, Aruṇā, Medinī, Jayinī, Sarveśvarī, Kauleśī; or of certain aesthetic and sexually charged tropes, viz. *abhisārikā* ('a woman on the way to a tryst with her lover'), *vāsakasajjā* ('a woman awaiting her lover/husband in her boudoir'), *utkaṇṭhitā* ('a woman yearning for her lover'), *vipralabdhā* ('a woman whose lover has failed to meet her'), *khaṇḍitā* ('a woman whose lover/husband has been unfaithful'), *kalahāntaritā* ('a woman separated from her lover as the result of a quarrel'), *svādhīnabhartṇikā* ('a woman who has control over her lover'), and *proṣitabhartṛkā* ('a woman whose husband is away'). It is possible that Bankim intended one of these groups, since there is an erotic tension running through strands of the narrative.

'the seven Mothers': *sapta mātṛkā*. The seven (female) personified powers of various gods. According to one list these would be: Brāhmī, Vaiṣṇabī, Aindrī, Raudrī, Bārāhī, Kauberī, and Kaumārī. D. Kinsley (1998:32), who gives a number of different names, describes their origin as follows: "In the course of the battle [against demonic forces], Durgā produces several goddesses to help her. She brings forth Kālī while confronting the demons Caṇḍa and Muṇḍa, and calls upon her again for help in defeating Raktabīja. During the battle a group of seven goddesses, collectively known as the Mātṛkās, is created from certain male gods to help defeat the demons. They are Brahmāṇī, created from Brahmā; Māheśvarī, created from Śiva; Kaumārī, created from Kārtikeya; Vaiṣṇavī, created from Viṣṇu; Vārāhī, created from the boar *avatāra* of Viṣṇu; Narasiṃhī, created from the man-lion *avatāra* of Viṣṇu; and Aindrī, created from the god Indra."

'the ten Mahāvidyās': *daśa mahāvidyā*. Personifications of the Śākta Great Goddess or Devī, sometimes identified with Kālī herself. For detailed information see D. Kinsley (1998).

'Mount Kailash': viz. *kailās*, the mountain-domain of Śiva in the Himalayas.

'Brindavan': *bṛndāban*, the forest near the north-Indian city of Mathura (south of modern-day Delhi), in which the young Krishna disported with the milkmaids.

'Lanka': the island-kingdom in the south of the subcontinent (identified by some with the island called Sri Lanka today) of the ogre-king Rāvaṇa. The God Rāma's wife, Sītā, was abducted to this island by Rāvaṇa and rescued after a great battle (one of the main events of the ancient epic, the *Rāmāyaṇa* (*c.* 300 B.C.E.–300 C.E.).

'Indra's abode': *indrālay*. The god Indra's sorrow-free and heavenly abode, a land of eternal spring, inhabited by the gods and other heavenly beings (also called Amarāvatī). In Vedic mythology, Indra is the ruler of the gods.

'the Elephant made of Nine Women': *nabanārī-kuñjar*. A motif apparently originating from the concept of various creatures (including the elephant) being formed from an array of animals, and depicted in Mughal miniature-painting. By the sixteenth century this had transmuted, in one of its traditions, into the Hindu, particularly Vaishnava, theme of depicting nine cowmaids from Vrindavan, led by Radha, contorting their bodies and joining together in the shape of an elephant to transport their beloved, Krishna, who rides on top. Thus four women become one leg each of the elephant, four make up its body, including the tusks (two arms!), and the ninth becomes the trunk. In the art of the time, the elephant made of nine women seems to have been the terminus of a series of similar compositions (e.g., the bed/divan made of four women, a knot or ring of five, a gateway of six [*chaynārītoraṇ*], a horse of seven [*saptanārīturaṅga*], a chariot of eight [*aṣṭanārīrath*], and the elephant of nine). It is possible that Bankim had the Vaishnava mode of the elephant-motif in mind here, since it is associated in the list with the well-known scene of Krishna removing the cowmaids' clothes while they were frolicking in a river. It is worth noting that the Vaishnava forms of the motif had erotic variants; in its non-Vaishnava modes it has been depicted in sexually blatant ways. See Syamalkanti Cakrabarti's illustrated book (in Bengali) on the subject (1999).

'and the Removal of the clothes' ": *bastraharaṇ*. This probably refers to a famous incident in Krishna's exploits with the cowmaids in Vrindavan, described in the *Bhāgavata Purāṇa*, Canto 10, ch.22. While the cowmaids were frolicking in a river, Krishna surreptitiously removed their clothes from the bank and made them expose their nakedness before handing back the garments. This is interpreted as the need to expose oneself fully to the divine scrutiny in one's relationship with God. *DCB* mentions another possibility, viz. *bastraharaṇ* may refer to another famous episode, this time from the *Mbh.* (see Book 2, 61.37f. in the Poona edition), in which Duḥśāsana attempts (unsuccessfully) to strip the Pāṇḍavas' co-wife, Draupadī, naked in a crowded assembly-hall in an effort to humiliate her. Every time Draupadī's single outer garment is forcibly removed another garment is revealed underneath. *DCM* favors this interpretation too (see under the Glossary, p.5, first column); however, the expression *bastraharaṇ* by itself is usually associated with the first episode rather than with the second.

Most of the motifs in this list of paintings are Śākta and/or Tantric, viz. traditions in which the Goddess is the supreme personification of the deity, and a number of them have traditionally been depicted in a more or less erotic manner.

"a high throne—a divan of embroidered velvet...": *masnad- makmaler kāmdār bichāna.* It was large enough to enable someone to recline on it (see further in text).

"hubble-bubble": *ālbolā.* A kind of hookah. A distinction can be made between the "hubble-bubble" and the "hookah," but it seems that Bankim does not intend this since in the following chapter he refers to this instrument as a "hookah."

"with a smoking-pipe of clay, fired by cowdung": thus *porjarer saṭkā; por* refers to a process of baking with fuel-cakes made from cowdung so as to give the hubble-bubble's smoking-pipe the appropriately crisp flavor. I am grateful to Pradip Bhattacharya for tracking down this item of information. *DCM* provides no translation for this phrase.

"owner": *munib.*

"But since you're my servant...use your name either": the real reason for this reticence being the convention of the time discouraging husband and wife from addressing each other by their personal names.

"If your caste...with mine": *tumi jadi āmār svaśreṇī na ho.* Since the preparation and intake of food was a matter of ritual purity, for Brahmins in particular the cook had to be of a compatible caste.

"a Kulin—the purest kind—or some lower type?": *kulīn, nā baṃśaja.* The *kulīn* adhered to the strictest requirements of ritual purity in the making of marriage alliances; the *baṃśaja,* though retaining his (Brahmin) caste status, did not feel the need to do so. For a note on Kulinism see under Part III, ch.8.

"I'll have to make amends": *prāyaścitta karite haibe; 'prāyaścitta'* is an act of formal reparation.

"I'm truly a Brahmin's daughter": in fact Sagar is claiming that the solemn word of a Brahmin woman is as good as that of a Brahmin male, though the traditional texts tend not to back this up. Bankim seems to be making a bid for gender equality here.

Chapter 7

VARIANTS

* "and said at last...": *DCsv* continues with, "No one's been able to make a fool of me, but you lot have done so," then continues as in the standard text.

NOTES

"in Queen Debi's domain": *debī rāṇīr rājye.*

"the smallest item of your possessions": *āpnār jinispatra ek kaparddak*...: a *kaparddak* is a small shell used as currency, a cowrie.

"how will she get home?": this was not a straightforward matter. A young bride from a respectable home, especially one not living with her husband, had to leave her residence and return to it in a way that did not excite comment, that is, with the right people, in order to retain her caste-status and reputation.

"I knew that Debi was related to me by marriage": *debī—sambandhe āmār bhaginī hay, pūrbbe jānā śunā chila;* lit. "my sister by marriage..." Sagar does not let on that the common bond of their "sisterhood" is Brajesvar himself, as the husband of both women!

"your beloved": *tomār śyāmcāndke:* an implicit (if somewhat facetious) comparison to the amorous relationship between Krishna (*śyām*) and his lover, Radha.

"The Queen's brother-in-law": *rāṇīr bonāi*: in so far as Sagar is her "sister" through marriage (but without revealing that the Queen is also Brajesvar's wife).

"Hindu customs": *hinduyāni.*

"utensils": *taijasa.*

"But they easily get soiled": *kathāy kathāy sakḍi hay.*

"little pot-thing": *ghaṭi bāṭi*: both small metal pots/jars.

"clay vessels"; *dauḍ mālsā.*

"jugs": *kalasī.*

"*paan*": a small wrap of betel-leaf and other ingredients; see earlier, under Part I, ch.6.

"customary...gift": *dakṣiṇā*. The statutory gift a Brahmin must receive on various occasions.

Chapter 8

VARIANTS

* "But hell has no power over me": *DCsv* continues with, "Why don't you go to your father-in-law's house?"

NOTES

"bed-chamber": *śajyāgṛha.*

"meeting-room": *darbār-kāmrā.*

"small . . . divan": *kṣudra pālaṅka.*

"on an item of unadorned wood": *anābṛta kāṣṭher upar.*

"agitation": *cāñcalyamayatā.*

"paid him obeisance": *praṇām karila*—usually by touching the feet.

"both charged with lightning": *duikhānā . . . baidyuti bharā*: the lightning of suppressed emotion.

"bad deed": *kukarmma.*

"refreshment": *jalgrahan.*

"greatly enhanced my standing": *āmār baḍa maryādā bāḍiyāche*: the acceptance of food by an observant Brahmin when not under duress legitimates the social standing of the host.

"a ritually pure Brahmin": *kulīn*: the most pure stratum of a twice-born caste (see earlier).

"Neither the scion . . . a Brahmin priest": *kulīner cheler ār adhyāpak bhaṭṭācāryer 'bidāy' bā 'maryādā' grahaṇe lajjā chila nā.* By *adhyāpak bhaṭṭācārya* Bankim means a Brahmin well-versed in the practice of ritual. They were supposed to be constantly on the lookout for money for their services. But to preserve appearances, such fees were accepted as "parting gifts."

"God": *debatā.*

"in the service of God": *debatra*, viz. property or money set aside or endowed to cover the cost of service or the worship of a god. This is a significant way of putting it, for Debi is now using it to satisfy the need of her husband, traditionally regarded as a "god." Cf. the conversation between Nishi and Debi in Part I, end of ch.13.

"by March or thereabouts": *māgh phālgune.* Māgh and Phālgun are two months in the Bengali lunar calendar, corresponding roughly to mid-January to mid-February and mid-February to mid-March respectively.

"mid-May": *baiśākh māse.* Baiśākh corresponds roughly to mid-April to mid-May.

"Debi took hold of his hand to put it on herself": an intimate gesture, characteristic of the behavior between husband and wife, not in the time-frame of the novel but in the language of late nineteenth-century domestic reform.

"in control of his senses" *jitendriya.*

"Providence": *bidhātā*, the One who disposes things.

"a couple of hot tear-drops": *phoṭā dui tapta jal.* Hot tears have a special connotation in Sanskritic literary tradition. In an article analyzing such literature, entitled "Hot tears and cold tears," Minoru Hara observes that "these hot grief-tears (*śokāśru*) stand in sharp contrast to joy-tears (*ānandāśru*), which are considered to be cold....[T]he former appear in the context of separation (from one's beloved, kinsfolk etc.), while the latter in that of reunion": M. Hara (1998:343).

"gently...dear": both renderings of *mā* in Nishi's speech.

"Lord in heaven": *baikuṇṭheśvar*, that is, the Lord of (the heaven known as) Vaikuṇṭha, viz. Vishnu's/Krishna's heaven.

"bird": *pakṣiṇī*, viz. "female bird," hence "gracefully."

Chapter 9

VARIANTS

* "Prafulla's a bandit! Shame!": After this, *DCsv* and the first edition conclude the chapter with: "Why didn't I—or Prafulla—die?"

NOTES

"What kind of sister?": as in other eastern cultures, the words for "sister" and "brother" in Bengali are used with much wider connotations than in the West. Sometimes in translation this is expressed by the curious phrase "cousin-brother/cousin-sister," but even this doesn't indicate the full extent of the possible relationship, viz. that it can include individuals related either through blood or by marriage.

"Through family": *jñāti*.

"as a favor from God": *debatār bare*.

"in such grand style": *ata āmiri*.

"the broken fragments of rice-grains": *khud*.

"clothes made of coarse cloth": *gaḍā*. Debi is still mindful of the discipline Bhabani Pathak instilled in her.

"In Farsi": *phārasīte,* viz. Persian, the courtly language of the Muslim rulers in Bengal. Sagar's way, perhaps, of getting Brajesvar to inspect the inscription.

Chapter 10

NOTES

"coarse cloth": *gaḍā*.

"The lacquered iron band...a married woman": *kaḍ*. A custom outmoded in urban society today.

"garb of Ganges clay...deity": *gaṅgāmṛttikār sajjāy debatār mata....* Images of deities made for worship in the home and during festivals are made of clay. The rivers of greater Bengal are regarded as offshoots of the Ganges.

"the region was covered": the region around Rangpur in the northern parts of the greater Bengal of the time.

"the Punjab Wars...the Marquess of Hastings": Francis Rawdon-Hastings (1754–1826, not to be confused with Warren Hastings), the second Earl of Moira, was created the first Marquess of Hastings in 1816, and was Governor-General of India from 1813–23. He was engaged in many campaigns of subjugation mainly in the north and west of the country, which extended to the region of the Punjab.

"the good sort": "*bhāla mānuṣ,*" with quotation marks in the original.

"There was no blame or shame attached to banditry then": if that was so, why did Brajesvar mutter "Shame" with such disappointment when he thought of Prafulla, at the end of the previous chapter?

"Diba": this is Nishi's ("Night's") sister, the Diba ("Day") mentioned at the end of ch.13, Part I.

"shrine": *debālay.*

"lamp": *pradīp*, viz. an oil-lamp.

"Shiva linga": for the mythic and iconic dimension of this "mark" (*liṅga*) of the deity Rudra/Shiva, see S. Kramrisch (1988:ch.VII).

"A Brahmin": no doubt his sacred thread was visible.

"ritual of worship": *pūjā.*

"sat down": the text simply says *basilen*, viz. "sat down," but in the shrine she would have been sitting cross-legged.

"ritual ablution": *ācaman.*

"Child": literally *mā,* "mother" (see earlier explanation).

"a great sin": *mahāpātak.*

"honest": *dhārmmik.*

"wicked...good": *duṣṭa...śiṣṭa.*

"unrighteous": *adharma.*

"live in Kashi": "Since there was no possibility now of family life, Debi wished to live a life dedicated to virtue (*dharmajīban*) in a place of pilgrimage (*tīrthasthān*)": *DCB*, Notes, p.64. Kashi/Benares was (and is) one of the most famous centers of Hindu pilgrimage, especially for a woman who wished to live a solitary life. On the sanctifying power of this ancient city, see Eck (1983).

"In the pursuit of duty": *dharmācaraṇe.*

"How can you renounce self then?": *ātmabisarjjan haila kai?*

"What need did you have of him?": The reader will remember that Debi consistently refused to reveal her past to Bhabani.

"the caste of a Brahmin": *brāhmaṇer jāti.*

"holding court": *darbār kariyā.*

"fighters": *barkandāj.*

"Debigarh": lit. "Debi's fort," apparently the name of a place.

"sixty strong men": *ṣāṭ jan joyān.* Previous references speak of fifty.

"What a life of renunciation . . .": *kirūp sannyās.*

Chapter 11

VARIANTS

* ". . . thick poles of silver": after this sentence, *DCsv* continues with, "Below that a large, thick rug had been spread, and on the rug stood a smallish silver throne" etc. as in the standard edition.

* ". . . particularly gorgeous today": *DCsv* continues with, "But this time she wore a proper sari. The sari had a floral pattern with diamonds" etc. as in the standard version. Bankim emphasizes the sari to contrast with Debi's attire on the moonlit night when she was playing the *vina.* On that occasion Debi "was dressed not in a sari, but in a white, filmy Dhaka wrap" (see Appendix B, *DCsv* ch.3). These distinctions do not occur in the standard version.

NOTES

"held court or sat in judgment": *debī rāṇīr "darbār" bā "ejlās."*

"about a hundred acres": *prāy tin śata bighā jami.* A *bighā* is a square measurement of land in Bengal. 3.025 *bighā*s=1 acre.

"marquee": *sāmiyānā.*

"sandalwood dais": *candankāṣṭher bedī.* Sandalwood is a fragrant, rather uncommon wood, used for special occasions.

"surmounted by a cushion also fringed with pearls": *masnad pātā—tāhāteo muktār jhālar.* Here the cushion on which Debi sits is a sign of authority. In modern parlance, the *gadi.*

"the autumnal Goddess": that is, Durgā, whose great feast is celebrated in autumn with particular pomp in Bengal.

"mace and sceptre-bearers... silver rods": *copdār o āśābardār... rūpār āśā*. The mace/sceptre/rod (=*rājdaṇḍa*) is the traditional sign of royal authority to rule and punish. For information on its symbolism, see for example., A. Glucklich (1994:ch.9). All the trappings described in this passage indicate that Debi really symbolizes a rule that asserts its legitimacy against competing claims (especially those of the British).

"red turban and jacket... red pointed shoes": *lāl pāgḍi, lāl āṅgrākhā, lāl dhuti mālkocā mārā, pāye lāl nāgrā*. Rival claimants to power—the British in particular—dressed their native soldiers and their own officers in items of red clothing; hence this is the act of a defiant claimant to authority (cf. the reference to the red turbans of the guards on Brajesvar's barge in Part II, ch.4). Nevertheless to show their indigenousness, Debi's men wear native dress in contrast to the Western attire of their rivals, that is, loincloths and pointed shoes.

"a song in praise of Debi": *debīr stuti* (or was it a song in praise of the "Goddess," viz. *debī*, whose surrogate Debi was perceived to be?).

"devoutly made a full prostration": *bhaktibhābe sāṣṭāṅge praṇām karila*, literally, "devoutly made obeisance with eight parts (*aṣṭāṅga*)" (of the person). There are several ways of counting these eight parts, viz. the (two) hands, (two) eyes, forehead, throat, breast, and waist; or the hands, eyes, forehead, breast, and knees with feet; or these parts (suitably enumerated) with speech and mind. Eight is a number of completeness in Hindu tradition. Thus there is a form of traditional yoga called *aṣṭāṅga-yoga*, or the Yoga of eight parts/limbs (also called *Rājayoga* or Royal Yoga), described in the *Yogasūtra*s of Patañjali; see I. Whicher (1998:190–99) and G. Feuerstein (1979:78–99).

Chapter 12

VARIANTS

* "and made obeisance at his feet": after this, *DCsv* and the first edition take a different turn, though still sharing a fair amount of material with the standard edition. For a translation of this chapter with these changes underlined, see under Appendix B.

NOTES

"By Durga, I'm saved!": *durgā, bāclem!*

"ancient ethical codes": *prācīn nītiśāstre*: the ancient codes concerning right and wrong—not specified—which Brajesvar had been taught. No doubt this was Brajesvar's interpretation of how to act in the situation; this is indicated by Bankim's use of *bhāḍābhāḍite* with *bāp*, both colloquial terms for "prevarication" and "father" respectively. Brajesvar suppressed the fact that Debi was his father's daughter-in-law, Prafulla.

"sainted money": *japtaper ṭākā*: money derived by or set aside for performing "prayer and penance" (*japtap*), as for example, priests or religious devotees might do.

"Kaibartta by caste": *jete kaibartta*. Traditionally a mixed, low caste that engaged in such occupations as fishing, cultivating, etc.

"not to share food with him": viz. not to eat off his plate as a wife, since by doing so she herself would lose caste. Sagar, of course, is laying it on.

"the accommodation reserved for Sagar": *ijārā-mahal*, literally, the "leased" accommodation; somewhat sarcastic, viz. the quarters kept apart for Sagar when she came to the house.

"formally take the girl in": *baraṇ kare ghare tulba*, viz. by performing the *baraṇ* ceremony which formally welcomes the new bride into the house.

"Nayan Bou . . . herself scarce": because the familiarity of meeting or consorting with one's husband during the day was not allowed.

"marries her and settles down in the proper way": *biye kare saṃsār dharma kare*. Though Brajesvar's parents didn't believe that he had married again (leave alone in the manner rumored), they were prepared to give him his head to some extent if he chose to remarry.

—PART III—

Chapter 1

NOTES

"on the sixth day": *ṣaṣṭhīr din*, that is, on the sixth day of the bright half of May—the day before the debt was to be cleared.

"in a sedan-chair": or palanquin: *śibikārohaṇe*. *DCM*, misleadingly, "In a carriage" (p.185).

"In those days, the Collector was also a keeper of the peace": apparently the same Richard Goodlad encountered earlier (see Part I, ch.8). In the job-description quoted in the endnotes to that chapter, we have seen how policing his District was a necessary part of the Collector's duties.

"renouncer": *sannyāsinī*, viz. a female renouncer.

"fearful ogress": *bhayaṅkarī rakṣasī.*

"by traveling downstream": *bhāṭi diye*, here and subsequently. *DCM* has, oddly, "up the river/up the stream" (p.186–7).

"'fighters'": *barkandāj*—really, *lāṭhiāl*s or fighters with staves. They bore this name more or less as a private army of mercenaries.

"Alas, O Staff...": *hāy lāṭhi... DCB* calls the staff the former "national weapon" (*jātīya astra*) of the Bengali (Notes, p.74). The *lāṭhi* was a narrow but very strong and inflexible rod of bamboo, about four to five feet long. The *lāṭhial* was adept at wielding it, often in anger but sometimes in stick-play (twirling it rapidly around his body and over his head etc.) to exhibit his skill. The *lāṭhi* is still used as a weapon or sign of authority by police forces in India. *DCB* says that the passage that follows is famous in Bengali literature, and that it was written by Bankim to encourage nationalist consciousness in the "weakminded" Bengali (ibid.). The gloss may be doubtful, but the passage is a typical example of Bankim's sometimes over-the-top rueful humor.

"preserved the honor of our women": *ābru pardā rākhite.*

"the Muslim": *musulmān*: that is, the emissaries of Muslim rulers.

"indigo-planter": *nīlkar*. By the time the novel was published, the (Western, i.e., British and other) indigo-planter had become a symbol of greed, extortion, and oppression with regard to the *ryot* or Bengali peasant cultivator. For an account of the controversial system that gave rise to this perception and of a *cause célèbre* in connection with it (in which the British missionary James Long (1814–87) played a laudable part), see Oddie (1999:chs. 7 and 8). In his fictional but hugely informative narrative of (largely Hindu) Bengali peasant life in the early nineteenth century, Lal Behari Day gives a graphic description of the miseries a Bengali peasant could undergo at the hands of an indigo-planter; see Day (1874: Vol.II, chs.xlvi, xlvii, xlix).

"you broke one skull for the offense of another": *rāmer aparādhe śyāmer māthā bhāṅgite,* viz. "you broke Syam's head for Ram's offence." As Deputy Magistrate in the Bengal Civil Service, Bankim had ample opportunity to observe how the law could function in this way.

"the Rod": *lāṭhi*, that is, the staff as symbol of authority.

"The Staff is the remedy for fools": in Sanskrit: *mūrkhasya lāṭhyoṣadham.* That is, fools should not be borne gladly.

"Son!" "Child!": *"bāpu" "bāchā."* Bankim is lamenting the present indulgence of elders toward the younger generation.

"far-flung ancestors and family": *sagotra sapiṇḍa. Sagotra* corresponds to one's clan and descendants, *sapiṇḍa* to one's ancestors.

"Nanda's Son": that is, Krishna, whose foster-father was the cowherd, Nanda. Devotionally and iconographically, Krishna is associated with his bewitching bamboo flute.

"imperishable heavens" *akṣay svarga.*

"prop up... pleasure groves": *indraloke giyā nandankānaner puṣpabhārābanata pārijāt-bṛkṣaśākhār ṭhekno haiyā ācha.* The Amaranth is a flower that never fades.

"the fruits of virtue... salvation": *dharma artha kām mokṣarūp phal.* These four fruits are the traditional *puruṣārtha*s, or goals of human existence, provided they are pursued in accordance with *dharma* or right living. On the *puruṣārtha*s see Sharma (1982), Lipner (1997), and S. Mittal & G. Thursby, eds. (2004), Part IV.

"the tree... every wish": *kalpabṛkṣa,* a fabulous tree.

Chapter 2

NOTES

"the pier": *ghāṭ,* a landing-stage or point, usually with steps leading to the water.

"were smeared with fragrant sandalwood paste": Debi has put off her worldly guise of a Queen with wealth and power at her disposal, and presents herself in ascetic mode as a chaste wife—hence the sandalwood paste—awaiting, as the text will show, one last meeting with her husband and the end of her career as Debi Chaudhurani. The (unlikely) philosophical discussion she is calmly having with her two companions intimates this intended transformation.

"see the supreme deity directly?": *parameśvarke... pratyakṣa dekhā jāy?* "Seeing," or rather, experiencing God directly in some way had become something of an issue at the time the novel was being written. There was a perceived conflict among some sections of the Bengali intelligentsia between the rationalist, positivist "scientific" temperament allegedly mediated by English education on the one hand, and the supposed intuitionism and emotionalism of prominent features of traditional Bengali Hinduism on the other. Examples abound; here is but one: much has been made of an early meeting between the Bengali sage, Ramakrishna (1836–86), and his most famous disciple, Narendranath Datta (who was known later as Swami Vivekananda, 1863–1902). I quote from an official biography (Narendra is reminiscing about his meeting with Ramakrishna): "...I thought, 'Can this man be a great teacher?'—I crept near to him and asked him the question which I had asked so often: 'Have you seen God, sir?' 'Yes, I see Him just as I see you here, only in a much intenser sense.' 'God can be realised,' he went on, 'one can see and talk to Him as I am doing with you.... If one weeps sincerely for Him, He surely manifests Himself.' That impressed me at once. For the first time I found a man who dared to say that he had seen God, that religion was a reality to be felt, to be sensed in an infinitely more intense way than we can sense the world.'" Advaita Ashrama (1960:47). It is not clear if the conversation which follows among the three women in *Debī Chaudhurāṇī* actually reflects Bankim's view.

"*seeing* directly... *perceiving* directly": *pratyakṣa dekhā... pratyakṣa karā.*

"There are six kinds of perception": *pratyakṣa chay rakam.* The six kinds of perception spoken of are based on the numeration of the original Sāṃkhya system, attributed to the sage Kapila (*c.* second half of the first millennium B.C.E., though the formulated or so-called classical system of Sāṃkhya comes to us in the text of the *Sāṃkhya-kārikā,* dated to about third–fourth century C.E. and attributed to Īśvarakṛṣṇa).

"visual perception": *cākṣuṣa pratyakṣa.*

"aural perception": *śrābaṇa pratyakṣa.*

"olfactory perception": *ghrāṇaja pratyakṣa.*

"tactile perception": *tvāc pratyakṣa.*

"gustatory perception": *rāsana pratyakṣa.*

"organs of knowledge": *jñānendriya.* The means by which we get direct knowledge, viz. reliable cognition, from the senses.

"and the hands, feet... five organs of action": The hands (*pāṇi-*), feet (*pāda-*), speech (*vāc*), anus (*pāyu*), and generative organ (*upastha*), are the counterpart organs of action (*karmendriya*) to the organs of knowledge, viz. the direct bodily means by which certain basic actions are effected. See, for example, the *Sāṃkhya-kārikā* vr.26: *buddhīndriyāṇi cakṣuḥ-śrotra- ghrāṇa-rasana-tvagākhyāni/ vāk-pāṇi-pāda-pāyūpasthān karmendriyāṇy āhuḥ//* viz. "The eyes, ears, nose, tongue, and skin are called the organs of knowledge [here *buddhi* instead of *jñāna*], while speech, hands, feet, anus and generative organ are said to be the organs of action." Debi enumerates and explains the organs of knowledge but doesn't do so for the organs of action, perhaps out of delicacy with respect to the last two.

"the internal sense or *manas*... is of both kinds, that is... an organ of knowledge as well as an organ of action": Strictly speaking, in this view, the *manas* is not the intellect, but is reckoned to be an *internal* sense (in contrast to the five *external* senses) which acts as a kind of "gate-keeper" or control of the external senses and organs of action. One of *manas'* primary tasks is to *focus* attention on the activities of one or other of the organs of action or knowledge so as to prevent "cognitive-overload" in the attending organism. C. Bartley, while commenting on the function of *manas* in the philosophical system of *Nyāya-Vaiśeṣika* (2005:86), writes as follows: "[The] sensory receptors (*indriya*) transmit a range of information about the objective environment to a physical faculty called *manas* which operates as a central processor coordinating that information and selecting what is relevant... the *manas* is instrumental in the conversion of some stimuli into feelings, the translation of some items of cognitive input into conscious thoughts with practical applications (storing some as memories), and the transformation of some affective responses into acts of will." This would apply to the Sāṃ khya system as well. Because of this function *manas* is regarded as "of both kinds," viz. as an organ of knowledge as well as an organ of action: cf. the *Sāṃkhya-kārikā* again (vr.27): *ubhayātmakam atra manaḥ saṃkalpam indriyañ ca sādharmyāt:* "In this context, the *manas* has both natures; it discerns the object (=*saṃkalpa*) and it is also an organ in that it shares the latter's characteristics" (medieval Scholastic epistemology in the West gave the *sensus communis* a function analogous to that of the *manas*).

"God is the object of mental perception": *īśvar mānas pratyakṣer biṣay.*

"Because there is no reliable way of doing so... prove God's existence" till "... not because there is no reliable way of doing so": as Bankim goes on to observe, this exchange in Sanskrit draws on a line of argument found in the well-known *Sāṃkhya-Pravacana-Sūtra*s ("Aphorisms declaring the Sāṃkhya [system]"), attributed to Kapila (but assigned to a much later date: *c.*9th–10th century C.E.), and in the *Bhāṣya* or Commentary on it by Vijñānabhikṣu (16th century). The author of the *Sūtra*s has defined perception (*pratyakṣa*) as that knowledge which, having been in conjunction with an object, represents the form of that object (*yat saṃbaddhaṃ sat tadākārollekhi vijñānaṃ tat pratyakṣam:* Bk.I, vr.89; B.D. Basu [1915:138]). If an objector were to reply that this definition does not apply to God's (*īśvara*) mode of perceiving, because the divine perception, not being *in* time, cannot first *have been* in conjunction with the object so as *to give rise* to the act of perception later, the author of the *Sūtra*s would respond that the definition is not at fault "because God has not been proven to exist" (*īśvarāsiddheḥ,* Bk.I, vr.92; ibid.p.142), that is, the objection is irrelevant in so far as God has not been assumed to exist in the first place (so that it is not incumbent on the author of the *Sūtra*s to make his definition apply to the deity). On this verse the commentator glosses as follows (using Nishi's words in part): "The answer to the objection would be: the definition is not at fault because you've offered no proof that God exists (*īśvare prāmāṇābhāvād adoṣa ity anuvartate*)." Note the difference between Nishi's and the commentator's words: Nishi says that God cannot be proved to exist because there is no reliable way of proving the divine existence (*īśvarāsiddheḥ—pramāṇābhāvāt*). The commentator says that no proof has been offered for the existence of God (hence it is irrelevant to object that the definition of perception does not apply to God). Nishi has distorted the *sūtra* to imply that God does not exist. Hence Bankim's reference in the following sentence to Nishi's "cynical remark" (*vyaṇgokti*).

In her reply, also in Sanskrit, Prafulla defends the possibility that God's existence can be known. Her point is that God's existence cannot be known by the external organs of knowledge and action; both kinds of organ are deficient in this respect—not that there is no way of reliably knowing that God exists; hence, *sūtrakārasyobhayendriyaśūnyatvāt—na tu pramāṇābhāvāt.* The underlying assumption here is that Sāṃkhya was not positively atheistic; rather, it was non-theistic: it kept silent as to whether a supreme being existed or not in its arguments.

"Diba (who did not know Sanskrit) . . . keep that high-flown nonsense to yourselves!": actually Diba parodies the Sanskrit: *rekhe dāo tomār hābāt mābāt:* "keep your *habat mabat* to yourselves" (echoing—*śūnyatvāt . . . prāmāṇābhāvāt*).

"form—external objects": *rūp, bahirbiṣay.*

"internal": *antarbiṣay.*

"without help or some prop": *sāhājya bā abalamban vyatīta. abalamban* is a more technical term than *sāhājya,* referring to an epistemological support.

"Shall I give you an example . . .": Bankim neatly turns the abstract philosophical discourse to the situation of the moment.

"They don't know we have a spyglass": again a stress on Debi's "scientific" progressiveness. In her person, she marries tradition and progress; this chapter is a kind of transition from Debi as bandit-Queen outside the conventional social system to Prafulla the restored but socially transformed wife—hence Bankim switches from "Debi" to "Prafulla" and back again when identifying her as the speaker in the text.

"land-sepoys . . . escape by land": *ḍāṅgār sipāhī . . . ḍāṅgā-pathe palāite pāri.*

"'Yoga' was the reply": *jog* (in Bengali); an interesting use of yoga. Yoga is the disciplining of mind and body so as to achieve one's full psycho-physical potential; this could release special powers or *siddhi*s ("accomplishments") such as perceiving without relying on the external sense organs, attenuating the body in one way or other, and so on. The goal of "classical" or *aṣṭāṅga* yoga (based on the *Yoga Sūtra* of Patañjali, 2nd–3rd century C.E.), which was aligned with classical Sāṃkhya, was to attain *kaivalya* ("aloneness"), viz. complete detachment from one's psycho-physical complement and its travails. However, the term *yoga* also had a wider application, implying the following of a particular discipline (by using the techniques of classical yoga in general) so as to attain specific goals. See further.

"all those practices of focusing…tricks": "focusing": *nyās(a): nyāsā* (Skr.: "superimposing upon, depositing"): a ritual process in various forms of yoga by which the adept effects a kind of identification between self (or some of its parts) and external target-objects either visible or invisible, by acts of disciplined meditation (hence "practices of 'focusing' ": see A. Bharati (1992:273–4) (footnote 54); J. Grimes (1996:214–15).

"special breathing": *prāṇāyāma:* in yoga practice, controlled breathing. "Control of breath has three aspects: inhalation (*recaka*), retention (*kumbhaka*), and exhalation (*pūraka*). The practice of *prāṇāyāma* aims at making the span of *pūraka, recaka,* and *kumbhaka* longer. There are also *prāṇāyāmā*s for purifying the blood, vitalizing the inner organs, etc." (Grimes: 1996:240). Bankim next mentions *kumbhaka* (which I have subsumed under "special breathing"). Its meaning is given under *prāṇāyāma* above.

"the mumbo-jumbo, tricks": *bujrukī, bhelkī.* These are not technical terms of yoga, of course, but Diba's way of intimating what she thinks of yoga's special exercises.

"practice": *abhyās*, disciplined practice.

"the yoga of knowledge…of devotion": *jñāna-yoga, karma-yoga, bhakti-yoga.* A well known triad, emphasizing disciplines of knowledge, action, and devotion respectively, variously interpreted.

"the yoga of complication": *goljog*: Bankim humorosly turning the conversation into word-play.

"pinnace": *pānsī.* A small boat with a wooden deck for carrying passengers, driven by sails and/or oars.

"yoga of opportunity": *sujog*: continuing the wordplay.

"made obeisance by touching his feet": *padadhuli grahaṇ karila*, literally, "took the dust of his feet."

"sinful woman": *pāpīyasī.*

"wife": in this passage, *strī.*

"golden icon in the temple of my mind": *maner mandirer bhitar sonār pratimā….*

"following what my elders told me to do": *gurujaner ājñā pālon karitechi.*

"merit": *puṇya*, or good karma.

"You are my god": *tumi āmār debatā.*

❂ *Chapter 3* ❂

NOTES

"gun": *banduk*, a generic term for a firearm, but at the time of the novel, viz. in the late eighteenth century, likely to be a musket of some sort.

"and heard that you still love me": *tumi āmāy bhālabhāsa, tāhā śunilām:* a remarkable social statement for a serious novel of the time. Traditionally, Hindu (arranged) marriages were not so much about love (though, of course, this could blossom in time) as about the duty of procreation and the continuation of the line. Such intimate details were hardly the subject of matter-of-fact conversation between husband and wife. Thus this statement reflects the current Western ideal of marriage rather than that of traditional Hinduism. Hindu marriages were not based on courtship or its unpredictable consequences. On the role of "love" in marriage in late nineteenth-century Bengal, see Walsh (2004: esp.ch.5).

"the lady of my house": *āmār gharaṇī gṛhiṇī kariba.*

"by rights . . . in danger": *bipade āmii dharmmataḥ tomār rakṣākartā.*

"informer": *goindā.*

"*A father is heaven . . . when a father is satisfied*": see Part I, ch.14 (and relevant endnote).

"Debi wished him well": *debī tār maṅgalākāṅkṣiṇī.*

"selfless": *niṣkām*, viz. without selfish desire. Prafulla had imbibed the teaching of the *Bhagavad Gītā*, which Bhabani Pathak was fond of quoting, and which he had insisted become a primary source of wisdom in her preparatory studies (see ch.15 where the *Bhagavad Gītā* is described as the "best of all works" (*sarbbagranthaśreṣṭha*); see also relevant endnote).

"Whoever follows a code of selfless virtue": *jār dharma niśkām.*

❂ *Chapter 4* ❂

NOTES

"that religious fellow with the beard": thus *dāḍi bābājīr*. For *bābāji*, see Part I, footnote 28. Here the epithet is meant somewhat sarcastically.

"Debigarh": *debīgaḍ*, or "Debi's fort." There is mention of Debi's stronghold or fort in Part II, toward the end of ch.10.

"see how clever Nishi is": *niśir kauśal dekha.*

"rich man's house": *rājbāḍīte*; see Part I, ch.13, where Nishi explains her background to Prafulla.

"playing a few notes in the musical mode *Mallar*": *phu diyā mallāre tān mārila. Mallār* is a musical mode or *rāgiṇī* favored by Bankim. It is the mode in which the famous hymn, *Bande Mātaram* ("I revere the Mother"), now India's National Song (as distinguished from the National Anthem), was cast in Bankim's novel *Ānandamaṭh*, where it first appeared. This novel preceded *Debī Chaudhurāṇī* serially in 1881–2 in the journal, *Baṅgadarśan*, of which Bankim was the editor. *Mallār* is a lighter mode (*rāgiṇī*) of its lead musical mode, *Megh-rāg*, which is a mode expressing the mood of the rains or monsoons. For a fuller description, see the relevant endnote in my book on *Ānandamaṭh* (2005:243–4).

"greeted Debi with a blessing": Rangaraj is a Brahmin.

"fighters": *barkandāj*, the expression used to refer to Debi's army.

"But why?": *kena, mā*. Literally, "But why, mother?" For "mother" in this context, see Ch.11, Part I, relevant endnote (i.e., the comment on "and asked her kindly"), and also Bhabani Pathak's directive to his band of men toward the end of that chapter.

"Do neither of you have any idea as to what is right?": *tomāder ki kichu dharmmajñān nāi?*

"Do both of you...such a low opinion of me": *āmāy ki tomrā emon apadārtha bhābiyācha....*

"the right to stop you": *niṣedh karibār adhikār.*

"The Lord of the world": *jagadīśvar.*

"I have no right to destroy the lives": *prāṇ naṣṭa karibār āmār kona adhikār nāi.*

"this selfless code of practice": *niṣkām dharmma,* that is, derived from the *Bhagavad Gītā*.

"Conquer, O Lord of the world": *jaya jagadīśvara,* a Sanskrit invocation derived, no doubt, from another text favored by Bankim, Jayadeva's twelfth-century Sanskrit love-poem, the *Gītagovinda,* where the expression, *jaya jagadīśa (hare)* (Conquer, O Hari, Lord of the world), occurs often at the beginning of the First Canto.

"She picked up a conch-shell and blew into it": it was (and is) a common custom in Bengal for women to blow a long blast or two on a conch-shell in the teeth of a storm. This is an invocation to the "gods" or celestials presiding over the storm to give protection against the elements. Here, apparently, Debi seeks their protection by invoking them to actually bring on the storm so that she can use it to escape from her enemies.

Chapter 5

NOTES

"the weapon typical...": *jātīya hātiyār*. An interesting use of *jātīya*, which began to assume the meaning of "national" at the time the novel was being written.

"white banner," and later "white flag": *sādā niṣān*.

"Don't you know the English...the white flag?": perhaps included in the narrative as an explanation to the reader, but curious that Brajesvar needs the explanation. This, together with Rangaraj's dismissive remark, "What are you, a little boy?," has the effect of showing up Brajesvar as ignorant and out of touch. Bankim is pressing the contrast in behavior between husband and wife: the one passive and uncomprehending, the other pro-active and in charge.

"I've plenty of money": yet in ch.3 Debi has informed Brajesvar that she has "distributed all [her] wealth." Perhaps she is engaging in subterfuge here, or the ornamental treasures of the barge are meant.

"the Lord": *bhagabān*. A familiar, Hindu term, for God.

"with familiar respect": thus *mā*, the diminutive form of "mother" (as explained earlier).

Chapter 6

VARIANTS

* "'I'm Debi,' said Debi": the first book-edition adds the following paragraph before the story continues: "Here we're bound to say that if we were to judge this reply of Debi's in accordance with modern western ethical codes (*ādhunik pāścātya dharmanīti śāstrānusāre*) it would have to be regarded as highly objectionable, for her words came across as false. Whilst that's against the western ethical codes no doubt, the reader must judge whether it is permitted by western ways of acting! Nevertheless, it can be said on Debi's behalf that she made no pretence of speaking the truth. It's in pretence that appalling untruthfulness lies. May the Almighty preserve the human race from conflating unsubtle ethical codes and abstruse moral manoeuverings." A somewhat abstruse passage in its own right!

NOTES

"the Englishman": thus *sāheb*, here and elsewhere in the chapter. *Sāheb* was used for a white man, and designated respect or authority; the equivalent for a white woman was *memsāheb* (both terms can now be used for non-whites).

"mistress": *prabhu.*

"iron bracelet": *kaḍ.*

"Sir": *sāheb.*

"We Bengali girls...": *āmrā bāṇgālīr meye.*

"The curse of Jesus Christ on you": *tomār jiśu chrīṣṭer dibya:* an awkward expression.

"stratagem": *kauśal.*

"reveres his Queen and is devoted to her as a mother": *se rāṇījike mā bale, rāṇījike mār mata bhakti kare.*

"evil woman": *pāpiṣṭhā.*

Chapter 7

NOTES

"Canakya's sound advice...": Cāṇakya (anywhere from 400 B.C.E.–400 C.E.), also known as Kauṭilya/Kauṭalya and Viṣṇugupta (not to mention a few other names), is famous for many worldly-wise sayings attributed to him. The one mentioned in the text runs as follows: *nakhināṃ ca nadīnāṃ ca śṛiṅgiṇāṃ śastra-pāṇināṃ/ viśvāso naiva kartavyaḥ strīṣu rāja-kuleṣu ca//* "One shouldn't trust creatures with claws, rivers, horned beasts, people with weapons in their hands, or women and royalty." This is given as vr.267 in Sternbach (1963:166).

"about a mile": *ardha krоś.*

"wretch of a bandit-woman": *ḍākāit māgī.*

"Listen old chap": *hā bāpu mājhi.*

"password": *saṃketbākya.*

"My humble salutations...in good spirits": *bandegī khān sāheb! mejāj sarif?* A Muslim greeting. Why this form of address is not clear—perhaps a reversion to the courtly etiquette of the time and to indicate that Haraballabh had now entered the *durbar* room of a Queen.

"(in the most appalling Hindusthani)": this is not in the text, but is indicated by the bad Hindusthani used. Brenan seemed to know good Bengali but bad Hindusthani.

"Mister": *sāheb,* since Brajesvar continues with the familiar "you" in aggresive tone—*tomār bajrā...* etc.

"Why? You low fellow...:" again in bad Hindusthani.

"an almighty slap": *birāśī sikkār ek capeṭāghāt*, lit. "82 silver rupees (*sicca*) of a slap." The *sicca* was a (notional) silver rupee in circulation at the time of the novel. "The standard weight of a rupee was theoretically one *sicca*, equal to 179.5511 grains troy; the standard fineness was 98/100 pure silver" (Hunter 1897:299, note 93). But there were in fact many kinds of *sicca* in circulation with different degrees of purity. See further, Hunter: Appendix N.

"about seventy-five feet": *pañcāś hāt*, viz. fifty "hands." For this measure of distance, see Part II, under ch.4.

"The Englishman had just raised his fist...": but where was his weapon? Bankim has said earlier (ch.6) that he had mounted the barge "armed" (*saśastre*), and accompanied by a sepoy. There is evidence of neither here.

"pointed shoes": *nāgrā jutā*, though we are told earlier that no fighter from Bhabani Thakur's army had brought shoes. Perhaps Rangaraj has been given shoes for effect here, again to poke fun at Haraballabh.

"invoking the Goddess": *durgānām japiyā*... lit. "repeatedly calling to (the Goddess) Durgā under one's breath."

"shooting-star": *nakṣatra*.

"Lord": *bhagabān*. A Hindu term.

"It's the Lord who's finding a way to save me": In *DT* there is a reference to the way Debi escapes which illuminates Bankim's intentions. In chapter 19 of the *DT* Bankim explains how selfless devotion to God allied with the requisite spiritual discipline (*anuśīlan*) enables extraordinary things to be done by the devotee. "The devotee becomes able," pronounces the Guru of the text. "When all the devotee's capacities (*vṛtti*) are fully disciplined (*anuśīlitā*), the devotee becomes extremely proficient in doing things. If, over and above this, such a person receives God's help, is it impossible for him or her even when in grave danger to save his or her life with the assistance of a natural law?" The footnote to this passage reads: "It is to prove this very thing that Debi Chaudhurani's escape from the hands of the sepoys was devised by the present author [viz. Bankim]. The gathering of the clouds at a particular time was God's grace, but the rest was the devotee's own skill."

Chapter 8

NOTES

"rolling about like pumpkins": *kuṣmāṇḍākāre gaḍāgaḍi diyāchilen*.

"twisted his sacred thread around his thumb": the sacred thread, the mark of Haraballabh's Brahmin status, hung diagonally from around the left shoulder across the chest and back up under the right arm. Haraballabh seeks to exercise the spiritual power of this status.

"began to mutter Durga's name again and again . . .": *durgānām japite ārambha karilen.* The verb *japā* refers to a silent intoning or recitation, or a repeated muttering under one's breath. The idea is that the sacred name itself becomes a *mantra,* with the inherent power to rescue or save.

"Master": *hujur.*

"gentleman": *sāheb.*

"we're Hindus": *āmrā hindu.* Note Bankim's use of this generic description—an indication of the way Hindu identity was being standardized at the time.

"When the Englishman saw Brajesvar's devotion . . . shook it warmly": a typical stereotyping of the Englishman's character: choleric but generous and quick to forgive when the circumstances were right; "devotion to his father": *brajeśvarer pitṛbhakti.*

"who had not the least idea what shaking hands meant": *brajeśvarer caturddaś puruṣer madhye kakhana jāne nā, sekhyāṇḍ kāke bale*: lit. "fourteen generations of Brajesvar's ancestors wouldn't know what shaking hands could mean . . ."

"to lose caste": *tomār jāti jāy.*

"*Dakinir Smasan*": *ḍākinī* refers to a band of terrible witch-like followers of Śiva and his divine consort Umā or Pārvatī, or indeed to a fearsome form of the Goddess herself. Either way, we are not talking of pleasant characters. *Śmaśān*: a burning or cremation ground.

"the sin": *pātak.*

"lowlife": *narādham.*

"Give me Ganges water . . . *tulsi* leaves": *gaṅgājal tāmā tulsī dāo.* According to one view, copper (*tāmā, tāmra*) was produced from the semen of the deity Karttik; it was supposed to have healing properties. Ganges water and *tulsī* leaves (see under endnotes for Part I, ch.14) are also sacred objects. This was a particularly potent, sacred combination, especially suitable for the taking of solemn oaths and vows.

"Will you put your hand on Brajesvar's head and swear": putting one's hand on the head of a loved one to take an oath was a terrible form of oath-taking, calculated to bring about harm or death to the loved one if for some reason the oath could not be observed. Even the self-serving Haraballabh draws the line at this; at least he genuinely loves his son.

"I come from a very strict *kulin* family": *āmi baḍa kulīner meye.*

"suitable husbands": *pātra.*

"There are many *kulin* girls like her": because it was not easy to get suitable husbands. The age of 25–30 for an unmarried girl at the time gave rise to the prospect of social ostracism. But it was a husbands' market and the demands for dowries and marital stipends by potential husbands, often in the face of genuine poverty in the girls' families, could prove too exacting for many. For a scathing early critique of the Kulin Brahminism of the time, not least with reference to Kulin matrimonial practice, see the (ex-*kulin*) Christian convert, K.M. Banerjea's, "The Kulin Brahmins of Bengal," 1844. "The laws which regulate the marriage of Kulin females are cruelly stringent. These must not on any account be given to any but persons of an equal or superior grade.... An indelible disgrace would be affixed upon such a prostitution of a girl of birth and family.... No parent... dares to risk his daughter's virtue by allowing her to lead a single life.... The distress and perplexity of a *poor* (emphasis added) Kulin, when his daughter attains the marriageable age, are therefore inexpressible" (op.cit., 15–16).

"she'll have to marry beneath her station": *aghare paḍibe.* That is, she'll have to marry a non-Kulin.

"the same caste status as my father": *āmār bāper pālṭi ghar.*

"my father's family honor will be saved": *āmār bāper kul thāke.*

"Haraballabh was in seventh heaven": *haraballabh hāt bāḍāiyā svarga pāila:* lit. "Haraballabh reached out and grasped heaven."

"pomp and circumstance": *ghaṭā.*

"It's true. Bengalis are such liars": another stereotype, this time of Bengali character as perceived by the British. Rabindranath Tagore parodies this stereotype in his (later) novel *Gorā* through the words of Mahim (see end of ch.4, pp.30–1, in Viśvabhāratī 1977 ed.).

"I wanted to see... mother-in-law's role with him!": Nishi jokes that if by conferring with Haraballabh (Debi's father-in-law), she could have negotiated a marriage, she would be acting as Debi's mother-in-law, since parents confer to negotiate a marriage for their offspring.

"God": *debatā.*

Chapter 9

NOTES

"fine morning... good luck for Debi today": see footnote 12 in text of translation.

"The day I'm finished...": Is Nishi having a moment of doubt about the ascetic path she has chosen?

"is allowed to take his ritual bath...": *snānāhnike nāmāiyā dāo*. As a Brahmin, Haraballabh was obliged to perform a version of this ritual daily. A description of this ritual in an elaborate form (there were shorter versions) together with an analysis is given in Glucklich, 1994:71–5. In short, this was a regenerating ritual in the presence of the rising sun (though it could be performed later) and in flowing water, meant to purify the bather on a regular basis of the burden of wrongdoing. "The morning bath...was meant neither for hygiene nor for sport. Consequently it was presented by normative texts as a relatively complex ritual. And, as usual, variations and differences in the descriptions and prescriptions of ritualized bathing were unavoidable...all baths possess a utilitarian, "visible" (*dṛṣṭa*) aspect, which is directly related to physical cleansing, and a transcendent, "invisible" (*adṛṣṭa*) dimension....According to the *Viṣṇu Smṛti*, the best place to bathe is the Ganges, followed by river water in general, fountain or fresh spring water, a tank, a well, and so forth. The general principle is enunciated by the *Vyavahāra Mayūkha*, which states that river water purifies by means of its velocity or the force of its current. Still water purifies less effectively....The most important and obligatory bath—the routine daily bath—takes place during two or three transitional phases of the day: dawn and noon. The first bath begins shortly before the solar disk emerges above the horizon....The obligatory bath is universal but women and Śūdras perform it silently, whereas others recite Vedic *mantras*. The bath is accompanied by the use of several items including rubbing earth (*mṛt*)...," and so on (ibid.:72–3). There follows a detailed description with the inclusion of accompanying prayers.

"Why the hurry?": because the bath could have been taken later (see above). Nishi goes on to joke that Debi wants her father-in-law out of the way so that she and Brajesvar can meet again as speedily as possible.

"Don't you see the boy...Lanka?": *bāchādhan samudra laṅghan kariyā laṅkāy āsite pāriteche nā, dekhitecha nā?* This is an allusion to the story of the great epic, the *Rāmāyaṇa*, in which queen Sītā has been abducted across the sea to the ogre, Rāvaṇa's island-kingdom, which impels her husband, Rāma, to launch a campaign to get her back. Similarly, Brajesvar has been cut off all night from his wife Debi by the presence of the unsuspecting Haraballabh. Out of respect for his father, and to maintain the as-yet unknown identity of Debi as his wife, Brajesvar has stayed away. Once Haraballabh has left the scene, performing his ritual bath, Brajesvar can make his way to Debi/Prafulla in the "Lanka" or "promised land" of her inner chamber. As is common in Bengali conversation between *sakhi*s or close female friends, there is friendly though barbed humor. *DCM* adds a footnote in the translation here: "Apparently calling him [viz. Brajesvar] a monkey" (p.248). This is an allusion to another incident in the *Rāmāyaṇa*, in which Rāma's devoted monkey-helper, Hanumān, leaps across the sea to Laṇkā to find Sītā on Rāma's behalf. Brajesvar is likened to Hanumān. But Nishi is making a joke about two persons romantically linked and this emphatically does not apply to Hanumān and Sītā.

"By guards I mean . . . so that they don't obstruct the ritual": *pāhārā māne jal-ācaraṇī bhṛtya*: "servants of a birth-group from whom Brahmins can take water," *DCB::*Notes, p.94. That is, guards from a caste not regarded as untouchable by Brahmins.

"invocations": *mantra.*

"Go back to your own home . . .": *tumi gharer chele, ghare jāo.* An oblique message for the colonial regime, perhaps?

"Mister": *sāheb.*

❂ *Chapter 10* ❂

NOTES

"discreetly": *dhīre dhīre.* "Discreetly" because to all appearances he was going to the boudoir of a woman to whom he was not married, and who was not a close relative. Besides, his father, who did not know who Debi was, was in the vicinity.

"Brajesvar kissed . . . on the lips": an unusually intimate gesture for a "respectable" novel of the time. Bankim writes boldly in this respect from time to time (see, e.g., *Ānandamaṭh,* Part II, ch.1, where Jibananda kisses his wife Shanti "on the lips right there in the shade of the coconut grove . . .," Lipner, 2005:174). This is another affirmation of the dyadic relationship between husband and wife that reformers recommended at the time Bankim was writing.

"It will brighten up the house": *ghar ālo haibe,* that is, "you'll brighten our lives."

"witches": *ḍākinī beṭīrā.*

"*kulin*": see above.

"her father has the same ritual status as us": *or bāp āmāderi pālṭi.* In Bengali society, caste-status was patrilineal.

"*Kulins* must protect the honor of *kulins*": no one else could do it, since to maintain *kulin* caste status only an appropriate caste-marriage was acceptable; see K.M. Banerjea (1844).

"the lower castes": these are referred to by their caste-names, viz. *muṭe majurer ta kāj nay. Muṭe* (*muṭiyā*) and *majur* are castes who work as load-carriers and laborers.

"boubhāt": same as *pāksparśa.* See footnote 11 of this Part.

"married in the proper way": *jathāśāstra,* viz. according to the sacred texts.

❂

"honor...social standing": *kul, śīl, jāti, mārjyādā.*

"rightfully our due by way of dowry": *āmāder jeṭā nyājya pāonā gaṇḍā.*

"muttered Durga's name": so that he could have a safe journey.

❁ *Chapter 11* ❁

NOTES

"Ma": as we have already seen, a term of respectful endearment or affection in some contexts.

"residence and property...which she had dedicated to the deity": *debīgaḍe prafuller ghar bāḍi, debsebā, debatra sampatti chila.* This meant that Prafulla did not own the wealth and property for her own gratification, but that she had placed herself in trust over it to use it in the name of the deity.

"and live off the offerings...": *debatār bhog hay, prasād khāiyā dinpāt kariyo. Debatā* is a deity in a temple or shrine; *bhog* is the ritual offering(s) made to this deity, while *prasād* is the offering returned to the worshipper with the deity's blessing (for a more detailed explanation of how the *prasād* works, see Fuller [1992:esp.74–81]). "What an amazing piece of advice! A most forceful man, the exponent of extraordinary valour, is supposed to spend his days in inaction, just living off the offerings to the deity!" (*DCB*, Notes, p.97).

"And do not take up the staff again": Prafulla, formerly the uneducated, untrained girl, is now in a position to give people advice as to how to live their lives.

"God": *īśvar.*

"obeisances": *praṇām*, or humble greetings.

"Will you go to your in-laws' house without ornaments?": unthinkable for a bride conscious of her (and her family's) standing in the community. Such ornaments would be a mark of her social worth.

"This is a woman's prize ornament!": *strīloker ei ābharaṇ sakaler bhāla.* The reverse of what men would say of their wives according to the old mentality. Actually, Prafulla is showing that she is still really in control. She has so much self-worth that she is prepared to forego the traditional ornamental trappings and hold up her husband as her prize ornament. Perhaps Bankim also wants to indicate the need for a reciprocal relationship between husband and wife. If a wife could be treated as an ornament of her husband (the traditional approach), then why not the other way round?

"dowry gift": *jautuk.*

❁

"grandee's wife": *rājmahiṣī.*

"Nishi had started them off... the sobbing continued in earnest": *niśi... sur tuliyāchila; dibā tatkṣaṇāt pō dharilen. tār par pō sānāi chāpāiyā uṭhila.* The metaphor here is a musical one. Nishi's sobbing starts the tune, and Diba's weeping provides the accompaniment; then the three of them wail together in the way a *sanai* (a wind instrument resembling a clarinet) forcefully accentuates the melody.

"There Prafulla took the dust of Diba and Nishi's feet...": since both were of Brahmin stock and older than she.

"parting gift": *upaḍhaukan.*

Chapter 12

NOTES

"and quite an old one at that": *baḍa nā ki dheḍe bau.* Generally, girls were married off very young, and not in full maturity; if they were married off when mature, this was "old" by comparison—the idea being that as a wife Prafulla was no "spring chicken."

"So every woman who could—young or old, the one-eyed and the lame..." etc.: what follows is another vignette of village life and sentiment, charmingly described. These finely etched cameos give us an accurate insight into Bengali rural life of the time, some of which is relevant to the present day.

"hurried to catch a glimpse of her": this is not simply curiosity. "Catching sight/a glimpse of" has special significance in Hindu, not least Bengali, tradition, both religious and social—with special reference to women. Note the frequent allusions here and elsewhere to the screening of the face with the border of the sari (otherwise thrown over the shoulder) in certain circumstances. This indicated the appropriate modesty where men and the public gaze were concerned; observance of social and family hierarchy, in particular with reference to relationships between senior and junior females; and also an acknowledgment of an element of personal vulnerability. Once you caught sight of the woman's face in the appropriate formal context, you acknowledged that a social barrier had been crossed and that you were jointly members of a particular community. In religious context, catching sight of the (image of the) deity in a temple or shrine in an appropriate manner (*darśan*), gave helpful access to the deity (see Eck [1996]).

"on the eating-leaf": *pāte.* It was the custom at the time, especially in villages, for food to be served on a large leaf (usually a banana leaf). This was cheap, hygienic, and ritually pure (since the leaf could be disposed of after each meal and there was no need for already used—and, where purity was concerned, ritually ambivalent—crockery).

"fish-gravy dish" *mācher jhol.* As noted before, a fish dish was, and still is, a favorite of Bengali cuisine.

"Granny": *āyi.*

"without so much as a by-your-leave...": *bhrātṛbadhu mānila nā*. She was there to serve the men as a good housewife, but catching a glimpse of the new bride was more pressing.

"The Goddess of modesty": *lajjādebī*—a trope; no particular Goddess is intended here.

piri: viz. *piḍi.* A small, low wooden platform inches above the ground, for standing or sitting crossed-leg on (as for a meal). Bride and groom stand on the *piḍi* to mark them out for special ceremonial attention as they formally enter the house for the first time as a married couple.

"during the welcome ceremony": *baraṇ karibār samaye.*

"These things usually happen in a *kulin*'s house": For an indication of what is meant see K.M. Banerjea's essay (1844) mentioned earlier.

"during her last rites": *ekṭi prācīnār antarjale tāhār pāṇigrahaṇ kariyāchilen.* "Last" indeed! Since the marriage rite took place while the old bride, who was on her deathbed, was being immersed in the holy waters of a river in preparation for her final journey.

"But let the *boubhat* be over first": so as to strengthen their case. The *boubhat* would be a significant event, drawing the family and their guests into social acceptance of the new bride. Haraballabh would then be faced with a *fait accompli*, which he would not easily seek to undo.

Chapter 13

NOTES

"Creator": *bidhātā*; the Disposer, the all-Provider.

"had gone to make friends": *bhāb karite giyāchila*: to create a rapport, to be of one mind.

"a proper marriage or hitched up with some Muslim woman": *ke jāne, biye ki nike. Nike* or *nikā* referred to the Muslim ceremony of marrying a widow or a divorcée, the last thing an orthodox Hindu would want to do since there were no proper rites for this.

"Shudra": a person of the fourth caste-order, born to serve the three higher castes.

"People keep a sense of dignity": *āpnār jāt bāciye sabāi kathā kay*; that is, "hold on to (the dignity of) your caste (*jāt*) and speak."

"With pudgy cheeks like Gobind's mother": a figure of speech describing the bloom of good health.

"Then who are you now?...The new wife": Didn't the new wife have a name? That is not the point: she is indeed the "new wife" of Bankim's reformist imagination.

"the right life for a woman": *strīloker dharma*.

"Women aren't born to rule": *dharma* again, viz. *rājatva strījātir dharma nay*: literally, "to rule is not women's *dharma*." *Dharma* refers to the way of life prescribed for one, by way of caste, stage of life, gender, and so on. See the Introduction for an analysis of this passage.

"It's the family life...that's a hard duty": *kaṭhin dharma-o ei saṃsār-dharma:* literally, "And this *dharma* of the family is also a hard *dharma*." Various nuances of the term *dharma* emerge in this passage.

"form of renunciation" *sannyās*.

"virtue": *puṇya*: merit; that which creates good karma.

"follow your example": viz. "be your disciple," *tomār celā haiba*. Bankim's implicit call, perhaps, to his women readers in particular.

"You still haven't seen to my death rites": *āmāy ta gaṇgāy dili nā?*

"...you're a Bagdi": Tongue in cheek, Grandaunt says that because Brajesvar hasn't kept his word as a Brahmin, he's lost caste.

Chapter 14

NOTES

"household": *saṅsār*.

"qualities": *guṇ*.

"for she had practiced the path of selfless action": *niṣkām dharma abhyās kariyāchila*.

"true renouncer": *jathārtha sannyāsinī*.

"She had no selfish desires...was to engage in work": *tār kona kāmanā chila nā—kebal kāj khũjita*.

"The goal of selfish desire ... the happiness of others": *kāmanā arthe āpanār sukh khôja—kāj arthe parer sukh khôja*. Bankim is invoking a distinction, enshrined in the *Bhagavad Gītā*, that has resounded in Hindu ethics to the present day, and which Hindu activists in his time, both social and political, sought to apply. The interesting thing here is that its exponent is a (lowly) woman, and its context, daily family life. So Bankim is trying to say that this foundational distinction is universally applicable in the new Indian polity. Work/action is the appropriate context for selfless service; that is what true renunciation consists of, not the life of a wandering mendicant or solitary yogi (see Introduction for further discussion).

"intent on work": *karmmaparāyaṇ*. See previous note.

"easily cut through ... family life": *saṅsār-granthi anāyāse bicchinna karila; "granthi,"* a knot, entanglement, is a term used already in the early Upanishads in this context (see, e.g., ChUp. 7.26.2, and KaUp. 2.3.15, viz. "When all the knots (*granthayaḥ*) of the heart here are severed, then a mortal becomes immortal ...").

"a great teacher" ... a most learned person": *mahāmahopādhyāy ... parama paṇḍit*.

"household duties": *gṛhadharma*.

"display knowledge": *bidyā prakāś*.

"A woman's husband is her god": *strīloker pati debatā*.

"to serve you too": *tomāke orā pūjā karite pāy nā kena: "pūjā,"* to correspond to *"debatā."*

"the head of the house": *kartā*.

"the poor and needy": *kāṅgāl garibke*.

"hostel": *atithiśālā*.

"an image of the Goddess Annapurna": *annapūrṇā-mūrti*.

"*Debinibas:* 'Debi's Home'": a pun on *debī,* since the hostel was endowed by Debi, and had an image of the Goddess or *debī* of Plenty installed in it.

"penance": *prāyaścitta:* formal reparation, for he was a bandit with a conscience, robbing to right wrongs and give to the poor. His conscience demanded reparation for his acts of violence.

"that he be transported for life ...": a punishment meted out by the British to subversives in particular. In later times, the Andaman Islands were a favored destination for this punishment. But as noted in the Introduction, *Debī Chaudhurāṇī* was not intended to be a historical novel. In fact, Bhabani Pathak did not die this way. "He died in July 1789 in a battle with sepoys in the employ of the British, not by going to some island after giving himself up (further, at the time the custom of transporting prisoners to the Andamans hadn't begun)": Jadunath Sarkar in his Preface to the Centenary edition of the novel, p.i. See under B. Bandyopadhyay and S. Das (eds.): 1950:i. On this punishment for Bhabani Pathak, *DCB* says, "This is not Bankim the novelist speaking, but apparently Bankimchandra Chattopadhyay the Deputy Magistrate, whose task it was to mete out appropriate punishment to the convicted" (Notes, p.107).

"keeping both joy and Prafulla in his heart": thus the compound expression *prafullacitte*, since *prafulla*, while meaning "joy," seems also intended to refer to Prafulla herself, who as Bhabani Thakur's leader, influenced the later portion of his active life so much.

"I am not something new.... Voice of the past": *āmi nūtan nahi, āmi purātan. āmi sei bākya mātra*. As the following lines will show, this is the Voice of the Lord Krishna in the *Bhagavad Gītā*.

"To protect the good... in every age": a famous verse from the *Gītā* (4.8), proclaiming the repeated descent of the deity in embodied form. This passage of the *Gītā* runs as follows: "You and I have passed through many births, Arjuna; I know them all, but you do not (4.5). Though I am unborn, with unchanging Self, the Lord of beings, I enter into Nature and by my wondrous power take birth (4.6). For whenever right order (*dharma*) declines, I create a self to uphold right order (4.7). To protect the good, to destroy the wicked, and to establish right order, I take birth in every age (4.8)." What is remarkable here is that Prafulla, in her new role as "true renouncer-in-action" is identified with the descent of the deity. In this way, all of us can identify with the divine being so as to act selflessly like Him for the welfare of the world. See the Introduction for further analysis.

Appendices

APPENDIX A

Earlier Version of Part I, Chapters 9–17

Part I

Chapter 9 (*DCsv: contd.*)

"[As she kept digging she heard a metallic clang. The hairs of her body stood on end, for she realized that the crowbar had struck the side of some jar or small pot.] Jar or pot? She'd be happy even if a small pot were unearthed, for she had nothing in the world except a single piece of clothing.

Prafulla began to dig, and the crowbar kept making clanging noises. No, this was not something small, it was a largish pot. As she kept digging the shape of the container was revealed. Good heavens! It seemed to be a large jar! A large jar of money! Prafulla couldn't believe it. Could so much wealth really be hers? Gradually the whole jar came into view—it was sealed with a concave lid made of clay. Prafulla tried to lift the jar, but to no avail; it was too heavy. So Prafulla was forced to open the clay lid. Her head spun when she looked inside. Not money, but a jar of *mohurs*![1] What in the world could she do with so much wealth!

Unable to lift the jar, Prafulla began to scoop out the *mohurs* and place them on the earth; she wanted to count how many there were. But because she didn't know how to count well enough, she was unable to arrive at a total. So she arranged them in heaps on the ground. When she had removed all the *mohurs*—dear God!—what was that that now came into view! Whatever it was shone like countless flames reflected from the embers of a wood-fire. Prafulla could see that there were diamonds, emeralds, rubies, etc.

Ten thousand times did Prafulla's mother come to mind! "Alas, mother," she thought, "I didn't get this money while you were alive! If I can hold on to it, I'll live like a Queen, but you, mother, died from starvation!"

Again she thought, "I had no idea there was so much wealth in the world. Still, let me keep it buried." She removed fifty gold coins and buried the jar again, then elated she began to climb up the steps. As she climbed up she thought suddenly, "Suppose there's more? But even if there is, what could I do with it? I've

---

What follows in this Appendix is a translation of the major text changes in the serial version of the novel, published in Phālgun and Caitra B.E. 1289, nos. 11 and 12 (February and March respectively, 1883), viz. from early in ch.9 till the end of ch.13 (Part I). The passage in square brackets under the heading is common to the standard edition and *DCsv*, and is given as a prompt, after which the text of the serial version takes over.

[1] *Mohur*: a gold coin.

enough riches to last a lifetime." So she began to ascend the steps again. But halfway up, her curiosity got the better of her. "I must find out if there's more," she thought. She took up the crowbar again and squatting where she found the jar, began to dig all round.

After some digging, the crowbar sang again—another clang! And another large jar with more *mohurs*, and below more diamonds, emeralds, and rubies like before! Prafulla thought she would die—no human could ever make use of so much wealth. "Let's see how much treasure Kubera, the Lord of wealth, has," she thought. She dug again. Another clang, another large jar with *mohurs* on top and diamonds, emeralds, and rubies below.

Prafulla carefully buried it all. "If there's more," she thought, "I don't want it. If I can hang on to what I've found, I can give the Queen of Dinajpur a run for her money!" She climbed up the steps.

Prafulla had worked hard; she went to the cowshed, milked the cow again, and drank some milk. Then she made a bed of straw and lay down. But she began to feel afraid lying there alone in that ruined pile in the jungle. We've given enough evidence to show how brave Prafulla was, still she felt afraid, especially since that very day someone had died in that room. Thinking that she couldn't sleep without a light, she began to hunt for some oil. There was no oil, but while searching she came upon two candles. She lit these, and lay down on the bed of straw again.

But she couldn't sleep! Were there more jars down there? No—surely there couldn't be even more wealth in the world! But if there was? Well, what could she do with more? Still, there'd be no harm if she found out! No, she wouldn't bother. But if she didn't find out could she sleep? Prafulla couldn't, so at last she lit a flame and went down the shaft. She took up the crowbar again and began to dig in the earth. Once more the crowbar sounded against a jar, and once more a jar of treasure was unearthed. In this way Prafulla found twelve jars of treasure.

It was past midnight when Prafulla washed her hands and feet and returned to lie down again. This time as a result of her exertions she slept a little. Suddenly she awoke in the midst of a great commotion; she seemed to hear a hundred people shouting "Kill! Kill! Cut and slash!" Prafulla rose from the grass bed, trembling violently. She listened intently to the noise; it came from the door—not "Kill! Kill" or "Cut and slash!" but without doubt the confused uproar of many people. What disaster to hear the noise of so many people in this jungle! Surely these were ghosts, or if not—even worse—bandits!

Amidst the confusion, Prafulla could discern one noise in particular. She had locked the door and lain down—it seemed as if a thousand people were now banging upon it, and the door was about to break open. Prafulla silently called upon all the deities! She thought of raising the trapdoor, going down, and hiding in the tunnel below, but even if she did that she wouldn't be able to hide the trapdoor by covering it with her bed. Those smashing down the door would see the trapdoor, lift it and come down, and get her. Prafulla realized that without showing courage she had no chance of saving herself. She was endowed naturally with a great deal of courage; besides, in recent times she had suffered many sorrows and travails and it was her great courage that had rescued her from the many dangers she had encountered. So trusting to bravery, Prafulla went and opened the door. The candles were still burning.

No sooner had she opened the door than twenty to twenty five strong men, terrible as the Lord of death, stormed into the room."

This instalment of *DCsv* ends here: *Baṅgadarśan*, Phālgun B.E. 1289, 101st issue (February 1883).

NOTES

"*mohurs*": "The official name of the chief gold coin of British India.... from Pers.[ian] *muhr*, a (metallic) seal, and thence a gold coin" (Hobson-Jobson, 2002:573). As this source goes on to note, the term *mohur* had been applied to gold coins since the beginning of Muslim rule in India in *c.* 1200 C.E, though the weight of this coin could vary.

"But because she didn't know how to count well enough...": As the standard text will go on to say, Prafulla had not received any schooling or education, so she couldn't count beyond a certain number.

"dear God!": lit. *hari hari!* "Hari" is another name for Lord Krishna or Vishnu.

"deities": *debatā*.

"terrible as the Lord of death": *kālāntak jamer nyāy. Jam* (Yama) in the form he assumes when he comes to claim a soul for the nether worlds.

Chapter 10 (*DCsv*)

"Since Prafulla didn't know who the old man who had died was, she had no idea where he acquired so much treasure. But we know his antecedents, so here we must say something about him.[2]

The old man's name was Krishnagobind Das. Krishnagobind was a Kayastha;[3] he had lived happily on his own, but after many years he fell into the hands of a beautiful Vaishnavi, and selling his heart to the insignia of her faith—the marks on her forehead and her tambourine—he took up begging and set off with the Vaishnavi for Sri-Brindaban. When they arrived at Sri-Brindaban Krishnagobind's Vaishnavi lady, taken by the sweet songs of the poet Jayadeva that the local Vaishnavas sang, their learning in the *Srimadbhagavata*, and their well-nourished bodies,[4] promptly applied herself to the acquisition of virtue in the service of their lotus feet. When he saw this, Krishnagobind left Brindaban

[2]Now follows a lengthy passage virtually identical to the text at the end of ch.9 of the standard edition. (For relevant notes of the shared passage, see under standard text).

[3]The Kayasthas are a respectable caste of Bengal.

[4]All with erotic connotations; see endnotes (under ch.9 of standard text) for further details.

with the Vaishnavi and returned to Bengal. He was still poor, so he went to Murshidabad in search of a living. Krishnagobind found a job, but news reached the Nawab's residence that his Vaishnavi was a real beauty. An African eunuch began visiting her at home to see if she would become the Nawab's wife, and out of greed the Vaishnavi was ready to agree.

Once more seeing the danger, Krishnagobind Babaji[5] took the Vaishnavi and fled. But where should he go? It was not desirable, he thought, to live among people with this priceless treasure; someone might snatch her away some day. So the Babaji crossed the Padma river with the Vaishnavi and began looking for a lonely place. During his travels he came upon this ruined mansion and saw that it was the very place to hide his priceless jewel from the gaze of others. For who else except Death himself could find them there? So that's where they stayed. The Babaji would go out every week to the local market for provisions, and forbade the Vaishnavi from venturing out anywhere.

One day, as Krishnagobind was digging into the earth to prepare a clay oven in a room underground, he found an old *mohur*, older even than those of his time. He dug further and came upon a clay pot full of money.

If he hadn't found this money, Krishnagobind would have had a hard time of it. As it was, the days began to pass easily, but now Krishnagobind had a new worry. After he had found the money, he remembered that many people had discovered a great deal of treasure buried in these old houses. He became convinced that there was more money here. From then on, Krishnagobind began to search daily for buried treasure. As he searched he discovered many tunnels, and many secret rooms below ground. Like one obsessed, Krishnagobind looked in all those places, but found nothing. After a year of such searchings, Krishnagobind reduced his efforts, but still he went looking from time to time in those secret chambers down below. One day, in the corner of a dark room, he saw something glinting. He ran forward to pick it up—and saw that it was a *mohur!* Rats had turned the soil, and had raised it with the earth.

Krishnagobind did nothing. He waited for the local market-day to come round. When the day came, he said to the Vaishnavi, "I'm feeling very unwell, so you do the marketing today." So she went in the morning to do the marketing. The Babaji knew that since she was given leave to go out that day, the Vaishnavi would not return in a hurry. He used this opportunity to dig in the corner, and twelve[6] large jars of treasure came to light!

In the past, in northern Bengal, powerful kings used to reign who belonged to the dynasty of a ruler called Nildhvaj.The last king of that line was Nilambar Deb. Nilambar had many capital cities and he built numerous palaces in many towns. This was one of them, and he lived here every year for a week or two. It so happened that the Muslim ruler of Gaud dispatched an army against Nilambar

[5]A title given to Vaishnava ascetics (meaning something like "Respected Father").
[6]The standard version has "twenty."

to conquer northern Bengal. If the Pathans, thought Nilambar, attack and capture my capital city, the wealth accumulated by my ancestors will fall into their hands; better to take precautions. So before the battle Nilambar secretly brought all the wealth from his treasury to this place, and buried it with his own hands. No one else knew where the treasure lay. Nilambar was taken prisoner in the battle, and the Pathan General had him transported to Gaud. After that, no one ever saw him again, nor does anyone know how he met his end, for he never returned to his own land. From that time his wealth lay buried there, and it was this treasure that Krishnagobind found; and after that Prafulla got it. The wealth belongs to one person, but someone else enjoys it!

Krishnagobind kept the jars carefully buried. Not even for a day did he mention anything about this treasure to the Vaishnavi. He was so miserly that he never spent even a single *mohur* from this hoard; he treated it like the blood from his own body. It was from the money of the clay pot that he eked out his days.[7]

After his discovery, he was in great fear of bandits. He would invariably come home from market after hearing stories about them. Furthermore, he kept seeing men who looked like bandits roaming about the forest—perhaps there was a den of bandits here. In fact, he was quite right. The bandits too noticed the ascetic emerge from the forest on a weekly basis to go to market, and then re-enter the forest. So they followed him and discovered the ruined mansion. They saw that this was where a Vaishnava and his Vaishnavi lived and that they passed their days comfortably without doing any work; consequently, they came to the conclusion that they had some means to live by.

So one day a few of them got together and arrived there to plunder the mansion. They looted the pot of money; then, demanding to be given whatever else he had, they tied Krishnagobind up and threatened to set him alight with a flaming torch. But Krishnagobind didn't give them anything. Rather, he supplicated them as follows: "I have nothing more. If you must kill me, so be it, but you'll get nothing more. However, if you let me go, you will get something. I do have money, but not here. I used to work in Murshidabad, and the money lies deposited in a merchant's house. Every year I go there to collect the interest. What I propose is that when I return with the interest, if you come here I'll give you some. I won't give it all. If you take the whole amount, I'll run away from this place, and you'll get no more. But if you're satisfied with what I choose to give you, then come here every year and I'll pay you on a yearly basis."

The bandits saw that this was not a bad arrangement—in any case, right now there was nothing else to take, so they agreed to the proposal and released the old man. The old man fixed a day and the bandits went away.

The old man carried on for a few days eking out an existence as before; then he removed some *mohur*s from a jar, stuffed them in a broken clay pot,

---

[7]From here, in what follows, *DCsv* branches out again.

smeared it with mud and showed it to the Vaishnavi, saying, "By the grace of Krishna, I've found something more." This is what they used to pass their days. When the bandits turned up on the appointed date, he would give them something.

In this way, a few years passed. The bandits began to trust Krishnagobind, and for his part, he began to trust them too—so much so that whenever a bandit was in difficulties, he went to Krishnagobind and borrowed some money at a small interest. The bandits cleared their debts if they could—otherwise they'd get nothing if they asked again. In this way, Krishnagobind became a creditor to their band. In the end he was reckoned as one of the gang. He was not required to take part in any banditry; all he did was to provide money when times were hard. Now he would receive back the sum he lent, but without interest. Instead of interest, he would get a part of each of their gains. This is the money he used to pass his days; there was no need to touch King Nilambar's treasure any more.

It was this band of robbers that now appeared before Prafulla."

NOTES

[For Notes on the passage shared with the standard text, viz. from "The old man's name" to "he eked out his days," see under standard text.

"a den of bandits": *ḍākātder ekṭā āḍḍā*

"ascetic": *bairāgī.*

"a merchant's house": *śeṭher bāḍī.* A *śeṭh* is a banker or successful merchant.

"creditor": *mahājan*, or moneylender.

Chapter 11 (*DCsv*)

"When the bandits saw Prafulla, they cried angrily, "What's this? Why are *you* here? Where's the old man?"

Summoning all her courage, Prafulla replied, "He's dead."

"What, the old man's dead?" they cried, "Who killed him? He wouldn't have died if we were here."

"He died of a high fever," said Prafulla.

"When did he get the fever? Lies! You've got him tied up somewhere!"

"I've buried him in the courtyard. One of you can go and check."

Two or three of them ran out to see. The rest began to harangue her. "Where's his Vaishnavi?" they asked. "Who are you?"

"His Vaishnavi took whatever he had and ran away."

"Damnation! How dare she! Where's she gone?"

"I don't know," said Prafulla.

"Who are you? Why are you here?"

"I'm Babaji's adopted daughter."

"Adopted daughter!" they cried. "He had no adopted daughter. We've never heard of one."

"He kept it secret for fear of the Vaishnavi," said Prafulla. "He hid me away in the house of an ostracized relative."

"So you've come now to take his money?"

"I heard he was ill, so I came."

"And who told you that?"

"The Vaishnavi talked about it in the market. That's how I heard."

"Oh yes? And what did you get when you came here?"

"Nothing. As I said, the Vaishnavi took it all."

"What about the money from Murshidabad? Who'll get that?"

"That's all lies," said Prafulla. She had no idea what they were talking about, so she proceeded on the basis of guesswork. But she was full of sharp intelligence and courage.

"Lies!" cried the bandits. "Are you trying to deceive us? So how could we borrow money on so many occasions?"

"You took money from what he had in the house," answered Prafulla.

"What! So the old man was deceiving us? And has that wretch of a Vaishnavi taken it all? Is that the end of the money we can borrow?"

"Not necessarily" answered Prafulla.

"But where can we get the money? Who'll give it to us?"

"I'll give it to you," was the reply.

"You? Where would you get it? So you *have* got the old man's money!"

"No," said Prafulla, "I got nothing. In fact, the old man didn't have much money. He had a certain knowledge, and that's what I got."

"What knowledge?"

"Why should I tell you?"

"We'll cut you up if you don't!" said the bandits.

"Go ahead," replied Prafulla. "If you do that, I'm dead, but then who's going to loan you money?"

"Right, so we won't cut you up. But what's this "knowledge"—no harm if you tell us."

"Will you tell anyone else?"

"No. Now tell us."

"He knew how to make gold," replied Prafulla. "He taught me before he died. He would make gold and give it to you."

"True enough!" said the bandits believing her. "We heard that he would change *mohur*s in the market. And he taught you that knowledge, my dear?"

"In a manner of speaking," replied Prafulla. "I tried today and found I can make gold."

"Then you must teach us," demanded the bandits.

"If you learn how," said Prafulla, "You might as well cut me up as soon as you do so, because if I teach someone this knowledge it'll be the death of me.

Still, I'm ready to teach you. Now who among you shall I teach? If I teach a number of you, this knowledge won't work. I can instruct only one of you. Who will it be?"

"Me!," "Me!," "Me!," "Me!" they all yelled. There was an uproar among them, and they were about to come to blows.

"No point in arguing and quarrelling," said Prafulla. "This incantation will work only if your horoscope's right. Babaji wanted to teach this knowledge to the Vaishnavi but she didn't have the right horoscope. So she flew into a rage, stole all his money, and ran off. Come tomorrow with your horoscopes and bring an astrologer with you. With his help I'll pick the right person."

The bandits began to look at one another. None of them had a horoscope. Prafulla said, "If you don't have a horoscope, that's the end of it. I'll die, and you won't be able to make it work."

So they thought hard and finally said, "Well, dear, then keep your knowledge to yourself. All we want is the money. Will you give us an annual payment?"

"I will," said Prafulla.

"And loan us money in good times and bad?"

"Yes," said Prafulla.

"And we'll give you your rightful share of our loot," they replied.

Prafulla said, "I don't want any share. I've no need. What Babaji lacked was courage. Because ghosts and evil spirits can get up to mischief in this regard, he didn't make much gold. But I'm not afraid; I'll make plenty. I'll take no share from you."

"Victory to you, lady! Victory!" cried the bandits in unison. "You'll not take interest?"

"No."

"Victory to the lady!" shouted the bandits again. "Did you try today?"

"Yes," replied Prafulla. "You're welcome to take what I made and go." She gave the bandits the hundred gold coins she had collected and kept aside. When they received the wealth the bandits were wild with delight. Some fell to the ground and made obeisance to Prafulla, others wished her victory and began to dance. Some said, "From today you'll be our mother, and we'll be your sons." Everyone began to sing her praises. Then the felon who had done most of the talking asked, "Mother, where will you live? Where can we meet you?"

"I'll live right here," answered Prafulla.

"But you're so young," was the reply, "Will you stay here alone in this ruined house in the jungle?"

"Well, if all of you are around," said Prafulla, "What's there to fear?"

"Don't worry, my dear. So long as we live, not even a thorn will prick your feet."

"I've not the slightest fear," said Prafulla. "I know plenty of spells and incantations."

"Very good. And you only have to command for us to obey."

"That you must do," said Prafulla, "Otherwise I shan't be able to stay here."

"Well now, tell us what to do," they said.

"Bring me four servant-girls tomorrow, and eight men to serve. They'll have to fetch water, cut wood, do the shopping and anything else I need. Bring people you trust. I'll pay them an agreed wage."

"You'll get them all tomorrow," the bandits replied. "We'll send folk from our own households. No harm if they serve you."

"And I want four guards."

"You need no other guards than us! We'll be your guards; just pay us something. Anything else?"

"You'll have to buy me some provisions from market, pots and pans, clothing and things for the household," said Prafulla. "And you'll have to repair this house."

"We can't do all that," said the bandits. "For that, we'll send Master Pathak."

"Who's Master Pathak?"

"Don't you know?" they replied. "He's the leader of our gang."

"Oh yes, Babaji mentioned his name. Send him along too."

The bandits bowed to the ground and departed. Prafulla closed the door and lay down once more. But she was unable to sleep again."

NOTES

"of a high fever": *jvarbikāre.*

"adopted daughter": *puṣyi meye.*

"my dear": *mā,* a more emollient form of address now; the bandits want to get on Prafulla's good side.

"incantation": *mantra.*

"horoscope": *koṣṭhi.* Horoscopes were (and are) a very important part of Hindu life: they help determine marriage alliances and other life-choices.

"Because ghosts and evil spirits can get up to mischief": *bhūt preter daurātma. Bhūt* is a more generic term for a disembodied spirit, while a *preta* tends to be a departed soul whose funerary rites have not been conducted or properly performed, or which is tied for a special reason to earthly circumstances and seeks release from this.

"dear girl": *mā.*

"the hundred gold coins": *je śata svarṇa mudrā.* Earlier on (*DCsv,* ch.9), there is mention of keeping aside "fifty gold coins" (*pañcāśat svarṇamudrā*).

"felon": *dasyu.*

"spells and incantations": *mantra tantra.*

"Master Pathak": *Pāṭhak Ṭhakur. "Ṭhakur"* is a term of respect.

"bowed to the ground": *praṇām kariyā.*

Chapter 12 (*DCsv*)

"Next day, early in the morning, Bhabani Pathak appeared before Prafulla. But before speaking of him, let us say something about the worthy Phulmani, the barber's wife. How could we suddenly neglect so virtuous a beauty?[8]

In making her escape, Phulmani the barber's wife entrusted her life, as a doe does, to the creature that was fleetest of foot.[9] For fear of the bandits Durlabhchandra ran on ahead, while Phulmani dashed after him. But so bent was Durlabh on escaping that he became "scarce indeed" for his beloved who chased after him![10] However much Phulmani called out, "Oh, please wait for me! Please don't leave me behind!" Durlabh cried in turn, "Oh God! Oh, here they come!" Through thickets of thorns, jumping over ditches, rushing through the mire, Durlabh tore on, breathless. Dear me! The neat tuck at the back of his loincloth came undone, one of his fancy shoes came unstuck somewhere, while his shawl attached itself to a thicket and fluttered in the wind like a banner to his heroism. The lovely Phulmani cried out, "Hey you vile fellow! Deceiving a woman like that.... Is that the way to go, you rascal, leaving me to the bandits!" Durlabhchandra heard this and thought that the bandits had got her for sure, so without wasting words, he ran even faster, while Phulmani screamed after him, "Hey you vile fellow! You wretch! You monster! You good-for-nothing! Rascal! Rogue!" But by then Durlabh had disappeared. So Phulmani stopped shouting and began to cry, and in the process had a number of uncomplimentary things to say about Durlabh's ancestry![11]

Then Phulmani realized that there were no bandits after her. She stopped crying and paused to think—no bandits after her, and Durlabh nowhere to be seen! So she began to look for a way out of the jungle. It was not difficult for someone as sharp as Phulmani to find a path. She easily made her way out to the main street, and seeing no one about, headed for home, furious with Durlabh.

It was very late when Phulmani reached her house. She saw that her sister Alakmani was not at home—she had gone to take her bath.[12] Without saying a word to anyone Phulmani closed the door and lay down. Since she hadn't slept all night, no sooner did she lie down than she fell asleep.

---

[8]Now follows, almost verbatim, virtually the whole of chapter 10 of the standard version (the differences worth noting are added in footnotes here). We reproduce the passage here for the sake of continuity (for further annotation, see also under the Notes for ch.10 of the standard version).

[9]That is, just as a deer when escaping with others singles out the fastest creatures to act as pacemakers, so Phulmani singled out the fleetest of foot when making her escape, viz. Durlabh.

[10]"Durlabh" means "hard to get."

[11]"ancestry": *baṃśābalī*. the standard version has "parentage" (*mātāpitā*).

[12]In the local pond or river.

Her older sister returned and woke her up, saying "So you've just come back?"

"What do you mean?" replied Phulmani, "Where do you think I've been?"

"Where indeed!" answered Alakmani. "You went off to sleep in the Brahmin's house, and since you didn't come back for ages, I'm asking you."

"You've gone blind, that's what!" said Phulmani. "I came back early in the morning and went to sleep right in front of you. Didn't you notice?"

"Oh really!" exclaimed Alakmani. "When I saw you were late, I went thrice to the Brahmin's house looking for you! I didn't see you there, nor anyone else either. So where's Prafulla gone today?"

"Quiet!" said Phulmani with a shiver. "*Didi*, be quiet! Don't speak about that!"

"Why not?" said Alakmani fearfully, "What's happened?"

"Let's not speak about that."

"Why not?"

"We're nobody. What have we to do with those gods, the Brahmins?"

"What do you mean? What's Prafulla done?"

"Well, is Prafulla still alive!"

Alakmani (again fearfully), "What do you mean? What are you saying?"

Her sister mumbled, "Tell no one, but yesterday her mother came and took her away."

"What!" Alakmani began to tremble violently. Phulmani told her some wild tale about seeing Prafulla's mother seated on Prafulla's bed very late at night. In a moment a great storm had arisen in the room, and then—there was no one to be found! Phulmani had fainted, lying there with teeth clenched, etc. When she finished her tale, Phulmani sternly warned her sister not to tell a soul.

"Promise me you won't," she insisted.

"Of course I won't," her sister replied. "How can I tell this to anyone!"

But then and there the said sister went out to make the rounds of the neighborhood, washing-basket in hand, on the pretext of having to clean the rice, and embroidering the story from house to house, warned everyone not to spread the news.[13] Consequently, it spread rapidly and finally reached the ears of Prafulla's in-laws."

NOTES (SEE ALSO UNDER NOTES FOR THE STANDARD EDITION)

"so virtuous a beauty?": *sādhucaritrā sundarī.*

Chapter 13 (*DCsv*)

"Early in the morning, Bhabani Pathak appeared before Prafulla. Prafulla had expected to see a bandit-leader with beard parted in the middle and turned upward, and the veins standing out on his wiry body. Instead, the person who

[13]The sentence after this deviates slightly from the ending in the standard edition.

appeared was clean-shaven, with sectarian marks on his forehead, and a well-nourished body; he looked just like a Brahmin priest. Prafulla was somewhat taken aback. When she saw him she asked, "Can you tell me why you are here, please?"

"Didn't you summon me?" he replied.

"The men who came here last night said they would send their leader. But who are you?"

"*I* am the bandit-leader," replied Bhabani. "What is it you need?"

Prafulla was speechless. During the terrible events of the previous night, surrounded as she was by numerous robbers and in the midst of their shouting, she didn't keep quiet—she spoke out bravely. But in front of this man she couldn't say a word. When he saw her consternation, Bhabani said, "You require things for the house, together with male and female servants?"

Prafulla remained silent. Bhabani said again, "I heard you need these things. But why? I understand you have money. How long do you think it will last?"

"Why do you say that?" asked Prafulla.

Bhabani replied, "Have you seen the men who live in this forest? How long, do you think, will they protect your money?"

"My money's not here," said Prafulla.

"It's useless to speak to me like that," replied Bhabani. "I've seen the old *mohurs* you handed out. Probably you got the money in this old house. Your money's here."

"Even if that's so," said Prafulla, looking dejected, "Are all of you going to take it away from me?"

"No, I shan't. And I've no idea who will. But you're a helpless girl. Forget the money, you wont be able to keep anything in this forest—your honor as a woman, nothing."

Prafulla was close to tears. But relying on the courage that had got her out of so many dangers, she said, "How am I helpless? I've got you for support."

"If I help you, you've nothing to fear, that's true, but if you don't listen to me how can I be of help?"

"What must I do?" asked Prafulla, apprehensively.

"You must do as I say. I give you my word that I shall never involve you in anything immoral. If I do so, don't obey. Otherwise you must do as I say."

Prafulla began to cry. "Why are you crying, mother?"[14] asked Bhabani Pathak gently.

Prafulla wiped her eyes. "You've addressed me as 'mother,'" she said. "So I'll do whatever you ask me to."

Bhabani said, "We shall both have to take a vow. But we can do that later. First let me give you good advice concerning your welfare. I'm saying this only for your good: don't accept this wealth."

[14]On the use of this expression, see under Notes for ch.11 of the standard text.

"Why not?"

"You've no protector, so how will you safeguard this wealth? Are you prepared to lose everything for its sake?"

"That's why I'm asking all of you for help. How did the ascetic manage to protect it for so long?"

"That's another matter. You're a young and beautiful woman without a protector. If you accept this wealth you'll either fall into danger or lead a bad life and go to hell."

"Is there sin in wealth?"

"Yes, if you don't truly offer it to Sri Krishna."

"Must I offer everything to Sri Krishna?"

"Yes, everything. If you do accept this wealth, then offer it all to Sri Krishna."

"All right, I'll offer everything to Sri Krishna. But who is he? And where is he? And how can he receive this wealth of mine?"

"Do you know how to read and write?"

"No," said Prafulla.

"Then today you will start learning to read and write."

"Who will teach me."

"I will."

"But why should I learn to read and write?"

"Because I want you to read some books."

"Why must I do that?" asked Prafulla.

"You'll learn how to give Sri Krishna back his wealth."

"If I give everything to Sri Krishna, there'll be nothing left for me. How will I survive?"

"I'll show you where I live. Every day you must come there to beg, and live on whatever you get."

"I have my own wealth, but I must survive by begging!" exclaimed Prafulla.

Bhabani replied, "If you don't offer this wealth to Sri Krishna with a cheerful heart, he won't accept it. And if *he* doesn't accept it, my gang of bandits will take it all!"

"But who *is* Sri Krishna?" asked Prafulla. "I see his image in the temple. How can such a thing accept this wealth? Does he have nothing of his own?"

Bhabani replied, "He is the Lord of the world. Everything belongs to him."

"Then why does he need my wealth?"

"First learn to read and write, and I'll explain it to you. For the present this is all you need to remember: that you're my 'mother,' and I'm your 'son.' I'll give you only good advice, not bad."

"Do you really live by banditry!"

"Yes I do. But we can discuss all that later," answered Bhabani.

"When will that be?"

"The day your instruction comes to an end," was the reply."

This instalment of *DCsv* ends here: *Baṅgadarśan*, Caitra B.E. 1289, 102nd issue (March 1883).

NOTES

"a bandit-leader with beard parted in the middle and turned upwards": *caugoppāoāllā . . . ḍākāter sardār.*

"and the veins standing out . . .": *śir-oṭhā pākān-śarīr.* The concept of the veins standing out as a mark of a hard or ascetic life is an ancient one in Indian literature. For a study of this idea in an early context see Hara (1995).

"just like a Brahmin priest": *bhaṭcājyi bāmun.*

"sectarian marks": *phoṭākāṭā.* Since Bhabani Pathak was a Vaishnava, these would have included a 'V'-shaped mark on his forehead (extending possibly to the bridge of his nose).

"honor as a woman": *jātikul.* That is, she wouldn't be able to preserve her "caste" (*jāti*) and "family respect" (*kul*) if violated.

"I shall never involve you in anything immoral": *āmi tomāke kakhana adharme prabṛtti diba nā.*

"my mother" [and later]: *mā.* See under notes for standard text, Part I, ch.11.

"the ascetic": *bairāgī*. A particular kind of Vaishnava ascetic (often with a female partner in his religious practice).

"lead a bad life and go to hell": *pāpācaraṇ kariyā narake jaibe.*

"I see his image in the temple": *ṭhākur ta mandire dekhi.* Here *ṭhākur* is the consecrated/worshipped image in the temple, viz. the image in which the deity is believed to be residing.

"The Lord of the world": *jagadīśvar.*

Chapter 14 (*DCsv*)

[Except for minor changes, this chapter is identical with ch.13 of the standard edition, Part I. For these changes see under "Variants" to ch.13, Part I in the Critical Apparatus.]

Chapter 15 (*DCsv*)

[This chapter begins a little over a paragraph into the text of chapter 14 of the standard version, viz. with the sentence, "It was a few days since Brajesvar had parted from Prafulla." The text then continues with, "Haraballabh's household carried on as before," as in the standard version. Thereafter, except for minor divergences in the body of the text and a significantly different ending to the chapter (which are recorded in the Critical Apparatus under chapter 14), the two texts are identical.]

Chapter 16 (*DCsv*)

[This chapter matches with chapter 15 in the standard version, with some differences which are recorded under "Variants" for chapter 15 of the standard version in the Critical Apparatus.]

Chapter 17 (*DCsv*)

"After he had finished teaching her for five years, Bhabani Thakur said to Prafulla, "It's been five years since your instruction began, and today it is over. Now you may spend your wealth as you please, I shan't prevent you. I'll give advice, which you can accept if you choose to. You need beg no longer; now you will have to fend for yourself. But let me say a few things first. I've said this many times and I'll say it once more.

"First, you've offered your wealth to Sri Krishna, so you have no rights over it any more. You can't spend any of it for your own happiness. You can spend what's needed to accomplish his work. Since you need to look after your own body to finish his work, you must spend what's necessary to care for your body. You must do the same when the need arises to clothe yourself, again so that you can accomplish Sri Krishna's work. But not a single cowrie for your own pleasures and comfort! So the first thing is, control of the senses. Now listen to my second piece of advice.

"Without selflessness you cannot follow the right path, for the Lord has said: "*Actions are always done by Nature's constituents, but the soul deluded by the ego thinks, 'I am the actor.'*" In other words, it is sheer egotism to think: "It is *I* who have done all these actions"—actions which have really been performed by the senses etc. You must never think that whatever you've done has been done by your power. If you do, your good actions become void.

The third piece of advice is this: you must offer the fruit of all your actions to Sri Krishna. Do not desire to arrogate to yourself the good fruit of any action. The Lord has said in Gita 9.27, "*Whatever you do, whatever you eat, whatever you offer in sacrifice, whatever you give, whatever penance you perform, Kaunteya, do it as an offering to Me.*" If you fulfill this threefold renunciation all the wealth will really be yours. You can then use it as you wish, I shan't say anything to prevent you. You can build a tall mansion, dress yourself in the finest clothes and ornaments—none of this will pervert your mind or bring about your fall from virtue. One can be a renouncer even if one is surrounded by worldly wealth. And that is the best kind of renunciation. Now do you understand who really possesses the wealth you have?"

Prafulla answered, "Well, the wealth belongs to Sri Krishna. We agreed to that long ago."

"The question is," Bhabani said, "Do you understand what that really means? Sri Krishna has said that if you give it to the afflicted you give it to him. In other words, when you spend this wealth to benefit others, you won't make the mistake then of thinking that by being generous to others you're acquiring merit. There's no merit in giving back to Sri Krishna the wealth that's his. This is how your actions can become selfless."

"So just being afflicted identifies you with Sri Krishna?" asked Prafulla. "What about those who have done wrong and must be punished? When they're being punished, they're afflicted too."

Bhabani answered, "All are Sri Krishna, whether afflicted or no. The entire universe is Sri Krishna. Wherever you give, Sri Krishna receives it right there. So give, and don't hold back. For the Lord himself has said:

'He who sees Me everywhere, and who sees all in Me,
I am not lost to him, nor is he lost to Me.
He who, based on oneness, loves Me as dwelling in all beings,
Howsoever such a disciplined soul acts, he acts in Me.
He who sees everything as his own self—as the same—whether in
pleasure or sorrow, Arjuna, I regard that disciplined soul as the very best.'"[15]

Prafulla said, "Master, I shall do exactly as you advise. But I have something to ask you first. If you don't take offence, I'll tell you what it is."

"You won't see me on a regular basis from now on," replied Bhabani. "Now it's up to you to carry out your work. So whatever you wish to ask, ask today."

"I wanted to ask this: you're the most learned of scholars, engaged in the performance of virtue. But the life of a bandit is the greatest evil. I've heard that this is what you do. Tell me if this is true, for you promised to answer my question."

"I engage in banditry. I've told you that before," answered Bhabani.

"Well then, why don't you keep some of the wealth I've given to Sri Krishna? Take it and live a virtuous life and stay away from bad deeds."

"But I too have no need of wealth," replied Bhabani. "I have plenty of it. I don't engage in banditry for the sake of wealth."

"Then for what?" asked Prafulla.

"Because I act as a ruler."

"What kind of rule is banditry?"

"He who has the power to rule is king."

"On the contrary, it is the king who has the power to rule," answered Prafulla.

---

[15]A footnote in the text here says: "Srimad Bhagavadgita, ch.6:30–2." See endnotes under ch.16 of the standard version for further comment.

Bhabani said, "There's no king in this land. The Muslims have been eliminated and the British are coming in. They do not know how to govern, nor can they.[16] It is I who subdue the wicked and protect the virtuous."

"By banditry?"

"Now listen, let me explain it to you."

Then Bhabani Thakur began to speak, and Prafulla to listen. It was with a powerful succession of words that he explained the terrible state of the land. He described the intolerable wickedness of those who controlled the land: how the officers of the local courts looted the houses of those whose dues were in arrears, broke into their homes, digging up the floor in search of hidden wealth, and if they found it, how they'd take not just their dues but a thousand times that, and if they didn't find it, how they'd thrash, truss up, imprison, burn, hack, set fire to homes, and kill. He described how they'd throw away the sacred relics of Vishnu from their household thrones, grab infants by the leg and dash them, knead and crush the chests of young men with bamboo rods, fill old men's eyes with ants and their navels with insects and then bind up these parts; how they'd take young women to their courts and strip them naked in front of everyone, beat them, cut off their breasts, and—in the presence of everyone—inflict the final insult on womankind, the ultimate outrage. After describing, in the manner of the Tantric poets,[17] this terrible situation with the most blazing combination of words, Bhabani Thakur said, "It is *I* who punish these evildoers, and protect the defenseless weak. Do you want to stay with me for a few days and see how I do this?"

Prafulla's heart had melted when she heard this harrowing tale of the people. She thanked Bhabani Thakur a thousand times and said, "Yes, I'll go with you. If I'm entitled to spend this wealth, then I'll take some of it with me, and give it to those who suffer."

Bhabani Thakur was well-satisfied. When he set out as a bandit with his gang, Prafulla accompanied him with the jars of treasure, and Nishi went with them too.

Whatever his designs might be, Bhabani Thakur had need of a sharpened weapon. So after whetting Prafulla for five years, he was now taking her with him as his sharpened weapon. It would have been better if she were a man, but no man was available with the various qualities Prafulla possessed, in particular a man with so much wealth. And the sharpness of wealth is sharpness indeed! But Bhabani Thakur had made one big mistake: he would have done well to get to the bottom of Prafulla's insistence on eating fish on *ekadashi* day. Still, now that we've launched Prafulla on life's stream, let us slumber for another five years."

This installment of *Debī Chaudhurāṇī* ends here: *Baṅgadarśan*, Kārttik B.E. 1290, 103rd issue (October 1883).

[16]The standard version has, "nor are they doing so."

[17]That is, graphically.

NOTES

(See also under endnotes for chapter 16 in the standard version)

"You have no rights": *tomār kono adhikār nāi.*

"not a single cowrie": *ek kaparddak o nay.* Cowries, tiny shells, were used as small change at the time.

"control of the senses": *indriyasaṃjam.*

"*Actions are always done*...": See the *Bhagavad Gītā,* 3.27.

"selflessness": *nirahaṃkār.*

"the right path": *dharma.*

"your good actions become void": *puṇya karma akarmatva prāpta hay.*

"threefold renunciation": *tribidha sannyās,* viz. giving up her wealth to Sri Krishna, renouncing her ego, and sacrificing the good fruit of her actions to the Lord.

"fall from virtue": *dharmacyuti.*

"merit": *puṇya.*

"actions... selfless": *karma niṣkām haite pāribe.*

"entire universe": *jagadbrahmāṇḍa.*

"the most learned of scholars": *mahāmahopadhyāy paṇḍit.*

"engaged in the performance of virtue": *dharmācaraṇe nijukta.*

"greatest evil": *param adharma.*

"virtuous life... bad deeds": *dharmācaraṇ... duṣkarma.*

"It is I who subdue the wicked and protect the virtuous": *āmi duṣṭer daman, śiṣṭer pālan kari.*

"the sacred relics of Vishnu from their household thrones": see endnotes for chapter 16 of the standard edition in the Critical Apparatus.

"in the manner of the Tantric poets": as noted in the footnote, "graphically," that is, without being reticent where sexual details were concerned (Tantra is not sexually reticent). The standard version has here instead, "like the poets of old": *prācīn kabir nyāy.*

APPENDIX B

Earlier Version of Part II, Chapters 1–12

Part II

Chapter 1 (*DCsv*)

This chapter is identical with ch.1 of Part II of the standard version. It appeared in *Baṅgadarśan*, Agrahāyan B.E.1290, 104th issue (November 1883).

Chapter 2 (*DCsv*)

Except for minor changes, this chapter matches ch.2 of Part II of the standard version. The changes are recorded under Variants for ch.2 in the Critical Apparatus. This chapter of *DCsv* was part of the 104th issue of *Baṅgadarśan*.

Chapter 3 (*DCsv*)

As there are a number of significant differences between this chapter and ch.3 of the standard edition, this chapter of *DCsv* has been translated here in full. It also appeared in the 104th issue of *Baṅgadarśan*. The changes from the standard edition are indicated by the material underlined:

> It was a moonlit night in the rainy season. The moonlight wasn't very bright—the softest moonglow tinted with darkness, like some dreamy covering over the earth. The Teesta river had swollen its banks with the flood of the rains, and the rays of the moon glistened upon the currents and whirlpools, and at times the little waves of the fast-flowing waters. In some places there were soft sparkles of light where the water bubbled a little, in other places the river glittered as it lapped against a sandbank. The water had reached the foot of the trees on the bank and was pitch black in their shadows, the swift current running over the flowers, fruit and leaves of the trees in the darkness. The waters gurgled and lapped against the banks in the gloom, and in the gloom that mighty stream sped, swift as a bird, in search of the sea. The countless murmuring sounds of the water along the banks and the deep roar of the whirlpools, echoed by the roar of the checked current, rose as a single deep sound, filling the skies on all sides.

There, on the Teesta, a barge was moored not far from the bank. And not far from the barge, in the shade of a large tamarind tree, lay another boat in the darkness. About this boat later—first let me speak about the barge. The barge was painted in various colors—how many shapes and forms were drawn upon it! Its brass handles, bars etc. were plated with silver and gold. The prow was shaped like a sea-monster's head, also plated in gold. The whole place was clean, tidy, gleaming—yet silent. The deckhands lay under a sail on one side of the bamboo deck. There was no sign of anyone being awake—except for one person on the roof of the barge. In all, an amazing scene!

A small but thick rug, very soft, with clusters of roses depicted upon it, lay spread on the roof. A woman was seated on the rug. It was hard to guess her age: one could never find so shapely a body in anyone under twenty-five, nor for that matter that bloom of youth in someone older than that. But whatever her age, there was no doubt that she was the loveliest of women. Nevertheless, there was a flaw or two in her beauty.

In his depiction of the beauty who was "like the Creator's first creation among womankind," the poet Kalidasa begins his description of her form by calling her "slender."[1] If slenderness is required for beauty, then this woman was not beautiful. She was not slim—yet to call her "buxom" would be to do her a disservice. Still, if you insist, then I'll call her buxom. In fact, her figure was complete in every aspect. Just as the Teesta had now filled its banks, so did the fullness of her body reach its proper limits. We do not speak of some undeveloped girl here—her body was unusually tall and erect. And because it was so, we were unable to call her buxom. The flood-waters of youth's fullness were caught up in that lovely form without overwhelming it. Yet the waters that pushed at those banks heaved restlessly. Still, there was a flaw or two here. Perhaps her fingers were a little plump—as were the rounded cheeks and shoulders. So if you do wish to call her buxom, perhaps I'd agree. I shan't object. But you'd have to acknowledge this: if she didn't have so shapely a body those large eyes wouldn't have suited her, nor would those eyebrows, so black and thick. And if she didn't have such cheeks, where could her smile that flashed like lightning have played?

The beauty's attire dazzled, just as the splendor of her body did. Today cloth from Dhaka doesn't have the reputation it once had, though a hundred years ago its fine quality had the reputation it deserved. The woman was dressed not in a sari, but in a white, filmy Dhaka wrap, under which she wore a bodice studded with glistening diamonds and

[1]There is a footnote here quoting an excerpt in Sanskrit from the verse in question: "'*tanvī śyāmā śikhara-daśanā pakva-bimbādharoṣṭhī*' etc." See endnotes to this chapter under "the poet Kalidasa" for an explanation.

pearls. Her shapely form, adorned with diamonds, emeralds, pearls, and gold, shone brightly in the moonlight, and her body glistened like the play of light on the waters of the river. Her lustrous clothes were like the still river-waters enraptured by the light of the moon, and just as the moonlight sparkled on the water from time to time, the diamonds and pearls of her clothes sparkled too. Her body was not weighed down by ornaments after the fashion of the time, nor can I tell if she knew how to tie her hair in a coil at the back. Certainly there was no coil at present, for her hair fell disheveled about her. It hung in clusters of curls twisted this way and that over her back, shoulders, arms, and breast. The moonlight played upon their soft, glossy splendor and the sky was filled with the fragrance of their perfumed oil. A chaplet of white jasmine flowers encircled the back of her hair.

If I say what this bejeweled beauty was doing on the rug spread out on the roof, many of my readers will take it amiss. But what can I do? I must write the truth. She was absorbed in playing the *sitar*. Her complexion, like the moonglow, blended with the light of the moon, and with it mingled the sweet and plaintive sounds of the *sitar*. Just as the rays of the moon played upon the waters and the moonlight played upon this lovely woman's rich attire, so the sounds of the *sitar* played upon the currents of the air bathed in moonlight and fragrant with the scent of wild flowers. *Jhom jhom, chon chon, jhonon jhonon, chonon chonon, drim drim, dara dara*—I cannot describe the quality of sound and rhythm of the notes played on the *sitar*. Now it wept, now it grew angry, now it danced or became tender, or rose to a crescendo—and as the woman played, she gave a little smile. Oh, how many sweet musical modes she played—the *jhinjhit, khambaj, sindhu;* how many serious ones—*kedar, hambir, behag;* so many displaying her virtuosity—the *kanara, sahana, bagisvari.* Like a garland of flowers the sound floated away in the roar of the current. Then, adjusting a fret or two, this knowledgeable woman suddenly looked up and with renewed vigor struck the strings of the *sitar* with great force. Her earrings, shaped like peepul leaves, swung to and fro, the mass of curls on her head began to dance like snakes, and the musical mode *nat* was heard on the *sitar*.

Then one of those who seemed to be sleeping quietly in a corner wrapped in a sail, rose and came and stood silently by the woman—a tall, powerfully built man, about forty years old, with a thick beard parted in the middle and turned upward. A sacred thread hung from around his neck. He came up close and asked, "What is it?"

The woman said, "Can't you see?"

"Nothing," was the reply. "Are they coming?"

A small spyglass lay on the rug. At the time the spyglass was a new arrival in India. Without a word the woman picked up the spyglass and handed it to the man. He put it to his eye and scanned the river with it.

Finally, catching sight of another barge in a certain place, he said, "I've seen it—by the bend in the river. About a mile away. Is that it?"

"No other barge is expected on the river at present," the other replied.

The man once again began to peer into the distance with the spyglass.

Still playing the *sitar,* the young woman said, "Rangaraj!"

"Yes?" said the other respectfully.

"What do you see?"

"I'm looking to see how many men there are."

"Well?"

"I can't make out. But not many. Shall I untie it?"

"Yes—untie the longboat and go silently upstream in the dark. Approach from the rear."

Then Rangaraj called out, "Untie the longboat!"

NOTES

(For notes on material in common, see under chapter 3 in the Critical Apparatus to the standard edition.)

"the poet Kalidasa": Kalidasa (skr. Kālidāsa) is perhaps the most famous classical Sanskrit poet, who is generally believed to have flourished in the early fifth century C.E. Bankim is referring to a verse from his poem, the *Meghadūta* ("Cloud-Messenger"). The verse in full (with an English translation) runs as follows: *tanvī śyāmā śikhara-*[some authorities have *śikhari-*]*daśanā pakva-bimbādharoṣṭhī, madhye kṣāmā cakita-hariṇī-prekśaṇā nimna-nābhiḥ/ śroṇī-bhārād alasa-gamanā stoka-namrā stanābhyāṃ, yā tatra syād yuvati-viṣaye sṛṣṭir ādyeva dhātuḥ//*. "She could be there—like the Creator's first creation among womankind: slender, not too dark, with sparkling teeth, lips as red as a ripe bimba fruit, narrow-waisted and deep-navelled, with glances like a frightened doe. She'd have a languid walk from the weight of her hips and be slightly bent by (the weight) of her breasts." In time this description came to represent the ideal of the beautiful woman. It occurs toward the middle of the second half (*uttaramegha*) of the poem, different editions numbering the verse differently (e.g., in Edgerton, 1964, vr.78; in De, 1957, vr.79; and in Karmarkar, 1947, vr.84).

"buxom": *sthulāṇgī.*

"some undeveloped girl": *kharbbākṛtā bālikā.* A young girl who is still growing.

"not in a sari": *ihār paridhāne... ḍhākāi dhūti, sāḍī nahe.* Good saris at the time tended to be heavy, patterned, and ornate. Debi eschewed this for the occasion, and wore the finest Dhaka material (suitable for elegant men's *dhūti*s or sarong-like wraps) in the manner of a sari.

"if she knew how to tie her hair in a coil at the back": *khõpā bâdhite jāniten ki nā. Khõpā* is a coil or knot of hair generally tied at the back of the head (hence more particularly located than a chignon).

"Many of my readers will take it amiss...": because displaying her musical talents so uninhibitedly did not conform to the image of the demure Bengali lady. Debi was her own woman.

"sitar": "a long-necked Indian lute with movable frets" (the Concise Oxford Dictionary), which was associated historically with Muslim culture. In the standard edition, Debi is playing a *vīṇā,* not a *sitār* (also see endnotes under ch.3 of the standard edition).

Chapter 4 (*DCsv*)

This chapter is virtually identical with ch.4 of the standard edition, and appeared in the 104th issue of *Baṅgadarśan* in Agrahāyan B.E. 1290 (November 1883).

Chapter 5 (*DCsv*)

Except for a few minor changes, this chapter matches chapter 5 of the standard edition. The changes are recorded under "Variants" in the Critical Apparatus to chapter 5 of the standard edition.

Chapters 5–through 8 of *DCsv* appeared in the 105th issue of *Baṅgadarśan,* in Pauṣ B.E. 1290 (December 1883).

Chapter 6 (*DCsv*)

Except for a few minor changes, this chapter is identical with ch.6 of the standard edition. The changes are recorded under "Variants" in the Critical Apparatus to ch.6 of the standard edition.

Chapter 7 (*DCsv*)

Except for a minor change or two, this chapter is identical with ch.7 of the standard edition. For the changes, see under "Variants" in the Critical Apparatus to ch.7 of the standard edition.

Chapter 8 (*DCsv*)

Except for one minor change worth noting, this chapter is identical with ch.8 of the standard version. For this variant, see under the Critical Apparatus to ch.8 of the standard edition.

Chapter 9 (*DCsv*)

Chapters 9 through 12 appeared in the 106th issue of *Baṅgadarśan,* B.E. Māgh 1290 (January 1884). At this point the novel was discontinued in the journal. It was then revised, completed, and published in its own right (viz. the first published edition) in May 1884.

Except for one noteworthy change, ch.9 of *DCsv* is virtually identical with ch.9 of the standard edition. See under "Variants" for ch.9 in the Critical Apparatus to the standard edition.

Chapter 10 (*DCsv*)

Chapter 10 in this version is virtually identical with ch.10 of the standard edition.

Chapter 11 (*DCsv*)

Except for a minor change or two—recorded under "Variants" to ch.11 in the Critical Apparatus—this chapter is identical with ch.11 of the standard edition.

Chapter 12 (*DCsv*)

There is sufficient new material here to warrant a translation of the chapter in full. The new material is underlined. For notes on the shared material see under ch.12 in the Critical Apparatus to the standard edition.

"In due course Brajesvar appeared before his father and made obeisance at his feet. Brajesvar had resolved that this money which came from banditry would not be touched. "For then," he had thought, "we'd be party to that sinful woman's" (alas, Prafulla had now become a "sinful woman!") "that sinful woman's wrongdoing." But it was Brajesvar's devotion to his father that made him transgress this resolve.

After some pleasantries, Haraballabh asked, "Now tell me the real news! What about the money?"

When Brajesvar replied that his father-in-law had been unable to give any money, Haraballabh was thunderstruck. "So you didn't get the money?" he cried.

Now if Brajesvar had replied, "I didn't get the money," then this would clearly be a lie. If he were a child of today with an English education, I cannot say what he would have decided here about the "Lie direct"; but since he was a child of that time, he had no particular objection to a situation involving a "Lie direct." Nevertheless, wherever else he might be able to utter a falsehood—not in his father's presence! He had never done so in the past. Brajesvar was unable to say that he hadn't got the money, so he remained silent.

When he saw that his son gave no reply, Haraballabh despaired and sat with his head in his hands. Brajesvar realized that even his silence was equivalent to uttering a lie, for he *had* brought the money, but since he gave no answer his father thought that he had not. The foolish Brajesvar believed he was deceiving his father! But the subtle intellect of our smart, refined, elegantly shod English-educated student of today would have thought instead: "I've told no lie! Whatever little I've said is nothing but the truth! I'm not *obliged* to say anything about Debi Chaudhurani's money since there was no question of bringing that money in the first place, and there's been no mention of it. Besides, that money comes from banditry so if he accepts it the pater will be sunk in the mire of sin. So it's incumbent on a pure soul like me to say nothing about it. The main thing is I've not told an untruth. What can I do if father goes to jail!"

But Brajesvar wasn't such a pure soul, and he didn't think this way. His heart began to break at the sight of his father sitting there silently with his head in his hands. He could bear it no longer, so he said, "Well, it's true my father-in-law was unable to give any money, but I got it from another source. . . ."

"So you got it!" cried Haraballabh. "What took you so long to tell me? By Durga, I'm saved!"

"But I'm not sure," continued Brajesvar, "whether I should have accepted the money from where I got it."

"Who gave it to you?" asked Haraballabh.

Scratching his head and looking down, Brajesvar mumbled, "Can't think of her name now. . . . you know, that woman who's a bandit?"

"Who, Debi Chaudhurani?"

"Yes."

"How did you get the money off her?"

In the ancient ethical codes known to Brajesvar it was written that it's not wrong to prevaricate a little with one's father in such circumstances, so he said, "It came to hand rather conveniently. . . ."

"Bad folk's money!" returned his father. "How was the money accounted for?"

"That wasn't necessary," said Brajesvar, "Since it sort of came to hand rather conveniently. . . ." But so that his father wouldn't inquire into what happened more closely, Brajesvar immediately sought to suppress the matter by saying, "Whoever accepts sinful money also partakes of the sin, so I don't think we should accept it."

Incensed, Haraballabh replied, "Do you want me to go to jail if I don't take the money? I'll borrow it—irrespective of whether it's good money or bad. Who'd give me sainted money anyway? There's no point in making such objections. My real objection is this: the money belongs to bandits and it wasn't formally accounted for. My fear is that if I'm late in paying it back they'll redeem it by looting the house!"

Brajesvar said nothing.

Haraballabh asked, "How long before I've got to pay it back?"

"We've got till the moon sets on the seventh night of the bright half of May."

"And she's a bandit to boot," continued Haraballabh. "Where will she be so that I can send her the money?"

"After evening that day, she'll be waiting in her barge at Kalsaji pier in Sandhanpur. It'll be all right if the money gets to her there."

"Very well," said Haraballabh, "Then we'll send her the money there on that day."

After Brajesvar had left, Haraballabh turned the matter over carefully in his mind. Finally he came to the following conclusion: "We'll pay that girl back her money, all right! If we get the sepoys to catch her all my problems will be solved! On the night of May the seventh if the English Captain doesn't board her barge with his platoon of troops, my name's not Haraballabh! That'll see to her taking any money off me after that!" But Haraballabh kept this pious design to himself—he didn't trust Brajesvar enough to tell him about it.

Meanwhile, Sagar went to Grandaunt Brahma and spun her a tale about Brajesvar going off to the barge of some great Queen and marrying the lady: Sagar had warned him repeatedly not to do so, but he didn't listen. That wretch of a woman, continued Sagar, was a Kaibartta by caste, who had married twice already, so Brajesvar himself had lost caste. Accordingly, Sagar had solemnly resolved not to share food with him any more. When Grandaunt Brahma tackled Brajesvar about all this he admitted his offence and said, "In fact, from the point of view of her caste, the Queen's all right; she's father's paternal aunt. As for marriage, well, I had three, and now so has she!"

Grandaunt Brahma knew none of this was true, but Sagar wanted her to tell the story to Nayantara. And this was done without a moment's delay. In any case, Nayantara was vexed to see Sagar, and when she heard that her husband had married some old woman, she was incandescent. So for a few days Brajesvar kept out of Nayantara's way and frequented the accommodation reserved for Sagar.

This is exactly what Sagar wanted. But Nayantara continued to cause trouble; finally, she complained to the lady of the house. Her mother-in-law said, "Child, you're off your head! Tell me, does a Brahmin's son marry a Kaibartta? Everyone has a go at you, and you allow them to."

Even then Nayan Bou wasn't convinced. She said, "But supposing he really has married her?" "If he really has," replied her mother-in-law, "then I'll formally take the girl in. I can't turn away my son's wife again." Just then Brajesvar came by, and Nayan Bou, of course, made herself scarce. When Brajesvar asked his mother what she had been saying to her, she replied, "This: that if you marry again, we'll be glad to take your wife in." Without making any reply, Brajesvar went away thoughtfully.

That evening, as the lady of the house was fanning her lord and master, she tactfully put the matter to him. "What do you think?" he asked her.

"I think," she answered, "that of the wives, Sagar is not ready to settle down, and Nayan is not a wife fit for the boy. So if Braja finds someone suitable and marries her and settles down in the proper way, I'll be happy."

"Well, if you see that's what the boy has in mind, let me know," said her husband. "I'll summon the matchmaker and finalize the negotiations."

"Good," said his wife. "I'll see what he wants."

The task of seeing what Brajesvar wanted fell to Grandaunt Brahma. So she told him many stories about princes who were lovelorn or keen to marry, but none of this helped to reveal what Brajesvar was thinking. Finally she began to question him openly—but still she learnt nothing from him. All he said was, "Whatever my parents tell me to do, I'll do."

And that's where the matter was more or less laid to rest."

NOTES

"sinful woman's wrongdoing": *pāpīyasīr pāp.*

"devotion to his father": *pitṛbhakti.*

"the "Lie direct": given thus in English. Bankim is poking fun at books on ethics written by English moralists for study at school.

"But the subtle intellect of our smart, refined..." etc.: here Bankim derides Indian youths who are the product of English education. They have lost the traditional ways and values.

"the pater": *pitṛṭhākur mahāśay.* Bankim is being sarcastic, hence "pater."

"the mire of sin": *pāp paṅka.*

"pure soul": *biśuddhātmā.* More sarcasm.

"And that's where the matter... laid to rest": In *DCsv,* the novel is abandoned at this point.

❁ Bibliography ❁

Advaita Ashrama. *The Life of Swami Vivekananda by His Eastern and Western Disciples.* Calcutta: Advaita Ashrama, 1960 (6th edition).

Bandyopādhyāy, Brajendranāth and Sajanīkānta Dās (eds. of Bengali text). *Debī Caudhurāṇī* by Baṅkimcandra Caṭṭopādhyāy. Kolkātā: Baṅgīya Sāhitya Pariṣat, 1950.

——. (eds. of Bengali text). *Dharmatattva* [*DT*] by Baṅkimcandra Caṭṭopādhyāy. Kolkātā: Baṅgīya Sāhitya Pariṣat, 1941.

Banerjea, Jitendra Nath. *The Development of Hindu Iconography.* Calcutta: University of Calcutta, 1956 (2nd ed.).

Banerjea, Krishna Mohan. "The Kulin Brahmins of Bengal," in *Calcutta Review* II (3), 1844.

Banerji, Chitrita. *Bengali Cooking: Seasons and Festivals.* London: Serif, 1997.

Bartley, Christopher. *Indian Philosophy A-Z.* Edinburgh: Edinburgh University Press, 2005.

Basu, B. D. *The Sacred Books of the Hindus, vol. XI: Samkhya Philosophy.* Translated by Nandalal Sinha. Allahabad: The Pāṇini Office, 1915.

Bharati, Agehananda. *The Tantric Tradition.* London: Rider & Co., 1992 (1st ed. 1965).

Bhaṭṭācārja, Amitrasūdan. *Baṅkimcandrajībanī* [*BcJ*]. Kolkātā: Ānanda Publishing Ltd., 1991.

Bhaṭṭacārjya, Debprasād. *Debī Caudhurāṇī (natun pāṭhyakram anujāyī likhita).* [*DCB*] Kolkata: Modern Book Agency Pvt. Ltd., 1998.

Bijlert, Victor van. "Sanskrit and Hindu national identity in nineteenth century Bengal," in Jan E. M. Houben. (ed.), *Ideology and Status of Sanskrit: Contributions to the History of the Sanskrit Language.* Leiden: E. J. Brill, 1996.

Borthwick, M. *The Changing Role of Women in Bengal, 1849–1905.* Princeton: Princeton University Press, 1984.

Burg, Corstiaan van der. "The place of Sanskrit in neo-Hindu ideologies: from religious reform to national awakening," in Jan E. M. Houben.

Burnell, A. C. *Hobson-Jobson.* See Henry Yule.

Cakrabartī, Śyāmalkānti. *Nabanārīkuñjar.* Kolkātā: Pritonia Publishers, 1999.

Caldwell, S. "Bhagavati: ball of fire," in J. S. Hawley & D. M. Wulff (eds.), 1996.

Chatterji, Bankimcandra. *Dharmatattva* [*DT*]. See Brajendranāth Bandyopādhyāy & Sajanīkānta Dās.

Comte, Auguste. *Introduction to Positive Philosophy,* ed. (with introduction and revised translation) by F. Ferré. Indianapolis: Hackett Publishing Company Inc., 1988.

Crawford, S. Cromwell. *Ram Mohan Roy: Social, Political, and Religious Reform in 19th Century India.* New York: Paragon House Publishers, 1987.

Crooke, William. *Hobson-Jobson.* See Henry Yule.

Das, S. K. *The Artist in Chains: The Life of Bankimchandra Chatterji.* New Delhi: New Statesman Publishing Company, 1984.

Day, Lāl Behāri. *Govinda Sāmanta, or The History of a Bengal Rāiyat,* in 2 vols. London: Macmillan and Co., 1874.

De, Sushil Kumar. *The Megha-Dūta of Kālidāsa*. New Delhi: Sahitya Akademi, 1957.

Eck, Diana. *Banaras: City of Light*. London: Routledge & Kegan Paul, 1983.

——. *Darśan: Seeing the Divine Image in India*. New York: Columbia University Press, 1996a (2nd revised and enlarged edition).

——. "Gaṅgā: the goddess Ganges in Hindu sacred geography," in J. S. Hawley & D. M. Wulff (eds.), *Devī: Goddesses of India*. Berkeley: University of California Press, 1996b.

Eden, Emily. *Up the Country: Letters from India*. London: Virago Press, 2003.

Edgerton, Franklin and Edgerton, Eleanor. *Kalidasa: The Cloud Messenger*, translated from the Sanskrit, Meghaduta. Ann Arbor: Ann Arbor Paperbacks, The University of Michigan Press, 1964.

Encyclopaedia Britannica. Cambridge University Press, 11th edition, 1910–11.

Feuerstein, Georg. *The Yoga-Sūtra of Patañjali: A New Translation and Commentary*. Folkstone: Wm Dawson and Sons, 1979.

Fuller, C. J. *The Camphor Flame: Popular Hinduism and Society in India*. Princeton: Princeton University Press, 1992.

Gleig, G. R. *Memoirs of the Life of the Right Hon. Warren Hastings, First Governor-General of Bengal*. Compiled from Original Papers, 3 vols. London: Richard Bentley, 1841.

Glucklich, A. *The Sense of Adharma*. Oxford and New York: Oxford University Press, 1994.

Gonda, J. *Aspects of Early Viṣṇuism*. Utrecht: N V A Oosthoek's Uitgevers Mij, 1954.

——. *Ancient Indian Kingship from the Religious Point of View*. Leiden: E. J. Brill, 1966.

——. *Vedic Ritual: The Non-Solemn Rites*. Leiden: E. J. Brill, 1980.

Grimes, J. *A Concise Dictionary of Indian Philosophy: Sanskrit Terms Defined in English*. Albany: State University of New York Press, 1996.

Hara, M. "Transfer of merit," *The Adyar Library Bulletin*. 31–2: 382–411, 1967–68.

——. "A note on the phrase *kṛśo dhamani-saṃtata*," *Asiatische Studien/Études Asiatiques*. XLIX: 2, 1995.

——. "The losing of tapas," in Dick van der Meij (ed.) *India and Beyond: Aspects of Literature, Meaning, Ritual and Thought. Essays in Honour of Frits Staal*. London and New York: Kegan Paul International & International Institute for Asian Studies (Leiden and Amsterdam). 1997.

——. "Hot tears and cold tears," in R. I. Nanavati (ed.) *Purāṇa-Itihāsa-Vimarśaḥ: Prof. S.G.Kantawala Felicitation Volume*. Delhi: Bharatiya Vidya Prakashan, 1998.

Harder, Hans. *Bankimchandra Chattopadhyay's Śrīmadbhagabadgītā: Translation and Analysis*. New Delhi: Manohar, 2001.

Hawkins, R. E. (ed.). *Encyclopedia of Indian Natural History*. Delhi: Oxford University Press, 1986.

Hawley, J. S. and Wulff, D. M. (eds.). *Devī: Goddesses of India*. Berkeley: University of California Press, 1996.

Houben, Jan E. M. (ed.). *Ideology and Status of Sanskrit: Contributions to the History of the Sanskrit Language*. Leiden: E. J. Brill, 1996.

Hunter. William Wilson: *A Statistical Account of Bengal, vol. VII: Districts of Maldah, Rangpur, and Dinajpur*. London: Trübner & Co., 1876.

——. *The Indian Empire: Its People, History, and Products*. London: Trübner & Co., 1886, 2nd edition; reprinted by Routledge, London, 2000.

——. *Annals of Rural Bengal*. London: Smith, Elder, and Co., 7th edition, 1897.

Jayadeva. *Gītagovinda*. See Miller, B. S. and Siegel, Lee.

Jones, Kenneth W. *Arya Dharm: Hindu Consciousness in 19th-Century Punjab*. Berkeley: University of California Press, 1976.

Kane, P. V. *History of Dharmaśāstra*, Vol. V, Part I, 2nd ed. Poona: Bhandarkar Oriental Research Institute, 1974.

Karmarkar, R. D. *Meghadūta of Kālidāsa*, 2nd edition. Poona: Venus Book Stall, 1947.

Killingley, Dermot. (Ph.D. thesis) *Rammohun Roy's Interpretation of the Vedānta*. London: University of London, 1977.

Kinsley, D. *Hindu Goddesses: Visions of the Divine Feminine in the Hindu Religious Tradition*. Delhi: Motilal Banarsidass, 1987.

——. *Tantric Visions of the Divine Feminine: The Ten Mahāvidyās*. Delhi: Motilal Banarsidass, 1998.

Kopf, David. *The Brahmo Samaj and the Shaping of the Modern Indian Mind*. Princeton: Princeton University Press, 1979.

Kramrisch, S. *The Presence of Śiva*. Delhi: Motilal Banarsidass edition, 1988.

Leslie, I. J. *The Perfect Wife: The Orthodox Hindu Woman According to the Strīdharmapaddhati of Tryambakayajvan*. Delhi: Oxford University Press, 1989.

——. (ed.). *Roles and Rituals for Hindu Women*. London: Pinter Publishers, 1991.

Lipner, J. J. (ed.). *The Fruits of Our Desiring: An Enquiry into the Ethics of the Bhagavadgītā for Our Times*. Calgary: Bayeux Arts, 1997.

——. *Bankimcandra Chatterji's Ānandamaṭh*, or *The Sacred Brotherhood*, translated with an introduction and critical apparatus. New York: Oxford University Press, 2005a.

——. (ed.). *Truth, Religious Dialogue and Dynamic Orthodoxy: Essays in Honour of Brian Hebblethwaite*. London: SCM Press, 2005b.

——. " 'Icon and mother': an inquiry into India's national song." *Journal of Hindu Studies*, 1:26–48, 2008.

Lutgendorf, P. *The Life of a Text: Performing the Rāmcaritmānas of Tulsidas*. Berkeley: University of California Press, 1991.

Marshall, P. J. (ed.). *Bengal: The British Bridgehead. Eastern India, 1740–1820, vol. II, The New Cambridge History of India*. Cambridge: Cambridge University Press, 1987.

——. *India: The Launching of the Hastings Impeachment 1786–1788*, Vol. VI of Paul Langford (gen. ed.), *The Writings and Speeches of Edmund Burke*. Oxford: Clarendon Press, 1991.

Miller, Barbara Stoler (editor and translator), *Love Song of the Dark Lord: Jayadeva's Gītagovinda*. New York: Columbia University Press, 1977.

Mitra, Subalcandra. *Saral Bāṅgālā Abhidhān* [*SBA*]. Calcutta: New Bengal Press, 1984 (8th ed., reprinted, 1995).

Mitra, Subodhcandra (published under the name of Subodh Chunder Mitter). *Bankim Chatterji's Devi Chaudhurani Rendered into English*. Calcutta: Chuckervertty, Chatterjee & Co., 1946.

Mittal, S. and Thursby, G. (eds.). *The Hindu World*. New York and London: Routledge, 2004.

Monier-Williams, M. *A Sanskrit-English Dictionary*. Oxford: Clarendon Press, 1970.

Nanavati, R I (ed.). *Purāṇa-Itihāsa-Vimarśaḥ: Prof. S.G.Kantawala Felicitation Volume*. Delhi: Bharatiya Vidya Prakashan, 1998.

Oddie, Geoffrey A. *Missionaries, Rebellion and Proto-Nationalism: James Long of Bengal 1814–1887*. Richmond (Surrey): Curzon Press, 1999.

Openshaw J. *Seeking Bāuls of Bengal*. Cambridge: Cambridge University Press, 2002.

Raychaudhuri. Tapan, *Europe Reconsidered: Perceptions of the West in Nineteenth Century Bengal*. Delhi: Oxford University Press, 1988.

Sarkār, Jadunāth. "Historical preface," in Brajendranāth Bandyopādhyāy & Sajanīkānta Dās (eds.).

Sarkar, Sudhircandra. *Paurāṇik Abhidhān*. Calcutta: M. C. Sarkar & Sons, Pvt., Ltd., 2003 (9th ed.).

Sharma, A. *The Puruṣārthas—A Study in Hindu Axiology*. East Lansing: Asian Studies Center, Michigan State University, 1982.

Siegel, Lee. *Sacred and Profane Dimensions of Love in Indian Traditions as Exemplified in the Gītagovinda of Jayadeva*. Delhi: Oxford University Press, 1990.

Sternbach, Ludwik (ed.). *Cāṇakya-Rāja-Nīti: Maxims on Rāja-Nīti, Compiled from Various Collections of Maxims Attributed to Cāṇakya*. Adyar: The Adyar Library and Research Centre, 1963.

Stutley, Margaret and Stutley, James. *A Dictionary of Hinduism. Its Mythology, Folklore and Development, 1500 B.C.–A.D. 1500*. London and Henley: Routledge and Kegan Paul Ltd., 1977.

Tagore, Rabindranath. *Gorā*. Kolkātā: Viśvabhāratī Granthanbibhāg edition, 1977.

Walsh, Judith E. *Domesticity in Colonial India: What Women Learned When Men Gave Them Advice*. Lanham and Oxford: Rowman & Littlefield Publishers, Inc., 2004.

Whicher, Ian. *The Integrity of the Yoga Darśana: A Reconsideration of Classical Yoga*. Albany: State University of New York Press, 1998.

Wormell, Deborah. *Sir John Seeley and the Uses of History*. Cambridge: Cambridge University Press, 1980.

Yule, Henry and Burnell, A. C. New edition edited by W. Crooke. *Hobson-Jobson: A Glosary of Colloquial Anglo Indian Words and Phrases, and of Kindred Terms, Etymological, Historical, Geographical and Discursive*. New Delhi: Rupa & Co. edition, (1886), 1986, 2002.

Index to the Introduction and Critical Apparatus

Index to Debī Chaudhurāi (Including Variants)